W9-BZE-069

INVISIBLE SUN

INVISIBLE SUN

EMPIRE GAMES: BOOK III

CHARLES STROSS

TOR

A TOM DOHERTY ASSOCIATES BOOK
NEW YORK

This is a work of fiction. All of the characters, organizations, and events portrayed in this novel are either products of the author's imagination or are used fictitiously.

INVISIBLE SUN

A Tor Book
Published by Tom Doherty Associates
120 Broadway
New York, NY 10271

www.tor-forge.com

Tor® is a registered trademark of Macmillan Publishing Group, LLC.

The Library of Congress Cataloging-in-Publication Data is available upon request.

ISBN 978-1-250-80709-0 (hardcover)
ISBN 978-1-250-80711-3 (ebook)

Our books may be purchased in bulk for promotional, educational, or business use. Please contact your local bookseller or the Macmillan Corporate and Premium Sales Department at 1-800-221-7945, extension 5442, or by email at MacmillanSpecialMarkets@macmillan.com.

First Edition: September 2021

Printed in the United States of America

0 9 8 7 6 5 4 3 2 1

For Chelsea Manning and Edward Snowden

TIME LINES

TIME LINE ONE:

History diverged from our own around 200–250 BCE in Time Line One. Judaism, Christianity, and Islam are all absent and the collapse of the Roman empire into dark ages was complete rather than just partial. Since then, civilization in Europe re-emerged and quasi-medieval colony kingdoms sprang up on the eastern seaboard of North America. (The western seaboard was settled by Chinese traders.)

The Gruinmarkt, one such kingdom, was home to the Clan—rich merchant-traders with the ability to cross between time lines. As world-walkers, they made a good living as the only people who could send a message coast-to-coast in a day in time line one. They could also guarantee a heroin shipment would arrive without fear of interception in time line two. But all good things come to an end, and the vicious civil war that broke out in 2003 (by time line two reckoning) led to the Clan's discovery by the US Government. Their escalating cycle of retaliation ended in a nuclear inferno.

TIME LINE TWO:

This is a world almost identical to your time line, as the reader of this book—right up to a key date in 2003. Here, world-walkers from the Clan's conservative faction detonated a stolen nuclear weapon in the White House. They assassinated the President and forced the government to reveal the existence of parallel universes and the technology for reaching them.

Our story starts in time line two.

TIME LINE THREE:

This time line was discovered by Miriam Beckstein. In this alternate world, England was invaded by France in 1760 and the British Crown in Exile was established in the New England colonies. There was no American War of Independence and no French or Russian Revolutions. Therefore the Ancien Regime—despotism by absolute monarchy—shaped the world order until the Revolution of 2003. Here, the New British Empire's Radical Party overthrew the government and declared a democratic commonwealth. The country is now known as the New American Commonwealth.

The French invasion of England stifled the Industrial Revolution in its crib, so industrialization began a century later than in time line two. But economics and science have their own imperatives. And even before Miriam led the survivors of the Clan into exile in the Commonwealth, the pace of technological innovation was beginning to pick up.

TIME LINE FOUR:

Currently uninhabited, this time line is in the grip of an ice age—with an ice sheet covering much of Europe, Canada, and the northern states of the US.

But it hasn't been uninhabited forever. The enigmatic Forerunner ruins pose both a threat and a promise . . .

MAIN CHARACTER PROFILES

ERIC SMITH

Born in 1964 in time line two, Colonel Smith, USAF (retired) has been a government man all his life. He worked for the United States' National Security Agency, then inside a top secret unit within Homeland Security. It was tasked with defending the States against threats from other time lines; these included world-walkers, those who could cross between these alternative worlds and his own time line. Many might consider this easy—after all, most known time lines are uninhabited, or populated by stone age tribes at best. However, the exceptions are the problem. The notorious Clan and their world-walkers came from time line one. And contact with this secretive organization resulted in a national trauma—dwarfing both 9/11 and the war on terror.

Smith knows that there are other inhabited time lines out there—and they're hostile. At least one vanished civilization left relics far ahead of the United States' technology levels, evidence that they'd been fighting—and losing—a para-time war against parties unknown. And then there's the BLACK RAIN time line, where reconnaissance drones and human spies go missing and air samples contain traces of radioactive fallout.

Defending the nation is easier said than done, when you can't even be sure what you're defending it from. But you can make a good guess . . .

KURT DOUGLAS

Born in 1941 in time line two, Kurt Douglas grew up in the German Democratic Republic—East Germany—during the Cold War. Drafted at eighteen, he ended up in the Border Guards. Then, in late 1968, he escaped over the Berlin Wall to the West, and emigrated to the United States. Marrying Greta, another East German defector, he made a new life for himself.

Kurt raised a family, and lived quietly with his son, daughter-in-law, and their adopted children—Rita and River.

The East German foreign intelligence service didn't send Kurt to the West to spy on the United States. For a defector to infiltrate their host nation's intelligence agencies was considered impossible. But they had longer-term objectives in mind: to have children who would be US citizens by birth, raised and trained as loyal agents of the worker's state. They'd have the perfect backgrounds to infiltrate the NSA, the CIA, and the government. But the Cold War ended and East Germany reunified with the West before the plan could be carried out. Old skills don't fade easily, and Kurt has given Rita the best training he could for living in a police state. And she knows, if she ever gets in over her head, that she can count on Grandpa Kurt—and his friends—for help.

MIRIAM BURGESON

Born in 1968 in time line two, Miriam grew up in Boston, Massachusetts. She worked as a tech sector journalist before discovering, in her early thirties, that her mother had been lying to her for most of her life; mother and daughter were fugitives from the Gruinmarkt—a small kingdom in time line one, which had reached medieval levels of technology. They were women of noble birth, whose designated role was to produce more world-walkers and to serve the Clan. Miriam world-walked 'home' by accident and was expected to conform. But that had never been Miriam's style. So, in short order, she discovered a route to a new inhabited time line and built a business start-up—using it to import high-tech innovations into this new territory. This triggered a crisis within the Clan, reviving a dormant blood feud and causing civil war.

Now seventeen years have passed since the Clan and the Gruinmarkt were both destroyed. Clan reactionaries made a disastrous miscalculation that led to a very brief war with the United States—ending when the US nuked the Gruinmarkt. Miriam saw the writing on the wall and led anti-Clan survivors into exile in the new world she'd discovered. But here she found a revolution in progress—and a new vocation.

Miriam is now older and wiser, and a minister in government. She works for the New American Commonwealth, the ascendant democratic superpower of time line three. She'd taken part in the revolution that overthrew the absolute monarchy of the New British Empire, now defunct. And ever since, she's been warning the new government, "the USA is coming". For seventeen years, she's been working feverishly to ensure that when the US drones arrive overhead, the Commonwealth will be ready to meet them on equal terms. But she wasn't expecting them to be expecting *her*—and to have made plans accordingly.

RITA DOUGLAS

Born in 1995 in time line two, and adopted at birth by Franz and Emily Douglas, Rita was eight when Clan renegades from time line one nuked the White House. Growing up in President Rumsfeld's America, she has learned to keep her head down and her nose clean. But there's only so much you can do to avoid attention in a national security state when the government has you under constant surveillance in case the woman who gave you up for adoption (or her relatives) takes a renewed interest in you.

Rita has a history and drama studies degree, a pile of student loans, and no great employment prospects. At twenty-five years of age she doesn't really know where she's going. But that's okay. Because the government has big plans for Rita.

ELIZABETH HANOVER

Born in 2002, just before the revolution that overturned the New British Empire and sent the crown into exile in St Petersburg, Elizabeth Hanover is the only child of his Royal Majesty John Frederick the Fourth, Emperor in Exile of the New British Empire. Unmarried, she's a pawn in her father's dynastic plans, which will come to fruition on the death of Adam Burroughs, First Man of the Commonwealth. But her father's plans revolve around a royal marriage into the Bourbon dynasty, to a prince twice her own age (who possesses a mistress and, according to rumor, the pox). She's supposed to be the Queen of a restored British Empire of the Americas. But Elizabeth isn't stupid. She's been watching the Commonwealth's technological progress from afar, and laying plans of her own. Plans which will bring two nuclear-armed superpowers to the brink of war . . .

PRINCIPAL CAST LIST

UNITED STATES OF AMERICA

RITA DOUGLAS, struggling thespian

FRANZ DOUGLAS, Rita's father

EMILY DOUGLAS, Rita's mother

RIVER DOUGLAS, Rita's brother

KURT DOUGLAS, Franz's father, retiree

GRETA DOUGLAS, Kurt's wife (deceased)

SONIA GOMEZ, DHS agent

ANGIE HAGEN, electrical contractor, childhood friend

JACK MERCER, DHS agent

PAULETTE MILAN, a spy

PATRICK O'NEILL, Rita's supervisor

DR. EILEEN SCRANTON, deputy assistant to Secretary of State for Homeland Security, Smith's boss

COLONEL ERIC SMITH, DHS, head of the Unit

DR. JULIE STRAKER, Colleague of Rita's

NEW AMERICAN COMMONWEALTH (AND FRENCH EMPIRE)

MARGARET BISHOP, Party Commissioner

MIRIAM BURGESON (previously Miriam Beckstein), Minister for economic development and inter-timeline industrial espionage, Commonwealth Government

ERASMUS BURGESON (Miriam's husband), Minister for Propaganda, Commonwealth Government

SIR ADAM BURROUGHS, First Man (head of state)

THE DAUPHIN, Heir to the throne of the French Empire

PRINCESS ELIZABETH HANOVER, heir to John Frederick

JOHN FREDERICK HANOVER, the Pretender, King in Exile of the New
   British Empire

MAJOR HULIUS HJORTH (YUL), Brilliana's brother-in-law, world-walker spy

ELENA HJORTH, Huw Hjorth's wife

HUW HJORTH, Explorer-General

BRILLIANA HJORTH (Huw's wife), DPR (espionage agency) director

ADRIAN HOLMES, Party Secretary

ALICE MORGAN, Commonwealth Transport Police officer

OLGA THOROLD, Miriam's director of counter-espionage

PART ONE

SINGULARITY

Depend upon it, Sir, when a man knows he is to be hanged
in a fortnight, it concentrates his mind wonderfully.

—Samuel Johnson, September 19, 1777

Drowning in Berlin

Elizabeth Hanover scuttled along the grimy sidewalk, her shoulders hunched and eyes downcast, running away from the sour fear-stink of a rendezvous gone wrong.

She was two blocks away from the ground-floor apartment where the Major lay, bleeding and unconscious in the care of questionable strangers, when a thud that reverberated through her rib cage set her heart pounding. *Was that a bomb?* she wondered. It sounded like a bomb. She'd heard too many of them for comfort in her short adult life. She increased her pace as distant sirens began to rise and fall.

The streetscape of this other-world Berlin was disorienting and unfamiliar. *Her* Berlin was the fusty regional capital of the French Imperial province of East Prussia. *This* Berlin was apparently the capital of a united federation of all the Germanies, in a looking-glass world where France was a Republic and the Russias were splintered separate nations. And there was no respite, in any direction she looked, from the reminders of her exile. The people around her went hatless and it seemed both men and women wore trousers. But that was the least of the strangeness. *There are no horses,* she realized dizzily. No ever-present road apples with their sweet-sick smell of equine droppings, no boys with brooms waiting to sweep the crossings. *Did they eat all the horses? Is there a famine?* But there were no obvious signs of starvation around her. Indeed, there were signs of outrageous wealth: street-corner grocery stores boasted outrageous expanses of plate glass. Some of the pedestrians talked to themselves, muttering or mumbling as if they were mad, while others walked heedlessly, eyes downcast at small, glowing tablets like the one she'd taken from Major Hjorth.

She'd imagined a future of melted-looking automobiles and streetcars, of flying machines and towers, but the small differences were far more disturbing. An infant pranced by in shoes with soles that flashed blue at every step, its hand held by a mother dressed in a Hussar's jacket and tight trousers. A brightly lit advertising sign on a passing tram flared an incomprehensible message at her, then dissolved before her eyes into a picture of toothily smiling people. The unfamiliarity everywhere she turned her gaze was exhausting.

Liz gripped the torn messenger bag under her arm and moderated her pace to avoid attention. Her heart hammered as a green-striped vehicle roared past, blue beacons flashing from its roofline and siren wailing like a damned soul. Through its windows she glimpsed hard-faced men (or women) in uniform. It was heading towards the block she'd left behind. Major Hjorth's scheme had clearly failed, attracting the worst kind of attention this world had to offer, and now she was stranded without any idea where to turn for help. Her unease veered towards suffocating panic. The Major's proposal had looked so excitingly promising when she awakened this morning! But now it seemed like a snare into which she had thrust her head, and from which she could not withdraw.

Major Hjorth's plan had gone off the rails when he'd been shot by Elizabeth's guards. His body armor hadn't quite stopped the bullet he took during her extraction. He'd brought her to his apartment and collapsed so she'd taken the glowing slab of glass he called a phone, but it stopped working for her, demanding that she look at it or enter some sort of code. A stranger called Fox turned up, then called a medic, and then the doorbell rang again. Scared, Liz had grabbed the Major's bag with his holdout pistol and bolted through the back door. A minute later there had been an explosion, then the gendarmes converging behind her like black-uniformed wasps . . .

She came to a platform beside a streetcar stop. It had a rain shelter and some uncomfortable looking furniture. Liz paused and leaned gingerly against the unfamiliar plastic rails of the seat. The cumulative sense of strangeness, relentless and disturbing, threatened to drown her but she made herself take deep, measured breaths, and fought back the urge to panic while she took stock of her situation. *What should I do now?* she wondered.

She remembered the Major's words: "We're safe from Captain Bertrand, but this is not your world. There are other hazards. We'd best get you to a place of safety as fast as possible." Bertrand had been her chief bodyguard—a polite word for jailer. *There are other hazards.* This was the world the Commonwealth's exiled world-walkers had angered. The one that had hunted them back to their original home and cauterized it with corpuscular weapons, if her father's intelligence briefings were to be believed.

A peculiar flat chime like a recording of real bells announced the arrival of a sleek, glass-walled streetcar. Liz watched, careful to keep her face expressionless, as doors rippled open along its length. She saw no sign of a ticket booth or conductor before the doors hissed closed and the machine whined away. It was eerily quiet for a tram. An illuminated sign on the shelter wall flickered: **OSTBAHNHOFF 4Km**. Were there two main stations in this Berlin? She shook her head, the tight scarf tugging at her hair. The other people she saw wore very different costumes but paid her little attention, as if she was a servant. Maybe it was her skin color, not just the outfit the Major had provided? She hunched up a little then forced herself to straighten, irrationally angry with herself.

Take stock: she had a nasty-looking pistol she hadn't trained with, a magic mirror that didn't work, and a wallet containing some paper money and plastic wafers the size of playing cards (value: unknown). She also had a number of solid gold guineas she'd stitched into her underwear over the past three nights, not trusting the Major entirely, but turning them into local cash required some understanding of how things worked here. She could get by in German and Russian, as well as being fluent in French and English. Stacked against her were: the Major's posited enemies, whoever they were. (Presumably, they were the ones responsible for the explosion). Whoever Fox had been afraid of—possibly the grim-faced gendarmes in their trucks? And the difficulty of making contact with the Major's backers. *How can I—*

An angry hornet buzzed in her bag. Liz squeaked and clamped her elbow tight on it, panicking. The buzzing stopped: moments later it buzzed again. She exhaled, realizing it was a mechanism of some sort. She opened the bag and looked inside. The Major's phone was vibrating, and it lit up the interior of the bag like a magician's cave, flashing a cryptic message: INTERNATIONAL CALL, NUMBER WITHHELD. Relief and worry twisted her mind in knots as she fumbled the device out of the bag and held it to her cheek.

"Hello? Is that Elizabeth?"

It was a woman's voice, tinny and tentative. She spoke English, oddly-accented.

"Who is this?" She asked nervously.

"Hello? I can't hear you—"

Liz turned the device around, upside down, and tried again. "Who is this?"

"Are you Elizabeth? If so, can you tell me the date when you were born?"

Tumblers spun in her head as sleepy summer lessons from Dr. Henkel, her father's chief of security, slotted into place. "Only if you tell me whose phone this is, first," she challenged. "Don't use their name, just identify them."

"Why? Oh. This phone belongs to the Major, of course."

Elizabeth's shoulders trembled with relief and she recited her birthdate.

"Thank you, Elizabeth. I work for Control—we direct the Major. I understand something has gone wrong—"

"Tell me something I don't know!" she said crossly. "I'm not with the Major right now. Too many people came. I stepped outside and a minute later there was an explosion." She glanced around furtively, but nobody waited within earshot. "The gendarmes came running. I think it's too dangerous to go back."

"You're absolutely right." Control fell silent for a second or two. "Elizabeth, you should assume that the Major is dead or captured. We will honor the agreement he made with you if that is agreeable, but it will take us a few hours—possibly a couple of days—to get you out of there. Meanwhile we're going to make alternative arrangements on the fly. First things first: this phone is your lifeline. But it is probably going to need charging up in a couple of hours, and if its battery goes flat you won't be able to use it."

"I can't use it anyway; it doesn't recognize my face and it keeps asking for a password—"

"Not a problem if you can memorize this number?" Control recited a six-digit code. "That will get you in. But you absolutely must obtain a booster battery as fast as possible. Did the Major give you any money?"

Elizabeth chewed her lip. "Before I left, I took his wallet," she admitted.

"Excellent!" To her chagrin, Control sounded *approving*. "You think quickly: this might just work. Listen, you need to go to one of the S-Bahn or DB—main railway—stations. Use the Major's transit pass—it's a plastic card labelled BVG, you tap it on the ticket machine as you board a tram or catch the subway—then when you get to the station you must look for a kiosk. Ask the kiosk owner for a booster battery and get them to show you how to connect it to the phone. Younger ones, under fifty, they mostly speak enough English—"

"I can get by in German." *I hope.* "How much will this cost? I don't know how much money is worth here."

"Somewhere between five and twenty-five euros is about right. How much do you have?"

Liz rummaged through the Major's wallet. "Three notes that say one-hundred euros. And two fifties." Also some small change. She rummaged some more. "I found the BVG card." *I think.*

"You can buy a cheap restaurant meal and a drink for ten to twenty. Find a kiosk, get a phone charger, take yourself somewhere to eat, and I'll call you back within the hour with directions to somewhere you can stay the night. Can you do that?"

Liz looked around uncertainly. Another tram was approaching, its electronic chime sounding slightly flat. The moving sign on the front of the streetcar agreed with the sign on the shelter. "I think so," she said, setting her shoulders. "I'll try."

"Take care, then! Control out." The phone went dark as the tram drew up beside her. Liz slid it in her bag and stepped aboard. Moments later the doors sighed closed and the tram lurched into motion, bearing her away into the streets of East Berlin.

TEMPELHOF AIR FORCE BASE, BERLIN, TIME LINE TWO, AUGUST 2020

"This isn't public yet—we don't want a panic—but we just lost time line four. The Dome, the Bridge, and Camp Singularity: they're all gone."

Colonel Smith, formerly of the US Air Force and then the NSA, now led a shadowy unit within the para-temporal division of Homeland Security tasked with countering intruders from other time lines. He stared at his boss's face on his tablet screen. He'd started the conference call expecting to share some good news for once—a captured enemy agent, just one loose end left to collect—with her. The change of track was jarring. "Damn! How? What's the impact assessment? Is my side of operations intact or do I need to re-plan?"

His boss, Dr. Eileen Scranton, cut across him. Their conversation was time-lagged by the satellite link across the Atlantic. "It impacts *everything,* Eric. Over a thousand people got out of the research facility at Camp Singularity—just in time, luckily—but now several thousand more people know what happened there. It's going to leak, there's no way to keep an alien invasion secret—"

"—A what? Excuse me, but I could swear you just said the words *alien invasion?*" Eileen Scranton didn't play games. At least, not with her core staff: "*What?*"

Dr. Scranton glared through the video link. Smith shut up, chagrined at his lapse. After a couple of seconds she resumed. "I was supervising an operation at Camp Singularity." The camp, in time line four, was an archaeological dig site of military significance. The dig was excavating the high-tech ruins of a destroyed para-time fortress. These included a still-functioning gate to a time line where the Earth had been destroyed—compressed down to a planetary-mass black hole—by an as-yet unidentified enemy. "I was there in person. We dropped a space probe through the Gate on a flyby of the hole. It was a reconnaissance mission, but it woke up some kind of weapons platform."

"A space probe? Which one?" There were at least three probe projects Smith had heard of, all with different goals and factions promoting them. None had been green-lit for launch before now, and he was mildly irritated to find himself on the outside.

"ERGO-1." A joint Space Command project, with lots of interest from the Air Force. "They were testing the black hole as a tool for gravitational slingshot maneuvers. It case they needed to launch a first strike against the Commonwealth, sending warheads through para-time." Dr. Scranton looked mildly disgusted at the scheme's lack of subtlety. "The headbangers on the National Security Council want a bigger club. As you have to liaise with the Commonwealth directly, you were kept in the dark for plausible deniability."

ERGO-1 was a modified maneuvering bus from a Minuteman ICBM, the platform that aimed and released the nuclear warheads the missile carried. Loaded with instruments instead of bombs, they'd sent it through the Gate as a test. It had been built in a hurry on a budget of mere hundreds of millions of dollars, peanuts for a nuclear weapons program. The objective had been to prove it was feasible to place missile warheads in close orbit around the planetary-mass black hole in the uninhabited time line. If so, they'd be available to carry out a para-time nuclear strike, arriving over their targets without any warning. So the Camp Singularity crew had pushed the test-bed through the Gate between worlds, letting it fall on an orbit passing close to the planetary-mass black hole that had replaced the Earth in that time line.

Viewed with 20/20 hindsight, perhaps it hadn't been such a good idea after all.

"We accidentally tickled a dragon's tail, and the dragon woke up." Dr. Scranton looked as if she'd bitten a chili pepper by mistake instead of a plum tomato.

"What kind of dragon?" Smith asked, fascinated. The alien relics they'd found in the Dome at Camp Singularity had been junk, corroded into inactivity by two thousand years of exposure to the elements. Nobody had expected anything but trash to survive in the high radiation environment close to a black hole.

"It launched some kind of interceptors. They destroyed ERGO-1, then invaded through the Gate. Current consensus is that there was some kind of dormant alien weapons platform down there in the gravity well. In hindsight—we should have anticipated this. I mean, it was on the other side of a gate leading from a multi-dimensional fortress that was destroyed centuries ago. But it was asleep until we accidentally woke it up."

Crap, crap, Smith swore silently. Eileen's increasingly rattled delivery suggested that she was really worried: last time he'd seen her like this . . . "What do you want me to do?" he asked.

"For now? Be aware of it, while continuing with the operations in Berlin and New York. The media blackout is holding, but I think it'll leak to the public within days at the outside and then we'll have to re-plan *everything.* We're desperately short of information right now, although steps are being taken to remedy that on the ground. Meanwhile, the potential for embarrassment in front of the Commonwealth is extensive. I'm bringing it up because we showed Rita Camp Singularity." The corners of Eileen's mouth turned down. Smith had recruited and trained Rita Douglas as a world-walking agent of Homeland Security. She was currently assigned to a diplomatic mission in the Commonwealth. There she'd met her birth mother, Miriam, who was high up in the Commonwealth government and also, for unrelated reasons, at the top of the FBI's Most Wanted list. Her psych profile said she was loyal and she'd been carefully primed to mistrust Miriam—and the Unit had her on a leash via her family and girlfriend—but Smith knew better than to trust anyone unconditionally.

"Do we have reason to believe the Commonwealth know about time line four?" Eric asked cautiously.

"It's not impossible. There were signs that world-walkers from the Commonwealth visited the Dome before we discovered it. But the mess could have been made by their people—or by someone else. Maybe there were survivors from the Dome's garrison?" (She clearly assumed that the archaeological evidence suggesting the Dome was a para-time fortress was correct.) "Or it could have been our fault. The initial survey team's first reaction was to block the Gate—it was venting air from time line four directly into the vacuum on the black hole's side—and they didn't realize how sensitive the site was until later."

"Ouch." Smith winced. "Okay, thanks for the heads-up. Meanwhile I've got an update for you."

"Oh good. And how *are* things going in Berlin?" Scranton asked pensively.

Smith smiled like a shark. "Ms. Milan is cooperating, and the dominos are falling into place. NSA identified her time line two contact. As we suspected, it was Major Hjorth. They then handed us *his* lamplighter—" the local assistant, tasked with preparing safe locations and supplies for an agent in the field—"codename FOX. FOX turned out to be a local fixer for drug smugglers. He didn't know the safe house he was preparing was for world-walkers. Our NSA friends had tabs on him already, so we hauled him in and he sang like a canary. Hjorth had spun him a story about industrial espionage—the Indonesian biosynthetic rubber trade—and used him to buy a light plane, lease an apartment in a very specific area of East Berlin, and buy weapons, body armor, and second-grade identity documents—not watertight, there were no biometrics—for an Elizabeth Hanover. Hjorth then turned up at the apartment, shot with a large-caliber pistol and in the company of an unknown woman."

Scranton's eyes widened. "Hanover: isn't that the name of . . ."

"Yep: if it's the same Elizabeth Hanover who's mentioned in Rita's reports, she's the heir to the royal family that the Commonwealth kicked out during their revolution. And the *only* heir at that. A princess."

"Please tell me you've got them both in custody?"

"Ah." Smith's smile slipped. "We caught Major Hjorth. He's stable in hospital under guard. But the woman gave us the slip right before we arrived—she can't have been gone even two minutes, we were *that* close. We've got fingerprints and DNA samples that don't match anybody on record, the federal and local cops have an all-points out, but we haven't picked her up yet. The good news is, she didn't have Hjorth's fake ID. If she's just come over from the Commonwealth time line she's bound to be utterly disoriented. So it's basically a waiting game: hours, a day or two at most until we reel her in. It'll be interesting to hear what the world-walkers were doing with her, won't it?"

Dr. Scranton's face was still, but the Colonel could see her mind whirling. "With the Commonwealth in crisis, this could be all the leverage we need to nail the world-walkers."

"Yup. Best case, we might be able to roll up all their espionage operations over here *and* implicate them in a conspiracy to seize control over the Commonwealth by reinstalling the monarchy. Or we hold the heir, who is presumably of value or they wouldn't have set up such an elaborate overseas operation. Either way, we gain freedom of action, and they lose it." Eileen cracked a tense smile. "Get me the girl, Eric—alive—and I'll have the lever I need to move worlds."

"Yes ma'am." *Speaking of worlds,* a parting thought struck him: "Are you thinking of arranging a game of 'let's you and him fight' between the aliens and the Commonwealth? As a Plan B, in case the Commonwealth doesn't manage to shoot itself in both feet when you hand them the ammunition?"

Dr. Scranton's cheek twitched. "While it's interesting that you might think that, I couldn't possibly comment. *That* kind of caper is way above your pay grade—or mine." As Scranton reported to the Secretary for Homeland Security, who in turn answered directly to the President, it was obvious who she meant. The Commonwealth had zero friends in the US Administration, not least because they'd absorbed the Clan of world-walkers who had nuked the White House seventeen years earlier. *Never forgive, never forget.* "Let's just say I'm juggling live hand grenades right now, and I'm relying on you to keep this particular one from exploding in my face."

BOSTON, UNITED STATES,
TIME LINE TWO, AUGUST 2020

Rita's contacts had chosen her grandmother's grave in Boston for the rendezvous. *Very fitting,* Kurt thought. It was his second visit to his wife Greta's headstone this month. He wondered if he'd ever see it again.

Don't be silly. Rita wouldn't have agreed to contact you if she didn't trust them to keep their end of a bargain. Whoever they are. His adoptive granddaughter was nothing if not sensible, and she'd grown up with tradecraft in her veins, a third-generation spy raised on US soil. She knew better than to take anything at face value. A canny girl, even though she'd fallen so deep into the turbid waters of intrigue that she'd need sonar to see the surface.

The message had come via Angie, Rita's girlfriend (who was playing the part of her controller in the informal but deadly-serious Game of Spies Kurt was running). Decrypted, it read: HER MOTHER'S PEOPLE WANT YOU TO VISIT THEM. SAY IT'S URGENT. IF YOU AGREE, RDV DETAILS ARE . . .

Her mother's people. The Clan: World-walkers from a backwards, quasi-mediaeval time line, who had grown wealthy running a major narcotics trafficking operation. They had been discovered by the US government and reacted to their exposure with devastating, deadly force, provoking an even more violent response. (Action and reaction both involved multiple nuclear explosions.) The survivors were now living in exile in another parallel North America, having thrown in their lot with the revolutionaries of the Commonwealth—in a world where history had taken a wildly different path.

If you're going to dine with the devil, bring a long spoon to the table. It wasn't as if there were many alternatives, in Kurt's opinion. He was certain that Rita's employers in Homeland Security didn't have her best interests at heart: they were handling her like a disposable asset. And if they had even an inkling about who and what *he* was—or the way he'd seen to Rita's training, much less how she'd first met Angie—then the best he could hope for was exile in a foreign country at best: more likely, life in a supermax facility run by Homeland Security.

Besides, Rita's birth mother wouldn't have asked to meet with Rita's elderly adoptive grandfather if Rita—or someone else—hadn't told her birth mother altogether too much about him for comfort. *Cover: blown.*

Last time he'd visited Greta's graveside it had been raining. Today the weather was colder but drier, with a chilly wind from the east. *Autumnal,* that was the word. He left his wheels at the motel car park and caught the T, then walked from the nearest stop. He didn't bother to dodge cameras or disguise his approach, or cut the radio frequency labels out of his underwear: the best concealment was not to be caught doing anything strange in the first place. Visiting his wife's grave was—

If they could pull you in and interrogate you for visiting your wife's grave, then it was already too late.

"Hi, Gramps!"

He'd been expecting her, but it still made his chest lurch. "Rita."

Rita stepped out from behind a tree only a few feet away. She closed the gap between them and hugged him, hard enough that his old bones creaked. It had only been a few days since he'd last seen her, but it felt longer. Kurt's twenty-five-year-old adoptive granddaughter didn't look anything like him. Her hair was long and dark and straight, her eyes brown and her skin the color of latte—her birth father's sole bequest. She was dressed oddly, in some kind of tailored tunic-and-trousers outfit. "Let's see if you can ride me piggy-back? We need to make this quick."

"Ha! All right, let's try that." She'd ridden on his shoulders often enough when she'd been a toddler that turnaround was fair play. She crouched before him and Kurt laboriously wrapped his arms around her. Then she stood, wheezing under his weight, head bowed, shoulders hunched—

Kurt's ears popped slightly and everything changed.

There was no graveyard here, just a woodland hillside. It was covered with young trees that grew so thickly that it was impossible to see for any distance. The trees seemed to be of uniform age, which was curious because there was no sign of husbandry—the spacing was uneven, the undergrowth wild. It was warmer and cloudier than the graveyard, too. "Can't stay." Rita wheezed as he slid off her back. "Wait, don't move. And try not to touch anything. There's still fallout."

The skin on the back of Kurt's neck crawled. "Fallout? You mean, this is the . . ."

"Yeah, this is what's left of the Gruinmarkt." A mediaevalesque kingdom in the time line the Clan originally came from, before their reactionary faction picked a fight with the United States. "The trees and plants have grown back but the surface soil is lousy with Cesium-131. You wouldn't want to eat anything that grows here. Also, the DHS does regular drone overflights so we shouldn't hang about. Let me see . . ." Rita checked a boxy device like an old-time PDA. "We're on target. Okay, one more jaunt."

Another heave, and the world changed again, even more confusingly.

"Downtown Boston, Commonwealth remix. Grandpa, I'd like to introduce you to Inspector Morgan. She's my minder. Inspector, this is my grandfather."

Kurt nodded and smiled vacuously at the woman in the unfamiliar uniform, trying hard to look like a harmless old geezer. The Inspector was in her thirties, old enough to know what she was about, and she had the stony expression and constant sidelong scan of a cop. Sure enough, she wasn't buying his act.

"Mr. Douglas." (At least she started out politely.) "Thank you for agreeing to meet the Party Commissioner. Please come this way, there's a car waiting outside. You too, Rita."

They'd landed in a back yard surrounded by crumbling brick walls, half-overrun by a patch of raspberry canes suffocating in a tangle of bindweed. The house that the garden backed onto gazed down at them blankly, its windows covered with wooden boards. Going by the peeling paint and skewed tiles, it had seen better days. The Inspector was not the only uniform in their reception committee. She came with a side-order of muscle: two troopers in green wool greatcoats, unfamiliar-looking guns slung across their chests.

Rita stretched her arms overhead, clearly creaky from lifting her grandfather. She followed the Inspector along an overgrown path around the side of the house. Kurt trailed behind them, heart thudding as the two armed police guards took up the rear.

At first it had been just barely possible for Kurt to imagine they were in a regular New England town. But once the other houses on the street came into view—not to mention the vehicles—the illusion was shattered. The street was paved in cobblestones, with embedded metal rails and overhead wires for a streetcar system. The buildings were smoke-stained cinderblock row houses with shared walls, climbing three, four, or even five stories above the sidewalk. What had been a graveyard in Cambridge was now, it seemed, suburban sprawl. And as for the automobiles—

"Yeah, I had that reaction the first time, too," Rita said disarmingly. She slid across the bench-seat in the back of the limousine to make space for him. It stank of leather wax, gasoline, and stale cigarettes.

"It reminds me of . . ." Kurt shook his head. In his youth he once rode up-front in a VIP's Soviet-built ZiL limousine, wearing his dress uniform as part of the VIP's bodyguard. This time, the Inspector took the front passenger seat while he got to play the part of that long-dead Stasi official. "This takes me back," he said, taking his place beside Rita and groping for the seat-belt. He was half-surprised to find one in such an old-fashioned car. When the driver turned the engine over it wheezed and clattered for a few seconds then caught with a snarl, followed by the gurgle of fuel draining through archaic carburetors. "Where are we to go?"

"An aviation field," the Inspector cut in ahead of Rita. "Then we will continue by gyrodyne." Whatever one of those was. The Inspector sat stiffly: from behind, Kurt saw her hair was scraped back into a bun with military severity, pinned down like a beetle impaled in a naturalist's display case.

Kurt stared through the windows of the gas-guzzling behemoth as it roared through unfamiliar streets, past odd-looking vehicles and people in odder clothing. It was almost, but not quite, a reprise of his arrival in the United States, a year after he went over the wall and claimed asylum in West Germany. He'd made his run via a stretch of the border defenses where the landmines lacked detonators and the magazines in the border guards' guns fired blanks at his back, under orders from the Foreign Intelligence Directorate. (Richard Nixon had been president then, Elvis was still alive, and buzz-cut aviators played golf on the Moon.)

This time line's Boston seemed drab, grey, and lacking in vibrancy. It took him a while to realize what he was noticing was simply the absence of garish video hoardings. Nobody was light-bombing the roads with advertising. Other differences gradually emerged. There weren't enough cars.

The omnipresent Stars and Stripes flags flying over every federal and state building were absent. The police wore green. And there were a lot more streetcars. It felt oddly homely. All these tiny cues were alien, but the sum of the parts took him back to his youth. This looking-glass America resembled the GDR in so many tiny ways that it was felt more familiar than the home time line he'd just left. He wondered then if the resemblance ran deeper, echoed in the politics: or whether the superficial similarities concealed something even more alien than echoes of Communist East Germany, thirty years after the wall came down. But for now, the strange sense of déjà vu was almost comforting. He felt a small hand slide into his. "It'll be all right," his granddaughter reassured him: "you'll see."

NEW LONDON, MANHATTAN ISLAND, TIME LINE THREE, AUGUST 2020

The news that Adam Burroughs had finally breathed his last detonated under the bureaucracy of the New American Commonwealth's government like a torpedo beneath the keel of a battleship. Normal business was cancelled or postponed. Flags were lowered to half-mast, contingency plans activated, communiques released, and all-hands meetings called at which black armbands were issued and speeches made.

Adam, the First Man, had been many things: minor gentry, official in the Land Registry, political philosopher, dissident, revolutionary, and finally the father of the Commonwealth. In life he'd been its head of state. In death he became an abstract symbol, a rallying cry. Truthfully, he hadn't been significantly involved in the day to day business of governance since the cancer entered its final stages six months ago. But his followers were determined that his death would not be a joyful occasion for the enemies of this time line's first democratic republic.

And in some particularly zealous circles, where it had been decided that his death would serve as a mandate for change, long-laid plans were put into action.

An emergency committee was in session in a marble-fronted ministerial building, inside the fortified palace walls of New London, the government canton at the south end of Manhattan Island. It wasn't a large committee, but it was top-heavy with departmental heads from the Ministry of Intertemporal Technological Intelligence, MITI—the government agency responsible for using industrial espionage against parallel universes to speedily modernize the Commonwealth.

Sitting in on this meeting was Huw Hjorth, the Explorer-General, whose responsibility included the opening up of uninhabited time lines. Also present was Brilliana Hjorth, the Director of the Department for Para-time Research, the chief spymaster targeting the United States of America in Time Line Two. And chairing the meeting was Miriam Burgeson, the People's Commissioner in charge of MITI.

"Huw." Miriam stared down the length of the polished mahogany table: "How soon can you fly JUGGERNAUT?"

Huw stared right back at her. "Seriously?" Huw Hjorth—mid-forties, still somewhat gawky despite the assurance that came with age, seniority, and knowing damn well that he was right about most things—looked momentarily apprehensive. "The plans call for a two-month launch campaign, but . . . do you need me to give you a risk assessment for fastest-possible launch to orbit? Or just a guess?"

"I need to know how soon it can fly—the absolute fastest we can launch. Short answer first, then the details." Sitting to Miriam's left, the Director of the DPR, Huw's wife Brilliana, cast him a warning look. *Don't push your luck.* Miriam was all but twitching from the coffee she'd consumed during the meeting so far.

"Well then." Huw crossed his fingers under the table.: "*In principle* JUGGERNAUT can fly now, but there's about a twenty percent probability of a severity one failure. And 'now' means 'maybe this week, if we hit the ground running, work around the clock, and absolutely everything goes perfectly.' If anything at all goes wrong, you can add at least a month. If we detect any major hardware snags, add three."

"Ah." Miriam froze. "Severity one failure is the worst, isn't it?"

"It's a fatal in-flight accident, yes. Loss of vehicle and crew." A couple of faces around the table looked uncertain: directors from departments who hadn't been fully briefed on JUGGERNAUT yet. Huw cleared his throat. "JUGGERNAUT is a pulse-detonation powered deep space ship. *Not* just another rocket, like the ones our colleagues in the regular space program are working on. It drops atomic bombs . . . sorry, corpses—" he translated into the Commonwealth's older, pre-MITI vernacular—"and detonates them behind a huge, armored pusher-plate. The vehicle can make orbit on roughly eight hundred propulsion charges. That's eight hundred *nuclear explosions.* Once it's in orbit it's fairly reliable—the main risks are as it ascends through the lower atmosphere. Our computers just aren't good enough to model the dynamics with the precision we need to guarantee a successful launch." He paused. "We put an unmanned prototype into orbit eight months ago, but the production vehicle is bigger, heavier, and *way* more complex. JUGGERNAUT has a crew of twenty astronauts, including at least four world-walkers. If you want to deliver a thousand tons of cargo to the surface of Mars? We can probably scale up to that with the next vehicle. But this one isn't designed for deep space—it's intended to go on a twelve-month orbital exploration tour of parallel Earths, mapping time lines from space. In one year it can open up as many new worlds as we've explored in the past decade."

Several faces turned pale. "But—if there's a severity one failure on take-off, does that mean—"

"Yes, it means exactly what you think. We'd lose the launch site, vehicle factory, and quite possibly everybody on the ground too. It'd spray fallout—including forty tons of weapons-grade plutonium—everywhere. That's why we launch from an *uninhabited* time line—time line twelve, for this shot. The only people on the ground will be in a deep bunker—the launch control team. Once it's in orbit, the world-walkers aboard will jaunt it to whichever time line we want it to explore, taking it with them, so in *that* respect it's clean. In fact, the whole project is un-workable without world-walkers; if JUGGERNAUT fired up its main drive in low Earth orbit, it would fry our satellite communications and navigation infrastructure. To maneuver, it jaunts into an uninhabited time line. It navigates by making a cross-time line knight's move, basically."

"Assuming it works." This from the deputy director of the Institute for Tutelary Transfer: he looked unhappy with the whole idea.

"The components are flight-proven." Huw shrugged. "We based the test article on the American ORION study from the 1960s. The un-crewed prototype worked. So launch is feasible. It's the rest of the mission that worries me."

Getting up into orbit just involved detonating a few tonnes of plutonium: getting down again afterwards was the hard bit. They'd built a crew re-entry capsule and tested it on top of an ICBM, but nobody had ever ridden one down from orbit before. And explaining all these risk factors to outsiders, and giving them a realistic perspective, was hard.

"This is a huge gamble," said the ITT deputy; he seemed to have a compulsive urge to cover his ass. "Is it really necessary, or is a more gradual test program acceptable?"

Brill met Huw's eyes across the table. She shook her head minutely, then glanced at Miriam. "We are approaching a critical decision point," she said. "I don't know how closely you've been following developments with the United States, but it may be necessary to make a display of 'technical competence'—"

Miriam snorted. "It's time to park a battleship on the White House lawn." Not that the White House National Monument had much of a lawn: it had been at ground zero of one of the nukes on 7/16. "Pay a friendly visit to the International Space Station. Something showy to grab the TV news cycle and signal that messing with us is a bad idea, like the Soviets used to do with their May Day parades."

Miriam slowly rolled a pen between her fingers. "Our intel assessments show that the current US administration is almost certainly underestimating us. They know in the abstract that they're dealing with a nuclear-armed superpower from another time line. But unless we show them something they can't match, they'll assume we're just a regular opponent. Another 'Upper Volta with nuclear missiles,' as one of their presidents called the Soviet Union." Those of her audience who'd studied the history of the other time line nodded.

"They're a planetary hegemonic power with a very aggressive foreign policy, a tendency to project their own worst intentions onto others, and a system that makes it really difficult to back down from a fight. Any leader who shows weakness hemorrhages support with the electorate, and the foreign affairs hierarchy is structured to systematically filter out doves and promote hawks," she explained. "If they look at us and think we're weak they'll try to manipulate us, and if they look at us and see their own mirror-image—a nuclear-armed superpower with para-time capability and a revolutionary ideology—they may panic and attack. Possibly with a nuclear first strike. Those are their ingrained responses, and we've got to find a way to bypass that, a way to shock them into sanity. The Ministry of Propaganda thinks the best way to do that is to present them with a display of competence so far beyond their reach that their usual methods are obviously inappropriate. But it has to be a non-violent one, otherwise we risk triggering an automatic retaliation."

"*We* don't want to nuke them, either," Brill added helpfully, glancing around the table: "Speaking from experience, that never ends well."

"Do you want me to get JUGGERNAUT ready to orbit and transition to time line two?" Huw asked. "As a propaganda mission, rather than the exploration flight currently scheduled?"

"If necessary, yes, but to throw a diplomatic punch we don't need to actually step on their territory. An overflight of New London during Sir Adam's funeral should do it, as long as they've got observers on the ground and we can get video into their news cycle. And we're making damned sure that's the case—not just relying on Rita," she added. Low-key negotiations with the US State Department had been in progress for weeks: an actual diplomatic mission was expected to arrive any day now.

"Time scale?"

"The sooner the better. The First Man's funeral gives us a timetable, and is a good excuse to put negotiations with the United States on hold for a week. After we bury Sir Adam, they'll expect us to be paralyzed while factions jockey to fill the power vacuum. Their fingers will be tightening on the trigger, just in case the new First Citizen is *unreasonable*. That's the period of greatest risk: it would be the perfect time for someone to hold a coup d'etat. But showing off JUGGERNAUT during the funeral parade will certainly not hurt our credibility here, and ought to give the Americans cause to pause. If they don't back down, then we need to double down and send JUGGERNAUT to visit their own time line. If JUGGERNAUT *doesn't* fly and we get through the inauguration of the new First Citizen without any extradimensional crises, then—"she paused—"it means the Americans are being unexpectedly reasonable and you can stop worrying about an emergency launch. But I wouldn't bet on it."

Huw scribbled notes on the pad atop his blotter. "Anything else?" He asked tensely.

"Yes. You'd better tell the commissary at Camp Bastion and the launch site to expect an influx of visitors. MiniProp isn't going to let an opportunity like this slip through its fingers, so JUGGERNAUT is going to go public sooner rather than later. You're going to have journalists, correspondents, and visiting dignitaries coming out of your ears during the countdown. It's going to be a circus, and you're the ring-master."

"Oh joy." Huw rolled his eyes. "You know, that's almost enough to make me want to ride the thing myself." Or watch the launch from the bleachers overlooking the pad, without benefit of factor one million sun block.

"Don't be silly." Brill glared at her husband. "You've already assigned the flight crew!"

"Yes, and Rudi's due to take the helm. It would help if Hulius was around, though: I'm backup for the flight director's desk in mission control, but we need backups for everyone on the crew, and you stole my main candidate for the captain's slot. Consequently, I've been shadowing Rudi *as well*, and although there's some overlap between flight director and captain, holding down both chairs has been eating my life."

Brilliana's face froze. "Well, there's a problem with Yul." At his raised eyebrow she added, "nothing you can help with, I'm afraid. Nothing we can fix right now." She paused. "Hopefully we'll get him back soon, but probably not in time for JUGGERNAUT."

Miriam cleared her throat. "We'll just have to hope nothing happens to Rudi in the next few days, won't we?"

Brill snorted. "Nothing can possibly go wrong now. You'll see."

NEW LONDON, MANHATTAN ISLAND, TIME LINE THREE, AUGUST 2020

"It'll be all right," Rita had told her grandfather, with a degree of certainty that she didn't quite feel. "You'll see." Kurt raised a tangled eyebrow from the other side of the back seat: abashed, she subsided into silence.

It was best not to say anything: the car from the Commonwealth Ministry was almost certainly bugged. While snooping devices built in this time line were still relatively crude, the Ministry of Intertemporal Technological Intelligence had access to just about anything that could be bought off-the-shelf in time line two. And they'd have absolutely no compunction about using imported tools to bug the Minister's long-lost daughter—who was also a foreign agent of influence—and her adoptive grandfather.

Kurt had a momentary flashback to a rainy afternoon fifteen years ago. He'd been baby-sitting Rita for her parents. To keep her entertained, he'd played a series of classic cold war spy shows, pointing out along the way how implausible the secret agents' gizmos all were. (Rita had demanded a secret elevator in the hallway closet, presumably to take her down to the command bunker in the basement. He recalled that she was very upset when he explained about dead ends and killing zones.)

Years later she'd told him that what stuck with her, even then, was the clunkiness of everything. The toe-crushing weight of Maxwell Smart's shoe-phone, the size of the microphones and reel-to-reel tape decks in the original *Mission:Impossible*. So then Kurt had shown her a German website maintained by a guy who was into old Stasi bugging devices. The Stasi and their Soviet opposite numbers, the KGB, believed the gadgets in Bond movies were real. They'd set up factories dedicated to copying Bond's toys and making them work in the real world. They had little success: film props were not required to comply with the laws of physics, and in the end, the real world disappointed them just as badly as real human beings had disappointed the social theoreticians of the Communist Party.

When Rita was sixteen, as part of her ongoing education in covert ops, Kurt had laid Rita's phone on the kitchen table. Then he'd made her write down a list of all the ways in which it resembled an implausible sixties movie spy gadget. Encrypted radio. Encrypted email. Gyroscopes and accelerometers and satellite navigation (itself an exotic multi-billion-dollar fantasy, until long after the last Sean Connery Bond film). Cameras—a color video camera with stereophonic audio and zoom—cameras in the plural! The ability to remotely control a small quadrotor drone with its own remote camera! A computer that could run hacking tools! All it lacked was a concealed gun barrel loaded with .22 hollow-point cartridges (although if you really needed one you could buy it from a Chinese factory, at least until they criminalized bitcoin). "You must assume that everyone you meet these days has the wiretap and bugging resources of George Smiley," he told her. Which was emphatically true, even back in 2010—and even more so today. What was one to make of a world in which every two-bit small town sheriff could field an infantry fighting vehicle, and every college frat boy carried spy gadgets beyond the artifice of Bond's Q Division?

They rode in silence until they came to a gate set in a brick wall with a razor wire hairdo. There was a checkpoint at the gate, staffed by men and women in oddly functional comic opera uniforms. Documents were examined, faces scrutinized—briefly, with unnerving deference. Then they drove out onto a concrete taxiway that led past a series of aircraft hangars. Military aviation installations seemed to converge on the same basic architecture everywhere. The aircraft they approached was of a kind unfamiliar to Kurt—a hybrid vehicle with stubby wings bearing pusher propellers, capped by a huge overhead rotor, the blades of which ended in tiny jet pods—but evidently it served the same function as an Osprey tiltrotor. Men in uniform strapped them into seats and handed them headsets, then the overhead blades spun up with a banshee shriek. The gyrodyne was *impressively* loud even by military standards, but faster than a regular helicopter. Boston to Manhattan was two hundred miles, but the rotorcraft tore down the coast and began to descend only an hour after departure.

They alighted on a helipad in the middle of a plantation of neoclassical-looking government buildings. Another car was waiting for them. Kurt kept an eye on Rita: he worried that she seemed to be acquiring a dangerous insouciance about this level of VIP transport, as if it was the natural order of things in this world. It was clear that her birth mother was an important person here, but the degree to which the machinery of state tilted towards her alarmed him. This was Politburo-level servility, the trappings of imperial power assumed by the functionaries who had risen to the top after the people's revolution. Kurt had met a few such people during his youth, and while some of them were good men and women trying to do a thankless job, others were the same sociopaths who bloated corporate boardrooms these days—only with fewer brakes on their depravity. He desperately hoped that Miriam Burgeson wasn't one of that kind.

Some things seemed constant across time lines. Government buildings came with uniformed guards on reception, junior officials scurrying round busily, and senior functionaries pacing out measured steps. There was more marble and statuary than he could count, gilt-framed paintings of significant events and famous people lining the corridors, and at least one flag in every room. But the flag was unfamiliar to him. Neither the Stars and Stripes nor the Bundesdienstflagge Tricoleur of his youth existed in this time line: the flag of the Commonwealth featured a superposition of red diagonals on a gold field, its symbolism opaque.

They came to a pair of doors flanked by soldiers in dress uniform. They opened for Inspector Morgan, and Rita followed her as if it was her right. Kurt slouched in behind them, glancing sidelong at the guards. The red tunics and gold braid were fancy but the guns held across their chests were jarringly functional, and ceremonial duty didn't stop them from staring back at him, unblinking. *There are real threats here,* Kurt pondered. *I wonder what they are?*

"Hello! You must be Kurt? Rita has told me so much—I've been looking forward to meeting you!"

Rita's birth mother had a twinkling smile, and Kurt returned her greeting, reminding himself that it meant nothing. Stalin was said to have been friendly and avuncular, with an impish sense of humor, and collected jokes about himself—he had several prison camps' full of them. But Miriam seemed genuinely pleased to meet him, as if she'd been worried that he wouldn't accept her invitation. Looking past the strange clothes, he saw a tall woman in middle age, her hair silvering and the skin on the back of her hands loosening. She held her back straight, but her manner was open and friendly. And, yes, there was something of Rita about her: the bone structure, perhaps, if not the skin hue. "I'm pleased to see you, too," he said gravely. "I don't believe we met, but I knew your mother. I gather she passed away?"

Mrs. Burgeson nodded, her smile fading slightly. "Yes, about ten years ago. She had multiple sclerosis. The medical treatments here lag those back home, although we're getting better every year."

Back home, Kurt noted, was still the United States to Mrs. Burgeson. "I am sorry." Kurt reined himself in. He took in Rita's body language towards her birth mother. It spoke of growing familiarity. "It would have been good for Rita to know her."

Mrs. Burgeson's expression was peculiar. "Not really." She shrugged. "My mother was Machiavellian; she wouldn't have been a good influence. For example, my uncle, her half-brother Angbard, ran the Clan's internal security force for decades. He kept files on everyone, and she contributed to them. And after his death she saw to it that those files that could be salvaged followed us here."

"Files," Kurt said flatly.

"Perhaps we could discuss this over tea or coffee, Lieutenant?" Mrs. Burgeson gestured at an overly baroque sofa and two armchairs flanking a low table at the side of the room nearest the big bay window. "It's going to take some time to explain. Rita?"

"Yes?" Rita raised an insouciant eyebrow.

"Would you mind waiting outside?" Mrs. Burgeson had the good grace to look abashed: "I need to talk to your grandfather in private."

"Is this because—" Rita stopped. "I'll wait outside," she said tightly, and left.

Mrs. Burgeson nodded to herself. "Quick on the uptake," she said aloud. "She'll make a good diplomat one day."

"Thank you for not forcing her to compromise her loyalties. At least, not on the spur of the moment."

Mrs Burgeson's forehead wrinkled. "Oh, please: I've only just met her, I'm in no hurry to drive her away!" She met his eyes. "And I'm sure you could tell me more about where her loyalties lie than she'll ever tell me—at least while she's playing the part of a loyal Homeland Security officer. At your behest, I assume," she added coolly.

Kurt struggled for calm. "I have no idea what you're suggesting," he said stiffly. A cold flush of sweat chilled the small of his back. It had been *decades* since anyone addressed Kurt by that rank. It was the one he'd held in the Hauptverwaltung Aufklärung, the foreign intelligence service of the Ministerium für Staatssicherheit, the National Security Agency of East Germany—otherwise known as the Stasi. How much did she know? *Far too much for comfort.* What did she *want*?

"Please call me Miriam, and I can call you Kurt? I want to set your mind at rest: I have no intention of blackmailing you." He interpreted it cynically: *I considered it, and decided it was too risky.* "But I think we can be of use to one another." Translation: *Here's what I want from you.* "It should be obvious that it's in nobody's interests for the impending confrontation between the North American Commonwealth and the United States of America to turn into a new cold war, much less to go nuclear. But some factions in the US government seem to think that they can meddle in the NAC's internal politics without risk of consequences." Translation: *New time line, same old CIA assholes playing games.* "Unfortunately they've started by running a counter-op against an operation that some of *my* people set up, with potentially destabilizing consequences." Translation: *My ass is in a sling.* "You are in a position to help resolve this affair without it turning hot. In return, well, I'm prepared to offer whatever you want, within reason. Asylum and a pension for your entire ring, if they want it." Two possible translations: Either, *the stakes at this table are so high that I'm prepared to tip handsomely*; or, *you are not expected to survive.* (Kurt's money was on the former, but he was uncomfortably aware that he was an optimist.) "We know what it's like to be exiles in a foreign land."

Translation: *Meaningless reassuring sound-bite.* "And that's before we begin to consider the huge debt I owe you for looking after Rita so well for so many years." (Which was plausible, and with an extra four bucks would buy him a coffee.)

Kurt picked up his cup and took a sip. "Thank you for your consideration. But I have been content, hitherto, to live a quiet life." *A little white lie.* "I am an old man and the upheaval of moving to another country would be unwelcome." *Also, you haven't told me anything about what's going on.*

"Well, then." Mrs. Burgeson picked up her own cup and held it in front of her face, either unconscious deflection or a deliberate attempt to signal anxiety.

Kurt couldn't help but admire her professionalism as the silence stretched out. But they were wasting time: so after a minute, he cleared his throat. "I do not actively require asylum," he said. "But certain friends of mine might, and Rita will be among them if my suspicions about her employer's intentions are correct. My suspicions about their intentions towards her, I mean. That is my price."

Mrs. Burgeson took a sip of coffee and put her cup down. "Herr Lieutenant, if Rita wants asylum here, it's hers for the taking—as long as I have anything to say on the matter. Her friends and family, yourself included, also. There are no strings attached—you're not beholden to me in any way for this offer. However, if the matter I'm asking for your help in isn't resolved within the next week, it's quite possible that I won't be around to help. It really *is* that serious."

Kurt forced himself not to twitch. In his experience, politicians as smooth as Miriam weren't prone to melodramatic overstatement. "Are you sure?" he asked. "What is this job, exactly?"

Miriam glanced away. "Until the revolution seventeen years ago, this country, the Commonwealth, was an empire ruled by a king-emperor. Then . . . we had a revolution, but as I said, that was seventeen years ago. The First Man, Adam Burroughs—the Lenin of our revolution, if you like—died a bit over a week ago. His funeral is due to happen very soon. Our local hostile superpower, the French Empire—who gave the heir to the crown-in-exile a home after the revolution: unlike the Romanovs, they were allowed to leave peacefully—are trying to stir trouble. The Pretender to the throne is a handy lever. Some of my people"—Miriam rolled her eyes—"hatched a scheme to separate him from his sole direct-line heir. She was to be seen to be in New London at the funeral, to swear an oath of citizenship to the Commonwealth and disrupt the French plans. Willingly, I might add: we're not kidnappers. Unfortunately—" She shrugged—"we lost her in your time line's Berlin, where we currently have no significant assets," she added, her tone almost inhumanly controlled.

"The agent my people sent over, and his support team, were captured by Rita's controllers in the DHS. Elizabeth made contact by phone, but her battery is draining and the DHS is hunting her. We've got about five days to go until the funeral. So, Lieutenant. How much do you want for the use of the last operational Stasi spy ring—the Wolf Orchestra?"

TEMPELHOF AIR FORCE BASE, BERLIN, TIME LINE TWO, AUGUST 2020

Hulius slowly became aware that he was awake: and with awareness came pain.

The pain was dull and somewhat distant, like an awareness of thundery weather pressing on one's skull, a coppery taste in the mouth and an aching in the joints. His eyes were closed and he was lying on his back in bed. When his throat itched he tried to cough, but gagged violently as he felt a tube where no tube had any right to be. Something was clipped to his nose. Then his chest joined in the cacophony of pain. There was a livid, fiery ache in his ribs, as if he'd been kicked by a horse.

"Major Hjorth? Can you hear me? If you can hear me, squeeze my hand—"

Hulius felt fingers against his right palm, small and feminine. He tried to squeeze, weak as a half-drowned kitten.

"—That's good. You're in a hospital ward and you're going to be all right, but you were badly injured—"

He squeezed the fingers again.

"Yes?" The speaker paused. "You're awake now, so I think they're going to try to take the feeding tube out. Please don't try to dislodge the oxygen mask or the cannula in your left wrist: you need them. And the catheter. You're on a morphine pump, so if the pain gets too much you can self-dose. The button is under your right hand. If you can open your eyes, we'll get you a bit more comfortable . . ."

He tried to say "water," but the tube down his throat wasn't helping. He was gradually working it out. He'd taken the brunt of a cavalry pistol at point blank range. Cavalry pistols were designed to knock down horses, not men: the bullet had lost energy going through his ballistic vest but had penetrated, breaking his ribs, piercing the pleural cavity and collapsing one lung. *Pneumothorax.* A killer if you didn't get attention within some tens of minutes to a couple of hours. Obviously he had. Equally obviously, the only people in position to help him were his enemies.

His memories were a jumble. He'd carried the girl out of the ambush zone, brought her over to time line one, then here, to time line two. He'd got her into the car, tried to drive to the airfield, realized he wasn't going to make it, and diverted to, to . . . the safe house? A hospital? How had he gotten here? *How do they know my name?*

He opened his eyes in a moment of pain and brightness and saw a woman's face leaning over him, worry lines on her forehead. Her lips were pinched in a bloodless line behind her disposable medical mask. He'd known her for years, it seemed, almost half his life: her name was at the tip of his tongue—

The sudden sense of betrayal hurt even more than his oxy-mask dried throat or the shattered rib. "Paulie," he tried to say. *What are you doing here? Did you sell me out?*

It came out as a grunt, but she seemed to get the message. Shoulders shrugged in a gesture of studied helplessness. "The DHS snatched me last month, right out of my bed. It was Colonel Smith—you remember him? He's still hunting the Clan." She waited for a flicker of recognition in his eyes. He kept her waiting almost a minute: he was in pain, distracted, and finding it hard to focus. More to the point, he was anxious to figure out where this was going, how much of what Paulette was telling him was true, or whether she'd finally cracked and done a deal with the devil. The consequences of believing her if she'd been turned could be absolutely horrendous. "He brought me here," she said, her expression desperate. "He knew about, about you being in the other Berlin to bring back 'a person of interest to the enemy regime,' as he put it. He wants to negotiate. But she wasn't there when they raided your safe house. Do you have any idea where she may have gone?"

"She?" He blinked, tried to mumble around the tube.

"I'll get the nurse." Paulie receded from his face. He heard her talking to someone behind his head board. There was a handheld device with a button close by his right hand, on a cable. He pushed the button, heard the beep as the morphine pump released a measured dose. A red light began to pulse on, counting down the time remaining until it would let him release another dose to dull the pain. Hulius closed his eyes. Maybe if he kept pushing the button until he lost consciousness—

Fussing. Hands on his face, instructions to relax and lie still. A really skin-crawlingly *wrong* sensation in his throat, like throwing up but not, a few seconds of breathlessness leading to near-panic—then the tube was gone.

"Better?"

It was Paulie. He opened his eyes. "Better," he agreed. His throat was burning and sore, and he still wanted to cough, but it was good to have the tube out. Paulette looked concerned, but he couldn't read anything more specific into her expression. "We're under guard?"

"You're not going anywhere, except on a trolley: *I'm* under guard. Colonel Smith wanted you to see me." *Now* he got it. She wore the haunted expression of an involuntary verbal tightrope-walker. It went without saying that their conversation was bugged. Quite possibly the Colonel's people were monitoring his skin conductivity, pupillary dilation, and pulse as well, the polygraph leads concealed among the trappings of an intensive care bed. "He's got us both, Yul. He bugged our last rendezvous, they're trying to roll up the entire network in the USA. They've got enough on me to shove me in a supermax cell for the rest of my life. Or worse. As for you, you're a world-walker from the Commonwealth. You know what that means."

He would have nodded if his head wasn't packed with cotton wool and lead weights. To say that the Clan's world-walkers were *persona non grata* in the United States was a massive understatement. They'd taken the position of Nazi war criminals and Communist spies as bogeymen in the public eye, one step up from Al Qaida members with box-cutters now that the latter were all dead.

"The Colonel has decided he needs Elizabeth Hanover. He says he's willing to negotiate a prisoner exchange and hand us over to the Commonwealth *if* we can find her for him." She gave him a sidelong glance: *You don't believe him, do you?* he inferred. "She wasn't in the safe house when he raided it."

The kid ran and hid, he inferred. *Good for her.* But now she was alone in a strange country where she knew nothing about how things worked. *Not exactly safe.*

"It's a mess," he rasped.

"You can say that again." Paulie sniffed, morose. "I think he—or his bosses—have some idea about using Miss Hanover as a bargaining chip with factions inside the Commonwealth government."

Shit, meet fan. So the United States of America had discovered the New American Commonwealth. That was bad enough, albeit not entirely unexpected: plausibly, it could have happened years ago and been kept under wraps by both sides to prevent panic. But the DHS would have to be crazy to meddle in the politics of a nuclear-armed revolutionary superpower in the middle of its first ever succession crisis! *Haven't these people read their history books?* "Chest hurts," Hulius husked, playing for time. "Can't think." He squeezed the morphine pump button again. "Took her from, from the Schloss Britz. 'S a finishing school. Took her . . . to the safe house. Can't remember anything after." He closed his eyes and squeezed the pump trigger once more. Nothing happened. It was too soon. Breathing hurt, and the soft hissing stream of oxygen was drying his sinuses out. It felt as if there were shards of sharp-edged glass growing inside his nose. "If she's missing, I don't know where."

"Was she hurt?" Paulette asked gently.

"Shaken. Not physically," he added. *Squeeze*: the pump motor buzzed. "Did you find my bag in the flat?"

"Your bag? What kind? What was in it?"

"Messenger . . . messenger bag. Gun." He was giving too much away: was there a tongue-loosening drug in his infusion bag? Or was it the morphine? He'd seen injured men out of their head on morphine before, burbling happy nonsense as they bled out. Hulius tried to yawn. "Too tired."

"Bag. With gun. Okay, I'll tell him." Paulie squeezed his hand. "We'll get out of this, Yul. You'll see." But he could tell from her voice that she didn't believe her own lies.

NEW LONDON, MANHATTAN ISLAND, TIME LINE THREE, AUGUST 2020

Adrian Holmes, Secretary to the Central Commission of the Inner Party, had been unhappy for some time: and now he was growing more displeased by the minute. He sprawled in the wing-backed chair behind the desk in his private office, frowning at the briefing paper in his hand as if it were a court summons. Harrison Baker, his chief of staff, stood by at parade rest—an old habit, acquired during his head-banging days on the barricades during the revolutionary struggle, ingrained over subsequent years as an officer in the Commonwealth Guard—and waited patiently. He recognized the signs. Holmes was not one to rant and rave or take his resentment out on subordinates when thwarted. He was far too professional for that. *Don't get angry, get even* was his motto. And there was a lot of groundwork to prepare if he was going to get there.

Eventually, Adrian looked up. "Sit down, Harry. I don't need to worry about your knees as well as . . . as well as *this*." He dropped the papers in the middle of his desk, not bothering to tap them into tidiness: a sure sign of severe distress. "Are you *absolutely* certain about this report?" he asked.

"I think we can be as certain of it as we can be about anything that's happening in there. The source is golden: everything the American emissary says has survived independent confirmation." Baker was no happier than his chief executive. "The rumor about Mrs. Burgeson's alleged—claimed—daughter by a previous marriage arriving here as some sort of envoy from a rival US government agency is confirmed. An announcement is due to be recorded by MiniProp tomorrow, for television broadcast whenever the Burgesons are ready. Our source's accuracy has now been verified on one important issue, which means we should seriously consider his other allegations. Just how they've come by this intelligence is worrying enough, but I've set the matter aside until we have time for a full counterespionage sweep. The *really* incriminating stuff is the business about a certain Major going missing in Berlin on a mission for Mrs. Hjorth. If true, it's too much of a coincidence. It took place on the same morning that the Pretender's heir was abducted from her finishing school, under the very eyes of her guards—"

"Yes, but what does it *mean*?" Holmes asked waspishly. He sighed. "I'm sorry, Harry. This damnable puzzle supports multiple interpretations." He took a deep breath before he continued. "It might be a coup directed against the Pretender: I am sure if I was to ask Mrs. Burgeson directly, that is what she would tell me. Produce the princess, have her swear fealty to the Commonwealth and foreswear her claim to the crown—it would take the wind out of the sails of the reactionary faction, wouldn't it?

Pay no attention to the sacks of gold hidden under her skirts, it signifies nothing—especially after a few years—except that she's beholden to us. But there are other possible interpretations . . ."

"You mean a different kind of coup? Against the Party, I mean."

"Yes. An arranged defection might be a pretext to spirit the heir to the throne into the Commonwealth—just as it lies headless. It would be 1660 all over again: with Oliver Cromwell dead and his heir ineffectual, it was easy for the royalists to install Charles II in the name of restoring stability. And our own monarchists would deal with us just as harshly as their predecessors dealt with Cromwell's associates. Many would welcome a pretty young queen, her powers suitably reduced from those of her grandfather, don't you think? Her dissatisfaction with the match her father arranged for her is widely known, and she'd make an excellent figurehead—a solid rallying banner against the French. Unlike her whimpering playboy father she would be *popular*, and you know where that leads. Demagogues and flatterers and knights of the bedchamber playing favorites, shadowy manipulators lurking behind the throne."

The logic of counterrevolution and restoration was inexorable. Within weeks of Elizabeth Hanover's arrival and restoration there'd be a purge, followed shortly by a crop of gibbets sprouting along Ministry Road. The revolution would fade into history. Perhaps the trappings of democracy would persist for a while, but sooner or later the strain of the confrontation with France would tell and the new regime would revert to the old ways.

"We would be back to the rule of kings, common people bowing to their betters clad in ermine and silk, our blood and silver squandered on the petty arguments of princes, the rights of man trampled underfoot." His face slackened into a mask of near-despair: "Have we lived and fought in vain?"

Baker's expression hardened. "I have taken the liberty of preparing some options, sir. Nothing in writing," he added hastily, in response to a pointed look. "Just talking around the options."

Holmes inclined his head. "I have a little list, too. Let's compare them, shall we? Tell me if I've missed anything." He began counting off fingers.

"One. If it's a genuine defection, we let it run—it strengthens MITI and the Burgesons but it removes a greater threat to the Commonwealth. I can live with that.

"Two: it's a genuine defection but something has gone wrong and the princess is dead or detained. In which case, we can safely leave the entire mess in Mrs. Burgeson's lap. I see no downside to that option, it weakens the Pretender *and* the world-walkers. In neither of these cases are we compelled to act.

"*Three*—this is where we get to the coup—our American source hints that they believe the world-walkers intend to place Elizabeth on the throne as Queen. If the princess is at liberty on Commonwealth soil for any significant length of time without publicly renouncing her claim to the throne, we can conclude that this is the real plan. In which case we need to put a stop to the conspiracy. This assumes that the American diplomats are acting in good faith. For our part, we can act covertly, or with overt force, via the Commonwealth Guard: option four.

"Option four is a counter-coup. The covert one first: we'd have to assassinate the princess, ideally making it look like an accident, and mop up MITI's intelligence heads. I think we should try to avoid taking that route. A war of assassination creates an unsettlingly level playing field, and world-walkers have an unfair advantage. That leaves the overt option, option five: a coup by the Commonwealth Guard in defense of the revolution."

He paused and crossed his arms. "Have I missed anything?"

"Ah, um, that is to say . . ." Baker shook his head. "I can think of another, sir, but it's just a sub-type of counter-strike: instead of the Guard, we could exercise control via the judiciary. Bring charges of treason against the Burgesons and Elizabeth Hanover. Speedy trial and rapid execution, then resumption of normal government under a caretaker administration . . ." He trailed off. "What?"

"Too risky," Holmes muttered. Louder: "I've read the briefing the DPR prepared for Sir Adam—on the dismal history of failures of democracy, that is, of revolution, in the other time line. I'm not going there. Let me repeat that, Harry: I'm *not* going to put myself forward to be the new First Man and I'm not going to allow any show trials to take place. I do not intend to be a, what was he called, a *Stalin*. I think I can bring myself to applaud if Mrs. Burgeson's people have in fact managed to bring a Hanover to the revolution's side: I see no reason to rejoice in unnecessary deaths.

"But you've missed one angle, Harry. This is a *para-time* crisis. And our source is, not to be too blunt about it, a meddling agency of the United

States government. Their *State Department.* What will *they* do? What do they want? They have world-walking machines and thermonuclear weapons, just as we have air wings with world-walking bombardiers. They are watching us deal with a convulsive crisis of legitimacy, one that we have no experience of. The temptation to stab us in the back with a so-called 'first strike' while we are weak and leaderless is unavoidable. So I think we can't afford to lose any time in presenting a strong front to our enemies. Get me Brigadier Stevens. I want to see him here, as soon as possible, this evening at the latest." Holmes frowned. "Just so we aren't caught on the hop if option five proves to be necessary."

NEAR CAMP SINGULARITY,
TIME LINE FOUR, AUGUST 2020

The quiet of a boreal forest in the chilly Appalachians of time line four was broken by footsteps and voices, a sudden infusion of humanity who appeared out of nowhere beneath the spreading branches of spruce and larch.

A quiet command: then eight soldiers sought cover among the trees. They were kitted out as an understrength rifle squad, with helmets and body armor as well as backpacks and weapons, but their movements were uncoordinated, as if this was all very new to them. Their leader knew what he was about, but Staff Sergeant Jackson had his work cut out keeping his raw recruits on track with hand signals they frequently misunderstood or failed to observe. He counted heads. All seven had made the transfer between time lines using the single-destination tattoos he'd issued them with earlier. (Jackson himself couldn't jaunt, or transfer between time lines, at will. Instead, he had a one-man ARMBAND device. It did the same job, but it cost twenty thousand bucks and burned out after a handful of uses.) At least they'd all made it this far: he chose to interpret that as a hopeful sign.

The recruits moved uncertainly, like teenagers who'd signed up for a holiday camp paintball game, only to be handed M4s and live ammunition and sent to a war zone. Which was alarmingly close the truth. There were four boys and three girls, none of them old enough to buy a beer, and most of them barely met the minimal physical standard for service. They'd been swept up by the Selective Service System and conscripted into the secret training program for DRAGON'S TEETH: and they were, in Staff Sergeant Jackson's professional opinion, the worst clusterfuck of raw recruits it had ever been his displeasure to lead.

They were resentful, lazy, and uninterested in a career in the military, like a throwback to the bad old days of the Vietnam war, before the Pentagon pivoted towards professionalism and Congress ended conscription. If they'd arrived as normal recruits he'd have washed them out before the end of their first week in boot camp, and he wouldn't have lost any sleep over the decision. But he wasn't *allowed* to shitcan their sorry asses. These were DRAGON'S TEETH, and he was supposed to turn them into soldiers by any means necessary, because this shower of sullen Generation Z losers were, God help them all, world-walkers.

In Jackson's opinion the only place they were ready for deployment was behind the window of a MacDonald's drive-through. Even if they'd been regular recruits—biddable volunteers who actually wanted to be there—they'd have needed another four months working up, then additional specialist courses before a first tour under the guidance of a couple of experienced fire team leaders. But there were no world-walking E-5s, no experienced NCOs, and no small-unit para-time tactics to train them in. If they survived and shaped up, maybe one of them would eventually get to write the rule book for the next generation. But it didn't seem likely right now, because none of them were volunteers.

The US army had given up on conscripting the unwilling before Jackson and his fellow training sergeants were even born. His CO, Captain Briggs, had been working on a plan to train and motivate them, hitting the historic archives for obsolete training manuals. Jackson had been cautiously hopeful they'd get somewhere before the end of the second year. But when the shit hit the fan, the training schedule had gone out the window. Briggs had called him into his office the previous day and briefed him: take the kids to this time line and do this thing, come back with your shield or on it . . . so here he was, leading seven untrained world-walking teenagers on a children's crusade to shove a pointy stick up the ass of a suspected alien invasion.

Walk in the park, right? Nothing could *possibly* go wrong. Except half the army brass had a hate-on for anything world-walker related—these kids being a case in point, considered unreliable and suspected of holding treasonous sympathies because of their ancestry. The other half wanted to mold them into some kind of elite para-time death squad, and Jackson could tell already that just wasn't an option, if anybody had asked for his opinion. Most of the kids weren't up to minimum standards for walking and chewing gum, never mind qualifying for Ranger training and special forces.

Jackson scanned his surroundings carefully, barely drawing breath. The kids were mostly still, some of them maybe even doing what he'd told them to do: *observe* and *orient*, but leave the *decide* and *act* bits to their squad leader. The rest . . . as long as they kept their heads down, that was as much as he could hope for.

"Zuck," he called quietly. "Go left three meters—about ten feet—and take cover."

"Where—oh, gotcha." Zuck was a pudgy kid from Brooklyn, still round-faced behind his glasses despite the PT that was beginning to build up muscles under the puppy fat. He held the squad high score on Fortnite, but in real life he could just barely hit a water tower a hundred yards away. His scrambling slither through the undergrowth sounded like a stampede of elephants to Jackson, but at least he didn't drop his M-4 this time. And *finally* he was in position to cover Mikka and Jensen, without exposing himself to anything coming over the top of the ridge line on the other side of the valley, because he had all the woodland situational awareness of a blind hippo.

Mikka seemed to know what she was doing—she'd been in the Girl Scouts—and Jensen wasn't *too* terrible, but D'honelle tried too hard to live up to her parents desire for a princess, and as for the others . . . *don't start.* Sally was a classic mean girl cheerleader stereotype, Barry—J. Barrington Weiss III—was some kind of preppy freak with delusions of tactical genius from playing too many games, and Neckbeard Gary hung out on creepy websites and had eye-fucked all the girls continuously until they dragged him round the back of a classroom and gave him a good schooling (to which Jackson had turned a blind eye).

Half the problem with DRAGON'S TEETH was that they were con-scripts. The other half was that they were all children of privilege. Their parents had paid a high end fertility clinic/surrogacy service for perfect and well-formed designer babies. They'd all been born loaded, and none of them had a clue that they were getting the secret special sauce for free with their donor DNA until Uncle Sam came calling. There had been howls and threats of lawsuits, but gagging orders from the FISA courts had shut the parents down hard. However, the kids simply weren't promising enlistment material. Raised in leafy suburban McMansions, expensively educated and driving fancy cars—at least two of them had rolled up for induction in Porsches—until a couple of months ago, they'd been expecting to go to Ivy League schools or make the kind of marriages that were listed in the society pages. Getting drafted into the army had come as a rude shock to them, and they were still mostly not over themselves. *Spoiled* was the word that sprang to Jackson's mind, followed immediately by *brats*. Except Mikka, who had been planning to join the Peace Corps and do good works overseas because she was a Girl Scout at heart, and *maybe* D'honelle if she pulled her head out of her ass. But the rest . . .

"Team one, up and forward fifty. Don't bunch, don't get distracted, use cover, and keep the chatter down. Second team, prepare to follow me."

The first four kids rose and moved forward without tripping over their own bootlaces or starting a forest fire. So far so good.

"Weiss, you and the Cheerleader take point. Neckbeard, stick to my nine. Move, now." No way was Jackson letting Neckbeard Gary out of his sight. He'd put him on team two for a reason. He was the kid most likely to go full trench coat mafia at the drop of a white supremacist tract: and also the one most likely, in Jackson's opinion, to lose his shit on contact with the enemy. He was not merely unsuitable for service but an actual hazard and a liability—but Jackson needed more evidence before he could petition Briggs to shitcan Neckbeard from the program, because the brass were deadly serious about there being no washouts from DRAGON'S TEETH.

"Sarge, why cain't they just send a drone?" Gary whined as they picked their way past a deadfall.

Jackson gritted his teeth. "They did. Drone didn't come back."

"But why do we hafta—"

Jackson silenced him with a gesture, then froze in place.

"Listen up, everyone," he called quietly after a few seconds. "I told you this already, but if any of you didn't leave your phone behind, and *especially* if you didn't pull the battery, do it now."

"But why—"

There was no birdsong. Jackson had been warned about that, about the oddly specific mass extinction that had hit this time line a couple of thousand years ago, but it still spooked him. Birdsong was a useful warning sign: the silence of the songbirds meant trouble everywhere he'd been. The lack of noise had his skin crawling with subliminal dread even though he knew it didn't signify.

"Anti-radiation missiles, right, Sarge?" Zuck piped up, right on cue. Teacher's pet, too fucking smart for this job—he'd been tapped for MIT. Again: he didn't belong here, he belonged in some SIGINT hut where he could be useful without tripping over his own toes. "That's why our headsets are off too, isn't it?"

Jackson gritted his teeth again. You couldn't just tell these kids, you had to explain *everything*. Including how to wipe their noses. "We don't know. Maybe. Maybe not. But if you couldn't bear to leave your phone in your locker then you're carrying a radio transmitter, and if the bugs have anti-radiation missiles you just dialed in a strike on your location. So this is your last call to turn 'em off and I'll pretend you heard me back before we moved out."

Nearly half his squad furtively fiddled with gadgets that they shouldn't have had in the first place. "Weiss, collect all those batteries and bag 'em." Once bagged, Jackson intended to dump them: like all phone batteries these days they contained cheap bugging devices, and he was serious about emissions control. Meanwhile he scanned the ridge-line ahead, nostrils flaring as he strained every nerve for any sign that they weren't alone in the valley. He got nothing, which was alarming enough in its own right. The valley with Camp Singularity and the Dome lay only five kilometers away, across a couple more ridge-lines. It was mid-morning, and they would be there by early afternoon if they didn't stumble across hostiles.

"Listen up, everybody. We're going to move forward by teams. Keep a lid on it and pay attention to what's in front of you. If you see any sign of bugs, go quiet and signal me. I'll check it out. If you make hard contact, duck out *immediately*, tag your location, retreat to the staging point to pick up your return ticket, and report to the Captain. You're not here to fight so I want your fingers clear of the *what* have I fucking told you about trigger discipline Gary, I've told you a thousand times if I've told you once—if any of you even *think* about lighting up the landscape I will kick you in the ass so hard you won't shit for a week—your job is to observe, orient, and *run the fuck away* if we're attacked by bugs so that *somebody* back home can work out how far they've gotten. Paint cans? Show me your fucking paint cans!" Much fumbling, then seven left hands rose as one, clutching their spray cans. "Excellent! Now put them away again and get ready. Okay, team one—"

It's a fucking children's crusade, Jackson swore to himself as he got the kids moving forward in roughly the right direction and with a minimum of mishaps. *But nothing can possibly go wrong . . .*

Epicycles

Everything was different in this Berlin.

Although the city center roads bore tantalizingly familiar names, the roads themselves were surfaced in strange stone covered in inscrutable markings, and the traffic ran along the wrong side of the street. The strangeness of the vehicles and the drab exoticism of the natives' attire she'd half-expected, but the buildings were another shock. Some of the architectural styles were familiar but others resembled agricultural hothouses cross-bred with airships, all glass and polished metal. And the shop windows! The shops all had slabs of finest float glass instead of front walls, smooth and flawlessly clear, a fortune on display in even the meanest kiosk.

This is the future the Commonwealth are copying, Liz thought, increasingly angry with herself, her incompetent rescuers, and the world—whether this one or her own she couldn't say. She wasn't blind and she could see perfectly well that in the run-up to the revolution in the Americas, grandpapa had played the game of statecraft disastrously badly, blundering into every pitfall laid for him. And her exiled father was twice-burned and gun-shy, a comet falling into orbit around the Sun King's primary. But this wasn't *fair.* That the revolutionaries had seized the crown dominions of the New British Empire was happenstance, but that they should then ride to victory on the coat-tails of *this* world's knowledge? *That* felt like cheating.

"Hey! Watch where you're going!" Liz startled, jolting out of the way of a red-faced middle-aged man in a leather coat. She'd been so distracted she'd nearly walked into him. She looked around, hunting for a way down to the ground from the raised decks of the Hauptbahnhoff. The station was built on several levels, its elevated platforms laced together by gleaming moving staircases and cylindrical elevators walled with glass.

"Please, where is the way out—" she began, but he turned his back on her and pointedly strode away. Her anger swelled, but by the time she'd formulated a comeback he'd disappeared, leaving her frustrated with *l'esprit d'escalier*. She looked around again, at pains not to look up at the bridges criss-crossing the atrium overhead, vibrating beneath the sleek electrical trains. She finally noticed one of the moving staircases. Angry Man was halfway down it, descending. She waited until he reached the lower level then stepped onto it, clutching the moving handrail firmly.

There were bakeries here, recognizable equivalents of the street-side stalls of her own Berlin and St Petersburg. There were other shops too. Some sold brightly colored but flimsy clothes which they displayed on headless statues—or maybe they were selling the statuary, although that seemed less likely—and then she saw a display of phones like the one in her pocket, laid out like butterflies in a collector's cabinet. Wire racks at one side of the room held packets of odd-shaped items that on inspection proved to be cases and wires. She went in.

"Hello? I need to buy a, a booster battery. Can you help me?"

The boy behind the desk with the plastic-framed painting on it (unless it was yet another television, though why shop assistants might be allowed to watch television at work was beyond her) seemed anxious to help, and they negotiated the rapids of her fractured German and his rusty English together. "May I see your phone?" He asked. She handed it over.

"I left my charger"—that was the word—"at home."

"Of course," he said. "Can you unlock it for me?"

Oops. "Let me—" Elizabeth took back the phone and held it in front of her, touched the screen. A moment later, it unlocked. She nearly collapsed with relief: Control had reset it! "So, you have a battery?"

"Just one moment." The boy (not really a boy, she realized: just very clean-shaven, and not much older than she was) fetched one of the packages down from the wall of accessories. "It comes pre-charged; you can top it up anywhere, it comes with cables. That will be forty-nine Euros . . ."

The most perilous part of the transaction, after confirming that the phone was hers (did he think she'd *stolen* it?) was recognizing the money in her purloined wallet. But the fifty euro note she handed over did the trick, and with the salesman's help she wired the heavy metal battery up to her phone (lights flashed green and blue, indicating success) then placed them back in her bag. She ducked her head and shuffled out of the shop, silently cursing the Major. *They will think you are Turkish, maybe Romany,* he had said: not *auslander,* let alone *thief* or *vagrant.*

The phone shop was next to a women's clothing store. Liz narrowed her eyes, staring at the fashions on the statues as she approached. The price tags on the garments seemed ridiculously low. Looking past the glass doors, she saw rack upon rack of clothes. They appeared to be ready-made, to buy on the spot. She went inside and discovered numbers, some sort of arcane size system, printed on labels on every item. Guessing her size, she chose an outfit displayed on one of the statues (a long-sleeved top and a pair of thin, loose trousers) and went looking for its elements on the rails. The quality of stitching gave her pause—it was as low as the prices—but the sooner she looked like everyone else the better.

The clerk gave her a suspicious glance as she entered the changing room, but when she came out they willingly took her money. There were public toilets on the level above the store, and ten minutes later a very different dark-skinned woman slipped out of a cubicle, leaving a bundle of clothes buried in the trash. She felt glaringly conspicuous at first, wearing the plain, cheaply made, mannish garments. But within minutes she realized that nobody was looking at her. More importantly, when she walked into another store the attendants paid her no more attention than anyone else. She had clothes that blended in, a charger for the phone—her lifeline— and she still had most of her money. *I can make this work,* she realized, and was just about to start looking for a café when the phone began to vibrate.

NEW YORK, UNITED STATES, TIME LINE TWO, AUGUST 2020

Angie Hagen's life had been, if not simple, then at least manageable un- til a couple of months before. She'd fallen into a routine of work, study, discreet partying, and saving towards the down payment on an apartment in one of the suburbs of Philly that showed some hope of clawing its way back up from 'urban wasteland' to 'promising cheap neighborhood'. Then Rita Douglas had re-entered her life, blazing a fiery trail from horizon to horizon like a re-entering space capsule.

When Rita turned up and tumbled into her arms as if they hadn't drifted apart nearly a decade ago, she had brought trouble in tow: her shadowy employment by a black unit within DHS, tasked with spying on a frighteningly advanced time line (nuclear-capable, while all others found to date were uninhabited or Paleolithic). Then Rita's *grandfather* showed up, which brought all her kindergarten training-games and family folklore slamming back into focus, because Kurt Douglas was the Wolf Orchestra's controller—the hub of a Stasi spy ring orphaned by the end of the Cold War.

Growing up as a third-generation Communist spy on American soil had been just another part of Angie's childhood, along with going to grade school, playing soccer, and being a Girl Scout. (The Troop she and Rita had been in had a surprising number of girls with parents who worked in Langley and Crypto City and couldn't talk about their jobs. It also featured field trips to the National Cryptological Museum and merit badges in tradecraft. She later realized that it had sponsorship from some government slush fund, nominally to help with parent-child bonding—or maybe to cultivate the next generation of potential CIA/NSA recruits. Which, of course, also gave it considerable appeal to Wolf Orchestra parents.)

The Germanies had been reunified and the Stasi abolished before she was even been born. It was just part of her family history, like being a secret practicing Moslem in post-*reconquista* Spain. There were quaint family rituals and observances, practiced behind closed doors out of fear of discovery, and it was just another unremarkable aspect of her upbringing.

But now, thanks to the freak accident (if indeed it *was* an accident) of Rita's adoption by Kurt's son and daughter-in-law, the Orchestra had inadvertently fulfilled its mission. It had penetrated a beyond-secret American espionage organization. They had an agent just two links down the reporting chain from the White House! Colonel-General Wolf would be smiling, were there an Actually Existing Socialist Heaven for him to do so from. And they'd only just succeeded in time.

The citizens of the United States, terrified of their own shadows in the wake of the nuclear attacks of 7/16 and the War on the Multiverse, had built a digital panopticon. Its ever-tightening grasp was squeezing the gaps in which illegals like the Wolf Orchestra families could survive. Just as the Marranos and Moriscos had lived under the shadow of the Spanish Inquisition, the Wolf Orchestra families existed with the threat of discovery. It was only a matter of time before the DHS, FBI or other agencies realized that there was an old-school sleeper ring in their back yard. With no more

Berlin Wall, there was no prospect of a prisoner exchange at Checkpoint Charlie, no Workers' Paradise on the other side willing to ransom them from their supermax prison cells.

"I'm going to try and cut us a deal," Kurt had told Angie before he went to his rendezvous with Rita's birth mother. "This Commonwealth took in one group of defectors. Maybe they can find room for another?" He'd looked tired, his eyes sunken in crows-nest webs of baggy skin. "Or just for the retirees."

Angie had swallowed, looking him in the eyes: "what about Rita?" She asked. *And me?* She left unsaid.

"You and your parents are natural-born Americans," Kurt pointed out. "Not illegals. Only my generation, your grandparents' generation, are at actual risk, unless you engage in espionage. If you keep your noses clean . . ." He trailed off uncertainly. "You have options we don't."

While they'd intended the Orchestra to remain in the US indefinitely and raise children there—it was a *very* long-term program—nobody in the office complex on the Frankfurter Allee had considered the possibility that the first generation of sleepers would enter their dotage on hostile soil. Nor had they imagined that the Workers' Paradise would collapse and their agents still be living in the United States in their eighties, at risk of succumbing to dementia, babbling state secrets in nursing home day rooms. If anyone *had* given it any thought they'd have arranged to repatriate the pensioners before it got that far. But by the time the contingency arose, the German Democratic Republic no longer existed and the existence of the Wolf Orchestra had been frantically erased from the archives inherited by its successor state. And nobody wanted to murder their own grandparents to keep their history secret. It was a deadly quandary.

Angie was an American citizen and therefore free to stay. Mom and Pop, too. But her freedom was not unconditional: she was only free in those states that tolerated gays and had resisted the no-choicers' war on female reproductive autonomy. As for Rita, she was even more conflicted. Her grandpa was an illegal and her birth mother was a headline act on the Most Wanted list. Rita herself was no patriot: she was reluctantly under the Federal thumb, monitored and tracked and diligently surveilled. But would life in the Commonwealth be any better if the two of them defected? Would they be allowed to live openly as a couple, without fear of sanction merely for being who and what they were? And, if push came to shove, would Rita stand by the American flag, or put family and girlfriend first?

Angie had spent the night after Kurt's rendezvous with Rita sleeplessly pondering what she ought to do. And come morning she still had no answers. However, when she went outside she found a brightly-colored flyer jammed under the windscreen wiper of her truck. She pulled it out as she climbed into the cab, and was about to throw it in the trash when something caught her eye. There were instructions scrawled on one side in blue sharpie, in a code that would be meaningless to anyone else. The breath froze in her throat for an instant, and she instinctively looked around even though there was nothing to see. In the early hours of the morning some anonymous figure had walked along the street and through the parking lots, stuffing leaflets in the cold. All the cars she could see had been leafleted. *Got to make it look good.* For a dizzying moment, Angie imagined herself in an entire world of spies, where every sedan and truck windscreen wiper held down operational directives and cyphered commands for a different agent. But no: all this effort had been for her benefit, and hers alone.

She blinked, and read the incriminating scrawl on the leaflet again: SEND FIVE ACTIVE RDV TXL LANDSIDE DAY AFTER TOMORROW 1000 LOCAL.

She translated silently, *fly five active operatives to TXL to rendezvous at 10am local time the day after tomorrow.* That was the code for Tegel Airport, Berlin. It was a tight deadline: there was no time to lose. She thumbed the truck's start button, swiped in the location of her current work site, and stuffed the leaflet in her coat pocket. The big-block V8 rumbled into life and the steering wheel began to spin: "five," she repeated under her breath, then dry-swallowed. "Shit." She cancelled the auto-drive command, took back the wheel, and drove around the block then back to the front of her apartment. "I'll be late for work," she said aloud. In fact she was going to have to blow work off completely. She had her marching orders, for the first time ever. Kurt intended to conduct a symphony of spies. *He's cutting it close,* she realized. Then she was at her front door, walking to the kitchen in a daze to collect the tiny screw-top can containing the burner SIM cards Kurt had given her to hold, mentally composing the message she'd send the agents in her cell.

Marching orders. We fly at dawn.
The orchestra was going home.

NEW LONDON, MANHATTAN ISLAND, TIME LINE THREE, AUGUST 2020

Rita watched the glass-nosed trijet push back from the terminal building, engines belching smoke as they screeched into raucous life. Inspector Morgan stood beside her in a simulation of companionable silence. Rita didn't credit her with empathy: Alice lived for her job, and was certainly not above manipulating Rita for her mission's ends. A chill of isolation prompted her to hug herself. Kurt was strapped inside that silvery cigar-shape with sharply-raked wings, one of only a handful of passengers aboard the diplomatic courier—a converted jet bomber—taxiing towards the runway on the first leg of his journey to Berlin.

Alone again. Kurt had come to some agreement with her birth mother. Mrs. Hjorth—Brilliana, one of Mrs. Burgeson's world-walking spooks—had whisked him away to the military airport immediately thereafter, and now she was walking back towards Rita and Inspector Morgan, shoulders sagging slightly as if she had just discharged a burden of responsibility.

"Well, that's done," Brill remarked. "Let's get you to the Propaganda Ministry for your play date."

Rita trailed her towards the waiting car, rubbing at a patch of skin on her left arm. *What just happened?* she wondered. Her sub-dermal key generator itched—the programmable e-ink tattoo DHS had provided, that allowed her to flash up the knot-like trigger engrams that enabled her to jaunt between time lines. "Do you know what they want me to do yet?" she asked.

"It's an acting gig." Brill was even more taciturn than usual. "No biggie, we just have a script for you to read."

"A—" Rita's eyes narrowed. "I think you'd better explain."

"Inside," said Brill, as Inspector Morgan held the car door open for them. "I'll brief you on the way, the Inspector and our driver are both cleared."

Cleared for what? Rita wondered. "You know who I work for, right?" She asked slowly.

"Yes." Brill climbed in behind her and closed the door. The car moved off. "I, um. This is awkward." Brill paused. "Before you were recruited by

DHS, you were an actor, yes? Most recently doing sales demonstrations of HaptoTech's motion capture kit. We have an, uh, problem. We badly need someone who can drive a motion capture rig for a couple of hours on two or three consecutive days during the funeral ceremony. So that an absent guest can put in an appearance by proxy, as it were."

Rita closed her eyes. *Bend over, here it comes*, she thought.

Rita's position in the Commonwealth was ambiguous, if not downright dangerous. She'd arrived as a spy, a world-walker dispatched by the DHS Unit headed by Colonel Smith, to figure out just what kind of civilization the US para-time reconnaissance drones had stumbled across. Surprise: this time line turned out to be a close sibling of her own—closer than the ones stuck in the Paleolithic age, anyway. Populated by North Americans who spoke a dialect of English and built railroads . . . not to mention jet fighters and nuclear weapons. They'd swept her up with frightening speed and efficiency, only to present her to her birth mother Miriam, a leader in the Clan of world-walkers. The Clan survivors—from their progressive faction—were now living in exile in the Commonwealth, where they had fled after their rivals within the Clan picked a fight with the United States nearly twenty years ago.

Miriam was now a very senior member of the government, and Colonel Smith had used Rita to open up a back-channel for negotiations with the Commonwealth. But it was clear to Rita that her birth mother and her commanding officer were playing a perilously deep game, and as a double agent trapped between two rival agencies, Rita was constantly looking over her shoulder, anticipating betrayal. Her life was complicated enough even without factoring into account her training as an agent of the Wolf Orchestra.

"What does my mother want me to do?" Rita asked, "and how is it going to compromise me further down the line?"

Brill chuckled: "direct as always." She tapped one finger on the armrest, betraying tension. "I don't think this will compromise you with your employers in Homeland Security, but it's your call. What I can say is, we were making arrangements to receive a high-level defector from within the French Empire. The operation went pear-shaped and we lost track of her in Berlin. Your grandfather has agreed to help retrieve her, but in the meantime we need to—"

"Who is it?" Rita demanded.

Brill took a deep breath. "We want you to impersonate Princess Eliza-beth Hanover, the heir-in-exile to the throne of the British Empire. It'll be for three, four days, max, just until she gets here. We've got a studio with green screen and an imported HaptoTech motion-capture rig, just like the one you worked with—for deepfaking the TV broadcasts, both studio and live, so the French think she's arrived—"

Rita pinched the bridge of her nose. *What is this, I don't even*—"You want me to impersonate a *Princess?*" She paused. "What happens if I say no?"

"Well." Brill glanced away. "For starters, I get to deliver my resignation letter. Quite possibly your mother gets to draft *her* resignation letter, too. It'll be quite the biggest political scandal involving MITI. Your Colonel Smith will find himself dealing with new and entirely unfamiliar coun-terparts, who may or may not choose to continue negotiations. There are hard-liners in the Commonwealth government, people who think the es-tablished methods for dealing with the French Empire can be applied equally well to the United States. Methods that include nuclear brinks-manship.

"I can't say for sure how bad it will get: I might be overly alarmist here. But Elizabeth was betrothed to the French heir—not happily, that's why she's trying to defect—and the worst-case outcome of a failed defection is that the King-Emperor in St. Petersburg frames it as a kidnapping, blames the Commonwealth, and uses it as a pretext for war."

War.

Rita turned her head and glared at Brill. "I don't respond well to threats," she stated.

Brilliana leaned tiredly against the leather bench seat of the limousine. "I'm not threatening you," she said. "You're free to say no—"

"—But you're doing this to compromise me, aren't you?" Rita jabbed a finger: "Don't tell me you don't have dozens of actors on call who can—"

"—What? But we *don't!*"

Rita blinked. "Bullshi—"

"No, will you listen for a moment? This is not about us trying to put you in a compromising position. If we wanted to do that . . ." Brill flicked imaginary lint from her lapel: "we've got experts. But we don't need to. Frankly, as far as Homeland Security are concerned you were compromised from the get-go simply because you're a world-walker. So no, this isn't about you, for once.

"You're new to the Commonwealth so you had no reason to know this, but you are a dead ringer for Princess Elizabeth. You might have noticed some people giving you a double-take? That would be why. She's of mixed descent, like you. Similar hair, similar skin tone. You're a few years older and a couple of centimeters shorter, but that's nothing that can't be fixed with cosmetics and platform shoes. You can impersonate her for the dignitaries at a state funeral who've never met her, given a suitable wardrobe and a voice coach, as well as doing the video motion capture. Do you know how many black actresses there are on TV here? Not enough that we have a pool of talent we can dip into without risk of them being noticed. You're a clean face, which makes you a perfect fit for Operation Zenda. We've even got people working on a set of scripts for you. It's the acting role of a lifetime!"

Rita, having run out of immediate objections, was speechless. Brill took her silence for agreement: or perhaps she simply decided to steamroller Rita into compliance. Either way, an hour later Rita found herself facing off with a rumpled-but-intense looking television producer, across a boardroom table in a windowless office in the Ministry of Propaganda. She pointed skeptically to the list of scripted scenes on the white board off to one side. "These are public appearances! How do you script for spontaneity?"

"We have a set of scenarios, and a number of set-piece interviews and speeches," he raised a sheath of papers. "For the first day, it's cut and dried. Just you in a studio, or with an interviewer. Costume and make-up as Elizabeth." Rita twitched. Brilliana had left her with Inspector Morgan and this guy, after reassuring her that the Propaganda Ministry had approved him for 'Most Secret Disinformation Productions'—official fake news. Then she'd breezed out without giving Rita an opportunity to express her misgivings, much less refuse to cooperate. "We can do that very easily using a sound stage and green screen. We need to capture a lot of calibration readings of you walking around and shaking hands and talking as the subject, for later use.

"The fancy bit is what comes next, the First Man's state funeral scenes. Assuming the subject herself isn't available by then." It was *his* turn for cheek-twitching. "I've seen the, uh, *motion capture* equipment from the other time line, and it's remarkable. I knew they were ahead of us, but seeing developments in your own field really puts it in perspective . . ."

"Your point, Mr. Adams," Morgan prodded, showing just a flicker of impatience.

Adams shook himself. "Well, we need to broadcast footage of the princess in public, don't we? So we need to interpolate her into actual television broadcasts in public settings. But not *too* public. Using these motion capture gadgets—the Department of Para-time Research bought a complete HaptoTech system, I gather Ms. Douglas has used it before—we can set up a rendering pipeline. Say that Ms. Douglas here is standing on a podium with a group of dignitaries at some event—a horse race or a state funeral or something. An event where the dignitaries are not watching themselves on television, anyway. We point the cameras at the podium and track Ms. Douglas's kinematics, and feed them to the motion capture and real-time rendering pipeline, which replaces her with an entirely generated image of someone else going through the same movements. It works smoothly at thirty frames a second. So the dignitaries on the podium see Ms. Douglas, but the television audience see the princess instead. So we can present the appearance of the subject attending state functions even though she's not actually there."

"But what about the VIPs?" Rita asked. "What happens if someone tells them they were on stage with Princess Elizabeth? Or asks them what it was like to meet her?"

Adams frowned. "Not my department. I expect they'll be warned in advance that they're dealing with a body double. I will caution that this has to be used *very* sparingly, in very controlled circumstances—ideally where the DPR or the Ministry can brief the participants. And of course, we have complete control of the audience. In another decade it won't be possible, everyone will have those magic pocket camcorder things: but for now, you can't hide a videotape system under your coat. Especially if you're a French Empire wire service," he added with some satisfaction. "We're offering them full cooperation and providing a live conduit to the trans-oceanic cables for their own coverage of the funeral. As long as none of their people are on the podium with you, they won't realize we don't actually have the princess."

Alice Morgan's face twitched into something approximating a smile. "You mean you can work your magic on the *French* television broadcasts, as well as our own?"

"They're the primary target, actually." Adams's smug smile said every-thing.

Rita took a deep breath. "But first you need to install the HaptoTech mo-tion capture implants, don't you?" Itching and sore patches had plagued her the year before, when she'd signed up for the job of demonstrating their real-time video motion capture tech at trade shows. The HaptoTech kit was invisible and accurate to within millimeters, communicating wire-lessly with transponders hidden below the floor. Unfortunately it required the injection of a bunch of rice-grain sized capsules under the skin.

"Yes." Adams stood up. "And we have a doctor and a trained technician waiting to see you in the nursing station, right after lunch."

"And then you need to kit me out as Elizabeth and let me study her voice for the studio impersonation . . ." Rita trailed off. Somehow she'd be-come infected with enthusiasm for this illicit job, even though Colonel Smith would probably scold her for agreeing to anything without obtain-ing prior authorization. But it was an acting role! Indeed it was her first professional performing role on camera, on TV, in front of a genuine au-dience, ever. It was the job she'd always wanted—even if she wasn't going to get her name in IMDb as a result—and it was going to help Miriam Burgeson out of a hole. *Is this what being compromised feels like?* Rita pon-dered: *because if so, maybe I should do it more often.*

MARACAIBO COMMONWEALTH AIR STATION, TIME LINE THREE, AUGUST 2020

Huw flew back to Maracaibo immediately after his meeting with Miriam in the capital. It was a routine trip, and he spent much of it catching up on his reading—reports from the various JUGGERNAUT teams, from General Anders (who was deputizing for him in command at Maraca-ibo Air Station), and interminable Party bulletins about the state funeral plans. *Let's hope the new First Man lasts a bit longer,* Huw thought mor-dantly. The public holiday and celebration of the revolutionary leader's life followed the only model the Commonwealth had for a head of state's death, namely the death of a King-Emperor under the previous regime. The two weeks of funeral preparations and post-funeral conferencing prior to the formal accession of the new supreme arbiter was causing entire industries to grind to a standstill. *How the Americans can afford to do this every four years . . . !*

The all-encompassing chaos of the state funeral was sufficient to swamp his low-key anxiety over his younger brother's disappearance in Berlin and his anomie over his job, but it returned with a vengeance after touch-down, when he found himself back in his office. Seth, his adjutant, was preparing to go over a list of medium-urgent matters that had arisen during his absence—nothing that called for his attention in New London, but nothing that could wait, either, this close to the launch window. More paperwork, more endless committee meetings, more visiting parties of dignitaries poking their noses around the site and getting in the way. *I'm growing old*, he realized: they'd forced him to take an office job managing the exploration program a decade ago, and even though the work was important, it had become a source of stress rather than excitement.

Huw was doing his best to burn through Seth's stack of problems when General Anders knocked briskly and opened the door. "Ah, Explorer-General Hjorth? Do you have a minute?"

Huw stood. "Come in, come in." Seth saluted, then jumped to pull out a chair for Anders, who grunted as he sat. His eyes were baggy and tired, Huw noticed. "What's wrong?"

"It's base medical." Anders glanced at Seth. "Have you gotten to it—"

"I'm sorry, sir, it's a couple of items down my list . . ."

"Medical?" Huw tensed. "What's wrong?"

"Influenza, that's what's wrong." Anders shrugged. "Not at epidemic levels, thank god, but Colonel Klein—" the base senior medical officer— "has established an isolation ward and activated the medical incident plan. Eighteen cases so far."

"Eighteen?" Seth startled. "Sorry, sir, but this—" he flipped through his papers—"says nine?"

"I came straight from the hospital. Your list was issued this morning: the number of cases has doubled in under a day." Anders shrugged. "We've got more than six thousand people on base. It seems to be a relatively mild flu bug, but the real problem is that it's hit the flight crew. They've been logging lots of hours in the capsule simulators and they weren't in pre-flight isolation yet. It looks like one of the ground technicians cross-infected his watch shift. JUGGERNAUT is down three world-walkers, including Colonel d'Ost."

"Fuck," Huw said succinctly, and leaned back in his chair. *Fuck* barely began to sum up how he felt. This was a disaster. To be so close to launch, with an immovable politically mandated deadline, for such a tiny thing as a virus to derail the program . . . !

"Rudi is running a mild fever and swears blind he'll be ready to fly by the day after tomorrow." Anders' expression made it very clear what he thought of Rudi's self-assessment.

"What does Colonel Klein say?" Huw asked. Suddenly his heart skipped a beat as he realized the implications if Rudi was still in quarantine and unable to fly on launch day.

"He says it's flu. Colonel d'Ost may or may not be fit to fly in seventy-two hours, but he'll still be potentially infectious, so Klein's grounding him. Says most likely he won't be cleared to return to duty for two weeks. Which means it's fallback time." Anders was watching him closely, Huw realized. Looking for signs of undue unease, or maybe enthusiasm. "Sir, I've got to ask, what happened to your prime candidate?"

"Major Hjorth is unavailable," Huw said suppressively. *My brother agreed to run a special errand for the DPR and is overdue for check in.* But that was secret, for sharing strictly on a need-to-know basis. "Looks like there's no alternative but to go with our substitute line-up, then." His heart skipped another beat from nervous excitement. He tried to keep a tight lid on his emotion. It wouldn't do for the base CO to leap out of his chair and start ululating and punching the air. "You'll cover for me in mission control and I'll take the flight deck, assuming Klein clears me on medical and I pass certification. Yes?"

"Sir, you're the *Explorer-General*. With all due respect, you're not supposed to lead from the front—I'd much rather we schedule a two-week launch hold at this point? Then we can launch with our intended captain."

"Sorry, politicians say 'no'," Huw said lightly. "You're right: I'm not supposed to fly anything but this desk. But we've got a locked-in launch window. The ministers want a spectacle to go with the funeral procession, so unless there's a high risk technical fault we're going to launch on schedule. As it happens, I've been shadowing Rudi's training cycle, and I'm already command-rated for para-time exploration. If Yul was around—or any other world walkers with flight, command, and exploration ratings—it'd be a no-brainer to substitute them instead, but with Rudi ill, the buck stops here." Huw shrugged. "It can't be helped. Schedule a hand-over meeting for tomorrow, then I'll switch to flight duties full-time—unless Hulius surfaces or Rudi makes a miraculous recovery."

Anders frowned. "Can I note, on the record, that I think it's a really bad idea and I recommended a two week hold?"

"Be sure to cover your ass in writing." Huw couldn't contain himself any longer: he grinned lopsidedly. "While you're at it, *please* go over my head and complain to the Minister for Intertemporal Technological Intelligence in person?" Which was Miriam. "*She* won't be happy about me flying this one either, and if there's a political fix to avoid it, you can be certain she'll find it—but I'm betting she won't."

Anders sagged beneath the weight of realization. "Crap."

"You can say that again: we're in a corner."

"Bah." Anders hauled himself to his feet. "Well, I'll be seeing you tomorrow morning, then. Captain, Explorer-General." He touched his cap, then retreated from the office.

"Sir?" Seth was looking at him, wide-eyed. "You're really going to take command of JUGGERNAUT?"

"Only if nothing else comes up." Huw grinned again. *How am I going to break this to Brill?* Secretly, he wasn't scared of his wife's reaction—she was a professional too, and would be equal parts proud of and pissed at him. "A couple more cases of influenza among the crew, or a coup d'état in the capital. Who the hell knows? Any miracle will do in a pinch." His expression brightened slightly. "But at least there's a silver lining: I may be an Explorer-General, but I've gotten to do precious little *exploring* these past five or ten years . . ."

COMMONWEALTH COURIER JET, TIME LINE THREE, AUGUST 2020

Kurt remembered planes like the Commonwealth courier jet: big fast Tupolevs that roared across the skies above the Warsaw Pact nations, bearing VIPs with exit visas in their passports. The Commonwealth was technologically backward compared to the United States, but it was an eye-opener compared to everything he'd ever heard about other time lines. They'd either been uninhabited or sparsely occupied by stone age tribes, with the exception of the Gruinmarkt, which had reached the dizzy heights of late mediaeval technology. These people had cars and computers and satellites buzzing and beeping across the heavens. More: they had a Plan, and not a Gosplan-style Five Year Plan, a centrally-controlled economy like that of the Soviet Union. They'd given him a "Welcome to the Commonwealth" briefing booklet and there was some wild stuff in it: computer networks, real-time planning, a continuation and expansion of a thing called Project Cybersyn that had been suppressed in Chile in the 1970s by a US-ordered fascist coup—a plan to catch up that paralleled the way South Korea, Japan, and China had modernized in the twentieth century.

And they're going to make it, he realized as the jet banked across the Hudson and turned south. At this rate, in another twenty years they'd be level with the world he'd left. Not that he'd be around to see it, but Rita might: and Angie, and the other children and grandchildren of the Wolf Orchestra. *As long as there isn't another nuclear war.*

The woman sitting in the seat opposite him sighed and pushed the button to recline her chair. They'd brought her to the air stairs in a wheelchair. "Six hours," she said, glancing at him. Her eyes seemed to belong to someone two decades older. "Then we change planes."

"You should save your strength, Miss Thorold," Kurt suggested. Something like concern flashed through him. She was younger than Emily, Rita's mother. *Adoptive* mother, he reminded himself.

"Olga." Her cheek twitched. "Kurt."

"If you wish." He mustered the ghost of a smile. "Is this worth it to you?"

"It's my job. I'll have plenty of time to sleep when I'm dead." She was blond, with long hair and piercing blue eyes, her skin so pale it was almost transparent. She was young, to Kurt's eye, perhaps in her mid-forties, but she was clearly unwell. "That'll be sooner rather than later, damn it. But someone needs to brief you fully, and that's why I'm here."

"Why?" Kurt raised an eyebrow. "You're obviously very senior, M— Olga."

She gave him a look. "This is eyes-only material. Ears-only. I'm briefing you because I have personal experience of the adversary we're facing, and we want to keep this under wraps."

"This is old world-walker business, from before you all moved to the Commonwealth, isn't it?"

"You assume correctly." Olga took a deep breath. "There is a unit within the national security bureaucracy of the United States. Back in the early noughties, it was called the Family Trade Organization. It still exists, but these days even its name is classified: it's the blackest of black operations, embedded in Homeland Security." Kurt managed to suppress any sign of his startlement. "The FTO was tasked with hunting world-walkers down, back before 7/16—when a rival faction within the Clan stole a couple of nukes from the Americans and used them to assassinate the President and blow up Congress."

Kurt nodded grimly. He'd lived through the years of panic and paranoia the bombings of 7/16 had created.

Olga frowned. "Not stopping them in time was our worst failure. And of course it led to our homeland, Gruinmarkt, being utterly destroyed in response."

"*Failure?* For a gang of time line-hopping narco-terrorists—"

She ignored him and continued: "The Clan, the world-walkers living in the Gruinmarkt, were a *government*. The government of an admittedly backward realm, but still a government. I mean, the Gruinmarkt was a monarchy, roughly equivalent in sophistication to a mediaeval European kingdom. Over the 19th and 20th century, the Clan had used their ability to visit other time lines—your time line—to become incredibly rich. We ran things behind the scenes, and of course, but we had internal factions. One party, the conservatives—and by 'conservative' I mean monarchical and un-sophisticated, the ones who weren't educated in the United States—got it into their heads that they could seize power and 'send a message' to the US government. But they didn't understand that the United States didn't function like the nations they were familiar with. When you're dealing with a king, if you don't like his attitude you hit him with a sword until there's a new king and hope he's more amenable to your demands. Simple, right? Like hunting a mountain lion or a wild boar. But that . . . that doesn't work so well against a superpower. They went hunting with a spear, expecting a wild boar, and attacked a hornets' nest instead by mistake. Hornets armed with nuclear weapons." An expression of mingled grief and fury flickered across her face and she took a minute to regain her composure before she could continue.

"They're dead. We hunted them down and executed them, and any we missed will have died during the subsequent nuclear bombardment. But I want you to be very clear that we survivors, those of us who went into exile in the Commonwealth, are the other faction, the other party from within the world-walkers: the modernizers.

"But back to Rita's employers. The FTO, the Family Trade Organization, was absorbed by the Department of Homeland Security, which took on the FTO's mission of para-time security, with results you know. Protecting the United States from all possible threats emerging from parallel universes by building the ultimate surveillance state with inter-universe strike capacity. Meanwhile, bits of the FTO are still embedded inside the DHS, and they've been hunting us all that time. We're even dealing with the same people: Colonel Smith and his Unit. He's not a Colonel, by the way, that was just his retirement rank from the US Air Force before he moved sideways into the NSA, and then FTO. He's a spook, and a very senior one at that. His boss reports to the Secretary of Homeland Security, on the National Security Council. And his boss reports on the Unit's activities to the President."

"How do you know all this?"

"Because I'm his opposite number. Before the exile, I was the very new and very inexperienced successor to our—the Clan's—head of internal security. These days . . . like the FTO, we're embedded. The Commonwealth has a ministry, the Ministry of Inter-Temporal Intelligence, which Miriam runs. And within MITI, there is a Department of Para-historical Research. DPR is roughly equivalent to the Sixth Directorate of the pre-1991 KGB—Vladimir Putin's organization, the KGB's industrial espionage section. There's not really an exact US equivalent, but MITI seeds innovations gleaned by the DPR throughout the Commonwealth economy: DPR does the actual spying. You might think it's about stealing the blueprints to the latest top secret weapons or microprocessor, but it's mostly really boring—patent library searches, buying dinner for garrulous scientists, subscribing to scientific journals, snooping in the archives of venture capitalists. Still, it's been amazingly useful to our economy. Sometimes just knowing that a new technology is possible makes all the difference—and so does knowing which on-ramps lead to highways, and which are dead ends. And these days I mostly run independent operations within DPR, because I lack the stamina for the endless committee meetings and public role of the head of the organization."

Kurt stared at her, realization dawning. *"These* days?"

Olga smiled shakily. "I ran the DPR until six years ago, due to my illness. Multiple sclerosis, in case you were wondering. Anyway, I dislike interminable meetings. I much prefer a hands-on role, and it gave me an excuse to cut back a notch and tackle a more manageable workload. But Edgar—the current Chair—is aware that he will displease the People's Commissioner if he ignores my whims." The smile faded. "Unfortunately I won't be coming with you. I'm forbidden to leave Commonwealth territory: I know too much. So I'm going to to brief you, then you'll be portaged across to your own time line and put on a flight to Berlin."

*Markus Wolf himself—*herself—*has struggled from his sick bed to give you a personal briefing: how can you say no?* Kurt kept his face still, masking his astonishment. Olga was either an epically skilled spymaster, or a mass-murderer who had assassinated an American president and half the senate and supreme court, depending on whether she was telling the truth or not. Another realization crept in. *And this material is ears-only.*

"Am I disposable?" he asked bluntly.

She stared at him for a few seconds. "You're Rita's grandfather," she said eventually. "Rita will be very upset if she loses you, and her mo—her *birth* mother—is a People's Commissioner. Cabinet level. So no, you are *not* a disposable asset. We only ask this task of you because we have no better options.

"So, to business: we want you to prevent Elizabeth Hanover from falling into Colonel Smith's hands and bring her to the Commonwealth. By any means necessary."

NEW LONDON, MANHATTAN ISLAND, TIME LINE THREE, AUGUST 2020

"I think we've got another problem," Miriam remarked.

"Problem," he echoed. "What kind of problem?"

"Intel."

It was late in the evening and they'd retreated upstairs to prepare for bed. Erasmus sat on the edge of the bed. "An intel problem." He yawned again, then breathed deeply, trying to clear the fog from his head. "What kind of intelligence problem?"

"Brill hatched one of her schemes, Olga signed off on it, and it's gone bad."

"Oh." Erasmus slid his feet carefully under the covers. "The business with Elizabeth Hanover, I take it? That's why your people have been going behind my back and borrowing studio facilities? And Rita's mixed up in it too."

"You're as well-informed as usual. There's no surprising you, is there?" Her smile was only slightly sardonic. "Who blabbed?"

"Your former lady-in-waiting let it slip. Brill phrased it as it was more of a hypothetical, *what would be the consequences if* a certain princess were to turn up in New London *as if by magic*, repudiate her claim to the Crown, and swear allegiance to the Commonwealth. I told her the stakes were too high for my taste: a win at that table would be glorious, but a loss could break the bank."

His wife finished undressing, walked around to her side of the bed and sat down with a sigh. "Well, she went ahead and did it anyway—the kid was more than happy to run away from her betrothed, who sounds like a complete toad—but it went bad. Brill sent Hulius Hjorth over to organize the defection, but Yul got himself shot and captured. The kid's in the wind right now. Olga is sending a backup team to Berlin in world two to finish the job. If it works she should be here in a couple of days, none the worse for wear. But we needed cover, before her parents realized we didn't have her. Hence Operation Zenda, with the motion capture stuff and Rita pretending to be the princess."

Erasmus sighed unhappily. "*Where* was Operational Oversight when this was being set up? Sleeping under their desks?"

"Preoccupied." Miriam raised her hands briefly, miming surrender. "You know how small and under-staffed DPR is, compared to a real espionage organization. I mean, we've got a gigantic back-office operation dedicated to turning the intelligence take into product and disseminating it where it's needed, but the head-end has, at most, fifty world-walkers. Anyway, Olga's more used to thinking in terms of managing their jaunt allocation and avoiding exposure and arrest hazards than worrying about Brill—who is usually sensible—hatching a rogue operation. I have *no* idea what Brill was thinking: charitably, she was distracted by worry about Huw and his toy—"

"So Brill fast-talked Olga into doing something risky with inadequate back-up? And Olga nodded it through because she was busy and took her eye off the ball? And *nobody else*—" his expression said it all—"even noticed?"

"No, I didn't. But I'm pretty sure if I go digging there'll be a requisition somewhere. We have to delegate to our divisional heads, otherwise we'd never get anything done. And Brill kept it small. She sent one world-walker—an agent with bags of experience of covert operations, I shall remind you—to extract a willing teenager from a finishing school. The biggest expense was buying a second-hand light plane. She's got signing authority for projects that large without needing to do anything more than mention it in her monthly reports. There's a limit to how much oversight you can exercise on your executives before you make their job impossible—it'd be like you trying to approve every single episode of every television show broadcast in the Commonwealth."

"Individual television show episodes don't have the potential to start wars!" He snapped, before he forced himself to stop. "I'm over-stressed, love, please accept my apologies." He paused. "It's a such a huge problem. What to do if . . ." He trailed off.

"Relax. We're not going to let it start a war." She pulled the bedding up. "Worst case, *very* worst case, is we lose an agent, we look like idiots in public, the Pretender shouts a lot . . . oh woe. I'm more worried about losing Hulius, frankly. If it goes to shit, I'm going to have to hang Brill out to dry. Fire or suspend her. I might lose Olga too, which would be bad, *very* bad. But nothing I can do to Brill will be a patch on what she's doing to herself right now: Yul is her brother-in-law and she got him shot. There are some wild cards in the game—And what if the Americans get their hands on Princess Gimme—but that's not going to start a war, is it?"

"Princess Gimme?"

Miriam sniffed. "She asked for a princess-sized golden handshake, which is *definitely* above Brill's signing level and very naughty of her to have agreed to. But if it puts an end to the monarchists' plotting, I'm pretty sure the Commission will vote it through."

Erasmus shook his head. "I still think you're underestimating the impact."

She sniffed. "What? You think that ball-less wonder Holmes is going to do anything?" She reached over and turned out the light. "No, Adrian's not going to act up. He's ambitious but he's not crazy."

Erasmus lay awake thinking, long after her breathing deepened and became more regular. Miriam's judgement of character was usually good, sharpened by a career in journalism and honed on the whetstone of homicidal world-walker politics. If she thought Adrian, as Party secretary, didn't have the guts to stab her in the back, then she was probably right. But Holmes wasn't the only bureaucrat who confused loyalty to himself with loyalty to the Party, and loyalty to the Party with loyalty to the Revolution. *Who else knows about this scheme?* he wondered. *I know, because Brill asked my advice on a hypothetical. But who else did she ask? And,* more importantly, *who did* they *speak to afterwards?* He was on the edge of asking aloud: but then he heard a faint snore from the pillow beside him, and held his peace.

TEMPELHOF AIR FORCE BASE, BERLIN, TIME LINE TWO, AUGUST 2020

No plan survives contact with the enemy, Eric Smith reflected bitterly, *but this is ridiculous.* While he'd been aboard a government jet bound for Berlin, total craziness had broken out back home. If anyone but Dr. Scranton—his boss—had told him there'd be an *alien invasion* the moment he took his eye off Camp Singularity for a couple of days he'd have laughed in their face. But Eileen didn't crack jokes: not *that* kind of joke, anyway. So here he was, running what was supposed to be a simple job in Berlin. (In fact, he was only there because Eileen thought it needed someone senior enough to smooth ruffled feathers with an ally-in-name-only, if anything went wrong in the process of scooping up the Commonwealth's defector.) Meanwhile a three-alarm emergency had broken out back home, and the 'simple job in Berlin' turned out to be an utter clusterfuck.

"You *lost* her," he accused the Bundespolizei Major, who stiffened and frowned at him before he remembered his place.

"Now that is not actually true—"

"—Bullshit. My people had the apartment covered when I sent Milan in with the message, but by the time your boys cleared it out our girl—" Elizabeth Hanover—"had flown. Where did she go? You don't have a fucking clue! What is this, Toytown? Where are the video feeds? Where are the traffic records and the Stingray take?"

He'd pushed too hard. The Detective-Major's face froze over. "You will please listen to me, *sir.* Here in Germany we are required to respect the civil rights of the people. Those civil rights include a *right to privacy.* We cannot simply ignore the right of those not accused of any crime to go about their lives without surveillance. Stingray phone trackers are illegal and camera records are only available with a warrant signed by a judge. Now, if you provide me with evidence that this woman is a wanted para-time terrorist,

I can go to my Polizeipräsident and she will apply to, to the judiciary for a warrant. But if as you say this person you want to arrest is simply an illegal immigrant from another time line—"

"Bullshit." Smith subsided, fuming. He'd flown nearly 4000 miles and bust his gut to set up a snatch, only for a naive teenage girl to show him a clean pair of heels. And now he had a small-town cop (*all right*, he conceded: a major in the Bundespolizei, the German equivalent of the FBI: *not so small-time, but still a cop*) telling him that national security be damned, he couldn't infringe the civil rights of dog-walkers and passing delivery truck drivers by pulling the video feeds? "How do you intend to catch her, then?"

"She'll show up in due course." The Major was infuriatingly calm. "If she is an immigrant from another world, she will be baffled and confused. She is without money and friends. If you have a DNA sequence and visual referents, I will register her as a person of interest and append a request to check hostels, hospitals, and homeless shelters. We shall do this lawfully, Mr. Smith. *Unless*—" his voice hardened—"you are withholding important information about this woman, or misrepresenting the facts of the situation to us. In which case my superiors will be very unhappy, possibly to the extent of withholding cooperation."

Withholding cooperation was a euphemism. Smith's credentials as a senior officer in Homeland Security would once have compelled obedience from police departments all over the EU, much as a KGB general's badge would have caused Romanian or Polish cops to jump to attention during the Cold War. But the tighter the US ran the domestic ship of state, the more suspicious and frightened their former allies became. There had been excesses during the war on terror, faked-up extraditions, extraordinary rendition, and torture at black sites. Even greater excesses had ensued during the war on the multiverse. The blowback had eroded trust catastrophically. Outside the USA the DHS was resented and resisted these days, rather than respected and feared—especially in Germany, with its historic and horrible historical experience of secret police.

"Major Schenk," Eric said, forcing his voice into a more conciliatory tone: "I'm sure that won't be necessary. And I apologize for my intemperate words. But it is *very* important that we find this woman as fast as possible. She is not herself a terrorist or a security risk, but she is almost certainly being sought by such people. In fact—"

"Yes, I know. And on that subject, I want to discuss your guests." Schenk was from Cologne: he chose his words with extreme precision and care. "The injured Major from this new time line. And the woman, Ms. Milan. My präsident reported their presence, and I must warn you that the state prosecutor's office is paying close attention to their treatment. We were under the impression that all known time lines, save one, were uninhabited, or inhabited by stone-age tribes, and that the sole exception was bombed flat some years ago. This woman you are seeking, and the Major, do not appear to be cavemen. Or mediaeval nobles." Schenk stared at Smith. "Questions are being asked, Mr. Smith, *pointed* questions."

Smith forced his hand to unclench from the fist he'd been making beneath the interview table. "It's complex," he admitted. "Also highly classified. We want to avoid causing a public panic. The short version is that we have made contact with a developed nation in another time line. Delicate negotiations are underway—" His fatphone vibrated. "Excuse me." It was set to *do not disturb*: only a very short list of people could get through to him right now. A glance told him that it was Sonia Gomez. Agent Gomez was part of the small, very select team he'd brought with him to Berlin, currently assigned to handle communications. "Smith speaking. Report."

"Message for you from Dr. Scranton," Gomez said without preamble. "Kurt Douglas is missing."

"Shit." It escaped before he could bite his tongue. "Any details? Do we know when it happened?"

"Mr. Douglas went to visit his wife's grave this morning. He dropped off the grid somewhere in the graveyard between eight-thirty and nine o'clock. Totally blank. It's like he jaunted."

"Please tell me he had a heart attack and fell in an open grave?" Smith barely noticed Major Schenk staring at him. "*Shit*. Has Rita reported in?"

"Not since her last check-in the day before yesterday, sir."

"I . . . see." Smith took a deep breath and attempted to slow his racing pulse. It felt as if he'd been walking on solid ground and then an abyss had suddenly opened beneath his feet. "Kurt was . . . oh. Yes, well, then I am afraid that your suspicions about Rita may have been correct. Can you send me his file please? The, ah, speculative material? I think I know who to share it with." Smith paused for a second. "Please call home and ensure that they've got Angela Hagen in a box. We wouldn't want to lose her, too."

Smith put his phone down. "Well, Major. It looks like the opposition are on the move."

"Who *are* the opposition, Mr. Smith?" Schenk leaned forward. "And what do you mean, *on the move?* What has this got to do with our business here in Berlin?"

Hah! Got you. "They're a polity from another time line that calls itself the New American Commonwealth, Major. They're a Communist superpower with nuclear weapons and world-walkers. And as for what they're doing in Berlin . . ." He shrugged. "Tell me, does your department have access to the old Stasi archives? Because there's a name I'd like you to look up and add to your watch list. Just in case he shows up here."

NEW LONDON, MANHATTAN ISLAND, TIME LINE THREE, AUGUST 2020

If an institution with a million members and its own army can be said to have emotions, then during the weeks of Adam Burroughs' final illness and death, the Commonwealth Guard was gripped by depression. An almost palpable sense of dread for the future gripped its soldiers and officers as they tied black armbands around their dress uniforms and tried to conduct operations as normal. And the sense of uncertainty and fear was felt most acutely in the Commonwealth Guard headquarters complex in New London.

New London was a fortified palace-complex on the southern half of Manhattan Island, home to ministries and a former Imperial residence as well as barracks and a military airport. The cantonment was overrun by uniformed soldiers: both regular Army and members of the Commonwealth Guard, the gendarmerie created by the Radical Party to be its military wing, during the revolution that overthrew the Emperor seventeen years earlier.

The Commonwealth Guard was the mailed fist of the Deep State, the state-within-a-state that the Party presided over. It existed to preserve the revolutionary framework of Democracy from counter-revolutionary threats, both internal and external. (Democracy was a new and supposedly fragile ideology in time line three, which had missed out on the revolutions of the eighteenth century, never mind the nineteenth and twentieth.)

The Guard had started out fighting street battles with monarchist mobs, then faced down the heavily armed blackshirts of the Internal Security Directorate during the immediate post-revolutionary chaos. Eighteen years later the Commonwealth Guard had become a sprawling paramilitary bureaucracy with its own armored divisions, air support, and assault landing ships. Not unlike Hitler's SS and the Iranian Revolutionary Guards, it saw itself as an elite force loyal to Party over Nation.

General Minsky was burning the midnight oil. Despite his rank, he occupied a cramped office with a single window overlooking a gap between buildings, rather than a garden or parade ground. In the wake of his meeting with Adrian Holmes, he was receiving visitors late into the night. He rose to salute the latest deputation: Police-Brigadier Anton Richards and his adjutant, Colonel Jefferson. "Good evening, Citizen General." His visitor returned his salute politely enough. "And Citizen Colonel. If you'd care to take a seat? I have news some information to pass on, from the Party Secretariat."

Brigadier Richards took the seat opposite Minsky. His tunic collar was unbuttoned; dark bags under his eyes bespoke too little sleep over the past week. "What does Adrian want now?" He glanced at his adjutant: "Gary, sit."

"It's about the DPR. Mr. Holmes has confirmed that they are attempting to bring Elizabeth Hanover to the Commonwealth. They're using world-walkers to smuggle her out via the Germanies. She could already be halfway across the Atlantic by now: the most recent word comes via the unofficial embassy in Irongate. Adrian expects them to make a public announcement during or immediately after the conclusion of ceremonies. There is also some sort of surprise military display being planned for the funeral, organized by the DPR, to coincide with the regular armed forces parade."

The interment of the First Man was to be no mere burial. The leader of the revolution rated a gigantic military parade and a state funeral, attended by ministers (and in some cases heads of state) from all over the world.

"He says it's not clear why they're doing this. He *hopes* it's a defection, and they've arranged for Miss Hanover to renounce her claim to the succession. But it's possible that it's an attempt to restore the monarchy, backed by some of the Party Commissioners themselves. Treason, in other words."

"Well, we can't have *that*, can we?" Richards said briskly. He glanced at his adjutant: "Jefferson, are you getting this?"

"Yes, sir." The colonel patted the compact voice recorder that rested on his knee. Cassette reels turned, reflected light. The chrome-and-plastic gadget was an uneasy reminder of what they were up against, an intrusion from the future the world-walkers promised—locally manufactured, but only possible thanks to breakthrough technologies fostered by MITI.

"What does Adrian expect me to do about it?" Richards' lips stretched in something not entirely like a smile.

"We're to prepare contingency plans for men, machines, and formations to be deployed on the day. Only if it's necessary to restore legitimate authority, of course. It's a short-term response, in event of the worst-case scenario: arrest the miscreants, protect the constitution, then return to barracks when it's done." Minsky's cheek twitched. "He'd like us to take care of business—and a pony as well, I assume. It's much easier to say 'hold a bloodless purge, arrest the guilty, release the innocent, then go home' than it is to actually *do* it. Who's going to guarantee the troops immunity from prosecution afterwards? What if some of the Commissioners—the ones who aren't conspiring against the Commonwealth—denounce us for mutiny? Adrian might even be setting us up to take the drop for his *own* coup. I don't personally believe he's disloyal, but he is clearly certain he knows what's best for the Commonwealth. So who knows?" Richards shrugged.

Colonel Jefferson could no longer hold his peace: "We're soldiers, not politicians, sir!"

Richards snorted. "Are we not also the armed wing of the Party?" He countered. "Which makes us politicians by proxy. What was that saying? War is the sharpest expression of political disagreement. We obey the will of the party, but when the party is conflicted, it's our duty to choose sides. The hard part is to remember that we are its hands, not its head."

"Which side *should* we choose, sir?"

Minsky cleared his throat.

"I would say, whichever side is clearly *not* the enemy of the Revolution," General Minsky said slowly. "And if it's not clear, we should stay out of it." He looked at Richards. "Well?"

"Yes, agreed."

Minsky glanced at the Colonel, then back at the Brigadier. "Since you asked . . . we will ready our arms and transport schedules, establish supply dumps and lines of communication, and prepare contingency plans. But we will *not* activate them unless there are *clear* indications that the Party machinery has been subverted. And if we are forced to act, we will proceed with Cromwell's admonition in mind."

"Ah . . . ?" Jefferson paused.

"'I beseech you, in the bowels of Christ, think it possible that you may be mistaken,'" Minsky quoted. "We must be *absolutely* certain before we act, lest our enemies to trick us into attacking our own Party and doing irreparable damage to the Revolution in the name of saving it."

"Yes." Richards nodded. "Very well. Contingency plans only at this stage, good."

"I'll need you to provide me with forward intelligence, brigadier. I'll prepare high-level plans for a variety of contingencies: overt violent threat, covert subversive threat, variously pre-funeral, during the parade, and after the interment. Our exit point is the selection of the new First Man. Once the spine of command has grown a new head . . ." He raised an eyebrow at Richards.

"We can all stand down at that point. Yes, sir." Richards nodded.

"Make it so. Dismissed." Richards rose, followed by his adjutant, and left General Minsky sitting in his office, face slack, shoulders slumped as if he carried the entire weight of the Revolution on them.

A minute after the door closed, Minsky took a deep breath and sighed. Then he picked up the receiver of his desk telephone. "Get me the General Secretary's office," he said. (A pause.) "Yes, this is Minsky." (Another pause.) "Yes. I've given him his orders. Please inform Citizen Holmes that he was receptive, and will plan accordingly." He put the phone down, and sat in silence for another minute. Then he sighed gloomily and addressed the window overlooking the air shaft: "It begins—but where will it all end?"

Defection

The Ministry of Propaganda did indeed have a full suite of HaptoTech hardware squirreled away in their basement, behind locked doors secured by unsmiling soldiers from the Commonwealth Guard. (Who, Rita couldn't help noticing, caused Alice Morgan's face to freeze over.) MiniProp also had real-time video editing suites that wouldn't have looked out of place in a CNN broadcast trailer. And they had a doctor, a trained technician, and a row of neatly-lined-up injectors armed with HaptoTech transponders. Rita left the room feeling like she'd lost a fight with a nest of yellow jackets: despite a liberal application of novocaine, those suckers *stung* when they went in. Adams shoved her straight into a calibration suite without giving her time to recover from the repeated stabbings. "Your first public engagement is tomorrow evening: we've got to get the transponders set up in the palace this evening. We don't have a spare sound stage, Ms. Douglas, or time for do-overs: this is *it*."

She ran through her standard gestures in front of a green screen. Out of the corner of her eyes Rita saw a stick-figure on the central monitor of a bank of three mirror her motions: walking, bowing, curtseying, raising her middle finger. The monitor to its left showed Rita herself making the same gestures, with the green screen replaced by a crowded ballroom with people walking around her. And the monitor on the right showed a pretty, dark-skinned stranger in an elaborate gown going through the exact same motions, with the same background and people composited in around her. "Impressive," she remarked, as mirror-Rita and fake-Elizabeth moved their lips in sync. (Lips that throbbed and stung somewhat, still swollen from the implant injections.) "That's her, isn't it—the Princess?" She gestured at the girl in the posh frock.

"Yes. It's the best we can do without getting her in a studio: we built a 3D model of her from newsreel film taken at her last birthday ball, when they announced her engagement to the French heir. The technicians did a stitch-and-splice from the stills, superimposed them on top of a digital mannequin, and corrected it for her known measurements—good, isn't she?"

Rita squinted and moved closer to the camera, scrutinizing the close-up on Princess Elizabeth's face for rendering artifacts and visible polygons. "But is it good enough?"

"We're broadcasting in analog at 640 lines, Ms. Douglas. This isn't the United States: nobody here has high definition TV, although we—that is, the Commonwealth—should get there in another decade. The French are still on 384 line black-and-white for the most part, only just starting to experiment with color. As long as we don't do any close-in reaction shots we're home and dry—this production is 4K high definition video." He twitched. "At 30 frames per second we don't have a problem with micro-expressions, either. We've got a voice coach waiting to see you next—and auto-tune—then a choreographer to help you copy her mannerisms. But the video side is solid as a rock."

After her first session with the speech specialist, Adams walked Rita over to Wardrobe for a fitting. "I've got clothes—" She protested. Her birth mother had engaged Alice to take her to a high-end department store the previous week, where she'd been fitted with a wardrobe suitable for a politician's daughter.

"Sure. But we want you back here tomorrow morning at eight o'clock for animation capture, so we can skin *you* and run you as an avatar if necessary." *If you're not available*, Rita translated. "It's much easier to simply film you than to try to animate the fabric on top of a computer model of you—we could do it, but it'd take too long. Clothes lie in layers and they affect the way you move: it's very hard to get the real-time rendering models to work perfectly. I mean, even using the off-the-shelf computers we've been able to buy and import. The stuff we can build ourselves falls a million miles short of doing any of this. As it is, the seamstresses will be working overnight: you need evening dresses, a formal court presentation gown, and a couple more funeral suits." Adams twitched again. "There's no *time*."

Someone was clearly leaning hard on the director. Rita forced herself to smile. "Don't worry, I'll be there," she reassured him, deeply uncertain. *What the hell are you planning, Miriam?* she wondered. *Why* wouldn't *I be available?*

Inspector Morgan dropped Rita off at Brilliana's house around nine o'clock with a warning to be ready to leave by seven the next morning. Inside, she found the place half-deserted. There were cold cuts and bread in the kitchen, but no sign of Brill or Huw. "Sir has been called back to work, ma'am," the elderly housekeeper told her. She refused, when pressed, to say where work might have taken him. Brill finally arrived as Rita prepared for bed. She was clearly exhausted from a day of meetings. "Tomorrow," she said dismissively, brushing off Rita's attempt at conversation with a yawn. "You've got a busy morning, I saw your itinerary. Alice will bring you to the ministry at three and we can go to the state viewing together. You should wear full state mourning." She yawned again. "Go get some sleep. It's going to be a long day."

Rita was up at six, red-eyed and tired, but unable to get back to sleep. The morning passed in blur of rapid costume changes punctuated by repeating the same set of movements for the cameras—this time to animate her own avatar: the screens endlessly mirrored Rita walking, bowing, curtseying, waving, smiling, frowning, turning, sitting, standing. Inspector Morgan hovered, watching and periodically checking a chunky wristwatch. She had a page-long checklist for Rita blocked out in ten minute segments. Finally—after a hasty packed lunch, a change into a black mourning dress, and a visit to a make-up artist to ensure that her face and hair were camera-ready—Alice propelled Rita outdoors and into a ministry car. They drove to the former Imperial Summer Palace, where the Commissioners and their entourages were gathering. It was time for the public viewing of the First Man's coffin as he lay in state.

"You're in Mrs. Burgeson's party, along with a number of other officials—you'll be identified as Mrs. Burgeson's daughter. They all have clearance to know about your origin and employment." Morgan, in a dress uniform dripping with gold braid, handed her an incongruously laminated ID badge on a lanyard. Her own wild-eyed face stared out from it, looking trapped. It was the police mugshot Alice's officers had taken when she'd been arrested right after her arrival in the Commonwealth. The irony did not escape her. "I will be in the second group behind your party. Mrs. Hjorth—Brilliana—will introduce you to the Party Commissioners before and after the viewing, as your mother's daughter. Are you prepared for that?" She stared intently at Rita.

Rita swallowed. "I'll deal." Thinking of Miriam Burgeson as her mother was deeply uncomfortable, raising questions that she couldn't answer. Mrs. Burgeson didn't *feel* like her mother Emily, the mom who'd driven her to Girl Scouts in a town an hour's drive from home, compiled scrapbooks of every play she'd been in from school to college, made her lunchbox every morning before she started high school. Seeing Miriam with Kurt had been a disturbing experience, making her feel as if her different identities and loyalties were somehow trying and failing to mix, like water and oil, and it gave her an unpleasant pang, as she wondered if she'd ever see Emily and Franz, or her brother River, again. "What else do I need to know?"

"There's a full HaptoTech sensor system installed in the chapel where the First Man is lying. And another in the reception room. You'll be on camera the whole time, naturally, in-scene for the entire duration of the ceremony—but long shots only this time around, and no audio. Everyone Alice introduces you to knows who you are, but in the feed from the cameras we'll replace you with Elizabeth Hanover. So try to hold yourself like a princess, especially during the viewing. It's supposed to last an hour and a quarter, and there's a forty-five minute reception afterwards, but you can bet everything will run late."

Act like a princess. Right. Rita nodded, although she had only the vaguest idea of how real princesses acted: she was pretty sure that Disney movies weren't a good guide. "Miss Hanover hasn't turned up yet?"

Morgan shook her head, jaw set. "They're still looking for her."

"Anything else?"

"Yes. Don't make a fool of yourself, don't get drunk at the reception—" Alice paused, then smiled—"and break a leg!"

BERLIN, TIME LINE TWO, AUGUST 2020

"Elizabeth? This is Control. Are you somewhere you can talk without being overheard?"

Liz looked around. After finding the Hauptbahnhoff exit, she'd come to a bare plaza dotted with poor-quality sculptures, starkly abstract—hardly a place of beauty. Signs pointed across an access road towards the Reichstag, a building that looked nothing like any palace she'd ever seen. A crowd of people holding signs stood at one corner of the square, surrounded by men in ill-fitting blue uniforms (some of whom might have been women: she found it hard to tell). A *mob*, she speculated, but the lack of affray and the boredom of the gendarmes suggested it was weirdly routine. *Dissidents, allowed to gather in public? An act of worship?*

"I don't know if it's safe," she said hesitantly. "I'm outside the Hauptbahnhoff." She walked towards a broad road with heavy traffic thundering along it. Colored lights controlled a junction. On the far side, tall glass buildings sprouted like crystals from a concrete geode.

"We can talk, then, but only briefly."

"Why?"

"I can track your location when you use your phone, but so can others, if they know to look for you. The trick is to keep moving and keep our conversations short. I will call you back periodically."

Elizabeth headed towards the road, head swiveling as she identified buses, private vehicles, and huge boxy-looking trailers towed behind squared-off tractors. They were not so different from their equivalents back home, but they sped past frighteningly fast and very close together. When the lights changed, everyone stopped, despite their headlong rush! And then it all started again, in a different direction. How to cross without getting run down? She looked around again, hunting for other pedestrians. "I'm trying to cross a giant turnpike."

"Remember to obey the pedestrian lights." *Pedestrian lights?* Elizabeth frowned, peering at the small green-and-red stick figures at the other side of the road. "People in Germany seldom jaywalk"—*Jaywalk? What's that?*—"except in Berlin, especially the East, so if you try it the police might take an interest. That would be bad."

"I know that," Elizabeth snapped. "What do you want me to do?"

"I am about to send a special message to your phone, that will make it display a map—a moving map. Your position on the map is indicated by a flashing blue dot, and you should see a path outlined to a building about a kilometer away. Can you walk that far?"

"I should think so." A kilometer was nothing to an outdoors-woman like Elizabeth. "As long as I am not squashed by a hurtling motor carriage." How a telephone could display a map, much less a magical one that knew where she was . . . well, chalk it up to yet more scientific wizardry. Didn't the Major have something similar in his vehicle, come to think of it? But his car was very big. *If you could make such devices really tiny . . .* Liz hefted her stolen messenger bag speculatively.

"There is a hotel there. A room is reserved in the name of Elizabeth Jordan. We have registered a passport number with the front desk, and it is already paid for in advance. When you check in they will give you a key-card. They will want a deposit for room service, of course." *Key-card? Passport? Room service?* Liz made a mental note to ask what those were— later. "Now, this is important. You are required to provide an ID card when checking in. Obviously you have no such thing. So you will tell the front desk that you were the victim of a pickpocket who took your purse, but you kept your phone, and please will they use your phone as proof of identity. They might object, but you can insist: unlock it by showing it your face. You can offer to pay the room service fee with it as well—they will show you a reader device and you should place your phone on top of it. If it asks you to enter a number called a PIN, that is a code to unlock the money, enter 1–2–3–4."

"Phones contain *money?*" Her head was spinning from Control's strange argot. It was like another language, superimposed on the King's English. *I suppose new things warrant new words*, she thought, *but this is ridiculous!*

Control seemed to sense her incredulity: "You know it can store maps and recognize faces and make calls? It can act as a wallet and make payments too."

"But where do you put the coins—never mind." Liz suddenly remembered the people she'd seen paying for things in shops with those plastic rectangles. Like the cards in the Major's wallet. "I have the Major's wallet, it had some cards—"

"You can't use them. Biometrics." Whatever they were. "But the phone will unlock for you and you can pay using that, wherever you see someone else using a card. Do you think you can do that?"

"I can try." Liz felt very unsure of herself.

"Find a kiosk, first, and buy a bottle of orange juice or something to practice. Offer to pay with your phone. Speak English, they'll think you're a dumb American tourist who isn't used to contactless payments."

"Contactless payments," Liz repeated. Somehow the idea of a low-risk rehearsal made it seem less daunting.

"Yes. As I said, the hotel front desk will give you a card to open the door to your room—you hold it against the lock until you see a light flash, then turn the handle. When you're in, call me back. You do that by unlocking your phone then, on the home screen—"

"How do you *lock* a phone—is there a keyhole somewhere? What's the home screen?"

It took Control almost ten minutes to explain, but by the time she was halfway to the hotel, she was able to call Control back: a major triumph.

"*Very* good," Control concluded. "Now, one last thing. Our people are coming to meet you, but it will take them at least twenty four hours to get there. The Major has been detained by our enemies, who have agents in Berlin. We don't know if he's told them about you: if so, they may attempt to abduct you. I'll update you once you are in the hotel, but for now you should be circumspect in your dealings with anyone who appears to be American. In particular, if you see anyone you have already met, they are under the control of the DHS and are a threat to your freedom—"

"The who? What is the DHS?" *You've got enemies in this time line*, Liz realized queasily, *and they've decided I belong to you, and you're only telling me* now?

"They're the American secret police. Look, why don't you buy that orange juice, go to the hotel, then call me back when you're in your room? We've got a lot to talk about."

JUGGERNAUT LAUNCH PAD, TIME LINE TWELVE, AUGUST 2020

The concrete runways and windowless bunkers of the Commonwealth military aerospace port along the shore of Lake Maracaibo baked beneath the tropical sun. Huw Hjorth joined a swollen shift change waiting inside one of the larger bunkers—a transit hangar, where world-walkers ferried huge hover-barges laden with shipping containers to Fort Bastion in time line twelve. Three times a day, a couple of hundred engineers, technicians and officers would ride the passenger hovercraft across to the space launch facility in the other time line. Then roughly the same number would file wearily aboard for the five-minute trip back to their barracks.

But everything was different today. If all went well, most of these people would be coming home within a couple of hours rather than at the end of a normal eight-hour shift. And there were eighteen new faces on the commute this morning. The entire flight crew, in their powder-blue uniform jumpsuits and the paper masks required by medical quarantine, were going out to the pad—and they wouldn't be coming back.

JUGGERNAUT was ready to fly.

Huw had been back in Maracaibo for barely a week—a week of manic twenty-hour days, fueled by burritos and coffee bolted between medical appointments, power naps, and briefings. He *had* managed two trunk calls to Brill and the girls over the week, totaling almost half an hour at ruinous expense—intercontinental telephony was still a novelty to most people in this time line—and on the second call she'd conditionally forgiven him, but their pending year of enforced separation was hard for his daughters to accept. Yesterday he'd made sure to leave Fort Bastion, to go back to the barracks and crash on the camp bed in his office, to ensure he had at least six hours of sleep before the morning shift change.

The countdown was already running: it had been ticking for a month now, but with frequent holds, pre-planned delays while the ground crew ensured everything was in place. For the past three days, Colonel Manning's soldiers had been playing taxi service for the fuel elements—highly specialized nuclear bombs—ferrying them the final five miles from the windowless assembly bunker to the magazines deep inside JUGGERNAUT's hull. Overnight, more than a thousand tons of kerosene fuel had been pumped aboard the booster stage that would loft JUGGERNAUT to a safe altitude above the launch pad before they fired up the main drive: now the liquid oxygen tank was filling slowly. The weather reports were good, the countdown was into the final hours, and the flight crew were boarding the vehicle.

The morning passed in a blur of briefings, work crowding out any time he might otherwise have had to feel anxious or excited. Huw recorded a short talk for the state broadcaster, then handed over to the head of Launch Control. (There was no overall Mission Control, JUGGERNAUT being designed for largely autonomous operation.) Next, he proceeded to the pad, in time to watch as the pad team disconnected all the static lines and most of the umbilicals and stored them under thick blast hoods. He took a last awe-struck look up the gleaming flank of JUGGERNAUT, stacked aboard its booster stage like a magnum cartridge sitting atop a hearing aid battery. *This is actually happening,* he realized: *I'm going into orbit!* One gantry was still in place, with the precarious walkway for the crew connecting it to the crown of the giant bullet. Huw joined his team in the suiting room at the foot of the tower, then took the final elevator ride up to take his place on the flight deck, trying hard to conceal his pre-flight tension from his people.

Huw had worked hard to conceal his nerves from the thousands of specialists at Port Maracaibo and Fort Bastion. The successful flight of the uncrewed test vehicle notwithstanding, nobody had ever launched a spacecraft precisely like this before. He wasn't the only one of them with cold feet, of that he was sure: he'd had a third and final trunk call with Brill the previous night. It hadn't turned into a fight, but only because his wife had enough tight-lipped professionalism not to mess with his focus this close to zero hour. He doubted she'd sleep a wink until the launch was over and she knew he was safe. There were a lot of similarities between watching a space launch, especially a crewed one, and a public execution: only the launch wasn't foreordained to end in death. Now he was about to walk out onto the scaffold, put a brave face on it . . . *well, if it goes wrong it'll be over even faster than a hanging,* he told himself, then tried very hard to put it out of his mind.

Behind him, the pad technicians retracted the bridge and made their way to the trucks that would take them back to the Forward Control Bunker, three miles from the pad and buried under forty feet of reinforced concrete and lead shielding.

This is crazy, part of his mind kept yelling. But all the checklists looked good. If they'd done their jobs properly, if the propulsion engineers had got their calculations right, if the full-sized ship performed in line with the test vehicle they'd flown the year before, then in an hour's time they'd ride this thing into orbit—and in the process break just about every record in the history of human spaceflight.

Everything about JUGGERNAUT was outsized. One of the peculiarities of JUGGERNAUT's propulsion system was that it became more efficient the larger it got. JUGGERNAUT was powered by a nuclear pulse-detonation system. The USA had pioneered the design in the 1950s as Project ORION, but shelved it unflown in the 1960s when the Test Ban Treaty prohibited atmospheric nuclear explosions. The test vehicle Huw's team had flown the year before weighed eight thousand tons on the pad:

JUGGERNAUT, at forty thousand tons, was more massive than all the NASA Moon rockets and space shuttles combined, loaded with fuel. The first stage booster that would lift it two miles, safely out of range of ground-reflected shock waves when the first nuclear propulsion charge detonated, would burn through two moon rocket's worth of fuel in less than a minute. If it malfunctioned, the result would be a purely chemical explosion in the kiloton range. And as for the nuclear magazine . . .

If this fails, we won't get a second chance, Huw reminded himself as he followed the bridge crew to their stations. Not when a single flight consumed an entire year's worth of the Commonwealth's plutonium production. The arms race with the French would ensure there were no second chances. If JUGGERNAUT didn't succeed with flying colors on the first attempt, there would be no JUGGERNAUT TWO, let alone the proposed follow-up expeditions to Mars and the moons of Jupiter.

"One hundred seconds to launch." Huw tensed as the countdown announcer cut into the audio loop, from a shielded bunker several miles away. He'd been so focused on the countdown checklist in front of him for the past two hours that he'd lost track of subjective time. The announcer had been an air traffic approach controller for a Commonwealth carrier battle group and sounded positively bored. To him, a nuclear-powered space dreadnought that waited patiently for launch permission and wasn't trying to land in his lap with a payload of live missiles on board was nothing to get excited about.

"Hold for reports, all stations." Huw checked his panel then cued his mike. "Go ahead."

—"Booster nominal."—"Life support nominal."—"Sick bay nominal."—"Guidance nominal."—"Ground nominal, bunker sealed and on internal power, sirens running, deluge system running."—"Vertical Assembly Complex nominal, evacuation completed."—

Then the call Huw was waiting for: "Para-time crew nominal," He announced.

"We copy, JUGGERNAUT," said ground control. Rudi—Colonel Rudolf d'Ost, who Huw had replaced—spoke over the loop from ground control. He sounded hoarse and was still signed off sick, but nothing was going to keep him away from the control room for the flight he'd originally been scheduled to command.

Huw forced himself to smile at his companions in the bridge capsule:

world-walker Jenny Wu, and two pilot officers. There were four other world-walkers on the ship, all relatives of some degree. Like Huw and the other astronauts, they wore orange pressurized survival suits and helmets and were strapped down inside cramped escape/re-entry capsules resembling enlarged Soyuz craft. Four such vehicles, each holding five crew, were half-buried in the flanks of JUGGERNAUT. If something went wrong during launch, they could try to world-walk: they had parachutes and a heat shield to carry them to a soft landing. In practice, ejecting from a stricken spaceship—then world-walking to a safe time line and making a ballistic re-entry in an untried capsule—would be no walk in the park. *So let's get this right*, Huw told himself, and settled, resolving to do precisely that.

He cued his mike to the all hands channel. "Bridge here. Good luck, everyone, and good flying."

"End launch hold," the Launch Director on the ground announced. "Resume countdown."

Where normal space vehicles were built like precision instruments, fabricated from lightweight alloys with every gram of spare weight pared away, JUGGERNAUT was built like a battleship. The pusher plate it sat on was a steel plate thirty centimeters thick: the hydraulic jacks that absorbed the shock of the detonations taking place behind the plate were built like the legs of a deep ocean-drilling platform and ballasted with reinforced concrete. Coordinating the precisely sequenced release of sixty nuclear propulsion charges per minute—fed from the magazine down a chute, then ejected to detonate directly below the center of the pusher plate—was the job of a computer. But it was a very *strange* computer, made from the precisely machined steel gears, cams, and drive shafts of a battleship's analog gun laying calculator. No one was entirely sure how well modern microelectronics would handle several hundred nuclear bombs detonating nearby, and nobody wanted to find out the hard way.

Huw stared at the display screen in front of him, sweating bullets. The bridge was windowless, but he'd argued for a camera to provide an external view, to address concerns about motion sickness. Right now it showed a view of the pad, as seen by a camera mounted outside the aeroshell on top of the spacecraft. The curved side of a giant bronze pillar filled the bottom of the screen, sitting on pylons suspended above deep concrete trenches flanked by the pad deluge system. The deluge system pipes were already spraying water across the pad, to dampen the shockwaves when the first stage engine ignited. It felt oddly unreal to Huw, even though he'd been working towards it for years: he was more apprehensive about a last-minute launch scrub or a glitch in the TV feed that would go out to the entire Commonwealth in a few hours, than the prospect of a major malfunction in flight.

This wasn't the view of the launch pad he'd been expecting, and it felt profoundly *wrong*—simultaneously unsettling and frightening and glorious and exciting. Before Rudi got sick and Hulius went missing, Huw had expected to watch the launch from the bunker five kilometers away. There were cameras in armored mounts on the roof, protected by high-speed shutters that would slam closed a fraction of a second before each of the air bursts. Other high speed cameras ran constantly, using film stock so insensitive it would only register the light of a nuclear explosion. For backup they had old-school submarine periscopes with incredibly dark filters. If anything went wrong in flight, they'd capture his last moments—

In the near distance, beyond the pad, a lagoon lay still in the noon-day glare. A seabird flew lazily across the camera foreground then flapped twice, thrice, stooping towards the pad.

Huw blinked and forced his attention back to the checklist and the instrument panel in front of him.

"Sixty seconds."

A wisp of vapor drifted from the fat disk below the bullet. The liquid oxygen tank was warming in the sunlight, pressure valves venting super-chilled gas to prevent it from rupturing. Huw checked his master panel once more, noting the readings carefully. If launch was delayed for more than fifteen minutes they'd have to drain the booster's oxidizer tank: another ten and they'd have to de-fuel and shut down completely, then try again another day.

"Booster on internal power. Pad tie-downs retracted. JUGGERNAUT on internal guidance."

Huw licked his lips then addressed ground control. "JUGGERNAUT here, General Hjorth commanding. I have control. Request take-off permission." It was a formality: right now the computers were in charge.

—"Minus twenty seconds, pad deluge system starting—"

The Launch Director spoke. "JUGGERNAUT, on countdown completion you have permission to launch at will."

"Confirmed." Huw breathed out hard. "JUGGERNAUT: all hands, brace for departure."

A waterfall of steam engulfed the base of the stack, lit from within by a violent orange glow as the deluge system pumped hundreds of tons of water across the pad. Moments passed as the rocket exhaust brightened to a blue-white glare: smoke and steam blasted out from the trenches below the pad, then the launch stack began to rise with a deceptive, leisurely grace. There were no service towers by which to judge its height, but Huw knew it was a hundred and sixty meters high. It took almost ten seconds to rise its own height above the launch pad, and although it was gathering speed steadily, it must surely seem to observers accustomed to normal rocket launches that it was accelerating far too slowly, teetering on the edge of disaster.

Huw became aware of his chair vibrating, very gently, as a giant hand pushed him down against the back support and headrest. A tooth-rattling thunder surrounded him: it reminded him of Horseshoe Falls, the sound of thousands of tons of water every second rushing over a cliff edge, a noise so deep that it was felt rather than heard, deep in his bowels and bones. Five kilometers away, despite the blast doors and meter of reinforced concrete and topsoil above them, the noise would just be reaching the ground crew in the bunker. Soon they would have to raise their voices to be heard over the earthquake-like roar.

Ground control gave a running commentary: "twenty seconds. Altitude five hundred and ten meters, air speed four-forty kilometers per hour—" Huw worked his checklist, scanning status indicators, too intent for emotional engagement. It felt like a sluggish travesty of a launch, some kind of clockwork steampunk fantasy of space travel. A *real* rocket would be in supersonic flight by now, approaching maximum dynamic pressure as it soared into the stratosphere. Huw grimaced, lips pulling back from his teeth as he willed the JUGGERNAUT stack to climb. Somewhere, the ghost of Wernher von Braun was knuckling Freeman Dyson's specter on the forehead saying, *I told you, it vould not vurk.*

"Fifty seconds. Altitude one nine nine zero, air speed nine six five kilometers per hour. BECO in ten seconds—"

JUGGERNAUT hung in the air, trailing a blowtorch glare of flame: pure blue-white at the heart, surrounded by a smoky red halo of unburned kerosene from the coolant system that kept the engine nozzles from melting. Still subsonic, the giant ship would coast upwards after stage separation before firing up its nuclear drive.

"BECO confirmed, we have booster engine cut-off. Booster stage separation and retro-fire. JUGGERNAUT first light in ten seconds."

"Nuke crew," Huw called. "You have control."

He felt a distant push from the small separation rockets below the base of the gigantic pistol cartridge as the hearing aid battery began to fall away. The gap between JUGGERNAUT and the booster stage widened steadily. Major Saunders voice came over the loop from the nuclear engineering control team's capsule: "Drive is in start-up. Stand by."

"EMP shutdown," Huw ordered. "Going dark now."

The video screens darkened, filters sliding into place across the external cameras. "Shutters sealed, waiting for impulse," Jenny Wu called across her neighbor's spacesuit. "Check visors." She touched the lowered faceplate of her helmet in confirmation.

"Check." Huw touched his own helmet then lowered his hand to the armrest. "Ready." *This had better work*, he thought as his heart seemed to miss a beat again. He tensed: *wish I'd told Brill I love her this morning*—

Over the loop, Smith intoned, "ready for first light. Shutters opening. Fire one."

Then the bomb dropped.

EXECUTIVE OFFICE BUILDING, BALTIMORE, TIME LINE TWO, AUGUST 2020

All government agencies accumulate disaster contingency plans like obsessive stamp collectors, drafting them, filing them, and occasionally updating them. Even the most singularly improbable scenario rates at least a five-page briefing, setting forth the parameters of the disaster ("a pair of neutron stars a thousand light-years away have collided, producing a gamma-ray burst which has struck the Earth without advance warning"), the responses ("POTUS to address the nation: urges calm, prayers"), and the likely outcome ("distribute body bags from immediately available stock: all personnel to stay at their posts until the end of the world: continuity of government devolves to the senior surviving administrator in each time line: survivors may return to CONUS-PRIME and recolonize Earth at their discretion").

Eileen Scranton was holed up in an office in Baltimore, reviewing the disaster contingency plan of the moment. The loss of ERGO-1 and the evacuation of Camp Singularity definitely qualified as an emergency. While it wasn't *quite* as apocalyptic as the Earth being hit by a gamma-ray burst, the alien invasion of a neighboring time line came a close second. And to make matters worse, her inbox was filling up with increasingly querulous demands from the White House Chief of Staff. Apparently the POTUS was concerned that she might have to address the nation. The Chief needed to know just how much calm the President should be calling for in her speech, and why—not to mention how many body bags FEMA was going to need for this one.

"Do we have an update from the Bridge Control room in time line four?" She demanded. It had been evacuated when the alien invasion came through the Gate, but—"is the self-destruct system still online?"

"Let me check." Bart Samson, from the Facilities Operational Directorate, tapped his tablet. "My last report is an hour old. Alice Chu should have updated the wiki fifteen minutes ago, but it's stale. I'll call her—"

Eileen turned to Max, who had been in the control room with Jose and Julie when the ERGO-1 mission broke bad. "Any update on the magnitude of the flare the bogies triggered? How much energy did it release?"

"Lots." Max looked tense, as well he might. "I'm not an astrophysicist, but I dumped the numbers into Jupyter Notes—" a scientific laboratory calculator and notetaking app—"and it's really scary. If I'm in the right ball park, it was putting out as much energy as a fifty-megaton H-bomb every second. That's on a par with Tsar Bomba, the most powerful nuke anybody ever detonated, and it was still growing when we lost telemetry coverage. Whatever was going on, they were exceeding the entire energy budget of human civilization."

"What do we know about the bogies?" The maneuvering objects released by the alien debris orbiting close to the black hole that had intercepted ERGO-1, then attacked the Bridge.

Samson looked up. "They accelerated for over eight hundred gee-seconds. That's equivalent to going from a stationary start to orbital velocity at Earth surface level. No sign of any hiccups in their acceleration curve: If they were chemically powered, they'd have had to stage at least once—or dump boosters—so I'm pretty sure they had to be nuclear powered. The really scary question is what were they doing with their waste heat? We should have picked them up on infrared, but the Bridge sensors saw nothing. Oh, and they must have been radiation-hardened, naturally, otherwise they'd have been fried by the black hole even before it flared. And there are other questions—so many questions."

"Could they have been momentum-coupled to the hole in some way? Some kind of quantum-entanglement process? So that the flare was a, a side-effect of whatever propulsion system they were using . . ." Scranton stopped grasping at straws.

"That would make everything worse." Samson looked twitchy. "Though it *might* explain the observations . . ." he was whistling past the graveyard and they both knew it. Rockets, especially nuclear-thermal rockets—where the reaction mass was heated by a nuclear reactor—radiated a huge amount of waste heat. Even the small thermal cameras on the Bridge would have spotted them. The bogies emitted no waste heat and the black hole flared whenever they accelerated: it suggested new physics was at work. And new physics meant they were outgunned as profoundly as a bronze-age war galley being strafed by F-16s.

"We don't actually know how para-time displacement works: help me, people, in an hour's time I've got to go to the Big Tent and brief the President." The Tent—the Big White Tent—was the domed complex on the outskirts of Baltimore, erected in the aftermath of 7/16 to serve the Presidency as an Executive Office Building-in-exile until the White House was rebuilt.

Samson looked up. "Alice just sent me an update. We've lost the last telemetry from the Bridge Control Room. A mag-six quake hit the site twenty minutes ago. Seventeen people are still unaccounted for, out of a total of three hundred and five on site this morning. Maybe they're slow checking in . . ." He paused, reluctant to pronounce them dead. "Camera feed from the generators show . . . shi—all telemetry from the Dome is out, as of thirty-six minutes ago. And the cameras at the on-site generator show the Dome is down, repeat, the Dome is *down*."

"They slighted a para-time fortress," Scranton mumbled to herself under her breath, barely able to comprehend the implications.

"I'm sorry?"

"'Slighting' a fortress means to render it unusable—although why the hell the Forerunners had a fortress there in the *first* place—go on, please."

"The Dome covering the Gate has partially collapsed, and there's a wind blowing into it. We don't have a weather station at the generator park but the cameras show mist, condensation from the air streaming in that is quote consistent with an unshielded gate, unquote. I mean, there's hard vacuum beyond the Gate, so the pressure is dropping, that'd cause water vapor to condense out. There are ongoing aftershocks from the quake that hit Camp Singularity. It's a good thing we evacuated."

Scranton massaged her forehead with her fingertips. "Yes it is, isn't it."

We tickled the dragon's tail and the sleeping dragon woke up . . . ERGO-1 had been a necessary test for a bombardment system that might give the United States a first strike capability against the rival time line. Given the Commonwealth's manifest nuclear *and* para-time capabilities, it made lots of sense to acquire the capability to decapitate their leadership without warning. But the cost had turned out to be unacceptably high. Even with the worst-case risk assessments, nobody had imagined that they'd awaken sleeping war machines orbiting the black hole left behind by a murdered alternate-earth. And nobody had anticipated that the ancient weapons platforms would spring into life, successfully intercept a maneuvering ICBM payload, then backtrack along its path, seize the Gate to time line four, and mount an invasion. "Anything else?"

"Yes." Samson glanced down. "A note to tell you that a squad of DRAGON'S TEETH army world-walkers are on-site. Equipped for light reconnaissance, looking for signs of aliens on the ground, seeing our drones just go missing. Uh, there are some cautions about them still being in training, but they're all the forward capability we've got right now. The intruders are destroying any drones we send through. The President has authorized NNSA to release an atomic demolition munition for deployment, and a team of specialists from the eighty-seventh Airborne Division who are trained to emplace it are inbound." He raised an eyebrow. "I didn't know we still had any of those things."

Scranton frowned at him. "We don't, officially, and you never heard otherwise. Whoever put that on the open wiki needs talking to—"

"Then you want to take it up with General Ziegler, ma'am, it's his signing authority."

Dr. Scranton sat back. "Thanks for warning me." Ziegler was a three-star general. He wouldn't discuss the eighty-seventh Airborne Division receiving battlefield nukes for deployment unless—*this is going bad* really *fast*. "Is that all?"

"Next update from Alice is due in half an hour." Samson paused. "You want me to forward it to you?"

"Yes—no, wait. I'm out of here." Scranton pushed her chair back and stood, her knees creaking. She'd stiffened up since the emergency evacuation of Camp Singularity the morning before. Running for her life didn't come easy at her age. "I've got to go brief the Secretary for Homeland Security, and once he's up to speed, I'm doing a stand-up in front of the Homeland Security Council. Message me as soon as there are new updates. And copy John—" the Homeland Security Secretary—"while you're about it." *Because when I come out of that stand-up, I might not have a job any more. I might even be in handcuffs.* She didn't think she'd exceeded her authority, but presidents took a dim view of middle-ranking State Department officials who started wars by accident, never mind provoking alien invasions. "I'm out of here."

NEW LONDON, MANHATTAN ISLAND, TIME LINE THREE, AUGUST 2020

Rita was discovering that state funerals were theatrical performances with a cast of thousands. All the inner Party Commissioners and their senior staff were present, rubbing shoulders, offering each other their condolences on this occasion of their loss. (Whether it was the loss of a friend and mentor, or loss of job security, was often hard to tell.) The Commissioners' spouses and children were present in the second rank, respectively awestruck and bored. They were warily circumspect with strangers as they tried to remember who was an ally of their sponsor, or a rival, or of no consideration. Then there were the Magistrates, the peoples' elected representatives, come to see the old man laid out in state: and the ambassadors and diplomats. Lots of business got done at state funerals—the guest list effectively made it an unofficial summit meeting—but Rita saw very little of it.

"This way, dear." Brilliana offered her an arm and Rita allowed the older woman to guide her. Elaborate black outfits were the order of the day: many of the women were swathed in veils, like something out of a Victorian costume drama. "There's going to be a short memorial service in the royal chapel, then we pay our respects to the deceased. After that, the reception. Huw can't be here, so"—she patted Rita's arm—"you can be my escort."

"Where *is* Huw?" Rita asked, looking for the Burgesons. It was a futile gesture, she realized: the series of huge audience rooms had once held an entire Imperial court. Between the officials and their families, there had to be several thousand people here. As Commissioners appointed by the central committee of the Radical Party, the deep state that led the revolution, Miriam and Erasmus' status meant they would be near the front of the crowd.

"He was called away on urgent business." Brill's facade cracked, and for a moment she looked haggard. Clearly something was up, but Rita was too unsure of her position to push. "Come on, we have seats near the front but we could lose them in this crush." Brill glided forward with a grace Rita could only hope to imitate. She mentally kicked herself for getting distracted. *I need to get to my seat,* she realized. The MoCap sensors had a limited range. Then another thought overtook her: *why did she stonewall when I asked about Huw?* And then an even more interesting question came to mind: *what kind of business is so urgent it overrides attending a presidential funeral?*

Brill led her through the doorway into the royal chapel, which was larger than some cathedrals Rita had seen. The came to a pair of seats in the reserved section right at the front, among the middle-aged to elderly dignitaries and ambassadors. "Excuse me," Rita said, squeezing past a woman whose back was turned: "oh!"

"Good morning, Rita." It was her birth mother, almost unrecognizable in formal mourning. Miriam's make-up did little to conceal her exhaustion. "I'm glad you could be here."

"As a witness for my government? Or as me?" The words slipped out unfiltered.

Miriam gave her a knowing look: "Whichever you prefer." She picked up a printed sheet of paper. "Here's a program, you might find it useful. I knew him, you know. Before the revolution."

"What, you knew—" Rita glanced at the paper to conceal her confusion. The running order consisted of various speeches and commemorations by politicians, but no clergy. The royal chapel had been repurposed for a secular, or at least non-denominational, event.

"Adam was impressive. He wasn't just a revolutionary, he was a philosopher and journalist before he moved into politics. Then exile, after the crown violently suppressed the democracy protests of the 1990s. Erasmus"—she glanced sidelong at a gaggle of men in tailcoats and breeches—"was his secretary. Before I met him."

Rita shook her head, trying to come up with a metaphor to help her grasp what Miriam had just told her. *My birth mother married Lenin's secretary, then joined the politburo as commissar for industrial espionage.* It didn't seem like something she could write in one of her reports to Colonel Smith and Dr. Scranton. It was too enormous: eyebrows would be raised and they'd discount her reliability as a witness. On second thoughts, that might not be such a bad thing . . .

"He was a good man, or as good as anyone in his position can be. He always tried to do the right thing. When the revolution began to eat its children—there were early purges—he tried to stop it, even though his own position wasn't secure. I'd be dead if it wasn't for him. He put his own life on the line." Miriam sniffed. Her eyes were red. "Please don't think that I'd willingly serve a monster."

"I don't." Rita crossed her arms uncomfortably. *But you're saying* other people *will tell me he was a monster. Later, behind closed doors.* And despite Miriam's special pleading, what if he *had* been a monster? Was it even possible to lead an empire of a billion people without setting in motion wheels that would grind human blood and bones into paste?

"Look that way and smile," Brilliana hissed in her ear.

"Where? Oh. There." Rita saw the nest of cameras and turned to face them. She unfolded her arms, and allowed Miriam to take her right hand as she went into a practiced sequence of princess-mode smiles. She held her final pose for a few seconds, then turned to Miriam, careful to keep her side-profile in view. "This is the public shoot, right?"

Miriam nodded. "The broadcast cameras are too low-resolution to see your lips, so you can talk freely. What they'll see is Elizabeth Hanover smiling and talking to the Commissioner for Communication and Information Technology. The talking heads are primed to draw attention to you . . ."

"Have they found her yet?"

Miriam squeezed her fingers. "Still looking." People were moving at the front, towards the altar bearing the coffin. "Looks like they're getting ready to start. We should sit down now. Your knees will thank you later."

The event started. Rita sat (and occasionally stood) through the hour of speeches, trying to maintain a polite smile and an attentive posture. The eulogies dragged on interminably. A state funeral served as much to honor the living as to remember the dead. Fidgeting and face-pulling were utterly forbidden while she was on national television. Midway through, Erasmus stalked onto the stage. He gave a personal recollection of a fire-breathing civil rights campaigner, painting a portrait almost unrecognizable from the previous speeches. Halfway through, Rita became uncomfortably aware that Miriam's shoulders were shaking. Out of the corner of her eye, she saw that she was holding a handkerchief to her face.

The viewing itself was anti-climactic: she stood in the queue, shuffling past the open coffin and it was over and done in a few seconds. The body inside was so pale and thin that it might have blown away on a stiff breeze. Rita copied the people in front, ducking a brief curtsey, then leaving the dais to make way for the next mourner. Brilliana led her through an archway into a huge ballroom lined with tables swathed in black crepe, supporting an enormous buffet. "And we're off-camera." Brill removed her hat and tucked the net veil out of the way. "Grab a plate and eat, kid. In about twenty minutes, Miriam is going to hunt you down with a dance card full of VIPs you need to meet."

Introduced to—"you mean, as her daughter?" The point of no return was upon her. Henceforth she could either remain Rita Douglas, DHS employee and diplomatic go-between, or become Rita Burgeson, daughter of a powerful cabinet minister and Party Commissioner. The question of whether she could be both wasn't one that felt safe to ask—let alone one to which she could expect a truthful answer.

"Yes, as her daughter." Brilliana replaced her hat. "Trust me, you don't want to run the gauntlet with low blood sugar." She winked, momentarily shedding a decade of age, then grabbed a plate from the nearest table. "Just be grateful you're doing it this way rather than making your debut by being presented at a royal ball. None of the VIPs here are going to ask you to dance, then spend the rest of the evening leering at your cleavage."

"Royal—" Rita did a double-take, then closed her mouth. "Do you mean before the revolution?"

"No, I was unfortunate enough to have my coming-out in the Gruinmarkt. Things aren't perfect here, but at least we've got the franchise and a constitution that recognized women as citizens from the start." Brill's eyes flickered sidelong, as if she was worried about being overheard. "Your mother's not just steering a technological revolution, she's been quietly pushing a social agenda. More education, equal rights for women—in practice, not just in law. We're trying to quietly engineer a stage four demographic transition by being selective about what new technology we prioritize. Raising female workforce participation, pushing family planning services, nudging quietly from the sidelines." Brill looked across the room at a group of grey-haired male dignitaries, her eyes narrowing. "She's pushing too hard for some: we may be a revolutionary government, but there are still people who think that if somebody else benefits, it means they're losing."

The room filled up steadily as Rita scavenged a light lunch of unfamiliar, but mostly edible canapés. For the most part she recognized virtually nobody, and even fewer people showed any interest in her. But not everyone: as she dutifully demolished her plateful of finger food, a fellow approached her. Something about his appearance put her on alert. His hairstyle or his mannerisms seemed out of place here, not quite at home among the Commonwealth dignitaries. Everything about him screamed *foreigner* in the back of her head, but in an oddly conflicted way that puzzled her.

"Good afternoon, Ms. Douglas." He was in his fifties, amiable-looking and impeccably groomed in a preppy, Ivy League way, even thought he was dressed in Commonwealth formal mourning. Then the penny dropped: he didn't look foreign, he looked *American.* "John Kaminsky, State Department. I was told I could expect to see you here. How are you finding the Commonwealth?" He smiled, is if genuinely pleased to find her.

"I'm—" Her jaw flapped, wordlessly—"you're from State?"

"Yes."

"But I thought—"

"Oh, don't sweat it." He chuckled. "You may be DHS, but State will back your cover. Just don't be surprised if you run into more of us, sooner or later."

"There's an embassy now?"

"Not exactly: an embassy has a very specific legal status, and we haven't got there yet. But we're here by mutual consent, talking to our opposite numbers about a framework for establishing full diplomatic relations."

"But I—" Rita shut her mouth. *Of course.* *I'm not here to build a relationship with the Commonwealth government: I'm here to build a relationship with* my birth mother. She'd known it in the abstract, but to have her nose rubbed in it like this was unsettling. It raised disturbing questions: *why didn't the Colonel warn me? Do they know that the State Department has people here?* "I get it." She forced a smile. "Well, I should let you get on with the diplomatic ping-pong, shouldn't I? I'm supposed to be being introduced to people by, uh, my *mom.*" The word felt alien in her mouth. "You know about that, right? And you know how to get in touch later?"

"I believe so." Kaminsky nodded gravely. "Good luck, Ms. Douglas. And here's hoping for a long and peaceful relationship between the United States and the Commonwealth, based on our shared ideals." Whatever *those* were.

She'd barely stopped reeling from the encounter when Miriam caught up with her. "Rita!" She smiled amiably enough, but it didn't quite reach her eyes: "I'd like to introduce you to some of my colleagues." And before Rita could mention the man from the State Department, her mother thrust her into a torrent of political movers and fixers.

A tall, fat, sixty-something man was first, with a face consisting of contoured jowls dangling below a bulldog's mild brown eyes: "Rita, this is Jackson McDonald, secretary to the chancellor of the Commonwealth Mint—"Rita translated internally: deputy head of the Federal Reserve—"Jackson, this is my daughter Rita, by my first marriage. She's visiting from the United States." *Now* Miriam smiled, a slightly manic exaggerated grin that telegraphed the delight of a mother cat pouncing on a small squeaky snack for the education and entertainment of her kitten.

"I'm very pleased to meet you, Miss." Jackson gave her a slight bow, his gaze sharper than Rita expected. Jowls rearranged themselves in an avuncular smirk. "I must say, this is a surprise! I had no idea."

"I've been looking forward to introducing her to everybody for *years,*" Miriam announced. Rita froze, unsure whether to hug her or kick her shins. Miriam's smile broadened further: "Erasmus was of the opinion that now would be a good time. The other news being so . . . distracting, as it were."

Am I an embarrassment? Rita wondered, looking at her sharply: *or are you rolling him?* She couldn't tell. Which shouldn't be surprising, Miriam had been playing high-stakes politics since Rita was a toddler. The *by my first marriage* bit was flat-out untrue—at least, Miriam hadn't married her birth father until after Rita had been born and hastily adopted—but then she remembered Brilliana's apologia. Commonwealth social norms had diverged from her own world's some time in the middle of the eighteenth century, and in some areas they were quite backward. Was a child born out of wedlock a political liability to Miriam? Another penny dropped: *Erasmus was of the opinion*—which could be translated as: *my current husband is supportive.*

McDonald nodded at her again, an assessing look. "You have a most remarkable mother," he said, amiably enough. "Well, I must circulate— I'm sure we'll meet again."

"What," Rita demanded, tight-lipped, "was *that* about?"

Miriam took her elbow, replying in a voice pitched for her ears only: "Making damn sure anyone who moves against you knows they're moving against Erasmus as well—oh look!" The professional politician's smile was back, and Miriam moved her hand to Rita's forearm. A trio of men in tailcoats and breeches were approaching, led by a serious-faced fellow who looked barely any older than Rita. "Hello there! Rita, I'd like to introduce you to Adrian Holmes, secretary of the Party Central Commission." She dipped stiffly, something between a curtsey and a bow, in the direction of Mr. Holmes, whose mild-eyed affability struck Rita as utterly false. *This is the guy Olga warned me about.* The one with the arrest warrant and the secret police in his back pocket. Her skin crawled as he looked her over.

"Pleased to meet you, ah—"

"Rita Douglas." Rita extended a hand. Holmes reached towards her instinctively, then stopped and did a double-take. Rita copied her mother's smile. *Two can play at this game.* "Yes?"

"Aren't you—" Holmes' gaze suddenly sharpened as he turned it on Miriam. "Yes?" He demanded.

"Rita is my daughter, by my first marriage," Miriam told him with a smile. "Erasmus and I will be acknowledging her as my heir in due course."

"Well." His eyes widened slightly as he looked back at Rita. "I must offer my congratulations." His words were far warmer than his tone. He took Rita's hand, briefly dipped his head over her wrist. To her infinite relief, he refrained from kissing it. "It's a good thing that the Party abolished hereditary titles of nobility, ha ha!" Glancing back at Miriam: "well played, ma'am. *Very* well played." He ducked his head, then glanced at Rita. "Do you have an opinion of this happy family reunion?"

"Yes, but not for you." Rita smiled at him. "You can fuck off. And then fuck off again."

Holmes stiffened, but not as much as Miriam's grip on her forearm. "I suppose I deserved that," he said ruefully. "Well, I'm sure we'll meet again, once the dust settles. Be seeing you!" And he sauntered away in apparent unconcern.

"*That,*" Miriam said tensely, "was unwise." A moment's hesitation: "but he totally deserved it."

"*Are* you?" Rita asked. "I mean, are you planning on acknowledging me as your heir? Or was that just a bluff, to mess with his head? What does that even *mean?*" she finished plaintively.

"You know," Miriam said reflectively, "until just then, I wasn't entirely sure. I simply wanted to mark you as off-limits to conspiracies. But you know what? If you're going to *start* your career in Commonwealth politics by telling that little tin-pot Stalin to GTFO, I can't wait to see what you're capable of . . ."

FORT BASTION, TIME LINE TWELVE, AUGUST 2020

In a single split second, while the launch control bunker's main camera's shutter shielded its lens, all the fires of hell visited JUGGERNAUT's launch site.

Before the shutter had locked, the launch pad was a smoking rectangle of concrete, surrounded on all sides by marshland. Overhead, a huge rocket exhaust plume rose hazily towards the stratosphere, splitting the blue sky.

Blink. Half a second passed.

The camera behind the re-opened shutter stared into apocalypse. The sky above the pad was an angry red welt, glowing with the reflected light of a million grass-fires that had broken out all the way from the pad to the distant lagoon. Everything had turned from green and wet to red and black in a single heartbeat. Overhead, an unbearable brightness ascended towards the sky's zenith, framed by a roiling cloud of fire that swelled and rose as it gradually cooled. Of the rocket's expended booster stage there was no sign: it had been vaporized by the detonation of the very first drive charge.

Aboard JUGGERNAUT's command module, a monstrous clangor rattled Huw's teeth in his head. A jolt of acceleration forced him down into his seat and his vision faded to grey as his ears rang. The pressure rapidly eased over the course of a second, but then: *thump*, a second jolt came hard on its heels. *Thump*, and there was a third. As he grew accustomed to the rhythm of the jolts the buzzing in his ears subsided. Blanking briefly every second during each explosion, the video screen at the front of the capsule faded from white-out to a view of hell behind them as the ground receded below.

"JUGGERNAUT altitude two four four two, air speed one thousand four hundred and ten kilometers per hour, six point two kilometers downrange. Switching to altitude-compensated charges in five seconds—"

Thump. Thump. Thump.

Darkness alternated with light as the video window faded and flared repeatedly. Radiant heat raised steam from the surface of the lagoon kilometers below. A thermocouple trained on the ground beside the lake was showing nearly two hundred degrees Celsius, the surface waters rapidly coming to a rolling boil. The detonations rammed bodies into foam-lined bucket seats with bruising force, repeating once a second. JUGGERNAUT had massive shock absorbers to handle the recoil from the nuclear blasts, but the thrust surges were harsh and Huw's nerves were at the breaking point as he listened for any sign of lethal harmonics in the pogo oscillation—resonance effects that could shake the ship to pieces in seconds if they'd miscalculated just slightly.

"JUGGERNAUT altitude three seven zero zero, ground speed six hundred and forty meters per second, nine point seven kilometers down-range. Switching to third series drive charges—" the first two sets of propulsion bombs had been down-rated to single kiloton yields, to reduce the risk of ground-reflected shock-waves damaging the vehicle—"six seconds—"

Behind them, the first detonations had already sucked up a trail of debris, leaving a strange knotted-rope of fireballs rather than a normal nuclear mushroom cloud. It began to drift away from the launch pad to rain poison across the incinerated approaches. By the fiftieth explosion, less than a minute after lift-off, JUGGERNAUT was already reaching for the stratosphere, chasing the sun atop a chain of solar fireballs. The camera filters no longer closed for each detonation: above most of the atmosphere there was less backscattered visible light. Two minutes into the flight, Huw began to relax. The ship hadn't shaken itself to pieces, and the Earth was now showing a visible curvature. To the witnesses in the bunker JUGGERNAUT would be visible as a hypnotically flaring column of brightness rising from the horizon, pulsing jerkily towards low Earth orbit as if hammering on heaven's door.

Huw closed his eyes and counted bombs in his head, tracking the launch sequence. Each bomb added roughly fifteen meters per second to the ship's speed, and it needed to get to eight thousand meters per second to make orbital velocity. They had to hope that the shock absorbers would hold together, that the chain gun shooting bombs out once a second wouldn't jam or misfire, and that the drive computer would continue to detonate the propulsion charges dead center beneath the pusher plate. There were fail-safes, but sometimes fail-safes failed. Meanwhile Huw's head hurt. It felt like he was sitting inside a church bell tower: his ears rang, he had worsening tinnitus, and he felt groggy. Trying to focus on the panel in front of him was surprisingly hard, with gauges blurring and doubling in his vision. *Mild concussion?* he wondered. The flight surgeons had said it was a possibility: *any space launch you walk away from is a good one*, he decided.

Thump.

Thump.

Thump.

Silence—

"Nuke crew confirms ascent shut-off." Major Saunders' voice was shaky over the audio loop from the other capsule. "Flight deck? You have control."

Huw swallowed, his ears ringing. "Flight deck has control." He glanced sideways at the Pilot Flying and Pilot Monitoring. There was another checklist to run, if he could just force his eyeballs to focus on it. "Davis, Jensen, status."

"Pusher plate temperature looks good. Drive safed, bomb ejector in shutdown—"

"—Velocity nominal, altitude looking good, ground track nominal. We're in the right orbit."

The sound of muted applause—or at least twenty shaken sighs and groans of relief—came over the crew loop.

Huw keyed his mike. "Okay everyone, you heard it. Clear your initial checklists, report any medical or station issues, then take ten and prep for on-orbit station-keeping. EVA team, you're on in five hours for preliminary external inspection." That would be their first space-walk: an external visual inspection of JUGGERNAUT for launch-induced damage. "We're not jaunting for at least twelve hours." It'd take that long to prepare for the first para-time portage, to a time line with deep space tracking facilities already in place on the ground. "Then it's showtime for the First Man's funeral."

NEW LONDON, MANHATTAN ISLAND,
TIME LINE THREE, AUGUST 2020

"I'm losing my grip," Miriam complained to Erasmus as she rolled the glove off her right hand. She stood just inside the front hall of their town house. It was barely eleven o'clock at night but she was bone-tired from the day of public appearances. She and Erasmus had both been up since half past five that morning, out and on display since seven. "I nearly bit Adrian's head off in front of everybody when he congratulated me on my daughter."

The confrontation she'd anticipated and dreaded for days had taken place at the evening reception at the Chamber of Party Commissioners, after the official public viewing of the First Man lying in state. It should have been a discreet, informal meeting for the inner circle of the politburo, to give them space to chew the fat and share their thoughts about the afternoon's more public events. But canapés and wine had taken a back seat to bickering and ill-tempered back-stabbing. "It wasn't what he said but the way he said it . . ."

"Needling you is a tacit admission that he's lost the fight." Erasmus held still as Jenny, their housekeeper, slid the coat from his shoulders. "Going after Rita now would signal a public attack that he knows he'd lose. So it was just a display of sour grapes."

"Sour grapes make bitter wine." Miriam went to work on her other glove.

"Anyway, Rita gave him the scolding he richly deserved. How do you suppose she came through the rest of the day?"

"I'm sure she managed perfectly well: she's very self-contained. Brill would have called you if there were any other problems." Erasmus shuffled painfully through to the living room at the back of the house. His slippers were positioned beside his preferred chair, along with a red leather box containing tomorrow's briefings. It had been dropped off by courier an hour ago, while they'd still been disentangling themselves from the Commissioners' Reception. Now he took his seat and unbuckled his formal shoes, wincing with relief. "Any word from your German spy?"

"He agreed to the proposal and he's on his way to Berlin. I told Olga to pull out all the stops."

"Meaning . . . ?"

"Olga put him on a government fast courier to Maracaibo, where he was portaged across to time line two's Venezuela. Travel is faster over on the other side. He should arrive in Italy in another four or five hours."

"Why Italy? Border controls?"

Miriam followed him through the doorway. She'd shed her hat, coat and shoes: now she dropped into her own chair on the other side of the fireplace. "Ah, that's better. You have to show a passport to enter the European nations that share a common customs zone. Some are easier to bribe than others."

"I see. So Kurt isn't free to travel on his own passport—"

"I don't want his real passport to be on a computer system anywhere the US authorities might see it. Or his false passport, if it comes to that. We didn't have time to generate a solid false identity for him."

"They can see other countries' visitors?"

"The US, and their key allies, have an intelligence-sharing treaty. They see everything that happens within range of a camera, hear every phone call, monitor everything that happens on every computer anywhere on the planet. They have that time line increasingly locked down." Miriam shivered. "The intelligence assessments coming out of Olga's people are scary stuff, 'Ras. They see *everything*: only the lack of people to watch screens limits them, and they're making progress using artificial intelligence to fill the gap. It's why we can barely run agents over there anymore. And why they don't have political demonstrations or public signs of unrest anymore—"

"Yes, yes, I know." Erasmus winced. "Sorry, m'dear, I've been following the briefings. You remember the revolution here, but not so much what went before. It's simply the application of better technology to the same dismal ends as the monarchy."

"I saw enough of that." Miriam picked up her briefing box. "I got the picture. 'A tyranny is always at its most vulnerable when the hands that wield the lash start to slacken,' as Adam put it." She sniffed. "The US is a democracy in form and theory. But they developed a bureaucratic security apparatus dedicated to fighting wartime threats and allowed it to persist in peacetime. Now it's mostly self-perpetuating. No elected politician dares tackle it because it'll get you the enmity of the security apparat, the voters won't notice the absence of something they've grown used to, and if there *is* an attack, your opponents will crucify you. At least *our* deep state was designed to support democratic norms while they were becoming established." She snorted, by way of adding ironic punctuation.

"Let us hope for a better—" Erasmus looked round, hunting for Jenny. "Where's our—oh, thank you." The housekeeper reappeared, bearing a tray with two glasses and a bottle of port. He filled both glasses close to the brim. "You need a drink. Here."

"Cheers."

"Two more days of this. The Juggernaut circus, the military parade, and the high-profile defection—if we can get it back on track. Then a week of commemorations and interviews and memorials and the selection meeting—and it'll be done, and you can relax." Exhaustion lent a heavy emphasis to his words. "All settled."

"Not if . . ." Miriam searched through her box. "Aha." She found the folder she was looking for, began to skim-read with an efficiency borne from years of experience of parsing this particular daily briefing. "Not until the fat lady sings. Or rather, the fat prince."

"That's the daily strategic overview summary, isn't it?"

"Yes. And . . . oh look, the French are indeed on heightened alert. Can't possibly imagine why that might be? Their seventh fleet just put to sea, repositioning from Marseilles to the Western Approaches for, um, sea trials? That new aircraft carrier, their first atomic one. Speeches in the Palace of Lords. Other movements too. The second fleet is exercising in the Bay of Bengal. The Third Air Army is staging out to its dispersal bases in Kamchatka. *Someone* poked the hornets' nest. The gendarmerie in the Germanies are conducting a sweep for anarchist agitators and anti-monarchist subversives—"

"—Olga's got them stirred up about the princess."

Miriam glanced at him sharply. "Do you think they took the bait?"

"Rita did a great job in the studio and at the funeral, very regal. I saw some before and after comparisons from the broadcast: the computerized compositing machines are amazing. I knew who I was looking at and I *still* wondered if maybe Elizabeth had arrived in secret. The technical wizardry involved!" He shook his head. "It really drives home what we're facing. Even after all these years, it still surprises me." He returned his wife's sidelong glance. "You gave up a lot to come here."

She sipped from her glass. "It wasn't much of a choice. And—"she shook her head—"I haven't regretted it. Much." She gave her husband a half-smile: "Mind you, if Kurt can't find and retrieve Ms. Hanover before Adrian realizes what's happening that might change. We will be in *so much* shit."

"Is there anything else I can do to help? Beyond what we're already working on?"

"I don't know." Miriam slid the briefing to the back of her box. The other folders were mostly reports on her own ministry's activities, of considerably less immediate import. "If you could spin up a cover story to explain the lack of more public appearances by Elizabeth Hanover that might help. 'The runaway Princess is being debriefed at a secure location and will only do interviews via television,' something like that. But they'll get suspicious eventually. And that bastard Smith has got Hulius. We should assume he knows who Elizabeth is and what her defection means for us, so he'll see her as leverage, and he'll be desperate to work out where our pressure points are. If he gets his hands on her before Kurt—"

"If I was in his shoes I'd debrief her, then threaten us with a drone dropping leaflets all over St. Petersburg. Make a splash."

"Or not even threaten. He could initiate overt diplomatic relations with the Imperium by returning the Dauphin's runaway bride as a goodwill gesture. All they need is a green light from the Oval Office. If we lose Elizabeth to Smith, we will be royally fucked, no pun intended. Total loss of credibility in the middle of a succession crisis. Worst mess since the revolution."

Erasmus took a mouthful of port and swallowed. "This all boils down to leverage," he said aloud. "Smith thinks he's got leverage over you—via Rita. He thinks he's got leverage over Rita through her family and friends. Olga thought she could buy us leverage over Adrian by fetching Elizabeth Hanover, which in turn would give us a lever to crack apart her father and the Dauphin. Elizabeth wants leverage, wants a way out of being a pawn—All of us have something the other side wants, all of us are afraid of something the other side intends for us."

"We've accidentally created a circular firing-squad," Miriam mused bitterly. "You could make a TV sitcom out of it if the stakes weren't so high." Twenty thousand thermonuclear warheads on each side, bristling at the rival superpower just like the kind of confrontation the USA and USSR had gotten into in the 1980s. "I wish the guns were all loaded with blanks. The risk of someone going nuclear by accident is too high."

Erasmus sat up. "You just gave me an idea."

"What? About the nuclear—"

"No, back up a bit. Think about leverage. You're absolutely right: everybody is looking for a lever, and if they've got one they're looking for another one, or a bigger one, because what you use a lever for is to move something. But what if we've got it wrong, Miriam? What if we're all looking for levers when what we should *really* be looking for is a better fulcrum?"

"A—" she gave him a blank look. "A pivot-point?"

He sighed. "We've got all these levers working at cross-purposes, and nowhere to rest them. What we need to do is to get them levering in the same direction."

"Great idea. Show me how." He was watching her.

"I don't know, love. If I had all the answers I'd be running the show, wouldn't I?"

She gave a weak chuckle. "I thought you already were."

He snorted softly. "Not even close." He reached across for her hand, and after a moment she rested her fingers in his palm. "It's just a bluff. I don't really know what I'm doing."

"Do you think Adam knew what he was doing?"

"Not hardly." Her husband slowly closed his hand around hers. "It's not as if *any* of us know what we're doing, not really: we're just faking it until it feels natural. At least, that's what I've concluded after all these years."

It had been eighteen years since the revolution. Nearly nineteen years had passed since they'd met, fifteen since they'd married. And he still managed to surprise her from time to time. "I'm worried, 'Ras."

"I know." He leaned towards her. "You get tense and technical when you're stressed. You'll work yourself into an early grave at this rate."

"I wish—" She stopped.

"Yes?"

"—I wish I could just let it all slide," she continued haltingly. "I'm so *tired* of this."

He didn't have to ask what *this* was. "We'll take a vacation," he promised. "After the funeral and the selection and inauguration. A month somewhere warm and sunny, just the two of us with no interruptions and no business." He sounded wistful. In truth, a month-long vacation seemed as impossible as walking on the moon unless the next First Man fired them both.

"I'd like that," she said.

He reached out and shoved her pile of briefing boxes across the table away from her. "Start now. Try to relax."

"But if—" she rolled her lower lip between her teeth and reached for the boxes.

"Stop that." He blocked her hand. "The world will still be here tomorrow, whether or not you're fully briefed." He shifted in his chair. "I'm going to bed, and I think you should come with me. Tomorrow can take care of itself."

She stood at the same time as Erasmus pushed himself to his feet. Glancing at the clock on the mantelpiece: "it's almost tomorrow already, anyhow." She stifled a yawn, then stepped towards her husband.

"Exactly." He gathered her into his arms and they stood for a while, leaning on each other's shoulder. "You need to let me look after you, love. Otherwise, who else is going to do that?"

NEAR CAMP SINGULARITY, TIME LINE FOUR, AUGUST 2020

"What the fuck is *that*?"

Sergeant Jackson froze in place. The outburst from Barry set his pulse racing. Not a shout, but far too loud for safety.

"Ew—" began Sally.

Jackson cracked. "Quiet!" *What part of* go quiet and signal me *didn't you understand?*

Barry was slightly upslope from Jackson, peering out from behind a tree about ten meters away. Sally, in contrast, was crouched in the open like a stunned sheep. "Freeze," Jackson called before she could move. He slithered sideways towards her then paused and scanned for whatever she'd seen.

There. A flash of silver in the undergrowth upslope, almost on the ridgeline where the trees began to drop away on the other side of the slope.

Jackson raised his M-4 and peered through the optical sights. At 4.5 zoom the thing was clearly visible, scrabbling around in the undergrowth near the base of a giant hemlock fifty meters away. It was silvery but not metallic, with the sheen of oil on plastic, and it had too many legs with joints that screamed *wrong!* It was about the size of one of the robot sentry/patrol dogs the DARPA geeks were so keen on—a small Labrador or a large bloodhound, rather than a German Shepherd—but it looked to be based on some sort of insect. Cockroach crossed with a—*shit, grasshopper legs, that thing's built to jump*—only where a roach would have paired antennae, two clusters of tentacles fanned upwards, swaying and shimmying. *What the hell?*

It didn't seem to have spotted the childrens' crusade yet. Which was very good news, but liable to change in a hurry.

"Sally. I want you to *very slowly* get down on your belly and back up five meters. Barry, freeze."

Sally, for once, did *exactly* what she was told without asking questions. A miracle. Jackson glanced over his shoulder and made eye contact with Mikka, fifty meters across the slope. She noticed and signaled: *all clear.* At least someone knew what she was supposed to be doing. *Good girl.* Jackson looked back at the bug. It seemed to be rummaging in the undergrowth. *Eating? Taking a shit?* He kept his sights on it. Those tentacle-bunches creeped him out, waving in the breeze, almost like the sensory hairs of a—

He registered movement out of the side of his eye. Neckbeard Gary, crouched behind a fallen tree trunk, was also watching the bug through his sights. And his trigger finger—

"Hold your fire!" Jackson snapped angrily.

But Gary wasn't listening. The flat crack of an M4 shattered the quiet of the hillside.

Gary whooped: he'd hit the bug, which sprawled on the ground, legs twitching. He stood and turned, punching the air: "Hoo-ah! Did you see that? I totally—"

The bug stopped twitching and rolled on its back. Wing cases irised open, then propellers unfolded and blurred into a snarling whine as it lifted off, hovered at shoulder height, and turned to point tentacles straight at Gary. Who wasn't paying any attention to his 'kill,' having already dismissed it from his mind.

Jackson squeezed off a three-round burst, then another as the oncoming insect-drone bobbed and zipped into a side-to-side slalom like a *really* angry hornet the size of a bulldog. The Neckbeard was useless: he stood in full view, jaw gaping, slowly raising his rifle. *Too slow.* The Cheerleader was caught out of position, lying frozen on her belly with her carbine trapped under her. J. Barrington Weiss III was *trying* to shoot the thing, but his aim point veered dangerously close to the other fire team's position. The bug veered to point first at Jackson, then at Neckbeard. A crackle of full auto fire from across the slope lit it up, and its head exploded.

"Cease fire!" Jackson screamed, his ears ringing. For a miracle, everybody seemed to get the message. The last burst of fire had come from Mikka, and the bug was now lying on the ground about five meters away, burning—a smell of melted plastic and hot metal and blood—

Blood? Jackson quickly checked. Cheerleader and Weiss had taken cover and were peering at the wreckage of the bug, totally spooked. Further away, Mikka had her team in hand, which left—

A trail of blood flowed downhill, crimson in the afternoon sunlight, forming a river delta flowing from the headwaters of Neckbeard's torso. There'd be no more whining from that quarter, and no need to scream at his sorry ass for disobeying orders. The bug was down but not due to his team's shooting: the blast had been highly directional, an explosively forged projectile erupting from the front of the bug to turn Neckbeard's entire head into a spray of red. *Neat targeting,* the analytical part of Jackson's brain commented over the unmistakable sound of the Cheerleader throwing up.

"Weiss, get the fuck over there and join up with Bernstein's team. At the double." He raised his hand and hastily waved Mikka off, downhill and away. Then he held the Cheerleader's shoulders as she vomited, and turned her away from what was left of the Neckbeard. "Come on, private," he said, pitching his voice low: "get it together. You're out of here. I want you to go home, got that?" He pulled out his paint can and tagged the nearest tree, then punched a waypoint into his inertial navigation pack. "Swap navpacks with me. That's right, give me yours, take this . . . can you make it back to our entry point on your own?"

He waited patiently, even though his senses were screaming danger. The kids weren't remotely ready for this: they needed a babysitter, not a sergeant. Hell, he wasn't sure *he* was ready for this. After a few seconds she nodded, still unable to speak.

"Take the navpack. Show me your icon?" He waited for her to show him the temporary tattoo on the back of her wrist that would take her back to the rendezvous time line. "Good. Jaunt back to the staging line, head for the tent, retrieve the icon for home base, then let Captain Briggs debrief you. Tell him we lost Baxter, then turn in your helmet camera. Think you can remember all that?" She damned well ought to, but shock did funny things to memory. He hoped to hell she'd find her way to the tent in the staging—empty—time line, where the security-coded safe with the flash-paper knotwork to get her home was waiting. If not, she'd be MIA in para-time.

She nodded again, more emphatically. "I'm sorry," she sniffed.

Kids. "Don't be. Just go." He pointed downhill. "Jaunt immediately if you see any more of those things. Fast as you can, now. Your job here is done."

Which was a little white lie: her job wouldn't be done until she delivered her message. But she didn't need to hear that right now, barely halfway through basic training in a role she was wildly unsuited for, with a teammate's brains splattered all over her boots.

Fuck, Jackson swore to himself. Rage and regret with a side-order of resentment propelled him upslope towards the wreckage of the bug. If Neckbeard had listened, for *once* in his sorry life—but no. The guy was a loser: his singular talent was the only reason he hadn't been rejected out of hand by the recruiting office. Instead it had ensured he was drafted and dragged into infantry training for DRAGON'S TEETH, a role he was even less suitable for than the Cheerleader. Jackson still felt a merciless stab of guilt in his guts as he unfolded his sample sack and rolled the remains of the bug up in it. He was responsible for these kids' lives, even though he knew some of them would freeze and others would disobey orders.

Shouldering the sack he checked again for lurkers, than scrambled across the slope in the direction Mikka's fire team had taken off in. Time to send the next-worst recruit home with the dead bug, then reform the survivors into a single team. That way he could keep a closer eye on them. Maybe stop anyone else from committing suicide by alien killer robot.

Although what would happen if they ran into actual hostiles didn't bear thinking about.

Reaction Shots

After a brief corpse-viewing followed by a long afternoon of being introduced to political dignitaries whose roles she didn't quite understand (so
that when they smiled at her, she was uncertain whether they were expressing their sympathies or sizing her up for a coffin of her own), Rita found
herself back at Brill's house. She was already exhausted, but this was only
the first of three days of national mourning.

"Tomorrow is another early start. You have more studio interviews to
record." Inspector Morgan read from yet another checklist. She seemed
indefatigable, although the pace had to be wearing on her too. "Then there
will be another green screen session with full motion capture. You get three
hours off, then in late afternoon there's a formal reception for the commissioner for state—"

"I have to go home and report," Rita interrupted.

"Excuse me?" Alice stared at her.

"I have to report to my superiors in Baltimore." She leaned tiredly against
the wall of the hallway. "Seriously. If I don't check in every forty-eight hours
they'll decide I've defected or something, and my mo—Miriam will have
another diplomatic mess on her plate. It's non-optional."

Morgan cocked her head for a moment. "This way." She led Rita into
the parlor and gestured at a chair. "Wait here while I make arrangements.
I'm sure I can get this sorted out." Rita closed her eyes briefly: *too tired*,
she thought.

A minute later the Inspector was back. "Mrs. Hjorth is in a meeting but
I've left a message for her to call. We need to clear this—"

Rita tensed. "Alice, it would be a *very bad idea* to make Dr. Scranton
think something has happened to me. She probably already wonders if my

grandpa is missing—I need to keep her reassuringly briefed, even if it's just to say 'everything is on hold during the funeral' and 'Gramps sometimes goes wandering off-grid, I don't know why.'"

Her minder cocked her head on one side, watching Rita thoughtfully. "You," she began, just in time to be interrupted by the distinctive double-ring of a phone in the next room. "One moment."

This time she was gone for a few minutes, leaving Rita to stew in her uncertainty. *How did I get into this bind?* She asked herself. *Oh, right. I was born into it.* Both sides—the Colonel's Unit within DHS, and her birth mother's organization within the Commonwealth government—found it expedient to have an agent in the other's camp. Having *a* conduit (even one you knew the other side were deliberately using to gaslight you) was better than having *no* conduit—especially when the other side was a paranoid, nuclear-armed superpower.

But they've both got to trust me, otherwise it breaks down, she realized sickly. *I've got to keep the message traffic flowing, keep them talking.* The Colonel—yes, he *was* sufficiently cold-blooded—had hostages against her cooperation: grandpa Kurt, girlfriend Angie, her parents, even her foster-brother River. Miriam's coercion could be more direct—Rita was under no illusions about Inspector Morgan's willingness to slap a pair of hand-cuffs on her in a split second if she was so ordered—but on the other hand, Mrs. Burgeson seemed to think Rita was *family*, a word seemingly freighted with eerie occult significance in her mind.

Miriam is much less likely to decide I'm expendable, Rita realized, in a somewhat disturbing perspective twist. To the Colonel and Dr. Scranton Rita was simply an agent, but to Miriam Burgeson there was a personal dimension. Rita was her only child. Even though she'd been adopted at birth and raised by someone else, apparently at the behest of a now-dead grandmother. Rita glanced around the parlor, taking it in afresh. From the unfamiliar electrical outlets, to the spindly, rococo furniture, and the normal-for-this-time-line clothing they'd given her to wear, it was all strange—she was a stranger in a foreign country in another time. This world had skipped straight past the clean lines and concrete of the Mod-ernist period, lurching from nineteenth-century imperial baroque into the era of plastic, antibiotics, and moon-shots. But alien as it was, it was also a world where she was viewed by her—employer? patron? other mother?—as something more than just another interchangeable cog in a bureaucratic totalizing machine.

It hadn't escaped her attention that nobody had mentioned ID cards or biometrics to her, other than simple badges to access government buildings. There weren't many cameras either. Perhaps it was simply that they didn't have the technological infrastructure to build a national surveillance system, but she had the impression that they knew it was possible and had decided they didn't *want* to go down that road. (Over dinner a few nights ago, Erasmus had said something about emergent constitutional flaws and the balance between liberty, equality, and fraternity. What did that even *mean?*)

They'll appoint a new First Man, then sort out a treaty framework, and I can go home, Rita told herself. But it rang hollow even to her own ears. Would she *really* go back to being a DHS field agent? Assuming they'd have her back at all, that was. Once she was confirmed in public as the daughter of a high-ranking foreign politician: what would happen then? Wouldn't they view her as a security risk, a foreign agent of influence? And if they thought she was colluding with Kurt and Angie, they wouldn't just fire her. They could disappear her into the Federal Corrections Colony System, dump her in a concrete cell in a prison in an uninhabited time line. They'd hoover up all her relatives as a matter of principle: merely by existing, an uncontrolled world-walker was a clear and present danger, much like a terrorist ringleader in earlier decades.

The idea of defecting, of cutting all ties with the DHS and her home time line, had occurred to her before, but she'd carefully avoided thinking about it too much. The thought of losing all contact with her family back home—of never seeing her foster parents Emily and Franz again— was unbearable. Such a profound and permanent exile felt like a kind of death. So she had reacted by studiously kicking the can down the road, which required her to carefully *not* think about making such a move. As long as she could kid herself that her loyalty was undivided, she wouldn't actually have to make any irrevocable, unbearable decisions. But now she faced a dilemma. What if Kurt, Angie, her family, maybe the whole of the Wolf Orchestra, chose to seek asylum in the Commonwealth? What then?

Alice swept back into the room. "That was Mrs. Hjorth." Brilliana. "Get whatever you need, you're going to report in tonight. The rendezvous is in New York." Across the East river, in the other time line's Brooklyn.

Rita stood up. "Give me fifteen minutes."

Half an hour later Rita slid into the back of the ministry limousine behind Alice's driver. She'd changed from formal mourning dress into jeans and a hoodie. It was less likely to attract attention, but felt weirdly out of place here. She'd also collected her tablet and inertial mapper, which she'd need in order to find the crossing point. "All right," she said, leaning forward to catch the driver's ear. "Once we're across the causeway, I can give you general directions, but first, we need to get out of New London to the south east."

She held the tablet close to her chest. She'd kept a diary, so compiling a written report on the events of the past couple of days wasn't difficult. The hard part was the prospect of making a quick trip over without going home, not even seeing Angie, let alone spending time together. But if the Colonel suspected her of disloyalty, she'd be putting Angie and her entire family in danger. Worst case: they might begin to dig into her girlfriend's background, and Kurt's, and pick up the thread of the Wolf Orchestra; East Germany's longest-enduring spy ring on US soil.

I can't go on like this, she realized hopelessly. *But what can I do?*

TEMPELHOF AIR FORCE BASE, BERLIN, TIME LINE TWO, AUGUST 2020

"Good morning, Hulius. Or do you prefer, Major?"

Hulius rolled his head sideways, to better see who knew his name. The man in the visitor's chair was sixty-ish, bald, with crows-foot wrinkles around slightly sunken blue eyes. He wore his grey suit and open-collared white shirt like a uniform.

"Colonel . . . Smith?" Hulius frowned, pained. His chest ached fiercely today. They'd taken him off the morphine pump and removed most of the tubes. He was relatively lucid, but he wouldn't be running any marathons or even walking to the bathroom unaided in the near future. "I can't say I'm pleased to meet you."

"I'm not surprised." The Colonel's smile was at best polite. "Perhaps under other circumstances," he added with a victor's magnanimity. "Do you remember Ms. Milan's visit?"

I wish I didn't. He met the Colonel's gaze. "What do you want?"

"*Who,* not what, Major. You know exactly who I'm talking about. Age eighteen, height five foot eight, weight one-thirty pounds, black frizzy hair, medium-dark skin, upturned nose, high cheekbones. Your contact in Germany. Last seen in your company in Turkish Muslim drag—which she'll have ditched by now if she has any sense. Where did you leave your shoulder-bag, Major, and what kind of gun did she steal when she escaped? This is *important*," Smith added urgently. "I can sandbox you—and her— and organize some sort of prisoner exchange, but only if she doesn't go full Ulrike Meinhof. Shoot it out with the cops," he clarified in response to Hulius's blank-eyed look. "They're looking for her."

But only because you told them to, Hulius thought.

"Why don't you tell me about her?" Smith asked. He laced his fingers together and leaned towards Hulius's bedside earnestly. Hulius couldn't help himself. He snorted instinctively: then took a couple of minutes for the searingly painful coughing fit to subside. The Colonel half-rose as if to summon help, but sat down again when Yul weakly waved a hand at him.

"Let me re-phrase." Colonel Smith waited another minute. "You are going to tell me about Elizabeth Hanover. We can do this the easy way or the hard way. The easy way: you give me everything you think I need to know, right now. The hard way: I tell you *why* I need to know, then you'll tell me everything. There is no *don't*."

Bait. Hulius could barely help himself. "Why should I?"

"She's a defector, isn't she? From a rival empire to your—Commonwealth." The pause was deliberate, noticeable. "She's part of the royal family of a European or Eurasian superpower. Obviously heavily guarded. Operating on their soil is a big deal, otherwise you wouldn't be playing elaborate ex- filtration games via alternate time lines. I would guess that *the princess* is of considerable value to you politically: the heir, or at any rate very close to the foreign monarch. *Very* embarrassing to have lost her. Even more so while the Commonwealth is paralyzed by a succession crisis."

Oh fuck you. The Colonel was deliberately showing his hand, and Yul's spirits sank. Smith had gotten some bits of the picture wrong, but what he'd got right was bad enough. If he captured the princess, he and his superiors wouldn't hesitate to use her as leverage against the Com- monwealth's Department for Para-time Research—blackmail, at best.

Orchestrating Princess Elizabeth's defection would have been an operational coup for the DPR, reinforcing the Commonwealth's revolutionary government right when it needed it most. But losing her, much less losing her to the United States, would be enormously embarrassing. Career-ending for Olga Thorold and Brilliana Hjorth: possibly also for their Commissioner—Miriam Burgeson. It would be a huge blow to the entire para-time bureaucracy of the Commonwealth. Colonel Smith could hold the threat of selling the princess to Adrian Holmes over their neck like an executioner's axe once he learned who the Burgeson's rivals within the Party hierarchy were. Even worse: he could wrap Elizabeth up with a bow and send her back to her father and fiancé in St. Petersburg, who could plausibly spin her defection as a kidnapping—and thus an act of war—while acting as an ice-breaker for negotiations between the United States and the French Empire.

The prospect of Liz Hanover being run over and killed by a delivery van while out of his sight was bad enough. Losing her to the enemy would be a royal disaster, raising the possibility of an alliance between the Commonwealth's two main rivals.

"We've got an all-points alert out for the princess," Colonel Smith added, rubbing it in. "The police are searching for her. They've been told she's a world-walking terrorist. There are cameras here, Major. Not as many as in New York—for example, at a certain diner where you used to meet with Ms. Milan to exchange packages—but enough."

Point taken. Hulius blinked first. "What do you want?"

"Short term or long—? Oh hell. Let's go with long term first: I want to *avoid a nuclear war*, Major, same as you do. Everybody's the hero of their own narrative, everybody wants to die of old age at home, surrounded by their family and friends. But we have to play with the hand we've been dealt, don't we? My people got dealt a really bad hand on 9/11 when a crew of fanatics murdered thousands of innocents. And when we were reeling, you world-walkers—I'm sorry, another world-walker faction, *the other faction* within your extended family—kicked us while we were down. Remember 7/16, remember those portable demolition nukes. Those *stolen* portable demolition nukes. My country, Major, takes a lot of stick because we're big on high ideals and often fall short on follow-through. We talk the talk better than we walk the walk. But at least we *have* ideals, even if we sometimes fail to live up to them. Our enemies have no such handicaps. They're hard men who are utterly unafraid to stab us in the back. The threat they pose to my people right now, and for the past seventeen years, is very great indeed. It's so great that when we stared into the abyss, Major, we blinked, and we collectively decided that perhaps abstract ideals like *freedom* and *democracy* could wait until our enemies weren't trying to murder us in our beds. I swore an oath to protect my country and its constitution: and I'm going to keep doing that until it's safe for democracy to resume. That's what I want. Does that answer your question? What do *you* want?"

Hulius stared at him. Then, slowly at first—despite the fiery pain in his ribs—he began to chuckle. Smith's eyes widened: but Hulius only laughed harder, until the tears of pain made it impossible.

"What."

"You want." Hulius wheezed, drawing a deep breath. "You want to save the United States—for democracy." And he was off again.

"What's so *fucking* funny?" Smith snarled, lurching to his feet.

"You turned your country into a prison camp, to protect it and make it safe for Democracy—" Hulius wheezed painfully, then closed his eyes and continued, gauging each word for effect: "You murdered everyone in my former homeland. Now you want to defend your democracy against *the Commonwealth* by sponsoring a hereditary dictatorship . . . have you looked in a mirror lately?"

Funny. He should have punched me by now. Hulius opened his eyes in time to see Colonel Smith's back receding. He'd met patriots like the Colonel before. To retreat in the face of such a baiting bespoke inhuman self-control. "Wait."

"I gave you a choice," said Smith, pausing but not looking round. "The easy way or the hard way. You've made it your choice and now I'm going to have to live with it. Thank you very much." He resumed walking, and Hulius heard the door close behind him.

ABOARD A JET BOUND FOR VENEZUELA, TIME LINE THREE, AUGUST 2020

The woman in the wheelchair flew with Kurt as far as Venezuela, but did not join him for the portage to his own time line and the onward journey to Berlin.

"There's an Interpol red notice out with my biometrics attached," she explained, looking slightly smug: "I made the Global Terrorism Top Fifty list!" She sounded like a pop star boasting that her latest album had gone triple platinum. In time line three Olga was a respected government official, but in time line two she was a candidate for drone strikes, extraordinary rendition, and SWAT teams. She might be able to bribe her way past the police in Caracas, but even a private jet wouldn't get her into the EU unnoticed.

"So I'm going to brief you, give you your documents, and turn you loose. Helmut will get you to the airport and fly with you—he's clean, he was only six years old in 2003—then organize your return trip to New London."

"What about my team?" Kurt tried to keep the worry out of his voice. After so many years—decades—they weren't just agents to him: they were lifelong friends, or their children and grandchildren.

"If they're compromised, they can travel back to the Commonwealth with you. Helmut will organize it. Otherwise, if they are clean, they can return to the United States. Most of them have families to collect: this is understood. We can extract them later if necessary, just as long as they have not been identified as persons of interest by the DHS. But Venezuela is as far as I can accompany you."

Kurt looked round, taking in the cabin of the Commonwealth courier jet. From the glassed-in nose (visible just past the pilots in their raised cockpit) to the rows of empty seats stretching out behind them, there was something oddly nostalgic about the plane's layout. It was like an echo of the 1960s Soviet Union, one that dredged up childhood memories of Russian leaders and Tupolevs in Aeroflot livery. A taciturn, broad-shouldered fellow who Olga had introduced as Helmut slept soundly in a seat right at the back. "Why do we have to use a different aircraft in my time line?"

"World-walking while airborne is difficult enough, but disguising a converted bomber as a Gulfstream is impossible. We'd be intercepted and shot down as soon as we crossed over."

They spent the next two hours rehearsing a packaged identity. Kurt was to be an Argentinian citizen of German descent. The passport was real enough, but his first level cover story was thin as rice-paper—he was a rich retired industrialist traveling on a whim—and there was no second-level cover story at all. He had a black Amex card and a wad of hundred euro

banknotes for bribes. Precisely what kind of retired industrialist would hire
a Gulfstream for an intercontinental flight—for a mere $9,000 per hour—
then rely on taxis for getting about Berlin was unspecified. File under Ec-
centric (subtype: Ingvar Kamprad) and move on. Out of deference to
Olga, who looked utterly exhausted, he didn't push back. This was clearly
a salvage operation and he'd have to rely on speed and improvisation.

Finally Olga yawned, running out of energy. "Helmut will give you your
phones on arrival and organize ground transport. Any questions, you can
message me but it'll take a couple of hours to get a reply. Your phone has
a number for a signals officer who can relay messages via world-walker.
It's a different control channel from our regular on-site people. We want
you insulated from the target in case someone has compromised Yul's—
her—controller." She sagged against her seat back. "Any more questions?"

Kurt frowned. "Nothing significant. You need to sleep."

She didn't reply, just closed her eyes and lay so still that for a moment
he thought she'd died suddenly. The jet thundered on through the stratosphere, its old-school turbojets bellowing hoarsely. Kurt glanced through
his paperwork one more time, then stowed it in the briefcase beside his
seat. He tried to blank his mind, seeking a centered state of relaxed readiness, but it did not come easily.

ST. PETERSBURG, FRENCH EMPIRE, TIME LINE THREE

"You wanted to speak, so I came directly. We—my wife and I—are dis-
traught, as you may imagine . . . is there any new intelligence?"

"Yes. It is definitely those fuckers from New London, to be sure. The
devils from another world. They took her."

His Majesty John Frederick the Fourth, by Grace of God rightful King-
Emperor of the New British Empire—not that he'd ever been crowned,
having fled into exile with his own father (dead these past ten years)—
shuddered from the top of his head to the tips of his highly glossed boots.
Raw fury flickered in his eyes, instantly suppressed. "What evidence do
your people have?"

"I am not your servant, sir!" Louis Philippe, the heir to the crown of
the French Empire and his interlocutor, was equally indignant. "Have a
care!"

"I—"John Frederick paused. The fires banked. "I am distressed and embarrassed and I spoke intemperately. Of course I do not ascribe any blame to yourself or your people, sir."

"Think nothing of it." Louis made a dismissive motion with one gloved hand. "I share your frustration. My fiancé—your daughter—a shared burden."

"But. What is the evidence?" John gritted his teeth. Louis Philippe's invitation had arrived over breakfast and he'd hurried to the summer palace at once, abandoning his table only to be kept waiting in a parlor for half an hour while the Dauphin remained cloistered with serious-faced men in staff uniforms. Evidently his position as prospective father-in-law and future brother emperor (in fact as well as in theory) was insufficient to justify an in-person briefing by the gendarmerie and police intelligence generals. Now Louis was in the foulest temper John Frederick had ever seen from him. "What actual evidence is there?"

"Oh, let me enumerate." The Dauphin began to pace. "Bullets extracted from the body of Lieutenant Gorki and his men are of unfamiliar caliber and type. The Directorate of Forensic Science further report that they are apparently formed of atoms not from this world—something wrong with their weight numbers . . . my people used magnets to separate them, very advanced stuff. The perimeter around the Schloss was not breached either, pointing to an intrusion from another universe, one of the para-dimensional world-walkers we have been hearing rumors of for so long." The tempo of his pacing increased, heels drumming on the marble floor. "And now the latest affront! Have you seen the news from New London yesterday?"

"New London? I confess I have been trying to ignore the traitor's funeral—"

"*She's there,*" spat Louis. He spun on his heel. "They are broadcasting the proceedings on the public televisor channels! We have people watching, keeping track of which vultures flock to the buffet, of course. And she *was* there." He bent over his desk and picked up a streaky grey print, brandishing it at John Frederick. "She was visible, in the company of the wife of the Commissioner for Propaganda! *That* woman"—he pointed to a figure in the background—"wears a Police uniform too."

John Frederick peered at the facsimile picture, adjusting his spectacles. It was blurry and indistinct, but one of the women did indeed bear a striking resemblance to his daughter Elizabeth, and standing behind her was another—in the tunic and braid of a junior officer. "She must be a prisoner," he murmured. "Else why have her under guard? They used this as an opportunity to parade her before our eyes."

"Yes, but *how*?" Louis Philippe's voice cracked. "She was only abducted yesterday! She can't possibly have arrived in New London already—"

John Frederick swallowed. A cold certainty gnawed at his stomach. "Don't be so sure they can't do that. Remember the rumors about where their devil's cornucopia of super-weapons comes from?" Rumors that had risen to a crescendo over the past few years held that the revolutionary Commonwealth had access to the science and technology of a more advanced world. "What if Elizabeth disappeared to, to wherever they get their satanic toys from? What if *that* place is so far ahead of anything we know, that *they* can fly her between continents in a handful of hours? We have jet motors now, after we saw what they could do. They don't have the range, but . . . what if the world the Commonwealth stole them from is even further ahead, so that we're only seeing what they can copy? Who knows what the originals can do? *Anything* is possible."

"But, Berlin to North America!"

"It's four thousand miles. A military aircraft *could* fly that distance in less than twelve hours if it had prepared refueling bases along the way. Or a squadron of them in relay, carrying a very important cargo. The Commonwealth's heavy bombardiers, never mind those monster war-rockets of theirs—"

"Yes, well." Louis Philippe stopped pacing. "Maybe I am advocating for Satan a little too zealously. But I think it is clear that if she was taken to another world, and popped up in New London so rapidly, then the powers in that world must be helping the Commonwealth. It takes immense resources to organize a high-speed flight between continents. *Someone* is definitely smoothing the way for her kidnappers."

"Damn them." The Dauphin's line of reasoning was an unpleasant surprise to John Frederick. "I dislike giving due credence to other worlds. I think I am going to develop a headache if I make a habit of it."

"In that, you are not alone," the Dauphin said heavily. "But you must understand this has implications for Plan Union."(The proposed restoration of the New British Empire, under appropriate—French-allied—rule.) He glanced round: footmen hastily brought up armchairs for the two royals.

As Louis Philippe sat, John Frederick carefully lowered himself into the chair opposite. "It is an intolerable provocation. It is clear that the Commonwealth took her as a hostage. This suggests that there has been a security breach—that Plan Union is known to the enemy, and they are prepared to retaliate. Our choice is therefore whether to escalate or to concede the round. And I do not know how you feel about it, but I am not inclined to decline a hand unless I know I'm losing—not when the stakes are this high."

JUGGERNAUT, LOW EARTH ORBIT,
TIME LINE TWELVE, AUGUST 2020

Floating in the loose embrace of his seat restraints, Huw finally had a free minute in which to get his dizzy euphoria under control. He concentrated on his breathing as he watched the ever-changing cloudscapes of time line twelve swirl past the command module porthole. *We did it*, he told himself. *We actually* did it, *and nothing major malfunctioned!* The bolus of uneasy guilt that had curdled in his stomach for months had vanished. *All I have to do now is get through the mission, the re-entry, and the recovery.* Then he would go home to Brill and the kids and *never* do anything this dumb *ever again.*

The Commonwealth's primary space program was an Air Force spinoff, using uprated first-generation ICBMs—traditional liquid-fueled multistage rockets—as launchers. It had orbited multiple satellites and sent beeping camera payloads past the moon, but had yet to launch a manned capsule. No-one—not the Commonwealth, not even the United States of America or their former Soviet and Chinese rivals—had sent astronauts into orbit aboard a nuclear spaceship. Huw's crew now held three records: they were the first astronauts from the New American Commonwealth, the first to launch to orbit on a nuclear vessel, and the largest crewed spacecraft in any known time line. And, arguably, a fourth: the noisiest, messiest, most gut-liquefyingly *terrifying* launch ever.

"I really didn't think we were going to make it," Jensen admitted ruefully from the next seat, just loudly enough to carry over the noise of the ventilation fans. "After the booster cut out and we went into free fall for a few seconds—"

"Don't," Jenny Wu interrupted tersely. She gulped and waved a hand at him: "Sick bag." They were in low Earth orbit, which of course meant continuous free-fall. About one in five astronauts suffered from nausea on their first flight. JUGGERNAUT's crew was large enough to gift someone in every crew capsule with projectile vomiting, and Jenny had drawn the short straw on the bridge.

They'd spent the first two and a half hours in orbit running tests to ensure that nothing had shaken loose during the ascent—or rather, to identify what *had* shaken loose, confirm that it didn't pose any imminent danger to their lives, and schedule what to fix first. Not to mention trying to get over the ringing in their ears and the residual dizziness from being strapped inside a giant steel yo-yo tossed around by an angry giant. There were minor injuries. Sergeant Erikson had a suspected whiplash injury: his seat head restraint had failed. Lieutenant Savoy had a burst eardrum—he'd been in the Eagle re-entry capsule at the end of Gantry Two during the launch. An unfortunate harmonic resonance had set up a low-frequency vibration that hit 150 decibels, threatening to shake that gantry to pieces. In the event none of the shock absorbers had ruptured, the pressurized modules and re-entry capsules had all maintained their integrity, and the crew radiation dose was pretty much as expected. Jenny's rebellious stomach was just motion sickness. But they were now a few thousand miles short of completing their second orbit, racing across the Pacific towards the sawtooth ridge of the northern Andes with a list of repairs to make that was as long as Huw's arm. And it was time to get ready for phase two of the mission.

"Launch Control, do you read. Launch Control, do you read. This is Commonwealth Deep Space Vehicle Juggernaut, over."

Now the hazards of lift-off were past, they'd left the escape capsules, moved into the main hull, and taken up their stations on the ship's flight deck—a row of recliners facing the main flight controls. Juggernaut—no longer Project JUGGERNAUT, but an actual space ship with a name— wouldn't undergo the stresses of a high-acceleration lift-off in atmosphere again. The next time they boarded the Eagle capsules, it would be for their final return to Earth at the end of the mission, abandoning the radioactive hulk in a graveyard orbit in an uninhabited time line. Still wearing their pressure suits, they pulled themselves hand-over-hand through access tunnels and across walls and ceilings, then strapped themselves to their stations before the main flight controls.

Huw glanced sideways at Sergeant MacDonald, the radio operator, who was intent on his console: "Launch Control, do you read—"

"Launch Control reading you six, Juggernaut. We have your telemetry coming through. Over."

MacDonald glanced up long enough to make eye contact with Huw: he grinned and gave a thumbs-up, then turned back to his console. "All systems green, orbit stable, two minor injuries, severity yellow, plus four medical severity green—all space sickness. Awaiting clearance for phase two. Over."

Huw checked his screens. Juggernaut ran on a curious mixture of hardware. The flight controls consisted of analog controls driven by physical relays and armored vacuum tubes, backed up by a modern fly-by-wire system. Some non-essential systems ran on imported hardware, sophisticated embedded controllers and SCADA systems made in China and Indonesia. There were no chips from the United States, but stuff of equivalent sophistication smuggled in from other sources. At a pinch, if the computers failed they could fly the ship by hand—not well, but well enough to survive, using systems derived from tech aboard battleships that had been built to survive the recoil of heavy naval artillery. Nobody had been certain that advanced microelectronics would survive the repeated shocks from nuclear detonations less than a kilometer away. However the computers were all running flawlessly, the ship's network backbone was performing well, and the data flowing across his console painted a hopeful picture.

"Jeff, what does our decay profile looking like?"

Jeff Fischer, one of the two orbital dynamics specialists, cleared his throat over the inter-capsule loop. "Drag is about where we expected it to be right now. We're going to have to reboost within three orbits or we'll begin to drop too fast—we're losing a kilometer on each pass right now and we'll de-orbit in six days if we don't correct. The beta flux residue from our launch detonations has dispersed—the radiation belts we created extend up to sixty degrees north and south of the equator. Peak intensity has passed but they're not dying down. Pretty much how we modelled them. If we reboost, we can expect rapid intensification, maybe more radio interference. I can't put any numbers on it just yet."

"Got it." The propulsion charges they'd detonated at high altitude had spewed high-energy electrons which were now trapped by the Earth's magnetic field. They formed an artificial radiation belt, just like the

American Operation Fishbowl high altitude nuclear test in the 1960s. It was a source of radio interference, and would only get worse when they made the course correction. "Switch to Launch Control please. Mac, I'd like a voice channel now."

"Sir. You have the command channel."

"Huw speaking. Is General Anders there?"

"Anders here, Huw." Anders, in charge of ground control, sounded proud. "Congratulations on a good launch. Rudi says hi. What's your situation up there?"

"We're a bit shaken, and we have a couple of minor medical issues, but nothing serious. Got a snag list of stuff that's shaken loose, and we're working on an EVA schedule to fix the worst of them. I'm not going to authorize a crew sortie while we're in the radiation belt, I want to walk Juggernaut over to an uncontaminated time line first. The actual fixes are probably screwdriver-and-duct-tape stuff. Good opportunity to work up best practices for later, but nothing we can't operate without at a pinch."

Huw paused to swallow. His throat felt unnaturally dry, and his face congested. The air was arid, a little too warm for comfort, and stank of metal and lubricants. "I also want to make an eyeball exam of the pusher-plate for signs of uneven erosion—that's a priority." The pusher plate took the brunt of the nuclear explosions that powered Juggernaut. Cracks or weakening could lead to a catastrophic failure. "But we need to let it cool enough to approach in a space suit. And it's going to eat a tenth of our entire mission EVA time."

The DPR's industrial espionage people had acquired several older Russian ORLAN-M spacesuits for study. They were generally recognized as superior to the equivalent American design, not to mention being a whole lot cheaper and easier to buy. MITI had set up an entire spacesuit factory under conditions of military secrecy, run by an experienced manufacturer of women's undergarments—again copying the Americans. (The Apollo moon suits had been made by Playtex, after the traditional aerospace suppliers failed dismally to come up with anything light enough and flexible enough to do the job.) The cover story was that they were developing naval diving suits. Secrecy was essential: *nothing* was guaranteed to freak out the Imperial French Armée de l'Air high command like the Commonwealth ordering space suits in battalion-strength numbers.

The results were impressive. Juggernaut was far less mass-constrained than a Soyuz or Orion capsule. The Commonwealth suits were a bit heavier than those of time line two, but had built-in maneuvering units and a host of creature comforts the Americans and Russians lacked.

But Juggernaut's launch orbit sent it through the radiation belts its propulsion bombs had created every forty-five minutes. An eight-hour space walk would expose the astronauts outside the hull to a higher radiation dose than an entire six-month mission inside the ship. A space walk—or EVA—needed two astronauts for safety, and Huw only had twenty-two bodies to juggle.

His headset beeped briefly as Anders tapped his transmit key. "I've got an update coming. Please hold."

Huw took the opportunity to glance around the flight deck again. Four astronauts clustered around the life systems station—two in their seats, two floating over their heads—discussing something. Over at the opposite wall, another pair were focused intently on the propulsion charge console: Wall and Gray. Gray, *Doctor* Gray—doctorate in nuclear weapons design—seemed particularly engaged, judging by the way she stabbed at a video touchscreen with one finger while anchoring herself to the back of Major Wall's chair with the other. "Holding," Huw murmured, just to remind Anders that he was aboard a gigantic bullet-shaped spacecraft hurtling across the heavens, in an orbit that would be sinking below the horizon, taking it out of contact, in only a few more minutes.

"Huw, Anders here. Launch control's consensus is, if you can complete the shakedown checklists, then conduct the reboost to your phase two orbit. Then you should prepare for first world-walk within the next twenty-four hours? The EVA can wait until after you arrive in a time line that doesn't glow in the dark."

Huw glanced at his mission plan. "Barring show-stoppers, yes to all that. As long as the destination time line is safe." *Why the deviation from the mission plan?* He wondered. "Do you have an update for me?"

"I've got a surprise visitor who wants to speak to you. Director, here's Juggernaut."

"Hi, Huw. Congratulations on your success." Huw startled at Olga's voice. He'd known her for many years—she was unmistakable—but he hadn't expected her to visit the launch control center in person. As the head of the DPR, she spent most of her time in the capital.

"Olga. I wasn't expecting you!"

"Neither was I: this is a last-minute visit at Mrs. Burgeson's request. I was in Venezuela on other business, and Miriam asked me to deliver her congratulations—and an update—in person. Ready?"

"Go ahead." Huw nerved himself.

"You're aware of the on-going state funeral proceedings in New London. It looks like the Central Committee is going to request a low orbit overflight of the capital tomorrow. After a suitable course adjustment so that you'll be visible to the naked eye." Huw tensed so hard he rebounded against his seat restraints. "I know, it's a last-minute change MiniProp requested in addition to the previously scheduled TV broadcast. Otherwise there'll be conspiracy theories and Juggernaut-deniers . . . Once we get final confirmation, launch control will update you with a flight plan that reflects the final funeral parade arrangements, including a maneuvering schedule that will put you overhead during a scheduled gap in the military aviation fly-past. The Commissioner for Propaganda will publicly introduce you, and you'll make a brief scripted broadcast from orbit. We'll uplink the text on your next orbital pass. Anyway, you're going to be famous, that's all. Now here's General Anders again . . ."

Anders came on the radio. "We're working up a revised mission plan right now. You'll reboost as discussed, transit to a cold time line, and conduct the EVA to inspect the plate and carry out essential repairs. Then, assuming all goes well and there are no exceptional circumstances—" and wasn't *that* a euphemism: Anders was clearly seeking a circumlocution for *assuming your drive isn't broken and the French don't shit the bed and start a nuclear war*—"you will execute the maneuvering burn and world-walk to time line three. You'll do three earth orbits and a broadcast, followed by an overflight of St. Petersburg *as well*, where you will repeat the broadcast. Then you'll proceed to mission phase three and time line Six-Alpha for sensor deployment testing. Then it's to Six-Beta for first Lunar fly-by, as planned—"

Huw noticed the pilots staring at him, slack-jawed. "Are the Commissioners *sure* they want us to overfly St. Petersburg?" asked Jenny. Relations with Imperial St. Petersburg were not exactly warm. Exactly how they'd react to the sudden appearance of a forty thousand-ton deep-space vehicle bristling with nuclear weapons was unclear, but they were unlikely to be happy. They were going to be even less happy when the implications of its para-time maneuvering capability sank in.

"Olga here. Was that Jenny? I really don't know, it was mooted by Commissioner Jervis as an adjunct to the primary funeral overflight, just to rub their noses in it. The committee is still arguing about it. Right now I'm trying to ascertain exactly what the consensus in New London is," Her tone was flat. "The funeral takes place tomorrow, and there are other diplomatic considerations that I can't discuss over an open channel. But I believe the opinion of those Party Commissioners who've been briefed is that current political challenges call for a peaceful, but emphatic demonstration of capability. You will not be called upon to conduct tertiary operations—" *tertiary operations* was a euphemism for the ship's offensive military capabilities—"that much is clear. But they want to introduce Juggernaut to the watching world, firstly with an overflight and salute at the close of the First Man's interment ceremony, and secondly, by showing the Emperor the consequences of any attempt at backing a restoration bid by the Pretender. As I said, I'm awaiting confirmation—"

"Signal strength dropping," MacDonald interrupted: "Two minutes to horizon black-out."

"Acknowledged," said Huw. "Olga, General, let's talk again in fifty-five minutes. We'll get more time once we've reboosted and deployed the repeater comsats."

"Acknowledged." MacDonald paused. "Juggernaut orbit three, ground chat over and out."

BALTIMORE, UNITED STATES, TIME LINE TWO, AUGUST 2020

The alien incursion into time line four progressed rapidly in the absence of effective opposition. It was largely bloodless because of Dr. Scranton's hasty order to evacuate Camp Singularity. Luckily time line four was, as far as anyone knew, uninhabited—at least now that the Americans had left. Any pre-existing hominid population had been wiped out around the time of the Forerunner war, more than two thousand years ago.

The DHS and the Air Force watched the invasion from afar. Initially they used the abandoned base's camera network. Later they had to rely on high altitude drones, as the intruders swept outward from the collapsed wreckage of the Forerunner Dome. But twenty-nine hours after the initial incursion, the drone overflights were terminated. The Air Force directed the last Predator UAV to fly out to sea until it ran out of fuel and ditched in the North Atlantic. The invaders were too powerful, the probability of attracting their attention too great, and nobody wanted to risk the capture of a surveillance drone with para-time capability and the coordinates of the home time line.

"Here's the sequence of events." Scranton stood at the podium in the briefing room, facing her stony-faced audience with her tablet plugged into the wall-sized screen. They looked as tired as she felt. Juggling two simultaneous crises—the diplomatic time bomb with the Commonwealth and an unanticipated alien invasion—was grinding her down. She was hitting the Provigil hard, but she'd crash sooner or later. *Just give me time to stabilize things first*, she prayed.

"Let's look at time zero: ERGO-1 is on approach to the black hole. It fires up its motor to execute an Oberth maneuver close to the hole—a gravitational slingshot. The black hole's accretion disk flares, emitting copious hard radiation. Mainly X-rays and gamma rays, but also heat, light, and radio waves. We had passive radar receivers on the Bridge, the repurposed space station module projecting through the Gate, that relied on the normal emissions from the accretion disk to track the orbital debris around the hole. According to our recovered telemetry, some of these objects—objects previously believed to be rocks or other space junk—began to accelerate."

She clicked on the first slide. A set of overlaid ellipses and circles depicted the orbital dogfight that had developed in orbit around the black hole on the other side of the Bridge. It wasn't much of a dogfight: it was more like a helicopter gunship shooting up a horse chariot.

"Here is T plus sixteen minutes. Signal from ERGO-1 is lost as one of the accelerating bodies intersects it. We realized pretty early that the accelerating bodies weren't emitting enough heat to be powered by rocket motors. Their acceleration profile wasn't right for a rocket motor, either. They were far too efficient—hinting at some new underlying physical principle at work. That's when I ordered a full evacuation." A general seated in the front row cleared his throat. "Yes?" Eileen asked.

"I just want to be clear about this—the bogies are definitely not rocket-powered?"

Dr. Scranton paused to collect her thoughts. "I can't guarantee it," she said finally. "But the delta-vee they expended would be impossible without multiple rocket stages, or a nuclear-thermal rocket—and we'd have seen the heat signature or changes in the acceleration curve from either of those. We didn't. What we saw was probably waste heat from on-board sensors and guidance systems. Some of my people are speculating about quantum entanglement between the bogies and the black hole itself—some sort of mechanism for transferring angular momentum via quantum gravitational coupling—but I've got to stress that's highly speculative and assumes breakthrough physics. For now, let's just call it an unfamiliar advanced propulsion technology and move on."

Next slide: a video clip from a high-definition camera, mounted on a mast overlooking a sub-arctic valley. A dark green carpet of pine trees blankets both the sides and floor, spilling across onto other mountains visible in the near distance. The peaks above the tree line are bare. In the middle of the valley sits a dirty white sphere, like a ping-pong ball a quarter of a mile in diameter. There is a huge crack in it, zig-zagging across one side, reaching almost as high as its uppermost pole. Tiny boxes litter the ground to either side of the crack.

"T plus forty-six minutes. At this point, Camp Singularity is being evacuated. Which is a good thing, because—"

A tremor shakes the camera, reflected on screen. A ripple passes through the trees around the Dome. Then a cloud of dust rising from the ground blurs the scene further.

"Magnitude eight quake. Epicenter is the middle of the Dome. We didn't have a proper seismic monitoring network in place, but we had plenty of acoustic mikes. Signal analysis strongly suggests that it originated within fifty meters of the Gate." Dr Scranton cleared her throat, suppressing a shudder as she recalled the panic the tremors caused. The Gate was an opening between the Dome and a time line where Earth had been replaced by a planetary-mass black hole surrounded by debris belts. "We now see a peculiar meteorological phenomenon. Let me skip forward an hour and a half."

Shadows jumped as the sun slipped towards an invisible horizon. The Dome was now surrounded by low-lying mist, condensate forming as air spiraled through the crack in the Dome. "This is much how we found it, fourteen years ago. Back then, the misting was caused by air venting through the Gate. Then we capped the Gate and installed the bridge airlock, which stopped the outflow. The mist signals that the Gate is open again. Now watch—"

A laser-straight bolt of painfully bright light splits the roof of the Dome, like a needle stabbing down from—or up to—the stars. A fraction of a second later, an ascending fireball shoots into the sky, following the path of the lightning bolt.

The double-crack of thunder takes seconds to arrive at the microphone attached to the camera. More seconds crawl past. Then another laser-bright spike of plasma wounds the sky. Another ascending fireball. The surface of the Dome is now blackened and scarred. Cracks begin to propagate across its surface. As a third lightning bolt erupts, the roof of the Dome slowly gives way, collapsing in a cloud of dust and debris.

Dr. Scranton glanced around her audience. They were silent, their tension speaking volumes. She moistened her lips before she continued.

"The initial stroke appears to be some sort of disposable shield emerging from the Gate, at a speed in excess of orbital velocity. Whatever it is doesn't survive passage through the atmosphere—it burns up rapidly. But it's followed a tenth of a second later by another object, which flies through the near-vacuum wake left by the shield. The bogies are clearly designed for rapid injection into orbit around Earth-like planets in other time lines. Sixteen of them come through over the next thirty minutes. Subsequent analysis suggests they're going into inclined elliptical orbits, with a period of half a sidereal day—"

An agitated Air Force general interrupts: "they're deploying GPS satellites! Seizing the high ground!"

He's interrupted in turn by one of his colleagues: "how do they synchronize their clocks? You need a master control station for the ground segment—"

"—But what if these objects provide relative, not absolute positioning? Peer-to-peer networking would enable them to agree on a consensus clock baseline—"

"Gentlemen and ladies. Please." Eileen showed her teeth, and to her relief they shut up much faster than a civilian audience would. "Yes, consensus here is that it's *probably* a positioning and communications network, but we can't be sure. There's no guarantee that they separate mission functions the same way we do. Nor do we have any ELINT capability in time line four, so we can't see exactly what they're doing. We don't even know if the satellites—if that's what they are—are emitting at all. Because of what happened three hours after the last intrusion . . ." And intrusion was a pretty mild word for it. The Dome was hardened to withstand a nuclear attack, but the Forerunner relics had utterly pulverized it. Not to mention toppling every single tree within two hundred meters of the edge of the Dome.

"Let's step forward again, to T plus five hours and forty-two minutes. Camp Singularity is now evacuated, all sensitive data storage decommissioned—" there were thermite charges molded into the server racks: the retreating Marine guards set them off on their way out the door—"And we're now retrieving our data dumps from the site monitoring station in time line four via store-and-forward shuttle." The para-time equivalent of swapping last-century floppy disks. "That was possible because the data shuttle jaunts at sixty second intervals. So we lost the critical minute prior to the final dump, but we still have some idea of what happened . . ."

The video skips ahead to late evening. The setting sun casts long shadows across the valley floor. The pulverized rubble of the Dome pokes jagged shards out of a pool of mist, like the remains of an egg from which a world-eating dragon has just hatched. The mist spirals around the heart of the wrecked Dome like a flattened, slow-motion tornado. Then, without any warning, a shock wave ripples out through the whirling fog, shredding the clouds. A roseate glow appears in the heart of the shattered Dome, pulsing and brightening from a pinprick to a swelling ruby bubble over the course of a few seconds.

"The Gate expands," Eileen announces. The glowing sphere ripples and wavers, then collapses in on itself and dims. It leaves behind a frozen model of itself, carved in a mirror surface that warps and confuses the eye. It ripples like molten mercury. "The new Gate is about forty meters in diameter, an order of magnitude bigger than the one we originally found in the Dome. They pushed it through from the other side. The reflective knot there appears to be some kind of hypersphere—a multidimensional surface projected into our spacetime—"

The invaders finally arrive.

They pour through the invasion gate. Or perhaps it manufactures them: they are as silver-shiny as the hypersphere itself. They drip from its surfaces with liquid grace, pushing through the meniscus that separates time line four from whatever lies beyond. But their resemblance to the hypersphere stops with their color. In form they're not unlike giant grasshoppers—grasshoppers with a meter-wide wingspan and strange arrays of sensors in place of mandibles.

"Fucking cockroach aliens—" a Marine Corps general brays, unable to contain himself. He's not the only appalled face in her audience.

"We think these are autonomous robots rather than life-forms. They're land-mobile and air-mobile. We're not sure about their power source but they don't appear to emit much heat or E/M radiation. The high albedo surface—we're speculating again—may be a passive countermeasure for a laser battle environment. This was suggested by what happened when the swarm encountered the sentry guns on the outer perimeter fence around Camp Singularity."

Thousands of the giant hoppers pour from the hypersphere and scuttle into the trees in a breaking wave of silver. A smaller number take to the air, keeping to treetop height as they zoom outwards, following the contours of the valley. Sunlight flashes orange-red from their bodies.

The screen switches to a view from a camera mounted atop an unmanned watchtower overlooking the razor-wire perimeter fence. The fence was designed to keep out bears, wolves, and other undesirable wildlife that might try to eat the base personnel. It's clearly overmatched by an alien invasion. A group of hoppers emerges from the tree-line a hundred meters away from the fence, pausing on the edge of a grass border clipped short by robot mowers. Two hoppers race towards the fence at ground level, then another two focus on the guard tower, dark eye-spots swiveling to orient directly at the camera viewpoint. There is a flare of ruby light, and the camera dies.

"Laser zap. Time from emergence from the forest to engagement with the perimeter sensors was under four seconds. Assuming they've never seen our kind of fence or watchtower before, that's a very fast, very aggressive threat assessment."

Dr. Scranton took a deep breath. "We lost all the ground-level sensors within six minutes of the hoppers making first contact. A couple of the sentry guns appear to have activated, but they dropped offline within seconds. At T plus six hours and eleven minutes, the last sensors in Camp Singularity went offline. And at T plus six hours and thirteen minutes, the store-and-forward shuttle failed to cycle home. After we lost Camp

Singularity, we sent in a Tier Two drone overflight, which took off at T plus nine hours twenty six—stealth and high altitude, the same stuff we used on the Commonwealth—and it went about as well as you would expect. While we got somewhere with oblique-angle observation from later drones, a decision was made to abort observation and ditch the UAVs to prevent the hoppers capturing them and reverse-engineering their para-time transport subsystems to backtrack on us. Which is when I requested early deployment of an experimental advance unit from a program you are about to be read into, called DRAGON'S TEETH—"

NEAR CAMP SINGULARITY, TIME LINE FOUR, AUGUST 2020

"That wasn't a combat bug," Jackson warned his charges. "The combat bugs have lasers. Blinding protection from here on, everyone."

It was bullshit, but superficially plausible bullshit, and if it motivated the kids to stay alert it was worth it. He had no idea if there were combat bugs out there, but the lasers were dangerously real. Captain Briggs had showed him the video from Camp Singularity once the spooks from DIA and Homeland Security had approved his clearance and read him into the Bridge program. The Bridge program didn't come out of nowhere—as a training sergeant in DRAGON'S TEETH he already had a pretty good idea that there were other black para-time programs—but alien super-weapons and killer robots were freaky, and the idea that they'd casually invaded a major research program just a hop away from the home time line was scary as hell.

They'd gone to ground about half a klick away from the contact site. Mikka had found a dip in the ground that would hopefully screen them from anyone—anything—looking for the missing bug-bot. Jackson had sent Sally on her way with Neckbeard's dog tags and the remains of the bug. By now she'd be over in the nameless 'safe' time line, hiking cross-country towards the base camp, where she'd punch her combination into the doc-ument safe to retrieve a copy of the knotwork to send her home. After Neck-beard, she was the least reliable of the recruits, and was safest out of the way. But the rest of the squad were distinctly squirrelly too.

"Listen up," Jackson continued, trying for a reassuring tone. "I ordered you to hold fire. Private Braxton—" Neckbeard—"didn't listen, and he found out the hard way why you *do not ever* light up a target without orders. So let me repeat what I said before we came here: this is *not* a combat mission, this is a scouting exercise." (Also a cynical headfuck because someone up the line wanted DRAGON'S TEETH blooded—there were safer ways to do recon, like sending in a forward observation team with ARMBAND kit—or so he speculated. But he wasn't about to tell the kids that: it would crush them.)

"We're here to look around, navigate the perimeter of the bugs' territory, and get the fuck out again. They must never know we were here. They've got air defenses and we think they've got navigation and observation satellites in orbit, so we're going to stick to the trees and keep our electronics off. If we spot an *isolated* bug, *if* I think we can take it, we will do so—but only on my command. Otherwise, if there's more than one, you *must* avoid contact, and if there is more than one and they notice you, you jaunt. I don't care if you walk head-first into a grizzly bear, I want no more shooting. Got that?" He paused. "Any questions?"

Zuck made eye contact almost immediately.

"Yes?"

"Sir, what about, uh, private Brax–Braxton?"

Oh you did not *just go there.* Jackson blinked slowly. "Son, he's *dead.* I'm trying to keep *you* alive." No way to sugar-coat this pill. "I logged his location. When it's safe, we'll bring his remains home." Assuming there was anything left to collect by then. (Their BDUs were impregnated with an experimental fungal/bacterial spore culture developed to accelerate decomposition. It was intended for ecological burials—cadaver suits, they were called. The suits weren't toxic, but if you died in the field, after a couple of days the sun and rain would turn them into a mushroom farm. Three weeks later there'd be nothing left but a skeleton sleeping under a blanket of compost.) "In the meantime—"

He squinted, gauging the wind direction. The afternoon was chilly and overcast, and the breeze was blowing from the ridge-line to the north. This time line was deep in an ice age, and although the ice cap was nearly a thousand kilometers north of here, the climate was distinctly colder than home. The air promised snow even though it was August. *So: they're blocked by the rise* and *they're upwind,* Jackson noted. "Bernstein—" Mikka—"take point, then I want the rest of you to trail her at twenty-meter intervals: Jensen, Weiss, Zuckerman, Mills, in that order. I've got your six." The trees were thick enough that keeping line of sight on each other would be a challenge. "Watch your neighbors and relay hand signals up and down the line. Like this: try it." He demonstrated, waited for his *hold position* to come back. They were rough, but it'd do. "Mikka, I want you to head uphill fifty meters to start with, then hold until I clear you to continue. Everyone, remember: watch your buddies front and back, if you see an isolated bug, drop and signal me, if you see a bunch of bugs or if they attack, jaunt and go home immediately. Okay, now get moving."

This was all stuff that was in their training program, but they weren't due to start orienteering and small-unit coordination until next month. They were so far behind the curve that he'd had to train three of them to tie bootlaces when they arrived. (Two of them, now, one of whom was on her way back to base camp.) So it was no surprise to Jackson that progress was halting at first, even with the former Girl Scout in the lead. After half an hour and three pauses in the cycle, they were moving more smoothly, in something that almost resembled a skirmish line if he squinted hard. Jackson took the time to drill them on a few basic hand signals beyond *stop* and *go* as they traversed the hillside. Losing Braxton had focused them: nobody was messing around or zoning out.

Close to the brow of the hill, or where Jackson expected the hill to peak going by the density of tree trunks ahead of him, the line stopped moving. Jackson caught hand signals from Zuck and D'honelle—he'd kept the two least-promising of the remaining soldiers closest to him—and sent back *stop and drop*. For a miracle, they did exactly what they were supposed to. But Bernstein was out of sight. Crouching, Jackson crabbed sideways along the hillside until he came up between her and Jensen, both of whom were prone and frozen in the undergrowth.

Jackson crouched and slowly brought his scope up, then searched the hillside. It took a few seconds to spot what Mikka had seen, off to the right, maybe thirty meters past her end of the line. He watched it for a minute, until he was sure it wasn't moving, then crawled towards her. "Report. What do you see?" He whispered.

"This is an uninhabited time line, right? I know it's not a bug like the last, but I figured . . ."

"You did absolutely right." A little positive reinforcement. Jackson peered at it through his scope. "It's too far out to be a perimeter sensor from the DARPA installation in the next valley. But it's definitely artificial."

The object was white, for one thing, not the flowing quicksilver of a bug. It was a rigid discus-shaped structure, like an antenna. It sprouted from the side of a tree trunk like a cyborg mushroom fifty centimeters in diameter, sitting on an organic-looking stem. It was a couple of meters above ground level, below the lowest branches of the spruce.

"What is it?" Mikka asked quietly.

"Don't know. Maybe a communication relay, or radar." *Form follows function* was a good rule of thumb, and probably good for aliens too, as long as they had to obey the same physical laws. *In which case*, Jackson thought, *it'll be like the border fence sensors in Afghanistan*. He'd spent a tour there, guarding the Afghan occupation zone from refugees out of what used to be the Tribal Territories of Pakistan before the nuclear war. You couldn't put a physical fence up—the locals would steal it and sell it for scrap within twenty four hours—but sensor masts every hundred meters defended by antipersonnel mines worked just fine. And it was on the ridge line, where it had line-of-sight back towards the Dome and good coverage of the valley Jackson and his squad had crossed. *Only question is, if it belongs to the aliens, did we trigger it?*

Jackson shook his head. *Obviously we didn't.* Otherwise the hillside would be swarming with bugs. Most likely if they'd been noticed, the watcher had interpreted them as wildlife. Wolves maybe. "I need to get closer," he told private Bernstein. "Sit tight, and if shit breaks bad, jaunt and lead everyone back to base camp." He patted her shoulder, then crawled towards the tree sprouting the alien intruder.

The forest floor was covered in debris, small branches and shrubs and a carpet of pine needles that made the approach a nerve-wracking experience. If the aliens could have scattered antipersonnel mines around the base of the tree, or even just a tripwire—but Jackson couldn't spot anything as he got closer. Ten meters out he stopped again and pointed his scope at the dish. No, this was *not* a sensor any human engineer had designed. It seemed to grow organically out of the pine, and its stem leaked a clear ooze of tree sap. But it looked too regular in shape to be natural.

Here goes nothing, Jackson thought. He quickly signed *take cover* at Mikka and waited until he saw her copy it: then he reached for a nearby fallen branch and tossed it at the stem of the mushroom.

A fungal growth would have wobbled or collapsed under the impact, but this one held firm. A flash of speckled ruby-red light caught his eye:

Jackson froze, then hurled himself down the hill. *Lidar,* he realized—laser radar—effective for short-range 3D mapping with millimetric precision, which meant—

"Jaunt now!" He shouted. "Go! Go! Go! Everybody get clear!"

Crashing and rustling broke out across the slope as Jackson loped away from the kids, who were scattering downhill back the way they'd come. *Damn.* "Jaunt!" He shouted, aiming for full drill-sergeant voice projection. He heard a low-pitched menacing hum like a swarm of hornets the size of bald eagles echoing off the walls of the valley. Something like a cloud drifted overhead, casting shade across the ground. Jackson reached for the trigger button of his single-shot ARMBAND device, his one-way ticket home, and looked up.

A squadron of silver-bellied robot hornets a meter long came roaring across the ridge line at treetop height, their triple-eyed heads glowing with viridian laser light as they scanned the ground beneath. Lightning flickered, lances of white stabbing between the trees below as panicked wildlife fled and drew the attention of the swarming slaughterbots. They moved faster than Jackson could hope to flee.

"Go!" He screamed one last time, then stabbed the button to take him to the fallback time line.

The trees blurred and went away. His ears popped with the sudden pressure change, hot air slapping his face, and the ground beneath his feet vanished. Jackson fell. The ground in this time line was almost three meters lower. He barely had time to brace and roll with the impact before realizing just how bad this could be. They were six kilometers from base camp in an uninhabited time line. The kids had minimal assault course training and zero parachute experience: they didn't know how to drop properly yet. Someone down-slope—the forest here was young deciduous trees—was already screaming.

Jackson winced, then picked himself up and headed for the screamer with the broken leg. It was going to be a long march home.

PART TWO

MANEUVERS

Of all those in the army close to the commander none is
more intimate than the secret agent; of all rewards none
more liberal than those given to secret agents; of all matters
none is more confidential than those relating to secret
operations.

—Sun Tzu, The Art of War

Best Laid Plans

The evening after the viewing and the Party Commissioner's reception, Adrian Holmes returned to his office in the Party Secretariat, which occupied a wing of the former Imperial palace in New London. The building was almost deserted thanks to the ongoing period of state mourning: routine business had been suspended for the duration. But the lights burned on in the small apartment Adrian occupied at the back of the building.

His man Pierrepoint was waiting for him in the drawing room, perched primly at one end of a chaise, legs crossed at the ankles, a black ribbon tied around one sleeve. "Sir."

"No need to stand." Holmes waved him back down then turned to the sideboard. His housekeeper had left out the port decanter, his usual evening nightcap. "Join me, Keith?" Pierrepoint nodded, so Holmes poured a second glass and passed it over before sitting in his armchair. "Any new developments at the DPR this evening?"

Pierrepoint sipped his fortified wine in silence for a moment, as if nerving himself. Holmes waited. "Our sources report a lot of chatter about the Juggernaut project," he said. An expression of distaste quirked his lips. "Miss Thorold flew to Maracaibo with an elderly American, who was dispatched back to his own world. She then disappeared for several hours. While she was gone, there was an extraordinary amount of inter-world message traffic—they tripled their world-walker duty staff on that shift, so it was clearly planned in advance. Then she came back, and according to the most recent report, her courier jet is being readied to return to the capital. But the only hard information we've got is a verbal report to the effect that Juggernaut is scheduled to make an appearance at the funeral parade." He frowned. "Whatever it is it's in Venezuela, so how it will get to New

London in time? Who knows? Maybe Miss Thorold is bringing it aboard her flight?"

Adrian thought for a few seconds. "I think not," he finally said. Pierrepoint, unlike Holmes, wasn't routinely briefed on alien para-time technology projects. "If they're going to reveal it tomorrow at the parade, it's a show of strength. No doubt aimed at convincing us that MITI is indispensable. Or at backing another power play."

"Well, about that, sir. MiniProp was buzzing with rumors this morning. Seems a dark-skinned young lady who bears a notable resemblance to one Elizabeth Hanover was seen being escorted around an interview suite equipped for recording news broadcasts. They kept her under lockdown, and the official word was that she's Commissioner Burgeson's daughter, if you can believe that, but the resemblance is there."

Adrian twitched. "Yes, I know: I was introduced to her at the reception." He took a sip of port. "Mrs. Burgeson says the girl is her daughter, Rita, by a previous marriage she's never spoken of previously. The girl backs her up quite spontaneously. However, Elizabeth Hanover *is* missing from St. Petersburg, and there *is* a resemblance there. A certain poise and polish."

"Suppose they haven't got the princess yet, wouldn't it make sense to record interviews and speeches in advance to roll out during an, ah, leveraged bid for power, sir? In which case this Rita woman is helping the Burgesons prepare the ground for Elizabeth Hanover's defection until she arrives and is ready to debut in public? They've got to know they can't get away with a bluff for very long, surely?"

"Correct." Adrian lapsed into a brown study, focusing on the dregs of his glass. "It's extremely disturbing. As is a worse possibility: what if the DPR *succeeded*? What if this 'Rita' is actually the Princess in disguise? It would be one way for the Burgesons to keep her under wraps until she's needed, while preventing other factions—unaware of her disappearance—from trying to kidnap or assassinate her. *And* there's Juggernaut. Hmm."

"Can you say what it is, sir? I mean, if it's going to be public this time tomorrow . . ."

Adrian looked up at Pierrepoint sharply. "It's a military project. A special technology to do with para-time, the kind of thing MITI specializes in. Can't say more than that, but if they *do* parade it in front of the cameras tomorrow, it's a show-stopper."

"A show of force, then, to soften everyone up for the unveiling of the heir to the House of Hanover?"

"I need to know what business took Miss Thorold down to Maracaibo with an American in tow," Adrian grumbled. "If she was exhibiting Juggernaut to agents of a foreign power, that would be grounds for . . . hmm." Holmes fell into a brown study.

Pierrepoint shrugged. "The American she was seen with is not one of the officially declared representatives of their government who the Ministry of Foreign Relations are currently hosting on the hush. But then, neither is Mrs. Burgeson's supposed daughter."

"The whole business sounds like a tall tale to me," Holmes mused. "What kind of faction within the American government would sniff out Mrs. Burgeson's child and train her as an agent in the first place? They'd have to have some sort of way of searching their entire population and locating world-walker by-blows! And they'd have no way of knowing that Mrs. Burgeson is a person of some importance here in the Commonwealth. They might have known her from before the world-walkers arrived here, if she was important to them . . . but this faction would have to be running their own private para-time intelligence service. No, it's too many implausible coincidences. No sane government would allow their own security organs to compete against each other that way! Only tyrants and autocrats allow warring fiefdoms to run wild, and they're supposed to be a democracy." Adrian put his glass down. "With the princess missing, we have to plan for the worst: this 'Rita Burgeson' girl is actually Elizabeth Hanover, and Mrs. Burgeson and her world-walkers are positioning her in readiness for a coup."

"Then you fear it *is* a restoration plot?"

"I hope not, but it's impossible to be certain that it isn't. In which case the logical time to activate it is right after the interment. The entire People's Commission and Chamber of Magistrates will be in attendance, all in one place and easy to round up. With Juggernaut flying overhead as a massive show of force, and the missing heir to the throne revealed to already be in New London . . . it all makes a horrible sense." Holmes sighed and put his glass down, then stood up and slowly walked to the door to his inner sanctum. "I have to make a telephone call, Keith. Feel free to show yourself out." He closed the office door behind himself.

Pierrepoint stared at the floor for a moment, then drained his glass and left. Behind closed doors, Holmes dialed the switchboard number, and waited. "General Richards please. Yes, it's General Secretary Holmes speaking. I have a query for you: it's for the US delegation. Can we get someone to check with them and confirm whether or not Mrs. Burgeson has a daughter in the United States? Name of Rita, Rita Bur—no, Rita Beckstein, daughter of a Mrs. Miriam Beckstein. It may be important . . ."

FEDERAL EMPLOYEE 004930391 CLASSIFIED VOICE TRANSCRIPT

DR. SCRANTON: Listen very carefully, Eric. We're in full scale crisis mode here. It's an emergency: as of yesterday neutralizing the Commonwealth threat is not even one of our top priorities. We appear to be facing an invasion from an unidentified hostile time line, and unlike the Commonwealth, they're way ahead of us on tech.

The Joint Security Council has gone into emergency session, VPOTUS has been moved to a secure para-time site to ensure continuity of executive government. Air Force and Navy nuclear response assets are on hot standby awaiting target assignments, and we're officially going to DEFCON One across the board. Ready for war, in other words.

COL. SMITH: *Shit* . . . sorry. That's a lot to handle.

DR. SCRANTON: I know, I know . . .

So, the other stuff I need to update you on. I requested—and got—a DRAGON'S TEETH deployment. We should hear back real soon now, assuming any of them survived: they're not even out of basic training yet. I'm just back from briefing John Irving and JSC—yes, the President was there and fully engaged—and I'm calling you because I'm pretty sure that once the situation is 'under control,' whatever that is taken to mean, the administration will commence a witch-hunt. POTUS is really pissed-off and this gives her the right caliber of ammo to take down very big game. Big Black will be the primary target—the research project that triggered the invasion wore a National Reconnaissance Office mission patch—but we'll be on the line too. I made the call to evacuate Camp Singularity so you may very well wake up tomorrow and find that you're running the shop.

COL. SMITH: Shit . . . sorry. I need a swear jar. About these . . . *aliens* . . . Are we getting into Fermi paradox territory here?

DR. SCRANTON: What, you mean "if they're so advanced, why aren't they already here?" I think we've been lucky up to now, but our luck just ran out. We've been playing empire games in para-time and it was inevitable that sooner or later we'd run into someone who was better at it than we are. Unfortunately the United States is structurally an imperial project, it's in our political DNA. We're always looking for a frontier to expand into, we can't back down, anyone who admits we're overmatched gets sidelined and booted out of office by an upstart who insists that we can never be defeated, only betrayed. So we can't work around obstacles, only power on through the fire. The thing is, confronting Ms. Beckstein's Commonwealth—or should I call her Mrs. Burgeson now?—is no longer the gold-standard nightmare scenario. The new gold standard is dealing with a paranoid Soviet-style nuclear superpower in the middle of its first succession crisis, *and* an invasion by para-time aliens—*simultaneously.*

COL. SMITH: The two great mistakes in warfare—never get involved in a land war in Asia, and never start a war on two fronts—needed a para-time update. Right? So which should we prioritize?

DR. SCRANTON: Glad you asked. Firstly, I'm going to ping you at least once a day, and you're going to do the same. If you don't hear from me, do not pass go, do not collect $200, just call John Irving directly and give him a sitrep, then await further instructions. If John isn't available, then you need to call the new SecHomeSec and give them a report. If there is no Secretary of State for Homeland Security and no placeholder, then you need to work your way up the reporting chain until you find someone who'll listen. Maybe the Joint Chiefs of Staff, or the Director of the FBI. Someone, anyone. Follow the chain of command all the way up to the President if necessary. But the first key point is, just because all hell has broken loose in time line four, it does not follow that we can take our eyes off the clusterfuck that is the Commonwealth succession crisis or the parallel clusterfuck in Berlin. Because we're facing a nuclear-armed adversary with para-time first-strike capability and no established framework for deterrence.

COL. SMITH: Well, that's nice and cheerful.

DR. SCRANTON: I haven't witnessed such a furball of crazy since I read the declassified reports on Kermit Roosevelt's coup in Tehran in the fifties.

Or maybe the Cuban Missile Crisis or the Able Archer confrontation in the eighties? This is like all of those rolled up in a single horrible mess.

COL. SMITH: Yes. I sometimes wake up in the early hours and wonder if we haven't totally misunderstood everything. Only . . . 7/16 happened. And we've got a clear mission directive. It just feels like we're playing hide and seek in the dark with nuclear-armed suicide bombers.

DR. SCRANTON: Welcome to the new cold war. You can have complete situational awareness or complete control, but you can never have both. It's almost as if surveillance proactively creates new threats. Sooner or later you've just got to let go of the ropes and hope everybody knows what they're supposed to do—even the other side—so we don't all go up in mushroom clouds.

COL. SMITH: So on that note, what's point two?

DR. SCRANTON: We still need diplomatic leverage on the Commonwealth government, and the defecting princess is a good bet. Rita may be harder to manipulate—I'm hesitant to rely on her—but if we can get our hands on Princess Elizabeth, I figure we can use her to discredit Burgeson. Or alternatively, put the Princess back in charge in the Commonwealth. Just as long as we don't get blamed later, the way the CIA caught it in the neck for re-installing the Shah in '53. What we *can't* risk doing is to scare their military chain of command into launching bombers. Which is why we're playing footsie like this. The DRAGON'S TEETH unit I signed off on for time line four are also available for use in the North American Commonwealth if necessary, but I'm reluctant to go there— worst case, if they were discovered it would be interpreted as an act of war. I'd much rather stick to our existing tools. As long as Rita contin- ues to file reports and the monitors indicate that she's being introduced in public as her birth mother's daughter, she's still provisionally running true to course. But if you suspect she's going native, bring her back or terminate her. Meanwhile I want you to retrieve the Princess from Berlin. There are a number of gambits we can play if we have her in custody: hostage, prisoner exchange, goodwill token.

COL. SMITH: If you are taken out of the loop, obviously my situation reports will tell whoever's in charge that this is what I'm doing . . . but it's going to take your successor time to understand the significance, is that what you're saying?

DR. SCRANTON: Yes. We've got a lot of balls in the air, and I want to ensure we see this through because I think events in the next few days are going to prove critical to achieving strategic dominance over the Commonwealth. The alien invasion might come looking for us, or they might not. But the Commonwealth know *exactly* where we live, and they've got more nuclear warheads than the Soviet Union ever had. I believe they're still the most immediate threat. But they need to be handled delicately.

Get the girl, Eric. Get me—or my successor—the leverage we need. Do it by any means necessary. Just don't get caught.

END TRANSCRIPT

EAST BERLIN, TIME LINE TWO, AUGUST 2020

The first thing that fully engaged with Kurt's lizard brain was the odor. Berlin smelled *different* these days.

Helmut pulled in and parked on the sidewalk of Naumannstraße, in a gap between the beech trees that shaded the pavement and the walls of the gardens. It was a cold, overcast morning, with clouds scudding overhead like the first harbingers of autumn. The leaves had mostly fallen, leaving the trees skeletal. Here and there, small municipal robots nibbled away at the residue of humus on the sidewalk like so many giant turtles. "I'll walk from here," Kurt told Helmut as he sniffed the air. "I know the way."

"Call when you need me." Helmut tapped his earpiece. He seemed remarkably un-fazed for a foreigner dealing with Berlin's roads for the first time.

"I shall do that." Helmut turned away and Kurt walked along the street, passing an ugly concrete-fronted convenience store.

History abruptly punched him in the nostrils. It wasn't that Berlin *looked* different. Here in Schöneberg in the east, *of course* it looked different—thirty years had passed since the Wall fell. From the cellular double-glazing in the windows of the modern buildings, to the bright display hoardings cycling through their adverts, and the densely parked modern automobiles, this was Berlin in the modern mold: the smugly self-satisfied capital of the beating heart of Western Europe. Well, not *entirely* smug: there were graffiti tags here and there, and old apartment blocks that had been upgraded to cheap urban dormitories for the poor and struggling—those who had been priced out of the western side of the once-divided city. East Berlin still had a slightly feral edge, as if it was waiting until your back was turned to go back to rifling the recycling bins for a prematurely discarded bottle of cheap schnapps.

But what took Kurt aback was the way that it smelled *wrong*.

The Berlin Kurt remembered was astringent. It stank of harsh, cheap tobacco and the heady oil-stink of two-stroke motors, the blue-grey effluvia of Trabants and the occasional Wartburg. The rasp of smoke from the omnipresent brown coal fires of autumn layered everything with a thin haze. This new model Berlin was too clean for Kurt to feel at home. Half the cars were electric, the other half were hybrids constrained by modern emission standards. Brown coal was banned, at least in cities, the old stoves replaced by central heating systems burning imported Russian gas. Cigarettes . . . there was a sign in the 24 Hour store's window: *e-cigs sold here*. Below it was another sign: *air fresheners*. A humorless smile tugged at Kurt's cheek. The smell of post-Communist freedom was, it seemed, no smell at all.

He came to a main road at the end of the tree-lined street and paused at a series of bus stops. He reached inside his new leather trench coat—*I need one*, he'd joked with Olga's people: *it's traditional*—and pulled out his new phone to check the transit app. His choice of garb was intentionally ironic. Who in their right mind would expect a modern-day spook to wear a uniform straight out of a cold war thriller? (Even though the Stasi dress code had explicitly forbidden such coats because of the lingering Gestapo vibe.)

He didn't have long to wait. A bus pulled up minutes later. He swiped his phone across the payment point and sat down as it whined and swayed off towards the Zoologischer Garten. It was 09:42 precisely, he noted, and he was not only on the right bus, but the right bus *at the right time*. They ran on schedule here, nailed down to within a matter of seconds. After decades of the authentic American public transport experience it came as a welcome change. In this country buses weren't just for poor people, and the German middle classes held them to the same standard as any other service used by the bourgeoisie: clean, efficient, fast, and frequent.

The bus made two stops. People got on and off: mostly older folks and mothers doing their shopping while the kids were safely in school. There were a few tourists—mostly they stuck to the U-bahn and S-bahn.

A pensioner with an aluminum stick and a blue scarf tightly knotted under her chin paused in the aisle behind him. "Hiya, Kurt."

He resisted both the urge to look round, and the parallel ghost impulse to pinch himself. He'd last seen Mona twenty-eight years ago in DC. She'd been in her mid-thirties then, with green-eyes and blond hair and a way of swinging her hips as she walked that drew the eye. Greta had ribbed him mercilessly afterwards, twisting his tail about the way his gaze had followed her sidelong (pointedly *not* staring). "Mona," he said quietly. "Long time no see." He moved over to make space for her. What was her husband's name? Grant? Garrett? Garrett. A heavy smoker, lung cancer, dead now, like his Greta. Both of them gone ahead to that final debriefing room in the sky. His body buried on foreign soil by those who would have rejected him, had they known what he was. A shared burden of experience. "How was your journey?"

"Purely horrible." She'd lived in the south long enough to acquire a trace of Charlestown lilt. "I haven't flown international since 7/16, the security reminded me of . . ." She trailed off. "You know: *us*. But I kept my papers clean against the day . . . Is it true?"

The bus stopped. Its suspension hissed as it knelt for an old man on a walker. People got on. The bus rose and moved off. "There's asylum and a pension if you want it. An honorable retirement. It's not exactly home, but they're a lot closer to it than the USA, in the right direction. Just this one job to tidy up first. It's top cover for a shell game."

"Who are the opposition?"

"DHS. A snatch team are hunting a girl." He felt rather than heard her breath catch. He kept his expression carefully blank as he surrendered to the impulse to look at her. Tried not to show any disappointment when he saw the same fine bone structure beneath skin that sagged from passing decades. The years had not been kind to Mona. Doubtless his face was equally shocking. A fragment of song stirred the dust of memories: *they sentenced me to thirty years of boredom.* "They're looking for a young woman. A teenager, really. She was defecting to our new employers' side when the extraction went bad. DHS picked up her minder and his controller, and they're going for the trifecta. Leverage against the, the other time line."

Mona's pupils dilated. They were still green as pond-water, startling as when he'd first set eyes on her. "Another *time line*? You mean, there's one where they're not stone age?"

Trying to change the system from within. "They've got computers and jets and nuclear weapons, so very much *not* stone age, no. They're led by a vanguard party, waving the flag of democracy in the face of kings and kaisers. They've offering us asylum in return for our help in this matter. I think it's the best offer we're going to get."

Mona stared at him. "What if I don't want it?"

"Then you can go back to America and never worry about seeing the rest of us again. This is the encore: one last performance before the Orchestra disbands for good." He paused. "There are certain residual assets. I intend to turn them over to whoever chooses to remain." Money the GDR had laundered and placed under the control of their senior agents. Not much of it— the Workers' Paradise hadn't exactly been rich—but they'd shoved it into real estate decades before the money laundering rules came in: it would suffice.

"Remain, feh." She looked away, towards the front of the bus. "Can you promise me they'll look after us?"

"If we do this for them, yes they will." He spoke decisively. Not saying: *if we do this for them, then Mrs. Burgeson will retain her office. If we do this for them, the cost of our pensions will be a fraction of the bribe they're offering the Princess. If we do this for them, we, too, are a propaganda coup to crow about.* He was secretly afraid that this might be the wishful thinking of a blind old fool who doted excessively over his granddaughter and placed too much faith in her birth mother's capabilities. Even now, he might be leading his followers up a path that would terminate in a windowless room with a dead-eyed executioner. But he hoped not.

"Well then. What's my part?"

"If you want in, you're our Lamplighter. You've got clean ID; I want you to go to the address on this note, book a hotel suite for a week, then buy the items on this shopping list." He passed a folded sheet of paper to her: she made it disappear. The veins on the back of her hand were blue, the skin freckled and loose from sunlight and time. "Here's how I intend to play it . . ."

TEMPELHOF AIR FORCE BASE, BERLIN, TIME LINE TWO, AUGUST 2020

Colonel Smith and his team had flown into Tempelhof Air Force Base on the outskirts of Berlin a little over three days ago, hot on the heels of an information leak.

Major Hulius Hjorth had been a Person of Interest to Homeland Security for years. He was a ghost in their national surveillance system: fingerprints and DNA traces captured from discarded ready meal wrappers and drink cartons, appearance matched from CCTV camera feeds. He'd been confirmed as a Commonwealth agent during Paulette Milan's interrogation. So when an advance passenger information record filed for a passenger aboard a flight from Venezuela to the EU matched his fingerprints, it was hastily passed to a DHS fusion center that processed suspected terrorist movements.

CCTV at Arrivals at Tegel confirmed the match, but the DHS only got confirmation some hours after the Major's arrival. Once they'd learned he was there, Smith prepared his team (and their reluctant informant) for immediate deployment. It took a while for Smith to get the local backup he needed—American orders didn't carry much weight in the EU, much less in a nation historically aware of the potential for abuse offered by Enabling Acts—but eventually the German Federal Police complied.

But he needn't have bothered with the borrowed SWAT team. An ambulance would have been more appropriate: when they finally arrested the Major he was at death's door. Unfortunately they missed the teenaged woman of color the Major had been after. She flitted out the back door, and thanks to the DHS team's lack of familiarity with East German housing scheme architecture he'd had nobody positioned to stop her. But she was alone in an unfamiliar city. How hard could it possibly be to track her?

Quite hard, as it turned out, even with the Five Eyes looking for her.

She's called Elizabeth Hanover, Smith reminded himself. Birthday: some time in 2002. Height: about five foot eight, plus or minus. Weight: one thirty pounds. Skin color: light brown. Hair color: black—*we think*—she'd left the house wearing a Turkish Muslim woman's outfit, a headscarf and coat worn over a blouse and long denim skirt. Which meant gait metrics were unavailable, and facial recognition was notoriously bad at handling skin tones darker than a typical whitebread silicon valley bro. (It went all the way back to the color cards used to optimize photographic film stock for white-skinned targets in the 1950s: algorithms embodied the prejudices and biases of their designers.) *At least we have fingerprints,* Smith consoled himself. Not that they were much use in hot pursuit.

But that was only the beginning.

Elizabeth Hanover *had no history.* She didn't have a bank account, home address, or driving license. In this time line she had no online identity, no AOLChat, Facebook, Google, LinkedIn, or other social media presences. She had no Amazon account, no Apple ID, no eBay history, no tracking cookies. She didn't even know the internet existed! Nor could the big networks recognize her by the hole she left in the social graph: Facebook couldn't auto-tag her in the background of her friends photo albums because she had no friends to tell Facebook about her.

There was just one ray of hope: the elusive Ms. Hanover had swiped Major Hjorth's fatphone.

Tracking people by their phones was the NSA's meat and drink. Indeed, staff at Crypto City jokingly referred to their phones as "tracking devices." A phone had GPS and a compass and microphone and a whole ton of memory and at least two processors—an application processor that ran the operating system and apps the user interacted with, and a far less visible thing called a baseband processor.

The baseband processor's job was to run all the radio hardware—GPS and wifi and cellular and bluetooth—that made a phone so useful. And the Five Eyes were *all about* baseband processors, because applications running on the baseband were invisible to the phone's owner but had unrestricted access to the hardware. Want to lead a drug trafficker into a trap? Just order their phone's baseband processor to lie to the Maps application about where they were going. Want to listen in on a suspect? Tell the baseband to switch on the mike and silently call you. Want to check who they are? Silently upload a stream of photos from the selfie camera. Of course all this required the willing cooperation of the phone manufacturers and operators, but that was easily obtained. Any corporation that wanted to stay in business understood the need to keep the government happy. And any phone company technician who wanted to stay out of jail understood a gagging order.

Unfortunately the Major's phone presented the NSA with other difficulties.

The Major's employers, the DPR, were a State Level Actor—the hardest kind of nut to crack. They were a scarily efficient government HUMINT agency. They did not make amateur level mistakes: their signals security was nearly watertight, and the fact that they were headquartered in another time line meant that ninety-nine percent of their threat surface—the intelligence perimeter they had to defend—was invisible. Near as anyone could figure out the Major had been provisioned with a couple of high-end blackphones manufactured in Korea or China, bought for cash at the factory back door. Their unique machine ID number or IMEI was cloned, matching some other (non-black market) phone elsewhere in the world. Worse: whoever sold them the phones had run off another couple of hundred clones with the same IMEI and scattered them around the globe just to make them harder to find. The Major had installed SIM cards for a local network when he arrived in Germany. The Germans were nosy with respect to phone cards and required official ID in order to buy SIMs. But the Major's minders had false identities and cash to burn—State Level Actors came with State Level Budgets. And a hotel room paid for with cash and a fake foreign driving license was enough to meet the residence requirement for buying a SIM card.

All Smith's people had been able to determine so far was that someone had—within the past six months, *probably*—checked into a hotel under a false identity somewhere in Germany, walked into a T-Mobile store, and bought a couple of SIMs. Or more likely they'd walked into a couple of T-Mobile stores, a couple of Vodafone franchises, and maybe a Cellnet shop, and bought SIM cards from *all* of them using various cards and identities, over a period of days to weeks. There was no telling which SIM the Major had put in his phone. Indeed, his phone might very well be a dual-SIM device with a field-reprogrammable IMEI. Illegal in the USA, such phones were nevertheless popular as drug dealer specials: if you had the right market contacts in Shenzhen you could buy them without any trouble.

The only lead on Elizabeth that the Five Eyes had so far was the wireless traffic in and out of the cell towers around the Major's safe house, both before and after his arrest. Unfortunately the towers covered high density apartment blocks. At the time of the raid, two hundred and eighty one devices had been in touch with the local base stations. Of those cellular devices, many or all might reasonably be expected to wander around the map of urban Berlin on a daily basis.

There had been sixty-two voice calls into that picocell in the half hour before the raid. None were from Venezuela or North America. Probably the DPR had a local controller bedded in somewhere in Germany, passing messages back and forth between the Major and whoever he ultimately reported to. Unfortunately it was not uncommon for people to phone their friends, get cut off in the middle of a call—if, for example, they were in a moving vehicle at the time—and redial, often some minutes later. Distinguishing the Major's controller from a random girlfriend or co-worker phoning an office-mate was virtually impossible. And German law had a blanket prohibition on recording voice calls without a warrant.

But trawling sixty-two phones was easier than cross-checking a third of a million dark-skinned faces, and the wheels were now in motion. Those phones were traveling around Berlin, and almost all of them were intermittently active, and the NSA was tracking them. *Eventually* they'd be able to narrow down the field until they could figure out which one Elizabeth Hanover was carrying.

Because Colonel Smith was certain of one thing: that the elusive Ms. Hanover would *not* return to the apartment complex. And by avoiding it, while the residents and their friends came and went and could be checked off one by one, she would ensure that her phone stayed on the list while all the others were slowly eliminated.

And then he'd have her.

JUGGERNAUT LAUNCH CONTROL BUNKER, TIME LINE TWELVE, AUGUST 2020

Olga watched Juggernaut from inside the telescope turret on top of the control bunker. The ship was currently visible as an unnatural star, moving fast across the angry red welt of the western horizon as daylight bled into darkness. The fallout plume had drifted out towards the ocean over the past two hours. The deadly hum of the scintillation counters had subsided to a crackle and then a foreboding buzz, as the radiation level inside the metal-roofed observation dome dropped back to something human beings could hope to survive, at least for a while.

In another month it would be safe to work there full time, albeit as long as the ground crew stuck to their hazardous environment protocol. In another year it would be time to begin refurbishing the bunker and launch pad for the next JUGGERNAUT-series launch. (Assuming the program wasn't cancelled: technical excellence alone was no guarantee that funding and a sufficiency of plutonium would be made available.) But right now, the urgent impulse to witness the next phase with her own naked eyes had prompted her to clamber laboriously into lead-shielded overalls, helmet, and respirator, then ride the freight elevator up the cement-walled tunnel to the cupola above the bunker. Fifteen minutes up there would eat up her entire permitted annual radiation exposure. But she decided she didn't really care. Rank had its privileges, and witnessing history in the making was one of them.

Now Juggernaut was about to make history for the second time in a day, and this time it was far enough away that she could see it without it melting her eyeballs.

"Juggernaut, do you read?" The disposable headphones Olga wore crackled slightly. The technicians had hooked her up to a repeater terminal inside the dome, along with General Anders and a gaggle of other personnel who were required for the next stage. Now, the radio operator repeated his call, minute by minute, as they waited for a response from orbit.

"Juggernaut here, reading you six," said the ship's radio operator. A knot of tension inside her chest eased. This was the third time she'd waited through it: each time it grew easier to believe that everything was proceeding normally. "The Explorer-General is coming on now. Over."

"—Radio desk, sir, do you want to take the mike?" (Their own radio operator, safely ensconced ten meters below the cupola, cut in.)

"I'll take the call," General Anders acknowledged. There was a click, and a subtle change in the background hiss. Olga watched the star-bright pinprick creep across the curve of the horizon. It was brighter than Venus, moving faster than anything in the heavens had any right to. "Launch control station, Anders here. Over."

"Huw Hjorth speaking." Huw sounded alert but Olga was certain he was tired. Four hours of pre-launch prep then the big fireworks display and then four subsequent orbits must have made for a busy day. "We've run our checklists and while we have a snag list, we've got a bravo-minus bill of health." A failing B-grade, in other words. Not great, but according to Anders it was above the threshold for continuing the mission. No need for a mandatory hold and a repair EVA. "Do you have any news for us? Over."

"Copy that bravo-minus, Juggernaut." Olga waited impatiently for Anders to continue. "Because you've made it this far, the launch monitor team have green-lit the public fly-by. Here are your instructions. You will commence the checklist for transit to time line fourteen immediately and execute unless you encounter a hold condition. You may maneuver to achieve the correct insertion orbit at will once you drop below our horizon. Once phase two orbit is confirmed, you are clear to transition to time line three and execute the fly-by sequences over New London and St Petersburg at will. Diplomatic channels—" Anders glanced at Olga, and raised an eyebrow.

"Olga Thorold here. The French embassy has been formally notified that a crewed spacecraft will be launched later today and will overfly New London during the funeral parade," Olga said slowly. "Contact Maracaibo Control on your arrival in time line three and update them with your orbital elements, and they'll inform the relevant parties so they nobody mistakes you for an attack. If at any point you encounter difficulties, you may abort or divert at will. Your objective remains to perform the public fly-by, then execute phase two of the mission—that's from the Commissioner's mouth direct to you. General?"

Anders nodded. "General Anders here. I think that's everything for now. Over."

"Copy that, launch control." Huw spoke slowly, as if aware of the gravity of his next works. "Let me confirm and clarify this: after correcting our orbital inclination and raising perigee, we are to maneuver to time line three and say hello to our friends on the ground, then stand by for further instructions from Maracaibo Control, pending execution of the public fly-by and then phase two. Is that correct? Over."

Olga paused until General Anders nodded. "Yes, General Anders concurs. I will transfer to Maracaibo Control in time line three once you're on your way, and I'll coordinate from there. Over."

"Copy all that, launch control. Okay, we're working our checklists now and should commence maneuvering in forty-eight minutes. Propulsion estimates they'll need eleven low-yield charges to position us for phase two orbit. Over."

"I'm delegating you back to launch control now, sir. Good flying and good luck: General Anders over and out." Anders keyed his mike twice, signaling radio ops to take back control, then glanced at Olga. In the minutes they'd been speaking to Juggernaut's flight deck, the moving star had risen almost to the zenith, shining above the bruised purple-and-green clouds of dusk. They weren't visible this far south yet, but tonight the sky would be dominated by ghostly aurorae, left-over radiation belts spawned by Juggernaut's initial launch as well as the burn the ship was about to execute to raise itself into a higher orbit. "Shall we go below?" He asked, with a pointed glance at the wall-mounted radiation counter's dial.

"That sounds like a good idea." Olga took a deep breath, straining to draw air through the respirator's filters. She unhooked her wired headset cable and handed it to a tech, who hung it over the console beside the sealed panoramic window. Another technician wheeled her chair back to the freight elevator and, once everybody else was aboard, they descended to the control bunker. It took a while: there were armored airtight hatches to traverse, and her ears popped twice as they entered the pressurized redoubt. Finally, they filed back into the control room through the door at the back. Heads turned. General Anders cleared his throat: "Juggernaut will commence phase two on schedule," he announced—somewhat redundantly, for they had all been listening in on the audio channel. "Command team will assemble in half an hour to return to time line three with me, once we get confirmation that Juggernaut has executed the burn. Major Moore, you will remain in charge until shift-change. Assuming all goes well upstairs, you can begin to close out the installation tomorrow."

Olga took in the round of polite applause, careful to keep her back straight and her face impassive. She was mindful that she represented the Party Commissioners today. Everyone else would draw comfort from her outward display of confidence. But inside, her apprehension was building again.

Juggernaut might have made contact exactly on schedule, but jaunting into low Earth orbit over the First Man's funeral—and into full view of the French Imperial military—wasn't without risk. And that was just the start of Juggernaut's hastily-revised diplomatic mission: the next step would be downright dangerous.

BERLIN, TIME LINE TWO, AUGUST 2020

Being born into wealth and privilege confers secondary, intangible, benefits. One of these is an unshakeable self-confidence: the conviction that in any social context one is *utterly right*, and that the carping critics and moaning skeptics should just shut up and mind their own business.

Accordingly, Elizabeth Hanover had acquired the self-assurance of a born con-woman before she learned to walk. It was an essential character trait for grifter and princess alike: and perhaps the two occupations were not that far apart. Minor royalty had only as much agency as the people around them believed they should have—and the same went for con artists. They had to stick within the roles they were playing, lest their audience question their character and their mostly-illusory power unraveled. But, just as grifters carefully chose their victims from among those who want to believe their story, so too did princesses come with a retinue of courtiers self-selected from among those who craved the mystical aura of royalty.

It was not an accident that, after practicing on a succession of retail staff, Liz successfully bluffed her way into a foreign hotel room. After all it had been booked and paid for in her assumed name, and who could *possibly* question her right to be there?

She spent the first half hour exploring her room's unfamiliar fixtures. It had lights that switched on or off and changed color when you doodled your finger across a panel. The motorized blinds on the windows were a lesser novelty, but still thought-provoking, as was the mattress with no springs, which appeared to be made out of some sort of rubbery foam. The television annoyed her until she finally worked out that the black plastic thing with the buttons was a controller, and found the "off" switch by pressing at random. (The universal symbol for a power key eluded her, for the design language of the universe she had grown up in was unrecognizably different.) The bathroom amused her briefly, the wardrobe surprised her by how tiny it was, and the odd sockets behind the desk—some electrical, others less clear—were just puzzling, until she worked out that one of them matched the charger for her phone.

Eventually she calmed down, plugged the phone in, lay down on the bed, and closed her eyes for half an hour.

She was awakened by the phone buzzing and rattling. Sitting up, she saw that it was displaying a call from Control. "Hello?"

"Hello, Elizabeth. Are you in the hotel room yet?"

She glanced at the doorway. "Yes. I can tell you the room number—"

"Please don't. Even if nobody is listening to this call, it's quite possible that every call in the city is being recorded right now. If they identify your phone, they will be able to replay everything you say. So! I have an update for you. Our people are on their way, but they will not arrive until tomorrow. In the meantime, please stay in the room if you can. The risk of being apprehended increases every time you go outside. You may want to get food, but you would be safer ordering meals from room service. There should be a menu on the desk in your room. Now, after we end this call, I want you to switch off your phone. You hold down the button on the side—" Control gave lengthy instructions, which Elizabeth tried to memorize—"you can turn it on again tomorrow morning, or when you leave the hotel. But try not to leave it turned on and stationary for long periods of time."

"Is that all?" She asked, irritated.

"Not quite. Tomorrow, there will be a letter waiting for you at the front desk. Don't open it in any public area—there are cameras that can read over your shoulder in the strangest places. Hotel rooms and toilets are mostly safe from surveillance, so take it to your room before you read it. The letter will tell you where to go next. You will need to leave the hotel, but do not tell them you're checking out. Can you remember all that?"

Liz bit back the impulse to snap: *I'm not a baby.* "Yes. Are we done yet?"

"I think so. Sleep well. And? Good luck."

The call ended, and Liz glanced at the glowing numbers on the frame of the television, which she inferred were a clock. It was only two o'clock in the afternoon. If Control thought she could hide in this room for the rest of the day, Control was going to be very disappointed. She was alone in an alien version of Berlin, and for once she was free and unchaperoned, unhampered by her usual retinue of guards and Imperial security. If that wasn't an opportunity for an adventure, what was? She turned the phone off and plugged it in to charge, as instructed—this being the extent of her willing obedience—then picked up her shoulder bag, hung out the DO NOT DISTURB sign, and set off to see just how different the capital of Prussia could possibly be in this universe.

EXECUTIVE OFFICE BUILDING, BALTIMORE, TIME LINE TWO, AUGUST 2020

Eileen Scranton came out of her meeting with the Homeland Security Council with both her job and her self-respect intact, either one of which was a better outcome than she'd expected going in. She was a little wobbly from the post-adrenalin crash but there were no handcuffs in sight, and she had the tantalizing promise of a blank-sheet Executive Order to back her up if needed. The President could turn on a dime with the chilly mental flexibility of a born political operator, and after establishing that this was very definitely *not* business as usual, she'd sent Eileen forth with orders to get the job done by any means necessary. It was a momentous victory, in terms of her usual scope. Eileen had given in to the impulse to pause for breath once dismissed from the Presidential presence—which might, in retrospect, have been a tactical mistake, because it allowed Secretary Irving to catch up with her.

"Eileen. A word, please."

John Irving, Secretary of State for Homeland Security, was her boss. Now he waved her alongside as he walked away from the meeting: "a word."

"Certainly, sir. What do you need?"

"Your plans, going forward. Not a recap from the rear-view mirror."

She took a deep breath. "Yes, that. I've got a DRAGON'S TEETH team on recon around Camp Singularity. I approved them because the facilities at the Dome were obviously designed for human world-walkers. I don't want to risk feeding the intruders any intel about our capabilities that suggests we're anything other than the Dome-builders' descendants. But the team isn't adequately trained—in fact they're raw recruits, and their readiness reports are deplorable, totally substandard. Also, we may need them for special ops in BLACK RAIN." The DHS's code name for time line three. "Against the Commonwealth."

"That's what I thought. Conflicting priorities are a bitch." Irving sighed. He turned a corner, ushered her into an office, and closed the door. Then he slid his lifelogger glasses down his nose, very deliberately powered them down, and transferred them to his jacket's front pocket.

Eileen copied him. "Are we in full isolation here?" She asked.

"We should be." Irving grimaced. The lifelogging glasses weren't just an intrusive measure aimed at policing the behavior of junior staff: at a high level they were auditing tools that could provide a solid alibi against accusations of conspiracy or collusion. Successive administrations had been tied up in court hearings for decades: the risk of intelligence leakage via discovery process or subpoena was so high that any trivial oversight might be seized on by the opposition in an election year. The current POTUS was of the opinion that the best way to survive a courtroom ambush was to have not done anything wrong in the first place—and to be able to prove it, which was a whole lot harder. Nevertheless, there were some subjects that were not to be discussed where outsiders—even officers of the Supreme Court—might overhear. Topics too sensitive to commit to computer storage. "I want your input about the Unit's activity in BLACK RAIN. And I want to know where we've got to with Colonel Smith's fishing expedition." He sat back, an avuncular, non-judgmental expression on his face. Waiting for her.

"Am I off the ERGO-1/Camp Singularity team?"

He made a noncommittal gesture. "Defending against alien invasions is Defense Department territory. They're going to make a bid to take control and, frankly, I'd prefer to focus on the game where we hold the most cards. The whole nuclear second-strike thing is coming to a head, and I think POTUS is considering using Camp Singularity to send a message to the Commonwealth."

"Okay." Eileen swallowed. If DHS was being eased out of the Camp Singularity task force, things were going downhill. And when you ordered the Defense Department to send a message—that was a very bad sign, because the kind of message the DoD was designed to deliver involved killing people and breaking stuff. "Everything came to a head in the Commonwealth last week. They're now in a full-blown succession crisis, and Rita is positioned to add value to a destabilization op. But there are contingency plans I haven't briefed you on, so you can maintain deniability. Do you want to open that can of worms right now?"

"I assume at this stage it's too late to clamp the lid on again," Irving admitted. "So enlighten me."

"Short version is, we're getting Rita established so we can use her to pull the rug out from under her mother. Who, you will recall, runs the para-time espionage agency that's been giving us so much trouble all these years."

"How's the op supposed to work?"

"Officially, we look like we're backing Rita all the way to the negotiating table, using her to cut a deal with her mother's people. But the State Department has established formal diplomatic links with a rival Commonwealth faction. They're asking State questions about things over here, and State is handling them, so I'm told. So once they've gotten their feet under the table, we're going to leak Rita's deal with Burgeson and hang her out to dry. At which point Mrs. Burgeson smells like shit."

"I see, a bait and switch tactic." Was that a note of approval in his voice? Eileen couldn't be sure.

"The plan is to use the world-walkers' enemies within the state to take them down for us," she persisted. "It's not hard to paint them a picture: Mrs. Burgeson is in the frame for entering back-channel negotiations with a hostile agency of a foreign power—us—without seeking the approval of her Party leaders. It'll look bad, very bad. Especially after we use DRAG-ON'S TEETH to black-bag her home office and plant incriminating evidence there: money, photos, whatever it takes. Then State can deliver an anonymous tip-off to her enemies, of whom there are many, because the Commonwealth is riddled with rival agencies, that makes Rita look like a very high-level spy or enemy agent of influence."

Irving thought aloud: "that paints State as the good guys, as far as the non-world-walking faction knows, when the dust settles. While significantly weakening the Commonwealth's para-time capability, but not actually attacking them directly. Any damage is plausibly self-inflicted." Irving slowly smiled. "That sounds reasonable." Eileen drew her first real breath since entering the room. "As long as they've got no idea DRAGON'S TEETH exist? Or about the DoD stuff?"

Eileen involuntarily tensed, then regretted it. He'd certainly have noticed: "That's an open question," she admitted. "I mean, they know that Rita wasn't an actual world-walker until we activated her. But she doesn't know any other operatives are ready to be deployed, and I've been careful to keep her bubble-wrapped. We've also trained her *not* to demonstrate her full capabilities—we've programmed Rita not to fully trust her birth mother, insofar as that kind of behavioral control is possible."

"Okay, I'll let that pass for now. And the DoD options?"

"Well, they must know by now that we've automated para-time transfer. The ARMBAND technology, pureed neural stem cells in a box, should be fairly obvious to them from where they're standing, even if they can't—or aren't willing to—duplicate it. So it follows that they've probably worked out what we can do with them: drones, planes, satellites, Trident missile warheads. It's another open question as to how close they are to replicating the technology—I've seen estimates ranging from five years to a century, depending on how advanced their tissue engineering labs are and how much access they've got to freshly killed world-walker brains. But for now we've clearly got an advantage, not relying on human world-walkers. Our best information on the Clan and their successors is that they could move a couple of hundred pounds per jaunt at best, and took hours to recover afterwards. That's got to be a giant bottleneck."

Irving doodled a cryptic note on his pad, his face unreadable. World-walkers were widely disliked within the administration—not to say demonized—but people could respond unpredictably when they learned where the ARMBAND technology came from. It had started out with brain tissue harvested destructively from living, conscious donors. Even though it was now derived from self-sustaining stem-cell cultures, in the early days numerous captured world-walkers had died horribly to make it work.

"Let's change the subject. How far along is Colonel Smith's side-quest?"

"He's in Germany, closing in on the crown Princess, who's on the loose in our Berlin. In addition to the Princess herself we're after her biomarkers: everything from fingerprints to DNA samples. We'll put them on the faked-up correspondence we're going to insert in Mrs. Burgeson's safe. That way, we can frame Burgeson for conspiring with the royal family in exile—right in the middle of a succession crisis. If that can't be spun as treason, I'll eat any hat you care to give me."

"Right. *Right*." A smile tugged at Irving's lips now. "Glory days are here again, it seems."

Eileen moved swiftly to take advantage, laying out the last plank of her plan. "It's above my pay grade, but I figure we might want to return the princess to the French Empire in order to open up a channel with them too, to use as a local proxy—"

Irving looked pleased. "So if we get the princess, you can Watergate the Burgeson faction within their own government? Right in the middle of a succession crisis, which is the *best* time. And if that fails, State can tie Burgeson up with a bow and deliver her as a goodwill gesture to the Commonwealth's rivals? And hand the Princess back to her folks for bonus points? Very elegant! It's low-risk but high pay-out . . . I like it."

The tension in the room had eased at last, but Eileen readied herself for Irving's inevitable cross-examination. "So . . . how do you rate the

Commonwealth's succession options once Miriam Burgeson is out of the picture? And how do you propose to handle this runaway princess once Colonel Smith captures her . . . ?"

NEAR CAMP SINGULARITY,
TIME LINE TWO, AUGUST 2020

The scale of the clusterfuck was clear by the time Jackson made it back to base. Luckily for him his CO, Captain Briggs, had his back. Less fortunately, Briggs was on the receiving end of a tanker-load of sewage pouring down from above him, as a bunch of high-ups who had confused politics with reality demanded to know what the hell just happened. And they were both up in front of the most junior of the high-ups, the one who'd been detailed to empty the chamber pot over their heads.

"Sir. Private Braxton disobeyed an express order, shot up an unidentified hostile drone—the one we retrieved. It killed him with some kind of explosively forged projectile. Private Flynn—" the cheerleader—"froze hard then lost her shit: that's why I sent her to the rear on messenger duty." *And got her out of the field.* "Preliminary medical report says severe PTSD, benched indefinitely. Private Bernstein—" *who you called a hippie chick*— "outstripped expectations and performed at an acceptable level. Privates Weiss and Jensen were injured during retreat—" a broken leg and a dislocated arm—"due to terrain anomalies, but otherwise performed nominally. The others weren't injured and didn't die."

Jackson braced and faced the screen while the loud noise, demands for an explanation, and thinly veiled threats of retribution washed over him. Eventually the asshole Major slowed down. "What the—were you playing at?" He demanded. "No, don't—"

Briggs threw himself on the grenade when the Major paused for breath. "They're dregs, sir. Six weeks into basic, and only two of them would have made the cut if they'd walked into a recruiting office—which they didn't— because *they're not army material.*" Jackson tried not to side-eye his CO. Briggs was clearly losing the battle to contain his anger and frustration. "This is basic Vietnam-era stuff, sir, you don't get good performance out of conscripts, *especially* if they haven't had time to cohere as a unit. These conscripts are *especially* bad: they're rich kids who expected to make a good marriage, or go to grad school and get a job in daddy's brokerage. Their parents all paid up to a quarter of a million for IVF to a clinic run by the Clan to manufacture potential future world-walkers. They're spoiled brats who never expected to be drafted." Which was unfair to some of them, but *might* get the Major to put his brain in gear. But then Briggs stopped, and the Major was off again.

"I don't care if they're Bill fucking Gates the fifth, why aren't they—"

Jackson screened it out. He was more worried about whether the squad was salvageable at all. Sally the cheerleader *might* eventually recover enough to be useful for something, as long as it didn't involve loud noises and walks in the woods. Weiss and Jensen would be down for the next couple of months recovering from their injuries, and Neckbeard was dead. To lose half the unit on a cross-country hike, first time out, was worse than disastrous: it was ridiculous. All he needed now was for one of the survivors to learn about conscientious objector status and sue and the job was fucked. (At least until the lawyers finished chewing on the twitching corpse of the program.)

"Sergeant! What's your opinion?" A new face on the screen, this time a colonel with a Ranger tab on his sleeve. Words were exchanged with the sound muted, and the Major departed speedily, his back straight and tense.

"They're not soldiers, sir," he repeated wearily. "They're untrained, unwilling, unsuitable, teenagers. Trust-fund kids with no experience and no aptitude and no desire to be here. If this was regular Basic, they'd all have washed out in the first two weeks—not that they'd have signed up in the first place."

The colonel gave him a look that Jackson instinctively recognized as dangerous. "What would you suggest, sergeant?" He asked, deceptively calmly. Oh, this one was dangerous all right: he actually sounded like he wanted to hear something other than his own voice.

Jackson froze for barely a moment. "Get me a squad of *real* soldiers, issue them with ARMBAND units, and I can have them worked up and ready in a week."

To his credit the colonel looked thoughtful. "You and I wish: ARMBAND isn't in plentiful enough supply to equip individual dismounted infantry." A single jaunt unit cost as much as an anti-tank missile. A regular squad would have burned out forty units in one go if they'd been given the mission Jackson had just taken the kids on. "It's not just the price tag, it's production capacity." Jackson's ears pricked up. He'd had no idea the world-walking black boxes were in short supply. Or maybe they were just in high demand for other projects.

"Is there no way to turn regular folks into world-walkers?" He asked.

"That's above my—and your—classification level, but I'm guessing the answer is a no, or we wouldn't be asking you to knock this bunch into shape."

"Well." Jackson took a deep breath. "In that case, we're stuck with them until someone up the line sends us some better conscripts. But this approach—treating them like regular soldiers—isn't working, and we're going to expend them fast. Maybe if HQ has a specific mission in mind that we could tailor training around? If you could give us some idea what we're intended to achieve?"

"Hold that thought," said the man on the screen. "Captain, sergeant, thank you for your input. Dismissed."

Jackson looked at his captain, confused. "What just happened, sir?" He asked.

Briggs drew a deep breath. "If we're lucky, the department of ass-covering just got its ass handed to it by the department of getting shit done. But don't bet on it. You don't make O-6 without getting political."

"*Is* this political, sir?"

"Do cows eat grass?" Briggs shook his head. "Only question is, what *kind* of political? If we're really lucky they're listening and we'll get new training objectives soon. But if not . . ."

"Right." Jackson paused. "Are we done here, sir? Because if there's nothing else, I'd like to get back to damage control." *And making sure I still have a job tomorrow.*

Funeral Games

The next day was the day of the interment. Rita awakened at dawn, yawned, and picked up the itinerary that Inspector Morgan had given her the evening before. It was three pages long. The graveside service itself would only take half an hour, but before that she had to get through two TV studio appointments and an interview as Rita Burgeson, the honorable Commissioner's daughter from the United States. Then there was a state banquet (an intimate affair for four hundred officials and relatives, hosted by the Minister of Propaganda) and . . . *a military parade?* She blinked. She was expected to sit in the second tier of the main reviewing stand, along with Commissioner's families and close friends.

This is going to be hellish, she moped as she brushed her hair. She took a quick snapshot of the itinerary and saved it for her report, then showered and dressed in the funeral outfit that had been laid out for her the night before. *Why am I meant to attend a freaking* military parade? *And then there's some kind of fly-past, and an announcement about the— waitaminute—about the* space program? *Followed by a briefing?* The latter note had been appended to her itinerary in crabbed handwriting after it had been printed, clearly a last-minute addition. Rita frowned, then tied her hair back. The Commonwealth had a space program? The Colonel was sure to be interested. *I'll ask over breakfast,* she decided. *Or figure it out later.*

She shoved her tablet, inertial mapper, and camera in her handbag, then made her way down to the breakfast room. Even though she was early, Brill had already eaten and disappeared. Instead she found an early-morning teenager—one of Brill's daughters—neatly turned out for the funeral in a black velvet frock. "Are you Commissioner Burgeson's daughter?" The girl asked her, her wide-eyed curiosity startling to encounter so early in the day. "What's she like?"

Rita flailed around for an answer. "I'm not sure," she admitted. "I only met her a week ago."

She was rescued from her interrogation (which was good) and her breakfast (bad) by the arrival of Inspector Morgan. Alice showed such good timing that Rita couldn't help wondering whether she had a man posted in the back yard, keeping an eye on the morning room windows to alert her to Rita's appearance. "Better finish that fast," she admonished: "we're already running late."

"But my first appointment isn't until nine!" Rita protested around a mouthful of cold toast.

"Yes, but there's heavy traffic in and out of the ministries today. Half the turnpikes in and out of town are closed for army units coming in for the parade. Even a Ministry staff car won't get you through a traffic jam of tanks." The Commonwealth had borrowed the American words for armored gun carriers and traffic congestion, it seemed.

"Oh hell." Rita pushed her plate away and stood up, shedding crumbs from her linen napkin. "Is it that bad?"

"You would not believe it." Alice Morgan's eyelids were saggy with fatigue. She covered her mouth briefly, fighting a yawn. "Come on now. You can sleep in tomorrow, but today's the big day."

Alice was right about the traffic jams. Despite leaving an hour early, they barely made it to the recording studio in time for Rita's first interview. She faced a tiresome stream of clichéd questions about life In the United States, delivered by an impeccably coiffed news anchor. She smiled inanely and gave perfectly vacuous, content-free but friendly-sounding answers, despite sitting under lights so hot that her sweat threatened to make her face powder run.

The second interview was very different. They had a dressing room where an elaborate costume awaited her. ("This gown is correct for the current fashion in the imperial court," she was informed, leading her to speculate that the Emperor's courtiers hadn't quite caught up with the eighteenth century yet, much less the twenty-first: it weighed about twenty kilograms and creaked when she breathed. "You need to wear it to get the posture and balance right.") There was also a sound stage with green screen, a full motion-capture system, and a teleprompter. This required *genuine* acting, and she had to think herself into the skin of an uneasy, but determined eighteen-year-old runaway princess, reciting a script from an unfamiliar device.

She was there as Her Royal Highness, Princess Elizabeth Hanover of New Brunswick, by Grace of God, Heir apparent to the Throne of the Americas and Imperial Dominions etcetera etcetera yadda yadda. And she was defecting to the revolutionary republic that had overturned her grandfather's throne, in return for a *full* amnesty, an absolutely *gigantic* cash settlement—and so she didn't have to marry a creepy older guy with wandering hands, a string of mistresses, and (allegedly) the pox.

In the end it took Rita over an hour to get through ten minutes of question-and-answer. Obstacles she eventually overcame included stumbling over her lines and staring at the camera like a deer in the headlights. (Although this might in fact have been a very realistic depiction of how the real Princess Elizabeth would have behaved when trapped in a Mini-Prop studio.) Lesser problems included coughing, someone opening the door at the wrong moment, and corpsing inappropriately at a rude off-stage gesture. Luckily the job warranted an imported (*stolen*, part of her whispered) HaptoTech motion capture rig and a digital editing suite, so there wasn't *quite* as much pressure to get it right first time. Even so, she was extremely glad when it was over.

After the interview, Rita changed back into her funeral dress for a Q&A session as herself, led by an unctuous emeritus newspaper columnist. Finally Alice drove her back to the Hall of Peoples' Magistrates for a gigantic sit-down banquet. The Inspector warned her not to get too drunk, then disappeared (with a promise to pick her up at the end of the banquet). Judging by her neighbors, a state of total legless inebriation was expected at these affairs. The invitees around her drank like fishes, as if anesthetizing themselves ahead of the grimly protracted formalities to come.

Rita ate her meal in a bubble of perfect isolation, surrounded by people in black mourning suits and gowns, none of whom she recognized. She tried to amuse herself by eavesdropping on the conversation to either side, but for the most part her neighbors were frustratingly circumspect, and besides, she felt faintly guilty. At least she learned one thing: institutional rubber chicken and cheap wine were apparently universal constants in every civilized time line.

The Inspector reappeared as everyone was leaving. Rita found her waiting near one side of the entrance hall. "Come with me," she told her. "Did you enjoy your lunch?"

"It was okay," Rita said diplomatically. Her expression contradicted her eloquently.

The Inspector ignored the unfamiliar Americanism. "Let's get you to the viewing stand. They're closing the approaches to Central Avenue in half an hour, assuming the audience have taken their seats by then—I think they're optimists if they think this shower will be in place that fast. You've got a spot in the first tier, second block—"

"Where's Mrs—I mean, where's my mother?" Rita asked. "And where is Brilliana Hjorth going to be? I mean, is it just me, or—"

"Your mother will be on the first block in the reviewing stand, sitting with the Commissioners of the People's Radical Party. They're taking the salute. Consider yourself lucky, they have to stand through most of it." Alice steered her through the throng in the courtyard towards a line of waiting limousines. "Would you mind walking rather than riding? It's less than quarter of a mile, and we'll get there much faster than by driving, what with this crush."

"I can walk." Her funeral outfit might feel like something straight out of a costume drama, but Commonwealth fashion didn't run to high heels and her ankle boots were unexpectedly practical.

"Good. As I said, there's not much room on the main stand. I'll be in one of the blocks for the regular audience: there are going to be thousands of people here."

"And Brill?"

The Inspector's face creased in worry. "She would be with us, but she sent a note. Something important has come up, and she's working in the office."

Rita stared at her sharply, but Alice gave nothing away. "Something big enough to keep her away from the most important state funeral in Commonwealth history?"

"Imagine that." The Inspector led her towards a gate opening onto the sidewalk beside the limos, then along the tightly fitted stone slabs. "I'm not privy to her duties. If you want to know more, you'll have to ask her yourself. She's donated her ticket to Nel instead. That's her daughter," she added, "whom you met at breakfast. If you could keep an eye on her, Mrs. Hjorth would undoubtedly be very grateful."

So I'm a baby-sitter now, am I? Rita wondered.

"It's only for a couple of hours," the Inspector continued. "There are bleachers, washrooms, and stands serving free refreshments. There will be music and civilian floats after the military part of the parade and the fly-past, and entertainments—at least, dignified ones suited to the occasion. It's intended to celebrate the better parts of the First Man's legacy, rather than drawing out the pain of his loss. I'll collect you in time for the funeral service afterwards."

"Okay, I've got this," Rita said as much to reassure herself as to inform her minder. Two more hours of boredom stacked on top of a day of tedium: *what can possibly go wrong?*

JUGGERNAUT, LOW EARTH ORBIT, TIME LINE THREE, AUGUST 2020

Juggernaut's flight deck was hot and noisy: the air smelled of burning metal and vomit. Somewhere frayed wires were arcing, and half the crew were busy pulling inspection panels that were warm to touch, checking for fire. Not everyone was available. A couple had sustained injuries during launch, and something that was trivial on Earth—like a nose bleed—could be a matter of life or death in free fall, where one risked asphyxiating on one's own inhaled blood. And then there were the space sickness cases. Those would mostly clear up within a couple of days, but in the meantime the crew were shorthanded.

Huw was busy holding things together, supervising as the duty watch prepared for the next time line transfer. Only hours had passes since they'd lit up the night sky over the Pacific with another display of nuclear fire-power, rebooting to a new orbit five hundred kilometers over ground. Now they were troubleshooting the most serious remaining faults, in preparation for their jaunt into orbit above the Commonwealth.

Over in the world-walkers' module, Bill Wolf was medicated and hooked up to the grounding rails. Jenny Wu monitored him while her own pre-jaunt dose took hold, keeping an eye on his blood pressure and ECG and relaying them to the flight surgeon. World-walking a spaceship that was already on-orbit was a fraught exercise: a one second error would put the ship ten kilometers off course. When they'd first started practicing in the mission simulator it had become clear that nobody could do it without a warm-up, and even with a countdown they couldn't reliably execute a jaunt with less than half a second of precision. So Juggernaut ran on certain rigid rules: no jaunts less than sixty seconds apart—enough to let the star trackers and inertial platform get a fix on their position—and always have one more world-walker ready to go than the plan called for, with a couple of propulsion charges armed and waiting. The latter, in case it was necessary to reboost in a hurry, because of some unimagined situation in their destination time line.

But reboosting in a hurry was *not* something anybody wanted to do over the Commonwealth, let alone over French airspace. Not when it meant firing off nuclear explosions above an enemy who had thousands of hydrogen bombs loaded onto bombers and missiles, their targets programmed, locked, and ready to launch on warning. The only way out was another jaunt. And so, Juggernaut operated with two or more world-walkers prepped and ready whenever it shifted time lines.

"Sitrep, Alan," Huw called over the open crew circuit. Alan Stevens ran the engineering crew, coordinating the hunt for the arcing wires.

"Still searching, skipper. Good news: maneuvering is clear. We've narrowed it down to a couple of breakers that are popping in life support two. It's the power circuit for the air circulation fans—you may have noticed it's getting kind of hot in here? Also, the primary ammonia coolant loop shows a pressure drop. We're tearing down those cable runs"—a pause—"Verity says she's found a hot panel. Hot voltage, not thermal-hot. We're isolating it now."

Huw wiped his forehead with one cuff and tried to look calmly confident when what he really wanted to do was punch the air and shout *we're not going to die!* It was not generally considered good form for a ship's captain to lose his shit over little things. He was meant to sail serenely over the small stuff—like an electrical fire smoldering behind the panels, a faulty life-support system, and crew members with handheld vacs playing chase-the-floater before someone choked to death in their sleep on somebody else's vomit. Not to mention the overwhelming sense that he and his people were undertrained and working way outside their comfort zone, having launched nine months ahead of their original target. *On the other hand . . .*

"Kudos to Verity. People, we're on countdown to the first transfer in two minutes. Does anyone need a hold?" He paused for ten whole seconds. They felt like hours. "Confirm countdown to first transfer, walker crew."

"Walker crew ready." Bill sounded so laid back he was positively supine, as if he didn't realize he was strapped to an acceleration coach inside a giant steel artillery shell hurtling across the Pacific ocean at twenty-eight thousand kilometers per hour.

"Comms and Nav."

"Ready." Huw took a deep breath. Sixty seconds to go. There'd be little enough to see if Bill did his job properly: no dramatic shift in the stars, nothing except the disappearance of the artificial Van Allen belt created by Juggernaut's launch. They would pick up a staticky hash of radio chatter, as the scanners on the Comms board suddenly found a civilized time line's worth of communications to eavesdrop on. Nav would take a star fix, then go looking for the carrier wave from the Commonwealth military comsat constellation, and Comms would broadcast their transponder code for the benefit of any twitchy fingers on the Commonwealth ballistic missile defense crews: *don't launch on us, we're friendly*. In fact—

"Comms. Switching on Band X transponder, squawking Juliet-prime. Testing. Confirmed."

"Thirty seconds." Huw glanced across the crowded room at Bill and Jenny. Jenny winked, turned her thumb up—following the local vertical, indicated by blue arrows on the walls. "Okay, Bill, you have the count. Commit to transition."

"Skipper, we found the short." Alan cut in over the general circuit. "Frayed wire in a duct between modules, part of the high-voltage rail to the primary ammonia pump." The pump circulated refrigerant through the radiator panels on the outside of Juggernaut, to keep the crew from cooking in their own waste heat. A space ship in Earth orbit without active refrigeration was a metal-foiled package of astronauts roasting in a solar-heated rotisserie. "We can splice it once we stand down from maneuvering stations." Despite the possibility that Juggernaut might have to light off its drive at very short notice, Alan's engineering crew had continued their search for the electrical fire, risking broken bones or worse.

"Good work. Get to your couches."

"Transition here: jumping in five seconds. Three. Two. One. *Ow*, my head—jump cleared."

The Comms and Nav crew were suddenly preoccupied, as their bulky CRT displays lit up with the signature of over-the-horizon missile warning radars. The audio spectrum analyzers were pulling in national radio broadcasts, the distant sizzle and hiss of TV stations. Snatches of patriotic martial music fizzed through the bridge speakers, mixed with announcements about the state funeral in progress. The Earth turned beneath them, visible on the big screen at the front of the flight deck.

"Nav here, we have a confirmed fix and we're on-orbit within twenty kilometers of target. Altitude nominal. We will be crossing the Californian coast on schedule in four minutes."

"Acknowledged." Huw took a deep breath. "Comms, get me a channel to Maracaibo. Walker crew, prepare for emergency exit then hold at minus one minute."

One minute. In their current orbit, five hundred kilometers up, that would give them plenty of time to bug out if they saw the tell-tale flare of anti-satellite missiles launching from silos at surface level. Huw checked their ground track again on the moving map. They'd crossed the coast a hundred and fifty kilometers south of Mission San Francisco. While there was a big nuclear-tipped SAM battery on Russian Point, it was all medium range stuff. Nobody in time line three had anything fast enough or big enough to touch Juggernaut.

"Command, I have General Anders on channel two for you."

"Put him on." Huw paused. "General, I bought you a battleship: whose lawn do you want me to park it on?"

"Hah, right. You had us all worried for a few minutes until you phoned it in, sir." Anders' voice was tense, but controlled. "I have you on track to overfly the capital in twenty-six minutes. We have formally notified the French Imperial embassy of your flight plan and the presence of a manned Commonwealth space vehicle in orbit. We should have a go/no-go for overflight of St. Petersburg in thirty-three minutes." If the French Imperial Air Armada threw a hissy fit at an overflight on such short notice, Juggernaut could jaunt back to its previous parking time line. But that might be worse, politically, than pressing forward with an orbital overflight of the Imperial dominions in Asia. "Meanwhile, we're sending up a task list for you to execute over the capital. Miss Thorold wrote the message you're to transmit in clear on public channels. Dog and pony show."

"Acknowledged." The teletype transmission showed up on his CRT seconds later. "Let's see . . . *the Department of Para-time Research pays its respects to the memory of the First Man. In his honor it sends the Commonwealth's first deep space para-time exploration vessel to bear witness to its loyalty to the principles of Democracy and Revolution.* That everything?"

"You got it. Everyone down here could do with a shot in the arm right now. Anyway, the next step after that is positioning for the St. Petersburg overflight. Oh, one last—"

"Any word from—"

"—Your wife sends her congratulations on a successful launch, sir. Hope that helps set your mind at rest."

". . . Ask me again when it's all over! But give her my thanks the next time you talk to her."

"I'll do that. Mission control over and out."

Huw cut the link and shivered. *Proceed with the next phase of the mission.* "Okay, you heard the man," he announced over the open crew channel: "we have an overflight to execute. All stations, report!"

BERLIN, TIME LINE TWO, AUGUST 2020

Angie stepped out of the airport arrivals hall and looked around for signs to the shiny new S-Bahn station. *So this is Germany,* she thought, feeling oddly distant—or perhaps it was the jet lag. She'd driven to Boston, then flown straight out of Logan Airport on a Lufthansa red-eye. It had been an eight-hour flight before she landed in Frankfurt, followed by a transfer and a half-hour connecting flight to Berlin—nearly twelve hours, door to door. But the west-to-east journey had crossed five time zones, and she'd been unable to sleep.

She dropped her messenger bag over the handle of her spinner and gave the stacked luggage an experimental twirl. (*Take a checked bag full of clothing you can afford to ditch,* Kurt had warned her. *Buy a return ticket.* Failure to do either of these things would alert the security bureaucracy.) The S-Bahn train was as impressive as expected, once she managed to convince the infuriatingly obtuse vending machine to sell her a ticket. She yawned again, then shuffled along the seemingly infinite articulated corridor of the train and tucked herself into a seat. It was five in the morning back home. She hoped Rita was getting the rest she so badly needed.

Worry gnawed at her as she rode the train through the endless Berlin suburbs. (Suburbs only by European standards: this would be a densely packed city anywhere in North America.) She worried about the passport that bore her name and her biometrics: it had been logged passing through the DHS checkpoints at Logan, and they knew she was involved with Rita so she had to assume they'd be monitoring her movements. She worried about Kurt: she was here because Kurt wanted her here, because the DHS had a team here, looking for someone Rita's contacts in the Commonwealth wanted. Kurt had given her a batch of instructions: *Buy this SIM, do this, do that, remember not to book your hotel until you arrive in Germany, stay* there *not* here. She worried about the adversarial nature of this job: *I'm exposed,* she realized, *there's no avoiding it.* The other bodies in Kurt's ad-hoc team were at least partially sandboxed. She'd delivered their instructions via burner phone, and they'd coordinate on the ground using old-school tradecraft. But she and Kurt were Persons Of Interest to the DHS, and their presence would be hard to explain. *I'm committed,* she realized. *But committed to* what?

She got off the train at the Hauptbahnhof and rode the escalators down to a cafe. Went inside, bought a double espresso, pulled out her tablet. There was free wireless, so a minute or two later, she logged onto the Web site of the Motel One across the main road from the station. Five minutes later she had a room. An hour after that—checked in, showered, no longer as rancid as she'd felt stepping off the trans-Atlantic flight—she blundered back out into the daylight and made her way towards her first rendezvous.

Spies (or agents, or streetwalkers, or HUMINT assets: whatever they were called these days) no longer identified each other in public with a red carnation through the buttonhole of a suit jacket, or a rolled-up copy of last week's SPIEGEL under the arm. (Suits were conspicuously formal, paper magazines unusual.) But they still needed a reliable way of hooking up in public without attracting attention. The preferred method was always to disguise your recognition signal as something unexceptional. You could both play for the same team in an augmented reality game. Or you could pretend to be bluedogging: set your phones to say you were looking for casual sex by broadcasting a distinctive bluetooth ID, then wait for your contact to zero in on you. Nobody would spare it a second glance: the worst risk you ran was that you might be casually propositioned by a complete stranger.

A hypothetical surveillance officer might have done a double-take if they saw the denim-clad woman with the shock of blue-and-green hair meet her contact. She found him loitering near the doorway to the giant Saturn electronics superstore, greeted him with a glad cry and fell into his arms for a conspicuous hug. *It takes all kinds,* the officer might have shrugged: so the twenty-something woman wanted to hook up with a seventy-year-old sugar daddy? *Or maybe he's her grandfather.* And they would have shrugged and turned aside, mildly embarrassed, and spared the couple (now walking arm-in-arm into the shop) from further scrutiny.

Which was exactly what Kurt and Angie were counting on.

"How was your flight?" Kurt led her past a row of dump bins full of this week's specials—unfamiliar power adapters, futuristic-looking kettles.

"The flight was okay." Angie yawned, her jaw cracking. "Couldn't sleep though."

"Then we must put some coffee into you right now." Kurt took a turn past a row of front-loading washing machines, then walked rapidly towards the up escalator. "Follow me."

They wove through the crowded store, dodging other shoppers, then rode two escalators up to a department full of electrical components that Angie itched to forage through. Alas, there was no time for shopping. There was an elevator tucked away at the back of the shop floor, battered and utilitarian. Kurt led her out into an upper-floor parking garage, walked down the up ramp, then entered another lift lobby. The stores all had cameras for prosecuting shoplifters, but they weren't networked and it was illegal for shops to film the passing public outside their premises. Kurt and Angie ghosted through multiple camera zones to muddy their trail, then rode the lift down to an indoor mall and made their way out through a department store. They exited only a hundred meters from where they'd entered, but on a different floor and with a reasonable degree of confidence that nobody would be able to track them. Finally Kurt led her into another mall, down a service corridor, past a public rest room, and into a lobby where there was a coffee shop. "Let's sit," he suggested. "How do you take your coffee?"

"Espresso. It's five in the morning back home. Give me all the espresso. *All* of it." Angie fought not to doze off while Kurt queued at the counter. He returned with two cups of coffee. He placed the smaller one in front of her. "Thank you," she husked, blinking against the glare of spotlights from the sportswear store across the aisle.

"Did all the party invites go out?" He asked, blowing on his cappuccino.

"Yes. All acknowledged." Angie's gaze was slightly glassy. "They should be calling in later this afternoon, once they arrive."

"Good." Kurt nodded. "The lamplighters are preparing fallback positions. Hotel suites, unfortunately. It's hard to get apartments or houses at a day's notice. But they're in the field and they're at work, which is the main thing."

Compartmentalization meant that Angie and her cell were not supposed to know the identity or location of Kurt's lamplighters. They were part of another cell, tasked with preparing accommodation and materials in advance. Kurt and Angie, as cell leaders, knew each other and coordinated the activities of their teams. Unfortunately there was no higher tier of management to keep them insulated, as would have been the case in a functioning intelligence bureaucracy. The Wolf Orchestra was the only surviving fragment of a long-dead agency: Kurt knew everyone, and could blow the entire ring if he was captured. But things would be structured to keep him as far from the opposition as possible. Direct contact was best left to the young, the dedicated, and the stupidly, recklessly angry—characteristics that weren't in short supply in the twenty-first century.

Angie took a mouth-burning sip of coffee. "So what's the plan?"

"Well." Kurt paused and slowly scanned the café, checking to make sure he'd spotted all the cameras, also double-checking that nobody was watching their table. "The first objective, getting the subject, this Elizabeth, will be easy. Our sponsors have her on line. Tomorrow their controller will tell her to rendezvous with you, and you will bring her to the primary location. From there, a cut-out will bring her to me and I will accompany her to the exit myself." Angie nodded. She had no need to know how Kurt and his employers planned to spirit Elizabeth Hanover out of Berlin. "That is the easy part of the mission," Kurt added gravely.

"And the hard part?"

Kurt sighed. "Rita's controller, this Colonel Smith. He is *personally* supervising the search for Elizabeth in this city. He has captured two of our employers' agents—a world-walker who was shot while arranging her defection, and another, whose position is unclear. A long-term resident, I believe, previously controlled by this world-walking major." Angie failed to suppress a tiny gasp. Kurt watched her gravely. The worst case in the

Game of Spies was for an entire network to be rolled up, cell by cell: and this was exactly how the process started, with a carefully-choreographed sequence of arrests. "I am led to believe that Rita's birth mother will be *personally* grateful if, in addition to retrieving Elizabeth Hanover, we can find a way to secure the release of these two. She—our employer—is loyal to her people. But the US government is unlikely to agree to prisoner exchanges involving world-walkers any time in the next decade."

Angie tipped back the remains of her espresso in one go and winced. "Great. Get the Princess? Sure. Then extract two prisoners from the opposition? That's another matter! Kurt, no offense intended, but have you lost your mind?"

Kurt smiled at her without showing his teeth, lips two pale parallel lines. "Absolutely not."

"But that's—"Her impending expostulation was punctuated by a titanic yawn—"you've got some kind of cunning plan, haven't you?"

"Yes." His smile slipped. "You're too tired for this right now. I said 'secure the release,' you heard 'engineer the escape.' These two things are not the same, Angela. I intend to motivate our adversary to release them. It may not happen right now, or here, but we will eventually make the dog give up the bone. But our first step is to ensure that the dog doesn't add any more bones to his collection, and you, my child, are so tired you are misunderstanding things. You're no use to anyone in this state. Go to your room and sleep for at least three hours: I will call you later and tell you where you can find the primary subject, and where to take her."

NEW LONDON, MANHATTAN ISLAND, TIME LINE THREE, AUGUST 2020

There were bleachers, just as Alice had promised: row upon row of benches erected on scaffolding, grouped into viewing stands spaced out along a broad boulevard. The buildings behind the stands were a mixture of ministries and palace buildings with neoclassical colonnaded fronts, all closed for the duration. Crowds of people in their best mourning weeds were politely waved through barriers by uniformed guards, whose deference failed to mask the care with which they checked every ticket. But there were no metal detector archways, no body scanners or sniffer dogs or camera drones, and the guards appeared to be unarmed. Rita felt curiously exposed when she noticed this. Alice Morgan gave Rita a ticket, patted her on the shoulder, then disappeared. She was clearly confident that everything was under control. Rita looked up at the stand. Despite a hazy overcast, the early afternoon sunshine was bright. There was an atmosphere of expectancy in the crowd: not cheerful—it was a funeral cortege, after all, not a ball game—but engaged.

Her ticket bore a seat number four rows back from the front and five seats in from the aisle leading to the exit. Rita found herself taking her place beside Huw and Brill's daughter. Apparently mid-teens were trusted to find their ways around crowd events unaccompanied: another datum Rita filed away. Definitely *not like home*, she thought. "Hi. Nel, is it?" she asked her neighbor.

Nel nodded. Dark-eyed with chestnut hair, in a black velvet dress with too many frills topped by a big hat with a net veil, she looked like the punchline of a joke about vampires and sunlight. "Is the Inspector coming?" She asked, fanning herself with her program.

"No, she's got duties elsewhere." Rita looked at her own running order. "Have you ever been to one of these before?"

Nel seemed surprised by the question. "A military parade? Yes, too many times. Daddy has to attend them. They're all right if you like tanks and soldiers." She glanced sidelong at Rita. "At a distance, I mean. Look but don't touch, mama always says. Are you a world-walker?"

Rita froze briefly. *Welp, should have seen* that *coming.* "Yes," she said.

"But if you're a world-walker, that means your father must have been one of us too. So who was he?"

"I don't know," Rita said as evenly as she could manage, biting back an acid urge to tell the kid the truth. Illegitimacy seemed to be a big thing here, at least as big as it had been a century ago back home. *The truth? You can't handle the truth . . .*

Nel's eyes widened as she misinterpreted Rita's reply. "Oh! I'm sorry, I didn't mean to pry. It's just that he must have been another relative, we might be cousins or something—"

Didn't mean to pry? Oh yes you did! "I don't think so." Rita paused, then flung herself on the truth anyway, hoping that the unexploded grenade lacked the fuse she feared: "He wasn't a world-walker. I was just a, a carrier, until they activated me." It wasn't as if her birth mother hadn't already worked it out. And everything Rita knew about the world-walking clan told her that encouraging them to speculate about her father could only end badly. But it was time for a conversational diversion, so: "can you world-walk too?"

"Oh yes! I took my test six months ago—" The crowd began to quieten, as an announcement crackled from loudspeakers at the back of the stands—"although I won't have to begin my service until I'm eighteen. Listen, they're starting." Rita heard a thudding, rhythmic and precise, accompanied by drums. Martial music rose over the chatter of conversation like breakers approaching a beach. She looked to the right, at the taller podium where the rows of Commissioners and their senior staff were seated. They were on their feet, at attention. *Glad I'm not up there,* she thought, as a marching band turned the corner at the opposite end of the mall, boots crashing a rhythmic counterpoint to the drumbeat. Ranks of soldiers in red dress uniforms with black armbands advanced at a slow march. Behind them followed further rows of soldiers bearing rifles tipped with bayonets, a rippling field of painfully bright steel blades gleaming in the sunlight. They seemed to take forever to reach the bleachers and inch their way past. As they approached the podium, those of them without weapons or instruments saluted in unison, receiving answering salutes from the mostly-male dignitaries.

Rita watched the slow-marching battalions for a quarter of an hour, growing bored. Rank upon rank of hunky men in uniforms might be of interest to some, but in her opinion there was such a thing as too much of a good thing. Judging by Nel's expression, even though she was on her best behavior, she was rapidly approaching her teenage boredom threshold. A spectacular outbreak of fidgeting was clearly only minutes away. "Let's go get a soda or an iced tea or something," Rita suggested. "This is going to go on for ages, isn't it? And it's going to be a long, hot afternoon."

"Oh yes, *please*—" Nel's relief was heart-felt. Rita felt smug: in one smooth move she'd redefined her role from adult chaperone to co-conspirator. (*Now if only I didn't feel guilty about how Dr. Scranton and Colonel Smith would expect me to pump her for information about her parents . . .* But there was no way to win that head-game.) They crouched and duck-walked past the seated people behind them, then headed down the aisle towards the stairs. There was already a queue at the refreshment stand.

"I don't have any money," Rita realized.

"Don't worry, the refreshments in this stand are free."

"Yes, but—"

A noise like a bed-sheet the size of Maine being ripped in half tore across the sky from east to west, dopplering down into a grumble like summer thunder. "We're missing the fly-past!" Nel squeaked, dismayed. "That's the best part!"

"Fly-past?"

Rita looked up, just in time to see a second formation of silvery delta-shapes hurtle overhead with a gut-churningly loud roar of jet engines. The nine arrowheads raced the length of the road less than a thousand feet up, followed seconds later by another wave, trailing flames. The metallic, oily fumes began to settle, stinking of unburned fuel. The military jets were so loud that Rita could feel them in her gut. The drinks queue inched forward as wave after wave thundered overhead—first the fighter aircraft, then ranks of swept-wing bombers making slow passes, shaking the bleachers. "Wow, this is special, isn't it?" Nel shouted in her ear. It was so loud that she had to repeat herself twice before Rita understood.

They reached the kiosk. Rita managed to order an iced tea, and before she could intervene, Nel asked for—and received—a wheat beer. Rita did a double-take before she remembered: *prohibition never happened here, and neither did Mothers Against Drink Driving.* Teenage drinking was normal. "Come on, once the infantry are past it'll be time for the cavalry guards, some tanks, and then the First Man's gun-carriage. And then the trade guilds and civilian floats . . ."

The deafening waves of warplanes became less frequent as they reached the steps, but now they found a queue of refreshed parade-viewers blocking the staircase back to their row. Rita spotted an empty stretch at the front barrier, and took Nel's arm. "Over here." The grinding screech of tank tracks on concrete was painfully loud this close to the boulevard, and the rumbling diesels spilled choking clouds of blue exhaust fumes across the stands. Rita couldn't tell one war machine from the next, but these were obviously special: big-tracked transporters, with gigantic green cylinders running fore-and-aft along their upper surfaces.

"Rockets," Nel shouted in her ear. "Probably atomic anti-aircraft missiles!" Rita managed not to swallow her tongue. Soldiers, their red dress coats and tall bearskin hats matched anachronistically to modern-looking assault rifles, marched alongside the transporters. They were followed in turn by row after row of infantry fighting vehicles in different colors, dark blue rather than field-green. "This is their Commonwealth Guard escort, they stop the missile troops launching without authorization—"

Rita sucked at her iced tea and glanced up at the VIP podium as the IFVs rumbled past. Nel seemed unusually well-informed about military affairs for a teenage girl. But with Brill and Huw for parents—"your father's military, isn't he?"

"Yes, and he's going to be overhead in twenty minutes!" Nel said excitedly.

"I thought he was in Venezuela?"

"He was! But mum told me what he was there to do this morning—it's being announced publicly today and there'll be an overflight!" Nel raised her wrist and pushed back a spray of lace to reveal a dainty wrist watch. "Think you can keep a secret for ten more minutes, until they announce it over the radio and the loudspeakers?"

"What kind of secret?" Rita asked, only half paying attention.

"Daddy's in charge of a program to develop world-walking atomic space battleships! The first one took off a couple of days ago and Daddy's on board, it's in orbit—"

"I'm sorry," Rita said, then paused and mentally replayed the last few seconds of Nel's excited monologue. "*What?*" The four-letter word slipped out before she could bite her tongue. "What did you just say?" It was so bizarre that Rita was certain she'd misheard.

"It's called Juggernaut and it's overflying the funeral!" Nel insisted. "I'm not making this up!"

She was about to say more when the speakers blared into life. "We interrupt our scheduled display now to announce a giant first step for the Commonwealth. Yesterday, our brave time travelers took their first steps into outer space! In exactly eighteen minutes, the Commonwealth's first interplanetary para-time space cruiser will rise like a star in the south-west—"

Rita pinched herself, but the crazy stubbornly refused to go away. She looked around frantically, gripped by a sudden sense of alienation. Formalwear on every side like something out of a costume drama, missiles on tracked launchers like something out of a North Korean propaganda broadcast: these she could just about deal with. But: *space battleships?* Reaching into her clutch she pulled out her camera, switched it to record full audio and video, and turned to face the direction everyone else was looking.

The announcer droned on over the speakers, all facts and figures about this Juggernaut contraption. She hoped the camera's microphone was catching it. The sky was clear, a pale blue with barely a thin haze of cloud overhead. Then near the horizon—Rita squinted—*is that Venus?* she wondered. But it was the wrong time of day, too low and too bright, and it was moving fast. People were gasping and pointing now. A familiar voice took over on the speaker, fuzzed by static, periodically interrupted by a high-pitched tone. It was Huw. "Fellow Citizens of the Commonwealth, this is the Explorer-General, broadcasting to you from low Earth orbit—"

Just when you get lulled into thinking they're quaint and a little old-fashioned, they do something like this. Rita fought back the urge to giggle nervously. She'd taken a couple of online history courses back when she'd still had delusions about being allowed into grad school. There'd been a unit on the cold war and the space race. The Sputnik Moment, when Americans awakened to a beeping sphere hurtling across the heavens and realized the Soviets had beaten them into outer space, had nothing on this. *Dr. Scranton's going to shit a brick,* she realized numbly.

The star brightened as it rose towards the zenith, brilliantly reflective. Juggernaut was enormous, far larger than her own time line's Space Station Freedom. Rita engaged the tracking on her light-field camera and zoomed in until the tiny dot almost resolved into an oval. Huw's announcement continued, a slightly stilted salute to the passing of the First Man and a declaration of lofty sentiments for the future. After a few minutes, the parade commentator took over again. Rita slid her camera back into the bag.

Nel clutched her forearm and turned shining eyes on her. "My daddy is a spaceman!" She announced, unable to contain herself.

Her joy was contagious and Rita found herself smiling back at her as the rumble of diesels heralded the arrival of the next formation of tanks and infantry fighting vehicles entering the boulevard. These ones were dark blue-grey, in heavily-pixelated nighttime camouflage with netting and tarpaulins covering their hatches. They were Commonwealth Guard units, in battle order rather than polished and gleaming for show. "Hang on." Rita's smile slipped. "That's not right—" The commentator was excitedly announcing the Marine Corps: evidently this was off-script.

Soldiers dismounted from doors at the back of the IFVs and ran past the main stand. Some of the VIPs on the stand were breaking ranks, gesturing and pointing as if puzzled. Rita looked at the soldiers again, squinting against the light. They wore dark-blue fatigues, helmets, and body armor with dazzle-pattern camouflage. They held grimly functional assault rifles at the ready. They didn't look like an honor guard at a funeral: they looked ready for action. Rita shook her head, half-deafened, choking on the fumes of the armor rolling past twenty feet in front of her. She tried to make sense of it all.

This is wrong, but what does it mean? Her knees wobbled as a terrified premonition settled over her. "Nel, do you have an engram on you?" She asked, pitching her voice to carry above the background.

"An engram? What's one of—"

"The world-walker knot." Rita fumbled with her left cuff, icy panic clawing at her spine. *If I'm wrong, I can laugh it off later. If I'm right*—she yanked her sleeve up, sending a button pinging off over the barrier. Then she clamped the fingers of her right hand around her wrist, pressing the sub-dermal contacts to pull up a trigger engram. "Don't look at this tattoo unless I tell you to, Nel—"

There was a rapid-fire popping like champagne corks, barely audible over the roar of engines and the screech of steel tracks on stone. She heard shouting. People were moving around. On the podium VIPs were falling over or rushing away from the front. Everything was confusing: there were more bangs, felt rather than heard, like doors slamming. The turrets of the IFVs traversed to cover the crowds, *pointed at each other*, helmeted heads ducking inside and hatches closing, more soldiers running with guns raised to shoulder height. More popping, louder now—

"What's happening?" Nel sounded confused rather than frightened.

"Hold on!" Rita grabbed her around the waist. "I hope I'm wrong—" The crackle of assault rifles a hundred yards away was drowned out by the thunder of a turret-mounted auto-cannon as she jaunted.

"Fuck!" She landed hard, falling as Nel instinctively pushed her away.

"Where *are* we?" Nel demanded angrily. "You world-walked, didn't you? You kidnapped me! Why did you—"She stomped round in front of Rita, pushing aside the knee-high undergrowth. They were surrounded by the narrow trunks of young trees on every side. Nel slowed as realization settled in. "That was gunfire, wasn't it? What's happening, Miss Burgeson?"

"Call me Rita." Rita tried to pick herself up. She felt a stab of pain in her left ankle. It smelled very *green* here, the scent of moisture and grass and growing things. The bark of gunfire had been replaced with bird song, faint among the branches. "The, the Commonwealth Guards in the blue uniforms? They were shooting at the Commissioners' podium and the other soldiers. Who began to shoot back. That's why I grabbed you."

Nel's eyes widened again. "Oh. Oh no." She leaned against a tree trunk, heedless of getting moss or bark on her finery. "But we—where did you take us?"

"Time line one." Rita raised her left wrist and double-checked the co-ordinates. "We can't stay here. What's left of the Gruinmarkt starts about a hundred miles north. The radiation's supposed to have died down, but we mustn't eat or drink anything—too much fallout in the soil. We need to go somewhere where there's no shooting before we cross back."

"They're trying to kill mama!" Nel burst out. "And your mother! What are we going to do?" She stared at Rita in horror. "I can't go to the United States with you!"

"Then we won't go there." Rita hefted her handbag. *They're trying to kill Miriam.* The thought was alien, savagely cold, inadmissibly weird, and oddly resonant—all at the same time. *They're trying to kill* my *mother.* Not Emily Douglas, who'd loved her and raised her, but her other mother, the one who'd turned her back on Rita to conceal her tears when they were first introduced. *She was on the podium, two stories up. She couldn't world-walk from there, not safely.* Rita shuddered with a pang of remorse for her earlier coldness towards Miriam. "Nel, your mother was at the office when this kicked off. Not in the stand. Where will she look for you? Will she expect you to go straight home?"

"No! Yes! I don't know!" Nel was panicky.

"Try and stay calm." Rita gritted her teeth then opened her clutch and pulled out the inertial mapper. Tapping the screen she typed in a waypoint marker: *viewing podium two, coup plotters.* "I hope your mother looks for you at home, because that's where we're going to go first. The government buildings are way too dangerous to approach right now"—a massive understatement—"and I don't have any other useful waypoints saved in this thing. But we'll jaunt over somewhere near to your parents' house, then if the way is clear we'll get you home, find a phone and try to find out what's happening."

"But what if there are soldiers?"

"Then we'll work something out."

BERLIN, TIME LINE TWO, AUGUST 2020

Nobody paid any attention to the black woman in jeans and a loose, embroidered top as she slid through the crowds of tourists and shoppers. She was unmemorable, with nothing to distinguish her from any other teenager or student. She clutched an olive-drab messenger bag to her chest. One end of it was marred by a scorched-looking hole, like a cigarette burn. Perhaps the way she paused at street corners, casting looks of guarded wonder at the shops and people, might have drawn the attention of a particularly bored observer. But Elizabeth Hanover's actions were almost indistinguishable from those of a tourist, because playing tourist was exactly what she was doing.

Liz had finally started to unwind. After the shock of her retrieval then the Major's injury and the raid on his apartment, she'd spent much of the morning in a state of terrified confusion. But she'd learned to buy things with a wallet full of alien money, mastered the phone, acquired a local costume, and checked in to a hotel. Now she had a place to eat and sleep she was beginning to relax, no longer in fear of hot pursuit by gendarmes and spies. In fact, she was perilously close to discounting the peril she was in, the deluge of new sights and experiences having desensitized her to the strangeness all around. She was inexperienced at tradecraft, so rather than obeying orders and going to ground, she spent the afternoon shamelessly wandering around shops, puzzling at the displays in front of cinemas and games arcades, turning up her nose at fashions that puzzled or surprised her, and killing time with a tall coffee and a plate of pastries in a café.

As the afternoon wore on, she became jaded. She was bored with people-watching, tired of directionless exploration. Some aspects of her new wardrobe were unsatisfying, so she checked out the shoe shops, but rapidly became confused by the variety of styles on offer for women. Unsure if she'd be making an expensive mistake, she finally gave up and switched to looking for a shoulder bag that wasn't quite as obviously damaged as Major Hjorth's. She spent many of her remaining euros on an oversized leather handbag. Retreating into a public rest room in a building similar to a department store, but with separate glass-fronted shops—indoor shopping malls were unknown to the Empire—she transferred the Major's gun and her other sundries into the new bag, then stuffed the old one in a trash can. She bought a pair of mirror-finished spectacles, the better to avoid direct eye contact—she had been disturbed by some ugly looks she received before she ditched the Major's disguise. Then she completed her ensemble with a short black jacket in some slick, flexible substance that looked and felt disturbingly like leather, except that it wasn't. She had seen that look around and liked the unapproachability, the attitude, the assumed arrogance of the (she had no name for them) punks and metal-heads hanging out just off the tourist drag. Nobody respectable, she felt, would mess with those people. And being *dis*respectable was exactly what she craved, having been forced to live her entire life until now in a cage of decorum.

While Liz drifted around the center of the capital, soaking up the atmosphere and indulging in recreational shopping, events were taking place elsewhere to which she was oblivious, but which would have far-reaching consequences for her future.

In a giant, windowless server farm in Cheltenham, England, racks of computers churned through location data leeched from the German cell-phone carriers. Whenever a cell registered the presence of a new phone, it added the identity of the phone to the distributed database used to route calls for a given number to the cell tower closest to the handset. The British GCHQ signals intelligence agency monitored all the European carriers' call forwarding databases and shared the data with the NSA. Today the roster of suspicious phones to track included all the devices that had been within a hundred meters of the Major's safe house when it was raided.

As the day passed, more and more of these phones and mobile internet routers updated their locations as their owners carried them around the city. As the afternoon dragged on into early evening, their owners headed back to their homes. If those homes were within the starting block, their phones could be crossed off the list of suspects. And by ten o'clock, only about twenty devices had not—at some point—returned to the apartment block in Pankow.

Now the field had been narrowed down, the search could move into top gear.

However, Elizabeth's shopping binge had put a spoke through the wheel of the Bundespolitzei team who were tracking her through the public CCTV records.

When Major Hjorth had extracted Elizabeth, his hurried departure left a clear trail of sightings for the camera trackers to follow. It was unavoidable, but it was taken into account by the original plan. Yul's mission planners had believed that by the time anyone could join the dots, Hulius and Elizabeth would be aboard a light plane somewhere over the Bay of Biscay. But then Yul was shot.

Elizabeth had fled the Major's safe house dressed as a conservatively-dressed Turkish woman. The Major had brought the disguise to her before the botched extraction. He'd selected it to account for her dark skin, and to spare her sensibilities. He hadn't planned it to frustrate deep learning recognition systems, but the headscarf had obscured her features from the nearest cameras, and the long denim skirt had blocked other biometric signifiers—particularly her knee/hip ratio—making it hard to track her gait.

The police team had examined the Major's rented BMW, and back-tracked its path to the Schloss Britz. But Hulius had led her out through service passages and rooms covered by a burglar alarm rather than public cameras. The fingerprints from the car and apartment were a bust, with no matches found in the crime database. All they had were some blurred, partial face shots of a dark-skinned woman taken from a considerable distance. This was not enough for facial recognition software, which was especially bad at handling non-white skin tones (reflecting the cultural biases of the programmers).

The first breakthrough in the case came the evening after they lost her.

A janitor working the commercial mall units in the Hauptbahnhof stumbled across a tightly-rolled bundle of clothing, misplaced in the paper recycling bin. Normally this would have attracted no attention, but as he bagged it, he realized he was holding a blood-stained blouse. Ten minutes later a pair of Schupos answered his call. Three minutes after *that* the public toilet was officially designated a crime scene, and an hour later the first tentative DNA sequence match came back—to a man lying in a bed in an American military hospital, with a drain in his chest and an INTERPOL red tag on his file.

Pay-dirt.

As soon as the match to Major Hjorth was confirmed, an urgent request went to the crime scene first responder: take forensic swabs from *inside* the garments, avoiding the bloodstains, and send measurements. By ten o'clock the investigators had confirmed the approximate waist, bust, and height of the suspect, along with a DNA sample for matching against future evidence.

Then the Bundespolizei team turned their attention to the cameras in the Hauptbahnhof concourse. They fast-forwarded through footage of the approaches to the public restroom until they saw a woman in Turkish dress enter and not come out . . .

Elizabeth Hanover didn't know it yet, but by failing to discard her disguise in the correct recycling bin she'd blown her cover. And while she ate her room-service dinner, showered, and tried to figure out the in-room television, the net was tightening.

NEW LONDON, MANHATTAN ISLAND, TIME LINES ONE AND THREE, AUGUST 2020

Rita and Nel were dressed for a funeral service, not hiking through the knee-deep undergrowth of a forest while avoiding snakes, spiders, deadfalls, and obstacles. On the other hand, Rita had her inertial mapper. Nel was fascinated by it, but dissatisfied by Rita's reply when she asked how it worked: "magic smoke."

"No, *really*, how—"

"I don't know," Rita cut her off irritably. "I just know how to use it. Do you know how a jet engine works? Or your father's spaceship? The battery's down to half a charge, and your mother's house is nearly three miles in that direction—" half way across the width of lower Manhattan—"and we need to get there as fast as we can."

If she'd been on her own, carrying an ID card and cash, she'd have jaunted across to her own New York and hailed a cab. But ID was mandatory in her time line, and money wasn't optional. Also, she had a sneaking suspicion that Dr. Scranton wouldn't permit her to return directly to New London if she knew what was going on there—especially with a teenage world-walker in tow. Rita had no intention of stranding Nel in a hostile time line with no way back. She was barely more than a kid but that wouldn't stop

DHS from finding a way to use her. It was another step along the path to losing faith with her employers, but it was a step Rita felt helpless to avoid. So she resolved to avoid the confrontation for as long as possible. "Come on."

A generation after it had been cauterized by nuclear fire in this time line, Manhattan Island had sprouted a verdant mass of undergrowth around clumps of new-growth trees. They were slender things that Rita could surround with the fingers and thumbs of both hands. Anything with an older, larger trunk had fallen, and was decaying slowly beneath the cover of ferns and shrubs. The deadfall mostly lay from north to south, with signs of charring on their upper surfaces. They would have presented serious obstacles to east-west travel, but the map was leading them north-east rather than due east, which made traversing the forest slightly easier.

"Is my mother going to be all right?" Nel asked as they picked their way past the carbonized corpse of a giant tree. "Those soldiers who were shooting, were they shooting at the Commissioners or the second tier? Or at their guards?"

"I'm not sure." Rita rubbed her wrist across her forehead. It came away damp. Her clothes chafed and sweat trickled down her neck. It had been hot in BLACK RAIN, and it was several degrees warmer in this time line. "I couldn't tell whether the soldiers from the parade were shooting, or whether it was the guards on the podium, or someone else entirely. But I know what gunfire sounds like and it's always bad—unless you're practicing, and even then, only if it's in front of you and pointing down-range. Which this wasn't. It doesn't matter where they're aimed, stray bullets are a—" *I'm babbling*, she realized, and forced herself to stop. Relief at being unharmed had been mixing in her head with a froth of anxiety and making her loquacious. *That's the last thing Nel needs from me.*

"My—" she stumbled over the next word—"my mother was supposed to be up on the Commissioner's podium." *I've only known her for a few days.* She felt a pang of self-pity and suppressed it mercilessly. "Come on. If your mom's safe she'll check in with your housekeeper as soon as she can. They'll be worried about you, too. There's no way we could find her back there—" *not in the middle of a military coup, anyway*—"so this is best." A thought struck her. "You're a world-walker. They tested you. Do you get a bad headache when you jaunt?"

"A headache? Oh, yes! I got one during my try-out. It was a killer. But

I jaunted twice in one hour without meds, and my blood pressure didn't go *too* high." Nel sounded as proud as if she was describing an athletic accomplishment. "How's your head?"

"I'm okay," Rita admitted. "I can carry you over once we get to your place, and if there's a problem—" *if there could be soldiers with guns waiting for us*—"I can bug out again immediately. I have very good blood pressure," she lied. Jigsaw pieces of a plan fell into place in her mind's eye. "We're about a quarter of a mile away from the, the park square a block north of your parents' house. I'm going to aim for that. Then I'm going to jaunt over—"

"—Wait! You can't leave me here? I don't have a knot!"

"I know." Rita took Nel's hand, trying for reassurance. "*We're* going to jaunt over. I'm going to carry you, and you're going to keep watch over my shoulder while we do it. If you see any bad guys tell me immediately and I'll take us back here."

"But surely—" Nel paused. "We've been here an hour, I understand, you can world-walk again. But twice in a minute? Wouldn't it be better if we swap over and I—"

Rita let go of her hand and tapped her forehead. "No headache. I can jaunt twice in rapid succession." And much more often than that, but Nel didn't need to know.

"The tattoo on your wrist, it would take us back here. How do you have it, anyway? I mean, it only takes you between here and home, and this place is no use to anyone—"

Telling the truth was opening a can of worms, but Rita was sick of lying. Lying only made things more complicated in the end. "It's not a tattoo." Rita unbuttoned her cuff and rolled her sleeve all the way up, wrapped the fingers of her right hand around the pressure points, then put the subdermal e-ink implant through its paces. "Try not to look too closely."

Nel's eyes widened. "Oh my God, what *is* that?"

"It's not a tattoo, it's a programmable e-ink display. It can store a bunch of trigger engrams. From here I can get to the United States, and also to a bunch of other time lines. Unfortunately none of them are any use to us except the Commonwealth, but . . ." She shrugged. "My bosses think the Forerunners used something similar, only more advanced."

The kid's eyes were like dinner plates now. "The Forerunners? Who are they?"

"Our long-lost ancestors," Rita said tightly. *Say hello to the meet-your-*

long-lost-cousins experience, everyone, she thought uneasily. *But if we met them, would they gather us into their arms or hunt us down like vermin?* "Come on, we're wasting time. Another half-mile and we can get you home." And find a phone and a change of clothes that wouldn't mark Nel out as one of the privileged funeral attendees, if she had to make a run to safety through New London while Rita reported in. Though Rita wasn't about to tell her that just yet. She wasn't even certain that she was going back to her own time line to tell Dr. Scranton that everything had turned to shit. At least, not just yet. She didn't have much to say—just uneasy tidings to bear, tales of gunshots, screams, and smoke. Her only real news consisted of some shaky video of a pinprick of light in the sky and a propaganda sound-track making implausible claims. *She'll think I'm mad.*

"Let's go." The lines on the map display converged on a clearing not far ahead. Rita found a suitable spot and braced herself, feet apart, ready to take Nel's weight on her hips. "Okay, this will do. Hike your skirts up and—yeah, like that. Ah. You're heavier than I thought. Okay, I'll jaunt and if you see anything bad behind me, just yell 'go' in my ear and we'll come right back. Got that?"

Nel mumbled something under her voice, then looked into Rita's eyes. "Got that," she said. "I'm scared."

"So am I." Rita took a deep breath as Nel grabbed her shoulders and tried to wrap her knees around her waist. "Oof."

"I'm slipping—"

"Hang on! Three. Two—uh. One."

Rita jaunted and the world changed color: then she saw the changes an hour had wrought—"Go!" Nel's urgent breath tickled her ear—and she jaunted back to the glade in the forest, just in time.

"Well *shit.*"

Nel slid from her arms and took a tentative step back. "What do we do now?" She asked, despairingly.

Rita took a deep breath and straightened her back, as she inhaled and tried to unkink her arms. "Not sure yet." There had been men in blue uniforms, guarding the smashed-in doorway of the townhouse with raised guns. "I think we may be out of options in New London." There had been a shattered pane in the window of the room she'd eaten breakfast in with Nel, jagged and gleaming in the sunlight. She took another deep breath: "I'm going to have to go over to the, to my own time line, and report in.

But I can't leave you here. And I can't guarantee your safety there. Unless you can suggest something else, we're fucked."

NEAR CAMP SINGULARITY, TIME LINE FOUR, AUGUST 2020

Unobserved by human eyes for the time being, the incursion in Time Line Four continued to grow.

Strange new structures were taking shape in the wreckage of the collapsed Forerunner Dome. The silver locusts that had taken the beachhead, swarming in through the three-meter diameter gate held in an unnaturally slow orbit around the planetary-mass black hole, had driven off the primitive hominids infesting the fortress of their ancient enemies. They'd hunkered down for shelter outside the Dome, while some of their number rotated the Gate until it pointed at the zenith. The battle stations orbiting the hole had dispatched small armored probes boosted to orbital velocity: threading the needle they blazed like meteors as they traversed Nova America Four's atmosphere, coasting into high inclination orbits with good coverage. Then a second wave of hoppers had arrived—surface foragers and prospectors. Finally a batch of robot queens arrived, gravid with the eggs from which the next generation of robots would hatch.

As the probes stabilized and settled into their chosen orbits, they conferred; and having conferred, they mapped: and having mapped, they agreed on a time sequence and location grid for this newly discovered version of Earth: and having agreed they went to work.

A human space agency, whether from the Commonwealth or the United States, would have assigned separate tasks to different types of satellite, whether surveillance or navigation or communications. But the intruders made no such distinction. It was all electromagnetic radiation after all, signals going in, signals processed, signals coming out. In structure the alien orbiters were nothing like human satellites, although they served approximations of the same tasks. They were the end product of billions of iterations of genetic algorithms fine-tuned to optimize for functionality, no two of them identical, with no obvious distinctions between subsystems that in a consciously designed machine would have been separated. They were metalloid life forms, or organically evolved robots: and as they looked down from on high, they provided a context for their ground-and-atmosphere-dwelling swarm-mates to learn the shape of the world they were to destroy.

Specialized bots fanned out at ground level to cover the approaches to the invasion gate. Some of them climbed trees, drilled into their trunks to forage nutrients, and sprouted relay and surveillance antennae. Others stuck to ground cover, taking a census of the local biomass. Most of the life on any Earth-like world with an oxygenated atmosphere and plate tectonic system was bacterial, deep in the crust and difficult to harvest. Of the rest, the vast majority by weight consisted of trees. The census locusts returned to the queens in their growing hive, bearing biological samples. Then the queens went to work, searching their genome libraries and other, more abstruse repositories of archived nano-machinery in search of promising replicators.

Somewhere in the midst of the self-organizing swarm, attention was drawn to the ongoing presence of hominids. A group was detected in the next valley over when they discharged primitive projectile weapons at a biomass sampler. The sampler neutralized at least one of the creatures, but was itself destroyed. The pack approached the valley, unintentionally awakening a sessile relay station which responded appropriately, summoning warbots, but the hominids withdrew—evidently they had retained a vestigial ability to jaunt—before samples could be acquired. Backtracking along their path, the warbots discovered the remains of a dead hominid and recovered samples which tested positive for the para-time infestation.

The detection of world-walkers agitated the swarm, and the half-awakened hives on the far side of the Gate shared their alarm. Packages of actinide metal were dropped into tight orbit around the hole and transmuted, then shipped up to the Gate: kilogram-sized pellets of plutonium began to arrive, to be fed to the digesters. (Bootstrapping all the way up to a matter-annihilation-based metabolism would take the swarm some considerable time, necessitating the construction of intricate fusion reactors and particle accelerators along the way. In contrast, plutonium fission was barely a step above banging rocks together.)

All this activity happened without comment, without conference calls and escalation and executives worrying about the next election cycle or security experts fretting about keeping it out of the public eye. Such things were alien to the swarm. The swarmbots lacked conscious ideation in any human sense. That was not to say that they were unsophisticated or lacking in complexity. They were a eusocial—hive—organism, divided into specialized castes of worker and warrior, much like a colony of ants or bees. But they were not of recognizable biological descent: their origins were lost in the depths of cosmological time, somewhere millions or even billions of jaunts away through the manifold of parallel universes. Whether they were a designed thing, or had somehow evolved in inconceivably alien circumstances on a world where nuclide-based DNA and RNA replicators had lost the race against organometalloid compounds, was now unknowable. But the hives existed. The hives were not limited by the constraints of carbon-based metabolism powered by sunlight: the hives burned hot and bright and dismantled entire planets, using their bones to build the black holes that opened the gateways they used to travel between time lines and star systems.

At some point in the distant past, the hives had arrived in Earth's solar system, and subsequently encountered humanity: lumpen hairless primates with their feet in the mud and their eyes on the stars. By a bizarre irony of path-dependent research, the civilization they first encountered—or bore the memory imprints of meeting, for they may have met and consumed many earlier hominid societies—had developed their own mechanisms for moving between time lines without gates. The human Forerunner empire was heir to primate consciousness and social behavior, and all the messy squabbles and inefficiencies that handicapped their ability to flourish in an essentially uncaring cosmos. Limited to just the one world and a limited environmental range, the Forerunners nevertheless iterated and prospered on a myriad versions of that planet. And at some point, centuries or millennia into their expansion, the Forerunners miniaturized their world-walking machinery and engineered it into their bodies, giving it the ability to self-replicate so that their infants were born with it. Like a new sub-cellular organelle, the jaunt nodes proliferated and replicated and their carriers flourished, threatening to become as indispensable as the mitochondria that had allowed humanity's first unicellular ancestors to exploit an oxygen-based metabolic cycle. The Forerunner civilization expanded across millions of parallel Earths, reaching heights of wealth and sophistication that neither the contemporary Commonwealth or United States could imagine.

They threatened the hives.

But the hives had ways of dealing with threats.

Off the Rails

Olga first learned of the developing emergency the next morning. She'd stayed in visiting officers' quarters overnight at Maracaibo: the courier jet she'd been flown in on was undergoing maintenance in preparation for its return to New London. After a brief evening call to Miriam's office (to send word of the successful launch, and to reassure Brilliana that her husband was safe and in one piece), she retired early.

The next morning she rose shamefully late and ate a light breakfast in her room. Then she summoned Jack to take her to the base administrative complex. Anders would have been up for a couple of hours now, and she wanted an update on Juggernaut before catching her flight north.

It had just turned eleven o'clock when she wheeled in the front door. She realized that something was wrong immediately. The lobby was half-filled by a posse of officers swarming around the base CO, buzzing like hornets whose nest that had been hit with a stick. Anders was talking on the handset of a bulky military cellular data link, a brief-case sized radio-phone carried by a communications officer. He paused and glanced at her: "ah, Director, I was on my way to see you." He looked tense.

"Has something happened to Juggernaut?" She demanded.

Anders shook his head and held the handset tighter. "Keep me informed," he said curtly, then handed it back to its owner. He turned eyes that suddenly seemed a decade older on Olga. "Juggernaut is fine. Ma'am, I think we should talk in private."

"What's happening?"

"Ears-only," Anders grunted. Then, in a move that chilled Olga to the core, he released the catch on his holster. "Follow me," he said, marching past the front desk, deep into the maze of security offices.

Behind her, Olga felt her bodyguard Jack go alert. "Did you see that, boss?"

"Yes. Let's do as the nice man says." Olga slipped her right hand under her rug and touched the pistol sandwiched between the seat cushion and the side-panel of her wheelchair. The MS attack she was recovering from had left her feeling particularly drained, and she doubted she had the strength to aim it accurately. Anders had turned his back on her, clearly not seeing her as a threat. But *something* had put him badly on edge and stirred up his staff. As Jack wheeled her along in his wake, she saw the General pause repeatedly to issue orders that sent his staff off in all directions. From the way they made haste—and the two guards she spotted, submachine guns shouldered, suddenly go alert for threats—something *really* bad had happened.

General Anders swept through areas where the usual mundane bustle of administrative business had been replaced by a febrile tension. There was a quiet undercurrent of whispered conversations, and Olga noticed furtive looks directed her way. Finally, after a whispered exchange with a messenger, Anders diverted into the admin block mess hall. "With me," he told her, then made eye contact with Jack. "It's on the TV."

Someone (possibly the Rec Office, possibly a MiniProp liaison) had set up a big projection screen television at the front of the commissary. It had been showing the broadcast of the funeral parade to a largely deserted room—most people at Fort Maracaibo were working to support Juggernaut's overflight, rather than watching the elaborate political opera unfolding in the capital thousands of miles away—when the shooting started in the capital.

Word had spread rapidly, and the duty officer hit the panic button. Around the time Olga had set out to see the General, Fort Maracaibo had locked down. The DPR troops assigned to guard the base had been issued live ammunition, then drove out to their defensive positions around the perimeter. The screen in the deserted commissary was frozen on a test card, martial music playing over the speakers as subtitles promised further information on the situation shortly.

Tired and, tense, Olga glanced at the screen then glared at the general. She had a sick sense of apprehension that everything was in danger of falling apart, just at the moment of the department's greatest triumph. "What," she demanded, "is going on?"

"Damn. We're too late, they've cut the broadcast. My office," Anders said, and turned on his heel.

Olga and Jack followed the General into his outer office. A rack of bulky scramblers, teleconferencing equipment and cameras—all home-built in the Commonwealth, decades behind the tech embodied by a cheap American fatphone, but far less prone to being rooted by enemies of the state—covered one wall. A group of officers waited around the table. "Paolo, brief us," Anders said crisply. "What's happening?"

Paolo Martini, the base intel officer, kept his face as immobile as a competition poker player. "Sir, ma'am, the Commonwealth Guard have held a coup d'état in the capital. They've formed a junta—they call themselves the Revolutionary Defense Committee—and have taken over MiniProp and all the TV and radio channels. They've arrested a bunch of Party Commissioners—taken them into protective custody for their own safety, by their account. They've got at least six Ministers in the bag, although they didn't show us all of them in their broadcast. They've taken over the main telephone switches but we still have teletype traffic, and the defense communications network is intact so far. Most recently, the rebel junta announced that they've declared martial law and imposed a curfew in New York. They're calling for calm. They're also denouncing elements of the army for shooting at Guard formations in the capital, accusing them of mutiny. One of the Commissioners they've arrested is Mrs. Burgeson. They're accusing MITI, and by implication her, of attempting to organize a coup of their own, to restore the monarchy." He looked directly at Olga. "Sorry to be the bearer of bad news, ma'am," he finished, with masterful understatement.

Anders swore under his breath, just loudly enough that Olga heard him. "Anyone else have any updates for me?" Hands went up. "Warren—" Anders' executive assistant—"are our guards still loyal? What action have you taken?"

"Sir! In accordance with standing orders I've brought the base to war state two and ordered full lockdown. Colonel MacAndrews' people are taking up their positions—they should be in place now. He's got the Commonwealth Guard barracks on base surrounded. We outnumber them substantially and as long as there are no infiltrators we should be secure."

"Further afield? What are conditions like in Maracaibo City?"

"Can't tell, sir. I was waiting for your instructions before contacting

Regional Defense Command. They haven't initiated contact with us. Everyone seems to be sitting tight and awaiting developments. There's nothing anyone down here can do to influence events in the capital, after all."

"Really." Olga cleared her throat and glanced at Anders. "What about Juggernaut?"

Anders looked at his watch and cleared his throat. "The funeral parade overflight actually went off without a hitch, ma'am, but nobody was watching because a bunch of *traitors* stormed the reviewing stand with small arms—anyway, Juggernaut won't be overhead again for a little over twenty-four hours."

"Is there no way to get them back faster?"

Anders was shaking his head. "Orbital mechanics, ma'am. They can't maneuver without jaunting to an unoccupied time line. It takes time to set up a maneuvering shot, and after that they've got to check for damage to the vehicle before they do anything. We're lucky it's not two to three days: orbital maneuvering is much slower than people imagine. As it is they're over Siberia right now, setting up to overfly St. Petersburg tomorrow morning—their time, a bit after midnight here tonight. We can't get them back without cancelling that part of the op, which I thought was a priority?"

Olga sighed. *Crap.* He was right: keeping the Empire from meddling was even more important now than it had been previously. But there *was* a coup. And the plotters had valuable hostages in the shape of Miriam and Erasmus. Maybe they genuinely believed Miriam was leading a secret cabal of monarchists. Or perhaps it was just a cynical power-play. But either way, as a loyal agent of the state—the irony would have given her some bitter amusement, if it had been any kind of laughing matter—her duty was pretty clear. First, ensure that General Anders was loyal (and if not, remove him from control). Next, brief Huw on the crisis and update his orders—

Crap. He'll shit a brick, she realized.

His wife and daughter were in the capital. They would have been attending the funeral parade. Brilliana was no push-over, even though her days of cleaning up messes for the head of the Clan's internal security force were long past. But if the plotters had captured or killed her—or worse, if they were stupid enough to use her and Nel as hostages against Huw— well, Huw commanded the largest single stockpile of nuclear devices in the Commonwealth arsenal. And he had autonomous release authority, because without it Juggernaut couldn't function.

Her stomach-churning moment of introspection was interrupted by a buzz of conversation, then a low-pitched call: "Sir? Front gate reports there's a visitor asking for you." The comms specialist appeared worried.

"Who is it? We're on total lock-down. Why are they even talking?" Anders barely kept his tone civil.

"The gatehouse say it's Overcaptain Berman from the Commonwealth Guard station in Maracaibo. He's, uh, he's demanding we open the front gate—"

"Well, we can't have that, can we?" Anders said with frightening geniality. He cracked his knuckles. "I think an example of what we do to mutineers is in order—"

Olga spoke up. "I'd like to have a word with Overcaptain Berman, if you can arrange it."

Anders paused. "Is that strictly necessary?" He asked, with an expression that suggested he'd much rather have the man shot.

"Yes it is." Olga took a deep breath. "We need to find out how deep this conspiracy goes. Right now all we've got to go on is what they're broadcasting, which reflects what they *want* us to believe. We need to know the real situation—who they've got, or claim to have, and what they want—before we decide what to do. And I'm afraid that, as the ranking civil authority here . . ."

"Understood." Anders nodded curtly. "Warren? Get Miss Thorold a close protection detail and transport. Send her—no, I'll come down with her myself." He looked across the table. "You're absolutely right: we need to get to the bottom of this before we point Juggernaut at them and pull the trigger."

BERLIN, TIME LINE TWO, AUGUST 2020

The sky above nighttime Berlin was dark, the deliberately-dim German street lights failing to reflect off the streaks of cloud high overhead. Elizabeth Hanover nodded sleepily in the armchair beside her unused bed, exhausted by a long and confusing day. She drowsed over a magazine that she'd bought, fascinated by the glossy hyperreal models on the cover. The photoshop wizardry of the photographers was a window onto another, even more alien reality. She was unable to tease much sense of out the articles inside. It wasn't that her German was inadequate: rather, the unstated assumptions about the women who presumably made up the magazine's paying audience were so bizarre that she found them fantastical. A woman had been Chancellor of this German Federation? There was a pan-European Union that didn't include Russia and lacked a crowned head to keep it in line? And while the politics was weird, it couldn't hold a candle to the domestic advice. One writer supplied tips for saving a failing marriage, as if divorce was easy and commonplace. Another piece offered helpful suggestions for mothers raising children while working, purportedly written by a woman who was an *engineer*—

It was all too much so she'd nodded off after a while. When she jolted awake, it was in response to her phone's angry insectile buzz. (She'd found it fully charged when she returned to her room, so switched it on again.) She picked it up. "Yes?"

"Elizabeth Hanover?" It was a strange woman. She spoke English with an oddly twangy accent. "Control gave me your number." *Number? What number?* "I'm in the lobby bar. Can you meet me there?"

"Meet—" Liz paused, trying to clear the cobwebs from her head. "Who are you?"

"No names over the phone. Meet me downstairs in the bar area in ten minutes and we can talk face to face. My hair is blue right now."

"Wait! Where's the Major—" The phone went dead, reverting to its twilight life as a rather dull vanity mirror. She used a word that would have shocked her ladies-in-waiting then cast around for her possessions. Jacket, handbag, boots, phone. She regretfully tucked her mirrored spectacles in a pocket of the bag. The denial of eye contact was an effect she enjoyed, but night had fallen and the lighting in the hotel was dim. She considered the Major's gun for a few seconds. She'd spent half an hour examining it when she got back, and was pretty certain she'd identified the safety mechanisms. She'd successfully removed the magazine—it held a ridiculous number of surprisingly tiny cartridges—cycled it, reloaded, and chambered a round without blowing a hole in the hotel wall. But she didn't relish using it, regardless of the pros and cons of shooting people while on the run in a foreign country. The only good thing about it, she supposed, was that whoever she was dealing with (both Control's minions and the enemy who had taken the Major) didn't know she had it.

She carefully safed the Five-seveN and slid it into the back of her trousers, made sure nothing was fouling the trigger, then slung the bag across her shoulder and slipped out of the bedroom.

The woman who said she was from Control might be watching the elevators, so Liz took the stairs instead. They were stark and uncarpeted and descended steeply. She left the emergency staircase at the mezzanine level, then cautiously inspected the lobby area over the edge of the balcony. There were no obvious sign of surveillance, no bodies in uniforms waiting to snatch her—but that meant nothing. It belatedly occurred to Liz that she ought to have called Control to confirm this contact. But if someone who *wasn't* one of the Major's people knew which hotel she was staying in, the game was already over. After a minute's indecision she strolled down the main staircase, chin up and shoulders back, with her right hand buried in her handbag as if fumbling for a lost lipstick.

The hotel lobby was nearly deserted this late in a weekday evening. Besides the two women on the reception desk, there were a handful of late-night barflies and a single bartender. The customers were mostly men in early middle-age, carrying the world-weary air of business travelers away from home. There were a couple of women: Liz wondered if they were prostitutes, then recalled how different fashion was in this place and gave a mental shrug. None of them looked like police, much less spies—

Her bag vibrated. She twitched in spite of herself. A moment later a woman with spiky blue hair looked at her and inclined her head in a fractional nod. Elizabeth's pulse sped up. She moved her hand behind her back nervously as the woman slid off a bar stool and headed towards the glass doors at the front of the hotel without glancing back. She wore a thin top with a scooped neckline, and the kind of mannish blue trousers that seemed to be ubiquitous here. She'd turned her back on Liz deliberately, making it clear she wasn't carrying a concealed weapon. Liz took a deep breath and slowly followed her contact, heart hammering.

People who smoked had to do so outside, apparently by law. Liz found Blue-Hair loitering in the smoking area, holding a silver-chased glass tube to her lips as she faced the street. It had rained earlier in the evening, and moving displays and blinking lights flickered in the water pooling in the gutters. They cast reflections, so that her contact's face matched her hair, jagged blue shadows and stripes criss-crossing her raised eyebrows.

"You must be Liz. Kurt was right: you look enough like Rita to be her sister. Fancy that. Here, take this." Blue-Hair offered her a white tube with a brown base that looked like a plastic toy cigarette. "You don't need to use it, just hold it like you're a smoker. Nobody will look twice." The woman yawned, which Liz found oddly annoying. Was she that unremarkable?

Liz held the artificial cigarette awkwardly in her left hand, keeping the handbag looped over her forearm and her right hand free to reach for her pistol. "Who's Rita?" She asked. Then she thought to add, "who are you?"

"You can call me Angie." She shrugged. "It's my real name. The way things work in this time line, there's no point trying to lie about your metadata to the authorities. It just attracts their attention. Anyway, you're not going to go to them."

Liz frowned, trying to understand. Angie was a little older than she was, built along functional rather than ladylike lines: one of the *working women* the magazine's authors had in mind with their lifestyle lectures. There was something disarmingly artless about her.

"Sprechen sie Deutsch?" Angie asked after an awkward moment's silence.

"A little." Liz considered her next words carefully. "Why?"

"In a minute we're going to finish vaping and share a joke for the cameras. Then we're going to turn left and walk across the next street crossing before turning left along the sidewalk. There's a bus stop there, and I have a ticket for you: in return, I need to take the keycard from your hotel room. I hope you brought everything you need, because you can't go back there."

"Why? What *exactly* is happening?" Liz stared until Angie looked right back at her, evidently perplexed.

"Your first contact was captured, so Mission Control asked my boss— the head of my group—to fly out here and rescue you." A telling pause. "Is that right? Is that what you're expecting?"

"Mostly. Tell me about these cameras. Why isn't it safe to stay here?"

Angie seemed to do a double-take. "You're *really* not from around here, are you? Huh, that's right . . . there are cameras *everywhere* in this time line, sweetie. Uh, television cameras? You know about television? Every shop, every hotel lobby, every sidewalk street corner. They're normally monitored by machines, but . . . you've got a phone, haven't you?"

"Yes, it was the Major's—"

Angie slowly reached into her clutch and pulled out a similar-looking magic mirror. "Once we start walking you're going to drop it down the first storm drain we come to. You've been carrying it for *way* too long, which means they're probably homing in on you by now. I brought you a replacement."

"They can *track* them?" Elizabeth only realized her voice was rising when Angie winced briefly.

"Let's walk, sweetie. Look, there." She pointed at the gutter.

Damn. Elizabeth realized she had a choice: let go of the grip of the Major's gun and ditch the phone, or make a song-and-dance routine out of rummaging two-handed in her bag. *Can I trust this woman?* she wondered. "One more question," Liz insisted. "What's in this for you? Why are you doing this?"

"What's in it for *me*?" Angie stared at her side-long. "Why do you even want to know?"

"Because." Liz shoved the e-cig into her bag decisively. "I've been doing some thinking. If you're just a mercenary I'd like to know."

"*Just* a mercenary?" Another impenetrable, opaque glance. "I'm here because my best friend's grandfather asked me for help. Rita—my friend—is impersonating you on television in the, the Commonwealth place, putting her ass on the line. The sooner you can take over and do that shit *yourself* the sooner she can quit being a target for assassins. That's for starters. And there's the other thing. (Turn left at the corner ahead.) You're trying to defect to the Commonwealth, aren't you?"

Liz nodded. The unfamiliar word, *defect*, she understood by context.

"Well, so are we. I mean me, my friend Rita, and a bunch of our relatives. We're from this world, from a country that no longer exists. If we can get to the Commonwealth safely, they'll take us in—as long as we get *you* to the Commonwealth safely. *Now* are you going to ditch that phone before it leads the bad guys to us, or do you have any more questions?"

Liz let go of the gun. She offered Angie the Major's phone. "Take it," she said before she could change her mind. Her companion bent forward as if to tie a bootlace. When she rose the phone was no longer in her hand. Liz added, "why do you want to defect to the Commonwealth?"

To her surprise, Angie laughed: a full-throated chuckle. "Oh girl, you ask the craziest questions! It's a long story and it all started before I was even born. The way I first heard it, I was four years old and my parents disguised the way the world worked as a fairy tale—except it was all true, in a manner of speaking. You see, once upon a time there was a magic kingdom, which had been conquered by an ogre. And the ogre was un-pleasant and bad-tempered and suspicious, and from time to time he ate people, but . . ."

NEW LONDON, MANHATTAN ISLAND, TIME LINE THREE, AUGUST 2020

General Minsky, leader of the Commonwealth Guards' task force defend-ing the revolution against treason, had established his headquarters in a former Imperial Constabulary barracks in the County of Queens, just across the water from the palaces of New London.

The first stages of the operation had gone smoothly and according to plan. The regular armed forces were busy with the pomp and ceremony of the First Man's interment. The endless triumphal procession of soldiers and tanks might have been problematic had they been issued with am-munition, but in the event they were toothless. Only a few military po-lice had been equipped to shoot back—and they mostly didn't. The Party leadership had helped things by congregating in one place, making them easy to round up. The ministries of state were under-staffed or closed for the public holiday. And so the reports reaching Minsky's desk were uniformly positive—at least until he received an update from the leader of the team responsible for the Ministry of Propaganda. It came by way of a harried-looking captain. And it was his first inkling that the plan was going off the rails.

"They're broadcasting *what?*" Minsky demanded incredulously.

"Sir, it's, uh, I've seen film of it. The take-off, I mean. They say it's real. And we're—"

"Sir?" An adjutant leaned across his desk anxiously. "It's the foreign min-istry, I've got Colonel Saunders on the line, he says it's extremely urgent, the French are screaming—"

"Put him on," Minsky grated. "Minsky. Report."

"Sir, the embassy in St. Petersburg says the ambassador has just returned from an audience with Le Roi, who is *really* upset. The French Emperor is accusing us of kidnapping the Pretender's daughter—yes, the Pretender-Princess Hanover—"

"Sir?" It was the other line, the one from the propaganda ministry. "About the space battleship, what *is* our position on extraterrestrial—"

Minsky took a deep breath. "Colonel, we have not—to the best of my knowledge—kidnapped any princesses. Tell the ambassador to await instructions, and that the new First Man will deal with it." He hung up. To the adjutant with the report from propaganda, peevishly: "*what* space battleship?"

"The one MITI announced this morning? It overflew the First Man's funeral parade!"

"*Battleship?*" Minsky glared. "Dammit, is this another of their artificial satellites? What did they do, mount an atom bomb on it?"

"Sir, I'm afraid it's a bit bigger than that." The captain frowned. "It's atomic-*powered*. Crew of forty, including world-walkers, and it carries several thousand petards. They say it's for peaceful exploration of other parallel worlds, but apparently it's got enough range to fly to Mars and back and enough corpses in its magazines to turn Europe into a radioactive desert. Explorer-General Hjorth is in personal command aboard this, uh, Juggernaut."

Minsky's face froze. "You're telling me MITI have a *battleship*? And nuclear weapons?"

"Sir, that's what I've been trying—yes sir. It came out of nowhere, they've kept it under incredibly tight secrecy! It only launched into orbit yesterday, apparently just for the funeral. A *surprise*."

Another phone began ringing, and another. The communications men on the tables lining the opposite wall were unable to answer them fast enough. It was a bad sign. The switchboard had been treading water handily for the first few hours. The team leaders in the field had their orders and knew what they were supposed to be doing: if things were proceeding to plan there was no need to call HQ for orders.

"Get me Police-Brigadier Richards," Minsky ordered. "Jefferson?"

His XO straightened. "Sir?"

"You're in charge the phones while I sort this out." Muttered: "Space battleships my *ass*." Busy in briefing rooms all morning and afternoon Minsky hadn't witnessed the overflight of the parade.

"Sir." Jefferson walked across to the switchboard operators. Seconds later, all but one of the phones on Minsky's desk stopped ringing. *That* handset he lifted.

"Minsky here—hello, Gary. Do you have the Burgesons in custody? Good. Listen, I want you to get to the bottom of this business about MITI having some sort of secret magic space weapon. Find out if it's true or is it just some sort of moonshine from MiniProp to make them look good? Also, the restoration plot, I've got tangential confirmation from the Foreign Office that the French are extremely upset. They've lost track of Elizabeth Hanover, the young Pretender. I want everything, and I mean *everything*, you can dig out of the Burgesons. Names, dates, how they were planning to organize the royal restoration, who's in on the conspiracy. Yes, you got it. Good! Dismissed."

Minsky hung up. Then a thought struck him. "Captain? Get me the Party Secretariat on the line. I need to talk to Mr. Holmes."

He glared at the pile of message slips on his blotter, and the humming beige computer terminal behind them. "Space battleships," he snorted quietly. "Pull the other leg, it's got bells on."

TEMPELHOF AIR FORCE BASE, BERLIN, TIME LINE TWO, AUGUST 2020

Hulius told the Colonel everything he wanted to know. It was not enough. Nothing would ever be enough: but Hulius's accounting was particularly deficient, because it turned out that Hulius didn't know very much at all. "If I knew anything useful to you I wouldn't be in the field, would I?" He pointed out. "I'm a glorified gopher, Colonel. I've got just the one magic trick that makes me useful to my managers." He took time out to breathe. Running on one lung made lengthy speeches difficult. "Well, I have a few minor skills. Stuff I picked up along the way. I have a private pilot's license, I've led small infantry units, I'm up to date on my firearms proficiency. I speak four languages fluently. But if I could tell you what you want to know, I'd be confined to an office, reading reports and attending meetings, wouldn't I?" He tried to grin mockingly, but it came out wrong.

Smith was imperturbable. "Well. Let's go over it one more time, shall we? Let's see if anything jogs loose."

And so they spent another hour going over everything Hulius could think of about Elizabeth Hanover, whose background and habits Smith seemed to find bewilderingly alien. *He clearly doesn't have teenage daughters*, Hulius told himself. *And he can't be an uncle either*. Hulius tried to leave daughter-wrangling to Ellie as much as he could, but even so, he knew more than a bit about how teenagers could act out or manipulate their elders. It came to Hulius that in his own way, Smith was another casualty of the para-time Cold War. He'd sacrificed his personal life to a higher cause, and it had crippled him socially. Long hours led to alienation and divorce, which in turn brought more long hours, a rising workload, and . . . well, it wasn't Hulius's job to criticize his enemy's work/life balance.

Eventually a nurse made it clear to Smith that he was exhausting the patient, and the lack of new insights finally convinced him to leave. Hulius lay back and stared at the ceiling. There was some sort of deep game in progress here, but he was damned if he could figure out the parameters. Smith was as much a pawn as anyone else, that much was clear. But for Hulius, the current round was over.

At some point he fell into a light sleep. When he awakened, his bed was vibrating. In fact it was moving, the ceiling unrolling before his uncomprehending eyes like a blurry vertical-scroller game of yesteryear. "Wha'?"

"We're transferring you to a different room," the porter told him from behind his head. (His English was German-accented.) "You are off the endangered species list for now." (His sense of humor was anything but.) "Not far to go."

The bed slowed, then entered an elevator which crawled slowly between floors. Going *up*. Which was bad news for Yul. (Someone obviously knew about world-walkers: If he tried to jaunt from a high floor it would end messily.) An infusion bag wobbled on a stand alongside him, like an amorous jellyfish fondling his wrist with a stinger-tipped tendril. *What* are *they pumping into me?* He wondered. The tip of his nose itched, something pinching it: a chilly breeze of oxygen tickled his mustache.

The porters finally parked him in a hospital room with a window that didn't open and a view of anonymous offices—or perhaps more hospital buildings—across a ground level park far below. Because of the drains in his chest and his half-collapsed lung, his nurses had elevated the head of the bed. Hulius was zoning out on a combination of fatigue and happy juice when the door opened and someone sat down beside him. "Yul?"

A woman's voice. One he knew. "Uh." *It's her.* "I thought I was hallucinating you. Earlier, in the safe house."

"Nobody would blame you if you were." She reached over and took his free hand, an intimacy which startled him into crystal-sharp focus for a few seconds. "You were a mess. I thought we were going to lose you."

Her voice was uneven, as if suppressing some emotion. "Why are you here, Paulette?" He asked, as gently as he could.

"I think Smith wants to keep all his eggs in one basket, at least until he's collected the extra-special one. Heaven only knows what he'll do with us once he's got the girl. Anyway, they moved me to the room next door. We're on a hospital ward, but there are guards. I think we're on a military base."

She still held his hand. Hulius closed his eyes, trying to order his jumbled thoughts. Their relationship, reversed: he'd been her controller for years, the go-between intercalated between her lonely mission to the United States and his superiors in the Commonwealth. Agents often imprinted on their controllers, becoming emotionally dependent on the rare contact that affirmed their sense that what they were doing was valuable. Here and now, he was as much a helpless prisoner as she. More so if anything, thanks to his injury. "Thank you," he said. "What did Smith tell you?"

"I believe he's going to use us to send a message. As the carrot, not the stick, I think. I *hope*."

Hulius opened his eyes. "Don't hope. Hope leads to disappointment. The room's certainly wired," he added. "They'll use anything we say against us. You know."

"I know, but I just don't care anymore." She shrugged. "They had me in jail, Yul. I was there for weeks. They could send me back there for the rest of my fucking *life*. I'd rather die."

"Not going to happen." He squeezed her hand briefly then let go. "Help me sit up more?"

"What did he want from you?" She asked as the motorized bed whined, its back creeping higher.

"Stuff I couldn't tell him because I don't know it. Insights. Where Liz will go."

"Liz—"

"Princess Hanover. Heir to the throne."

"The girl." Paulette reached behind him, adjusting pillows to stop them sliding down. "She's the heir to the New British *throne?*"

"Yes."

"What the fuck?" She was silent for a few seconds. "Well, at least that explains the chess message."

"Chess message?"

"Smith said he was going to release me into your custody, and you were going to take me back to the Commonwealth. I was to give Miriam a message—pawn takes queen." She chuckled shakily. "Guess someone up-ended the chess board."

"I hope so. Why do you think the US government want the heir to the New British Empire?"

"Because . . . oh hell, it means they're meddling in Commonwealth politics now, doesn't it? Which means they must have made contact with the Commonwealth already, through back-channels. They must have enough context to know what her presence means, mustn't they?"

"Guess so." Hulius shut up. Best not to speculate aloud in front of the Colonel's microphones. If he'd carried on, he might have observed that some DHS insider obviously knew more about what was going on in the Commonwealth than the Colonel himself. But saying that aloud might be a fatal move. *They can dangle us in front of Miriam as a lure, but they won't let us go unless they think releasing us will damage her.*

NEW LONDON, MANHATTAN ISLAND, TIME LINE THREE, AUGUST 2020

Miriam was dragged off the podium, roughly searched, then shoved into the back of a covered truck, along with a bunch of politicians ranging in rank from members of the inner cabinet down to their personal assistants. She could count herself lucky: there had been casualties, but neither she nor Erasmus were among them. The Commissioner for Coal, Oil and Gas Extraction had died, apparently of a heart attack. A Secretary to the Justice Commission was shot and bled to death on the stand (a stray round, according to their captors). Several others were beaten by the Commonwealth Guards in the process of their arrest. Their captors had threatened them with bloodthirsty collective punishment if anyone tried to escape—a threat that Miriam took seriously enough that she dared not jaunt to safety and leave Erasmus behind. Then the trucks drove for half an hour at breakneck speed (quite possibly in circles, it was impossible to tell), before backing onto a loading bay. Here the VIPs were ushered out at rifle point and relieved of their shoes, belts, and wallets. Then they were herded into a second-floor barracks room.

The barracks, built to hold a couple of platoons, was overcrowded, sweltering, and airless. The windows were boarded over and the lockers had been removed, although the bunk beds remained—without sheets, pillows, or mattresses. The toilets lacked cubicle doors and toilet seats, never mind sanitary supplies. There was a single water barrel with a tin mug chained to it, and the level was dropping rapidly. The guards had crammed nearly a hundred dignitaries into a building built for sixty: they were sitting on bunks and lying in corners, doubled up and sharing a couple of stinking toilets. Ominously, the coup organizers didn't appear to have made arrangements for holding prisoners for any length of time.

There was no food.

By early evening, the air stank of the fear-sweat of middle-aged men. Most sat on the wooden slats of the lower bunks. Several paced, some lay and groaned. A couple sprawled face-down and were ominously silent. One of the toilets was blocked and had backed up, adding a special miasma to one end of the room. But most of the prisoners clustered near it, because it was the farthest point from the entrance. From time to time the blank wooden door sprang open and hard-faced men with guns barked harsh summonses. If they weren't answered immediately a snatch squad would rush in and beatings would ensue. Those they called forward went through the door on their feet or on their backs—and whichever way they went, they didn't came back.

At least there were no abrupt volleys of gunfire. If the departed were being marched to their deaths, then their captors were doing it furtively, as if from a sense of guilt or shame.

At around nine o'clock Miriam Burgeson was sitting on the edge of a wooden bunk, next to her husband. After the first adrenalin-shock of fear and indignation had passed, they and the other prisoners had spent the first hours pacing and speculating, making plans and rehashing them. But boredom and apprehension—and a total lack of information to work with—had taken their toll on aged bodies. For the past hour, they'd mostly fallen silent. Over in the far corner, Cornell Irving was loudly mumbling a laundry-list of administrative housekeeping chores he intended to apply to the Census Bureau on his release. He was apparently in total denial of their situation, halfway to a breakdown, but Miriam was disinclined to interrupt him. Erasmus sat hunched beside her, his hands clasped, patiently waiting. "How can you be so calm?" She'd asked him. "Because they'll get to us when they're ready," he'd replied. "And I don't want to show them fear. Or be nervous. It only encourages worse behavior."

(Erasmus had spent years in the Imperial labor camps in decades past, then more years on the run and working undercover as a revolutionary quartermaster. It dwarfed her own experiences of captivity, however unpleasant they'd been. Three months mewed up in a baron's castle, a year in a revolutionary labor camp: Erasmus had a postgraduate degree in imprisonment to set beside her mere diploma.)

"It isn't the same," she'd said, then stopped when he took her right hand and gently stroked her wrist, not speaking or making eye contact. She bit her lip. After all these years together, she was pretty good at reading his mind, and what she could see in it now broke her heart. During a coup, they could have no expectation of due process. They were merely being held until their utility as hostages came to an end, at which time they could be disposed of safely. That she, personally, could escape was . . . well, it was an option. She was a world-walker, after all. They were on the second floor of the building. The drop would hurt, she might break a leg, but she'd be free. But if she fled, she'd have to leave Erasmus. Moreover, the coup plotters would interpret it as confession of guilt. It would not only mean deserting her husband: it would be a betrayal of every principle she held, of everything she'd tried to build over two decades. So she stayed and waited for the end of the world, sitting knee-to-knee with Erasmus while he held her hand.

"They won't come to shoot us until they're sure they've won," he reassured her, "and should the worst happen, I trust you will do your best. Escape, survive, witness, persist." She was about to remonstrate with him, but the door opened and three guards stepped inside, bayonets mounted and assault rifles at the ready.

"Burgeson and Burgeson!" Barked the squad leader, looking directly at them. He held his gun at waist height, shoulders tense, as if wishing for an excuse to shoot. "Over here! Move it!"

Miriam pushed herself to her feet. Beside her, Erasmus rose creakily: she heard a joint click loudly. "Where are we going?" She called.

"Over here! Move it!" The snatch squad leader glared at Miriam with angry narrowed eyes: she recognized the face of a man who wanted someone to hate. He was burning with a mixture of fear and resentment, jacked up on the thrill of the biggest day of his life. His expression put her in mind of fuming nitric acid in a glass bottle balanced on a table's edge, waiting for a bump on the opposite corner. She bit back a sharp retort for Erasmus' sake. She walked gingerly towards the door. Erasmus shuffled behind, then started coughing—the terrible hacking coughs he'd never quite thrown off, a legacy of tubercular lung-scarring from the labor camps.

Outside the door, an escort of Revolutionary Guards waited for them with handcuffs, a quite unnecessary humiliation. (What were two un-armed, middle-aged commissioners going to do to them? Club six burly soldiers unconscious with their own rifles? Make an intrepid escape from a locked-down base guarded by tanks and machine guns?)

They were led downstairs and out round the back of the barracks, then onto a paved square. A staff car, and blindfolds, awaited them.

"No blindfolds, please—" Miriam couldn't hold back: terrified apprehension forced it out of her mouth.

One of the younger guards who took mercy on her: "The Brigadier wants to talk. Our orders are that you're not to see where we're taking you." She went limp, allowing him to blindfold her and steer her into the back of the car. Even if it was a white lie, she badly wanted to believe him—*they won't shoot us until they're sure they've won*, she reminded herself over and over again, a despairing mantra.

She could feel Erasmus next to her through the frame of the seat. He didn't say anything, but he seemed to be shivering. *It's worse for the men.* He'd been raised to provide for and protect his families—both his first wife, who'd died in the camps, and now her. Blindfolded and cuffed, he'd be feeling doubly helpless right now. *But I've been here before. And I survived.* She'd survived seeing a lover shot to death in front of her. Survived a massacre at a wedding feast. Survived assassination attempts and revolution and war. *It's not over until it's over.*

NEW LONDON, MANHATTAN ISLAND, TIME LINES ONE AND THREE, AUGUST 2020

Nel's face puckered after the abortive jaunt. Rita was half afraid she was going to cry or pick a fight. But then she realized the younger woman was thinking furiously, eyes screwed shut. "I can world-walk, but I don't have a focus. You have a focus. Can I make a copy?" Nel opened her eyes and stared at Rita.

"A copy—" Rita suddenly realized she'd been absurdly obtuse. "Damn, if I had a pen and paper I could—"

"I do!" Nel produced a somewhat dog-eared notebook and a pencil from her clutch. "So can I copy the tattoo-thing off your wrist?"

"Yes, but don't look at it too closely and jaunt by accident while you're transcribing it. Or make a mistake and end up with an engram that takes you somewhere else entirely." There were drugs that could suppress jaunting—or world-walking, as the Clan descendants called it—but Rita didn't have any on her person. Nel looked at her skeptically. "I'm just worried it's dangerous," Rita said half-heartedly.

"Yes, but it's better than not trying at all. I'll only use it as a last resort, I promise!"

They found a fallen tree, and, after checking it for wildlife, they sat. Rita used her fingers to cover two-thirds of the design while Nel sketched the visible portion of the engram. After half an hour and a handful of false starts, they had a design that made Rita's vision blur and her head throb when she looked at it. It was clearly a working engram, and it wasn't obviously wrong, but she had a feeling something was missing.

Rita wiped her display and looked up. "Listen, I think this is a bad idea. I don't know if it's going to take you back home, and there's no safe way to test it. So we're back to square one. I need to go report to my boss. You can't go to your home . . . is there anywhere else in New London where you can go to ground? Any friends' houses you'd be welcome at? Anywhere you can hide for a day or two while the situation resolves itself, that isn't a government building?"

"There's always my old school—" Nel began.

Rita felt like kicking herself again. "I'm slow today. Where is it? How do you get there from home?"

"—It will be closed, because of the funeral, but it's only about two miles up-island. It's called St. James' College. On good days I used to bicycle there, but my father withdrew me last year when we moved south to live in Fort Maracaibo most of the time. But you can world-walk there, can't you?" Nel crossed her arms. "If we can get there without exposing ourselves, I know where to hide."

"Well then." Rita stood. "Let's get going."

It took more than two hours for them to locate Nel's school. First they sweated their way through undergrowth and across shallow streams. Then Rita unslung her tablet, launched the camcorder app, and jaunted—or tried to jaunt, where there were no buildings blocking her transfer. Each time she'd pivot swiftly in place, panning, and jaunt back immediately, like a submarine commander raising her periscope in dangerous waters. Stepping through the video clips frame by frame allowed them to spot warning signs—smoke rising over buildings, blurred glimpses of uniforms across the road—and more importantly, it enabled Nel to tell Rita when they were getting close. They'd walk another block, then Rita would jaunt and Nel would peer at the screen, frowning intently. Suddenly: "Stop! Yes, that building, right there! That's next door to the school, I recognize it."

"Okay . . ." Rita bit her lip. She flipped rapidly through video frames, looking for people. "We're in luck. No cops or soldiers here. Looks like everyone's indoors." Pulling up the video metadata she got a bearing on the sidewalk that ran alongside the school. "Right." She logged a waypoint on her inertial mapper and hunkered down. "All aboard."

"What are you going to do next?" Nel asked.

"I'm going to get you inside the school yard. Then once you're safe, I'm going to go report to my boss, then—I hope—come back again." Dr. Scranton would want to know all about the developing coup, Rita realized apprehensively. She felt a gut-deep sense of unease: anxious that her superiors meant Miriam ill, or that they held Rita herself in suspicion as a world-walker, that doing her job would somehow make everything worse. "Just wait for me. Can you do that?"

Nel nodded gravely. "But I can't wait long," she said. "I need to find my mother. She's out there—" for a moment she looked very young and scared. "We ought to find somewhere to leave a message for each other." She hugged Rita again, who stood up, grunting with effort under Nel's weight, and jaunted.

They were on a stretch of sidewalk shaded by elm trees. Brick walls rose to one side, punctuated by iron gates some distance away. A chapel or church, its doors shut, faced it from the other side of the road. Beyond it a pillar of smoke rose into a blue sky. The banshee howl of gyrodyne rotors reverberated in the middle distance, echoing through the stony canyons of the city. There was no thunder of artillery or crackle of small arms, to Rita's relief.

"Come on!" Nel slid down onto the sidewalk then tugged Rita's hand. She let the girl lead her towards the gates. "This is it," Nel said. "We need to be about ten feet over there." She pointed straight at the brick wall beside them.

"Right. Let's go." Rita grappled with Nel. She jaunted, lurched drunkenly past a couple of tree trunks, and jaunted again. Her knees gave way beneath their combined weight, but not before she registered that they had made it past the wall. Her shoulders and upper arms formed a chorus-line of dull-edged aches, warning her not to lift Nel again, *or else*. "Ouch. Are you all right?"

"Yes!" Nel shook her skirts out. "Perfect." She turned round, and Rita followed her gaze. "We're in the yard. Follow me." She marched towards an out-building round the side of what was clearly a school, albeit tiny compared to what Rita had been expecting. Rita paused to log another waypoint, then glanced round. The gates were chained shut, the buildings seemingly deserted. She followed Nel, then stopped dead as the younger woman marched up to a side door and hammered on it with her fist.

"What are you—"

"Seeing if the janitor's in. If he's away, you'll need to world-walk me inside."

Nope, Rita thought, *not doing that, not going there. Knees say nope.* Nel froze, then hammered again. As Rita drew breath she heard the click of a bolt being drawn back, and another far less welcome sound—the metallic crunch of a hammer being drawn back.

"Who's there?" A gruff voice demanded abruptly. "Who's that?"

"Mr. Stewart! It's Nel Hjorth! Mr. Stewart! Can I come in? I need to use the telephone. It's an emergency!" Nel spun in place and gestured urgently at Rita. Rita ducked to one side, then plastered her back against the wall below the skylight beside the door.

Mr. Stewart sounded a lot less aggressive the second time around. "Little Nel? I remember—didn't you be withdrawin' last year?"

"Yes, I was taken out of school, Mr. Stewart, but you see, it's an emergency, isn't it? I need to call my mother. I was caught out in the disturbance, I don't know what's going on—"

"It be another revolution, by the sounds of it." The door opened. "Ye'd better come on in quickly now." Rita held her breath, left wrist propped in front of her eyes, ready to jaunt at an instant's sign of danger.

"I have a friend," Nel said, facing the open doorway. "Can she come in too?"

"If ye'll vouch for her, aye, I suppose so." At last Rita heard the sound she'd been praying for: a soft click as Mr. Stewart carefully lowered the hammer on whatever engine of destruction he was holding. His voice faded as he called to someone inside the building: "Lissa! Lissa? We've got company!"

"Rita? Come inside."

Mr. Stewart, the janitor, and his wife, Lissa, the cook, were the only staff at the school today. They lived on the premises. Everyone else, staff and students, had been given the day off for the state funeral. The Stewarts, in their fifties, had lived through the revolution and civil unrest two decades previously. Hence the chained gates and the blunderbuss. Now they listened to the bellicose bulletins on their ancient radiogram. The endless loops of martial music were punctuated by increasingly strident announcements from some group calling themselves the Committee to Preserve the Commonwealth. The Committee insisted that everything was under control, that the counter-revolutionary elements had been arrested, that martial law was declared and a curfew in place. Periodic clattering and strobing buzz-saw noises suggested otherwise. Someone was trying to jam the national broadcast network, and had a transmitter with enough power to swamp the Committee's diatribes half the time.

Rita propped her tablet against the side of the radio during one of these bulletins so the voice recorder app could capture it for the Colonel. Meanwhile, Mrs. Stewart fussed over them, offering refreshments and wringing her hands because the telephone lines were all busy. Rita gratefully accepted a mug of tea and a plate of slightly stale cookies. She was exhausted from hours spent hiking through the forested reaches of time line one's lower Manhattan Island on a hot afternoon. Only her unease kept her alert. As long as she was learning something about the coup in progress, she could justify delaying her departure to report in by another few minutes—

"Miss Burgeson?" Rita blinked, then realized someone—Lissa Stewart— was addressing her. "Miss Burgeson?" She repeated, "Did you hear that?"

"Hear—" *Did I just doze off?* she wondered. "What—"

The radiogram was crackling, some kind of announcement about arrests and custody, traitors under arrest, the Party Commissioners for—

"Isn't that your parents?" Mrs. Stewart asked, peering worriedly at her face. "I'd have thought—"

"Wait." Rita stood up hastily, chair toppling backwards. Her pulse pounded in her ears. "I wasn't paying attention. What—"

"It was on again just now," Nel said, from the doorway. She'd gotten up while Rita was zoning out. "The Committee say they have half the People's Commissioners. They're calling your mother a traitor, and Mr. Burgeson an accomplice, even though he was the First Man's secretary during the first rising! Rita, what's happening?"

"I don't know." Rita picked up her tablet. "But I've got to go and tell somebody." *Dr. Scranton needs to know,* she rationalized. She was negotiating with Miriam. *My mother. If she's been arrested, this coup won't help the US government. Will it?* She wobbled on her feet, still struggling to come fully awake. "I need to get some fresh air," she said, feeling nauseous. She forced herself to smile at Mrs. Stewart. "Can I go outside for a minute?"

Mrs. Stewart wrung her hands. "Oh, I canna say as that's a good idea, sweetie, you'll be much safer indoors—"

"Don't worry." Rita tried hard to look reassuring. Lissa Stewart was short and dumpy, her greying hair doing its best to escape the headscarf she wore even indoors. Rita towered over her. "The gate's locked and there's a curfew. Nobody's on the streets. I'll just step around the back and everything will be fine, won't it?"

"But, but . . ."

"Let her," Nel urged. "She'll be back again soon enough, won't you Rita?" She gave her a significant look, then stepped aside to let her into the doorway.

"Yes, I will." Rita hurried along the short corridor that led to the sluice room by the back door. She took a deep breath and jaunted, then fell a foot to the grassy surface below. "Damn," she muttered to herself. The map overlay claimed she was somewhere around the location of West Houston Street in her America. Jaunting from here would probably fail—and a good thing too. The last thing she wanted was to come out in the middle of a busy New York street, or embedded in the wall of a building. (Not that the latter ever happened: some kind of exclusion principle blocked attempts to jaunt into another solid object.)

She was a quarter mile from Washington Square Park. However, if she jaunted into anywhere in Manhattan other than one of the pre-assigned safe transfer locations, the omnipresent networked security cameras would spot her arrival. They'd send SWAT teams and quadrotor drones screaming towards her within seconds. Ever since 7/16, the nightmare scenario for DHS had involved world-walkers jaunting into the heart of a major city with backpack nuclear weapons. However, with a curfew in place and a coup in progress, she had no way of getting to get across the Hudson or the East River. The designated transfer spots were out of reach. "I haven't thought this through," she muttered under her breath, then looked around guiltily. There were no witnesses: nothing but the insects of the new-growth forest, and the distant cries of birds.

She removed her tablet from her handbag again. Battery charge: 34%. "Damn," she muttered. She typed up a brief report on everything that had happened, including the announcement about Juggernaut and the subsequent coup, and flipped the tablet's wireless settings to 'on'. As soon as she crossed over, it would try and connect to the internet and send Dr. Scranton her email. How long would it take? How long *could* it take? She'd have to be fast to jaunt into a public park, have the good fortune not be shot at by a random beat cop, send her message, then jaunt out again before NYPD's finest arrived and did their best to turn her into a smear on the sidewalk.

She slid the tablet into her bag, consulted the mapper (battery charge: 51%), and began to make her way towards Washington Square with a dry mouth and a knot of fear in her guts. *I hope I'm doing the right thing.*

MARACAIBO COMMONWEALTH AIR BASE, TIME LINE THREE, AUGUST 2020

The main gate of Fort Maracaibo presented a forbidding face to the world. Set in a three-meter-high concrete perimeter wall topped with razor wire, its gun slits faced outward across a flat concrete apron. Inside, the gates opened onto a square surrounded by walls and guard towers on all sides. It was designed not merely to intimidate, but to meet invasion attempts with lethal force. As Fort Maracaibo took in shipments of nuclear weapons the way a supermarket absorbed freezer trucks, this was entirely appropriate.

Right now, an armored car in Commonwealth Guard colors waited before the gates, engine idling to keep the aircon running. It was alone: a single car, with no tanks or IFVs for backup. It didn't even have a roof-mounted machine gun. "Good, they're being sensible about this," Olga murmured.

"Ma'am?" General Anders leaned close. Jack shifted uneasily behind her wheelchair.

"They're obviously here to talk, not to fight." Olga paused. "It's your call, but I'd recommend hearing what they have to say."

Anders nodded. "See to it," he told the lieutenant in charge of the gate house. A lone guard left the base of the tower and walked across to the driver's window: words were exchanged, then the car's rear hatch swung down and a couple of Guard officers stepped out. A minute later, the guard room door opened again and a pair of soldiers led them inside.

Overcaptain Berman was a tall fellow with sunken cheeks and gold-rimmed spectacles. His manner was diffident, his pistol holster conspicuously empty. He reminded Olga of an academic librarian rather than an officer in the Commonwealth Guard's Special Counter-Espionage Police. "Ah, General Anders, sir?" He didn't salute, but he dipped his chin politely. Olga he ignored. "I have a message for you."

Anders stiffened. "Overcaptain Berman, may I introduce Miss Olga Thorold. Miss Thorold is the senior-most Party official on this installation. She's the Executive Director of Operations of the Department for Parahistorical Research. I believe any message your superiors have given you is a message for her, rather than for me."

Berman flushed. "I'm sorry, sir, but my orders are not for traitors to the—"

Anders didn't need to raise a hand: the troops behind Berman and his assistant grabbed him. Anders smiled. It was not a friendly expression.

"Let's get something straight," he said, keeping his tone conversational. "This base is operated by the Joint Commonwealth Military, which remains loyal to the government. I swore an oath, and my troops all swore an oath, to uphold the constitution, not any particular person—not even the First Man, were that post not currently vacant. We stand ready to honor our oath, and under the circumstances, I *really* wouldn't advise you to question anyone's loyalty. This base hosts a program operated jointly by the Air Force Space Command and the DPR, and *again*, Miss Thorold is the executive in overall command of it—and I believe she has *also* sworn an oath to uphold the constitution. The only traitors I am aware of are the ones who are attempting to overthrow our government right now, although I'm willing to hear you what you came to say. *Now.* This message: deliver it."

"I, uh—" Berman swallowed nervously, as if suddenly realizing he'd walked into a bear's cave—"all right, then." He slowly reached into a pocket of his tunic and withdrew a letter. "This is from my superiors. It's addressed to you by name."

Anders passed the envelope to Olga, who opened it and read. "Huh." She nodded to herself, then looked at the general. "We need to talk." She glanced at the sweating Commonwealth Guards. "Not here."

Back in the conference room, Olga slumped in her wheelchair. She looked worse than exhausted: a fish out of water, too tired to gasp for oxygen. "This isn't good."

"Summarize," said Anders. "What do they want us to think?"

"Pretty much what you'd expect. They say they've got half the Party Central Committee. They specifically mention the Burgesons, Erikson, White, and Brooke: probably more. They're accusing the captured commissioners of conspiring to restore the monarchy, and claim to be moving to defend the revolution."

"That's ridiculous."

Olga shook her head. "It's not as daft as it sounds, but—the good news is, Army Command North is firmly behind the Party. This appears to be a Commonwealth Guard action, possibly supported by—well, we haven't heard anything from Secretary-General Holmes, have we? Unless he's a prisoner too, although I expect they'd have named him if they had him."

"How bad is it?" Anders eyebrows furrowed. "Can you be absolutely certain there's no plot to restore the tyrant?"

Olga stared at him for an endless moment. "You haven't heard this. We—the DPR—had an operation in progress to do the exact *opposite*—to fatally undermine the royalist cause. It would have been a spectacular coup, timed to coincide with the funeral. Unfortunately things went wrong with Princess Elizabeth's defection—" She held up a hand to stave off the expected explosion—"the objective was to smuggle her into New London, where she'd swear loyalty to the Commonwealth, and *renounce* her claim to the crown. Thereby cutting off the alliance between the French and the Pretender, *and* putting an end to the direct Hanoverian dynastic claim. Instead it looks like someone leaked it to SCEP, who put two and two together and made five—they decided we were trying to restore the monarchy, not end it. So they decided to pre-empt one coup with another."

"What the *fuck?*" Anders looked as if he couldn't decide whether she was a genius, or mad. Or a mad genius, for that matter.

"That's partly why we moved up the Juggernaut launch: as a distraction while we got Elizabeth's defection back on track," she added candidly. "And to send a signal to both the French Emperor and the US State Department that the revolution will *not* be fucked with." *That's right, blab one state secret, might as well blab them all—at least he's got a top secret clearance.* "Anyway, that's what brought me down here in person."

"You were going to get *Elizabeth Hanover* to swear allegiance to the Revolution?"

Olga smirked. "You've never been female, eighteen, noble, and staring down the barrel of an arranged dynastic wedding, have you? Not all girls look forward to marriage, especially when it's the opposite of a love match. Her suitor is old enough to be her father, and famous for his mistresses. She's a bit of a tearaway and didn't take much persuading." Her smile faded. "Unfortunately the extraction went sideways and the Americans got involved. They want to weaken the Commonwealth. And if *they* get their hands on the kid, they'll use her any way they can."

"If they get—*how* would they manage that?" Anders' gaze sharpened. "Are they over here?"

Olga nodded.

"*Shit.*"

She held up a finger: "Worse, the princess is over *there*. In their time line. They haven't caught her yet, but it could happen at any time. In which case, we'll need all the leverage we can get."

"So that's why you wanted a flight plan for Juggernaut to visit the United States . . . *Fuck.*" Anders looked as if he was about to explode. "This is all connected, isn't it. *Fuck.* You shouldn't be telling me—"

"Agreed! But the normal rules went out the window the instant the Commonwealth Guard held a coup. I'm making a judgement call here: you're loyal, the Burgesons are out of play, I need someone who knows the score to hold things down in Maracaibo—and keep Huw in line—while I go back to the capital and sort this out."

"Huw—" Anders looked appalled. "Where are his family? Aren't Brilliana and Nel in New London?"

"Yes, and that's probably the best life insurance the plotters could hope for, isn't it? Huw will think twice about doing something stupid with them at ground zero." Olga's expression was sour. "I mean, if they haven't been captured yet. God help the plotters if they've hurt his family."

"All right." Anders picked up his notepad and began writing. "What are your objectives? Tell me what you need from me."

"I need to get back to the capital and talk the SCEP leadership down from the rooftops. It'll be a lot easier if my people succeed in rescuing Liz and get her in front of the TV cameras—the sooner, the better. But I also need a big stick to wave at them as backup. So . . . I need you to sit tight and relay messages between me and Juggernaut. Meanwhile, once my jet is ready, I need a list of all the bases that remain loyal to the government where I can land and refuel en route. I don't want to be shot down on approach into New York, either. Finally, if my people get Operation Runaway Princess back on track, she'll probably show up *right here* in the American's time line. They've got direct flights from Berlin," she added. "You're to keep the Commonwealth Guards from murdering her. And the Americans, if they show up in pursuit. Just get her on a courier jet to New London—hell, in the back seat of a fighter jet with in-flight refueling all the way if that's what it takes—and I'll handle everything else."

MANHATTAN ISLAND, TIME LINES ONE AND TWO, AUGUST 2020

On her first attempt to jaunt into Washington Square, Rita was nearly run over by a yellow cab. The road grid of Manhattan in her world did not align with the curves and boulevards of New London in Time Line Three, and her inertial mapper was prone to drift. An offset of just one inch per mile could add up to missing the sidewalk and stumbling into traffic. A blare of horns and an angry wave, then Rita was balancing on the curb, head swiveling like a frightened pigeon—

"Hey! You, freeze! On your face!"

The cop's face was an angry blur as he drew on her from across the street. But he was too slow. She jaunted back into the lovely but poisoned forest glade in time line one, heart hammering between her ribs.

She checked the tablet. Her email outbox was empty, and a copy of her report nestled in the 'sent' mailbox. Pulse slowing, she hunted around for a safe patch of grass to hunker down in, then sat to wait out the next half hour.

On her second jaunt across to Washington Square, there were no yellow cabs, no tourists, and virtually no pedestrians. Instead there was a deafening chainsaw buzz of quadrotor drones overhead, a weird rippling beat that seemed to orbit her head as the noise from the flying robots echoed off the buildings on every side. Police cruisers with strobing light bars blocked all the roads: the square was cordoned off.

A wall of guns and riot shields swung towards her almost instantly, but instead of jaunting, Rita raised her hands high. For a moment, nothing happened. Then a faceless helmet called: "Don't move! Identify yourself!"

"Rita Douglas, Department of Homeland Security."

"Ms. Douglas, don't move. All officers stand down, stand down." Rita stood still, a runnel of sweat trickling down her forehead as half a dozen officers moved in around her, hulked up in black body armor like storm troopers. "Hold still while we frisk you, ma'am." Rita gritted her teeth. They were fast and did a thorough, unpleasantly intrusive job of searching her, but compared with how much worse it could have been, they were gentle. There were no zip-ties, manacles, or spit hood: no gunpoint screaming in her face, no tasers. She was getting the VIP treatment. Finally, the one who'd spoken to her stepped in front of her, proffering an oral swab. "Open wide, one last check."

Rita opened her mouth, worked up saliva. The swab went straight into a ruggedized scanner and the result came back in under a minute. "Okay, we have a positive ID and it's a green light. Ma'am, we have orders to take you to—"

"—Can't." Rita lowered her arms and made a cutting gesture. "I've got to go back immediately, it's an emergency—"

"Ma'am." The officer flipped her visor up. Eyes as pale as blue sapphires stared at her, framed by head-up monocles and anti-laser displays. "They want you to brief the Presidential advisor *in person*." The noise of the gun-drones was subsiding, but a new throbbing roar was growing overhead. A Marine Corps Stealth Hawk helicopter slid into view, maneuvering perilously close to the archway at the north end of the park. It looked like a cubist rendition of a whale, all grey carbon-fiber and titanium.

"Oh hell." The chopper eased sideways and dropped slowly towards one side of the central fountain, spraying water across the plaza. *I've fallen into a River Phoenix movie*, Rita thought, teetering on the edge of hysteria: *when do the explosions start?* Then she realized that the explosions had already started—they were happening in another time line. "I *hate* helicopters," she whined under her breath. Before her kidnapping, she'd never been in one. Now they were a regular fixture in her life—ones that only showed up when things were going wrong.

"Over here—"

They waited at a safe distance as the troop transport landed and the rotor blades slowly blurred into visibility. The freight door slid open and a couple of marines jumped down, then unfolded a short stairs. A female figure climbed down the steps, then walked over to her, ignoring her escort. "Rita, we need to talk."

"What's going on? Where's Colonel Smith?"

Eileen Scranton glanced away, taking in the marble archway, the MRAPs and armored officers spread out around the streets on either side. They were holding the line against the ferocious hordes of tourists and students from NYU, as if afraid they might interfere with Rita's debriefing. "He's been called away. Something came up in Berlin. We're juggling live hand grenades right now, and it's not all about the Commonwealth." She gave Rita a penetrating look. "Let's walk." She took Rita's arm and led her towards the shade of the trees. "Your last email, half an hour ago. How stale is the report?"

"About an hour old when I sent it." Rita shuddered. "But it's based on what I heard on the radio. Things went to shit at the parade, and then Nel and I were running, mostly through Time Line Two. There was shooting. It all happened *really* fast."

"So you don't know for sure that Mrs. Beck—Burgeson is a prisoner of this junta?"

"They claimed they had her, on the radio—"

"—But you didn't hear her voice? So they might be lying?"

"Why would anyone lie about having someone in custody when they don't?" Rita asked, then instantly flushed, feeling like a complete idiot. "Sorry." However, Scranton nodded thoughtfully. *She probably thought I was being sarcastic*, Rita told herself. "It's a coup," she added. "I saw that

part with my own eyes. The Commonwealth Guard have imposed a curfew and they've got the Party leaders, but it's not a, a—" she found herself
floundering at the air in front of her, as if it could lend substance to her
thoughts—"not a done deal. Otherwise they wouldn't need to do that
stuff, the curfew and the martial law. They must feel insecure."

"Hmm. Your hosts, the Hjorths—their house was guarded, wasn't it?"
Scranton's attention slid sideways, eel-like, faster than Rita could keep up
with it.

"Yes, there were soldiers there—"

"Did you check the Burgeson residence?"

No!" Rita stopped. "Why?"

"When did you last see her?"

"She was on the main viewing stand in front of the parade. I'm pretty
sure I saw her in the second row, although it was a long way from where
I was sitting. That was before Nel talked me into going down to the refreshment stall. We were out of view of the main stand when the shooting
started, but I'm sure—"

"Rita, stop." Scranton's hand tightened on her arm, restraining her. "I
need a moment to think."

Rita waited while Dr. Scranton closed her eyes for a couple of seconds.
She looked round. Four SWAT cops waited patiently behind them. They
must make an odd scene, she realized, from worlds so different they might
appear centuries apart: Scranton in her power suit and heels, Rita in other-
worldly mourning dress and hat, the two of them escorted by soldiers in
futuristic armor, head-up displays flickering behind their visors.

Eventually Dr. Scranton looked at her again. "Okay, I think I've got
everything straight. Now I need you to tell me everything you know about
this Juggernaut thing they announced."

"Not much to tell." Rita pulled out her camera. "I recorded as much
as I could here. Tried to video it as well, but it was just a very bright dot,
moving fast." She scrubbed back to the beginning of the announcement
and hit play.

Dr. Scranton watched and listened intently, then made her re-wind and
re-play the sequence. It only lasted a couple of minutes: Juggernaut was
barely visible as a jiggling dot in the sky. Finally Scranton nodded. "I need
a copy of that," she said.

"Sure." Rita ejected the memory card and passed it to her.

"Rita. You've done a very good job so far, but you must realize this changes everything. We desperately need to know what's going on, and once we know whether the plotters are bluffing—or if there's actually been a transfer of power—we'll need to re-establish contact with the regime. I know you'll be safest if we agree to abort the mission at this point and recall you to Philadelphia, but you'll be doing us—"

"—But I don't—"

"—a great favor if you agree to go right back to New London and deliver a message. What?"

"Sorry. I meant to say, yes."

Dr. Scranton nodded. "Well, then. Our problem is where best to reinsert you. The school caretaker's residence is safe but useless for information gathering. If the Hjorth household was raided, we can be certain that the Burgeson's house will also have been hit. That leaves Mrs. Burgeson's office in the, uh, Ministry of Intertemporal Technological Intelligence. If the coup plotters are telling the truth in their broadcasts, then they'll be guarding that, too. If they're lying, her own people will be there. Either way, it would be an enormous service to us if you could report on who's there. If it's Mrs. Burgeson's people, we have a message for them. We've got a location for it—your earliest mapping trips logged it—are you prepared to go there?"

Rita's forehead wrinkled. "Let me be clear on this. You want me to black-bag the office of a cabinet minister during a coup?"

"Put that way, it sounds a little excessive, doesn't it?" Eileen lips quirked. "But actually, it's not that crazy. We can position you with a hydraulic lift so that you're right in the middle of her office when you jaunt. If there's anyone there, you can jaunt right back immediately—they won't have time to stop you. If the room's empty it'll be safe to take a look around, figure out the lay of the land. What do you think?"

The words, *I think you're nuts*, sprang immediately to mind. But then Rita had second thoughts. "If the coup plotters are lying, it's possible Brilliana will have secured the ministry compound."

"That's my thinking." Scranton nodded encouragement. "In which case it's important to establish a line of communication. Well?"

"I'll do it," Rita said, before she had time to get cold feet. Lives were in danger, people she'd come to feel some common bonds of kinship with.

Lives on both sides, come to think of it. She glanced up at the early evening sky. "Is there time for me to grab a shower, some food, and a change of clothes first? It's been a long day . . ."

NAVAL BASE KITSAP, WASHINGTON, TIME LINE TWO, AUGUST 2020

Kitsap Naval Base was the largest US Navy base in the Pacific North-West. Looking east across the waters of Puget Sound towards Seattle, the complex of fuel depots, dry docks, and shipyards was a small city in its own right. Home to a nuclear-capable shipyard with a dry dock capable of housing a Nimitz-class supercarrier, the base was also the home of the Pacific Fleet's nuclear submarines, including half the Navy's Ohio-class boats.

And right now one of these, the USS Maine, was scrambling to prepare for an abnormal departure with an experimental, untested payload.

The Maine was one of eight Trident SSBNs—large, nuclear-powered submarines armed with UGM-133 ballistic missiles—tasked with maintaining a continuous deterrent patrol in the Pacific. With twenty-four missile tubes loaded, and each missile carrying a full payload of twelve Mk-5 warheads, a single Ohio-class boat could devastate a subcontinent. Four of the boats were on patrol simultaneously at all times, running silent and submerged for seventy days at a time. Normally the Maine, having recently returned from patrol, would be laid up for a couple of months of refit and replenishment. But the blue and gold crews had been abruptly recalled for active duty just ten days into their on-shore cycle. And now the Maine was preparing to put to sea in a hurry for a special, top secret mission—just as soon as the yard finished their checklists and signed off on the replacement payloads for eight of her missiles.

The Trident II D5 LE missile system is designed to deliver a dozen hydrogen bombs across intercontinental distances. (Indeed, the solid-fueled multistage rocket has a *minimum* range of slightly under two thousand nautical miles.) It's so accurate that it can also be used to deliver low-yield nukes—or even conventional explosive warheads—to within a hundred meters of a target a third of the way around the planet.

For this special mission, the payloads of eight of the Maine's rockets were hastily being swapped out for missile buses featuring the same special sauce as the ERGO-1 probe that had inadvertently awakened the Hive orbiting the black hole. A derivative of the ARMBAND jaunt motor used for para-time travel, each of the modified upper states relied purely on inertial guidance and star sighting for mid-course guidance corrections. After the three rocket stages burned out, putting the bus on a sub-orbital trajectory, it would jaunt into a time line without a GPS cluster or ground-based reference points before releasing its dozen Mk 6 warheads. If called upon to do so, it could even jaunt more than once.

There would be no heat-flare of ocean-launched missiles lighting up the sensors of satellites high in orbit in the target time line. There would be no radar track of boosters crossing the coastline and accelerating towards the zenith. Just a stealthy drift of trash-can sized conical warheads, almost invisible until they lit up in the stratosphere with the blazing heat of re-entry, seconds before they detonated in nuclear fireballs seconds apart.

The Maine was not about to embark on a grueling seventy-day deterrent patrol this time out. Instead, the boat and her crew were going to run due west at a not very stealthy twenty knots for two days, until they were nearly a thousand nautical miles out—and far from the normal deterrent patrol zone.

Once on station, the boat would come to periscope depth and make contact with the National Command Authority. Safes would be opened and keys removed: checklists executed, a countdown executed.

Then the missile crew would wait for a coded presidential order that had been issued only once before in history: the order to conduct a first strike against an enemy in another time line.

Invisible Sun

General Anders returned to the base operations HQ, trailing a cometary tail of subordinates. He sent Olga to the base sick bay for a check-up while the air station prepared her flight for departure. Her proposed itinerary would have been exhausting even without her illness. "The last thing anyone needs is for you to collapse before you get back to the capital," he pointed out, and she grudgingly acceded.

Once at his desk Anders got on the phone immediately. "Get me a line to Supreme Command Southern Hemisphere, Continental Air Defense Forces. I need to talk to General Mendoza," he told the operator. From his headquarters in the regional capital of Greater Paraguay, Mendoza was responsible for all air defense operations over South and Central America. More importantly, he was politically astute. He'd know which way the wind was blowing in the high command. "If he's not available, get me whoever's deputizing for him. Or the most senior member of his staff." Anders grinned, lips pulling back from his teeth. "While you're setting that up, put me through to the public address system—"

The specialists manning the bank of communications gear went into action. One passed him a microphone while the others patched him into the base PA. He took a deep breath, then spoke.

"Attention, everybody. General Anders speaking, on behalf of the Explorer-General. By now, many of you will have heard rumors about events taking place in the capital. I regret to inform you that an armed mutiny broke out during the funeral parade. I don't have any details to share with you yet: suffice to say, we remain loyal to the Commonwealth, and our loyalist comrades are taking steps to restore order. Our task is to continue to do our jobs, to remain at our posts, follow orders, and defend democracy against its enemies at home and abroad." (*Whoever they are. And assuming the government that emerges from this mess doesn't think we're the enemy.*) "Let's hold it together, people. Remember, the job we're doing here is doubly important today. When the enemies of the Commonwealth see Juggernaut overhead, it will send them a message they can't ignore: we own the skies, and nowhere is beyond our reach."

As he keyed off the microphone, one of the other communications specialists stepped forward, offering a phone handset. "Supreme HQ on the line as ordered, sir," he said, stepping out of the way.

"Good afternoon. General Mendoza?" Anders sat up instinctively. Mendoza would almost certainly have discussed the coup with his cronies in order to decide which horse to back, before returning Anders' call. A *politically astute shit-weasel*, as Huw Hjorth once described him over one after-dinner brandy too many. That he'd phoned back almost immediately was probably a good sign, but—

The voice at the end of the line was faint but audible. "Explorer-General Hjorth? Explain yourself. What's going on? Your site has been off-line for eight hours now."

"The Explorer-General is unavailable. This is General Anders, I'm deputizing for him and acting under written orders. I was hoping *you* could tell *me* what's going on. I've got Maracaibo on lock-down. The Explorer-General is currently off-base, commanding the deep-space vehicle, Juggernaut. You might be tracking it on your ballistic missile warning radar? Huw Hjorth's been working on MITI's secret parallel space program for the past couple of years, and Juggernaut is the result. I'll have my people telex you the updated orbital elements to track after his next maneuver. Meanwhile, I'm seeking clarification of Army High Command's position on events in the capital. I've heard from the Commonwealth Guards: where do *you* stand?"

"Everyone here remains loyal to the Commonwealth." Mendoza's tone sharpened. "Precisely what that means is currently unclear, unfortunately. There's nothing any of us can do to influence the events unfolding, so there's no point speculating on whether this so-called junta will succeed or fail—"

Anders interrupted. "Assume for a minute that the junta does *not* succeed. Can the Party Central Commission count on your continued loyalty?"

There was a brief splutter of indignation before: "Absolutely! Anything else would be treason! I'm just observing that we have no way of influencing political events three thousand miles away—"

"You might think that, but my superior is about to prove you wrong." Anders glanced at his adjutant who raised a notepad, with some figures scrawled on it: ST PETERSBURG OVERFLIGHT IN 1H19M. "We've got just under an hour and twenty minutes to go before Juggernaut overflies St. Petersburg. It's a show of strength that should get everybody's undivided attention. When the French see it, they're they'll be on the hotline to New London so fast, you'll miss it if you blink—at which point we'll see if the coup plotters really have *any* clue as to what they've got themselves into. I suggest you tell everyone you're in contact with to sit tight, and keep them from going off half-cocked: if you do that, you'll be fine."

"What are you *doing*?" Mendoza asked querulously. "Overflying the enemy capital is insanely risky! We've barely got them to accept the principle of open skies! Whose idea was this?"

"It was approved by a subcommittee of the Party Central Committee before the coup, general. You see, we *do* have the ability to influence events over three thousand miles away. This so-called junta is going to be pleading for the commissioners to take back control before today is over . . ."

BERLIN, TIME LINE TWO, AUGUST 2020

Liz followed the green-haired girl through the dimly lit streets of nighttime Berlin, bag clenched under her arm. The hard edges of the pistol dug into the waist of her trousers, a lethal comfort to one adrift in a city that harbored hidden enemies. *I'm not going back*, Liz reminded herself, *not ever.* Commonwealth or bust. Angie blew a thin plume of steam into the night air, the baroque chimney of her e-cig puffing infrequently. "Nearly there," she announced, pausing to check the time on her phone. "Two minutes to wait."

"Wait for what?" Liz glanced over her shoulder. The street was dimly lit, the huge glass sheets of shop fronts shuttered by metal grilles. There was little vehicle traffic and fewer pedestrians.

"Our ride."

While Angie tapped her toe and whistled tunelessly to herself, Liz studied her. Her costume (and hair!) would have had her hustled off the street by gendarmes back home, but she wasn't particularly noteworthy by this Berlin's standards. Liz was either starting to acculturate or becoming numb to the strangeness around her. *Surely they wouldn't send an agent who stood out?* She pondered. "What are you staring at?" Angie demanded.

Liz glanced away, flushing slightly. "This world and everyone in it is very strange. I mean, compared to . . ." She trailed off.

But Angie seemed to understand. She nodded. "I can barely imagine. Were you expecting to come here?"

"No! No I wasn't!" Elizabeth was surprised by the vehemence of her own denial. "I thought there'd be a short ride in a motor carriage, through a different version of the city I was already in—then an aircraft."

"You have aircraft in the other time line?" Angie asked, raising an eyebrow.

"Of course! We're not backwards!" She paused. "We even have space rockets. The Commonwealth does, I mean. The Empire, not yet. But we— they—are working on it." It was a significant slip, betraying her own uncertainty.

"Well." Angie was about to say something else when her phone chose that moment to emit an oddly musical chord, distracting her. "Ah, here he is."

A low-slung automobile approached them. It slowed and pulled in nearby. Angie held up her hand, then leaned forward as the side window retracted. Then she opened the rear passenger door for Liz. "This is our Uber. He'll take us to the next cut-out." Angie took the front passenger seat. Liz climbed in—with some difficulty: the car's seating was ridiculously close to the ground—and they moved off. Ten minutes later they parked beside a tall glass-fronted building in a better lit area. "Okay, this is our stop," Angie told her. "Danke," she added as she climbed out.

"Where are we?" Liz asked.

"Our first cut-out. Now we walk a hundred meters and catch the U-bahn several stops."

"Why?"

"You might have noticed there are cameras everywhere? But the networks aren't joined up, and the opposition has to get a judge to issue an order before they can look at each separate recording. The laws here are designed to prevent abuse of power, and information about people is power. I think that's probably why the DPR tried to extract you through Germany. Anyway, we're leading the watchers on a treasure hunt." Angie flashed her a grin. "We're the treasure, but by the time they catch up with us, we'll be gone."

Over the next hour and a half, Angie led Liz on a seemingly-random tour of the city. They took an U-bahn to the east, walked a couple of streets, caught a bus, entered a different U-bahn station . . . then a train to the west, caught a street taxi and paid cash, S-bahn halfway to the suburbs, then another bus . . .

Liz was bored, footsore, and more than a little annoyed when Angie finally said, "that's enough. Our next stop is your safe house for tonight."

Liz nodded. Her stomach chose that moment to grumble indelicately. "Oh, you haven't eaten anything?" Angie's eyes widened. "Can't have that! I'll see what I can do when we get there."

It was near to midnight when Angie led Liz to the door of an anonymous-looking apartment building in Charlottenburg. "Oh thank heavens," she said as Angie unlocked the door and led her inside.

"Sorry, sorry," Angie said, sounding not even slightly repentant. "We're up on the fourth floor." She bounced up the staircase without waiting for Liz. Inside the building, everything seemed to be painted white except for the staircase treads and the handrail, which was made of a smooth, black substance rather than proper wood. It was an undecorated, drab space, as inhumanly functional as the Major's bathroom with its tiles and stainless steel fixtures. Suppressing a shudder, Liz hastened to catch up. Angie finally stopped on a landing where someone had made a pathetic attempt to lighten the severity of the stairwell by putting out a raffia door-mat and some sad-looking potted cacti. She knocked three times, paused, then knocked again. The door swung open and a middle-aged woman peered out at them.

"Maria? This is Liz," said Angie.

"Pleased to meetcha," Maria said, with an odd accent that Liz didn't quite recognize. She backed into the flat, making way for the new arrivals. "I made up both bedrooms an' stocked the refrigerator. Y'all have a good night and remember to set your alarms for eight." Maria ushered them along the corridor to a surprisingly large open-plan living area. It was a far cry from the hotel or the Major's apartment. The furniture had to be at least as old as the combined age of everyone present, with walls hung with framed paintings and prints—and the oldest person in the room was the dried-out looking fellow rising painfully from the sofa. "This is Kurt, he wants to talk to ya," she told Liz. "I'll be on my way now."

"Hi," Angie nodded at the old man. Clearly she knew him. Maria was already scooping up a coat and bag before Liz thought to open her mouth, but Angie got there first. "You pulling out already?"

Kurt cleared his throat. "The mice must scatter before the cat comes prowling," he said gnomically.

Maria spared her a twitchy look. "I'm out of here. I'll give you a call at eight-fifteen sharp and if all's well, I can drop by with the new travel documents, if they're ready in time." A nod at Liz, then she was on her way.

CENTRAL BERLIN, TIME LINE TWO, AUGUST 2020

"Well, *fuck*." Colonel Smith's mood couldn't have been described as good even before this latest news. Now, Agent Gomez thought, he looked as pissed-off as she'd ever seen him. "What does he mean, they've lost her phone?"

Gomez yawned. It was close to midnight here in Berlin, six in the evening back in Baltimore, and they'd been stacking long work days on top of jet lag. "Helmut confirmed that one of the phones from the block where we picked up the Major was present in the mall where suspect number one ditched her outfit. Same SIM, same IMEI—it's a perfect hit, both locations. So we know the princess was using Major Hjorth's stolen phone. And it was sitting in one place for six hours earlier today, but intel say it took two calls in quick succession and began moving around an hour ago—then went offline. Looks like she ditched it."

"Shit. Can we trace the caller?"

"Yes sir," Gomez tried not to sound impatient—Smith was old: he'd formed his habits of thought long before every member of the public began conveniently paying for the privilege of carrying their own bugging devices. "That's a standard standard call graph proximity search. The contacts were from another cellphone. Better still, it was in the same picocell as the subject's phone when it placed both calls. But that one's gone offline too. It was probably a burner phone, and her contact ditched both devices once he hooked up with her. So they've got COMSEC discipline."

Cellphone contact was as contagious as the common cold: if you were tracking one and someone else contacted it, you could track the contact, too. But cellphones were also dirt cheap, and it was easy to break the ring of contagion if you knew what you were doing. Using burner phones and ditching them after a single contact was simply good communications security. All you needed was a copious supply of new phones with pre-loaded address books that you could hand out at face-to-face hookups.

(There were ways a smart adversary could get around that, but it became exponentially harder if you didn't have a copy of that address book. Which changed constantly, every time the defenders added a new burner phone. Phones were like keys in a one-time pad cypher—as long as the defenders didn't re-use them, they could make life impossibly hard for snoopers.)

"Well, that's what you can expect when you're facing a state-level actor like the Commonwealth." Smith pushed himself out of the office chair he'd made his own, and walked over to the window. He stared morosely out through the venetian blinds, across the darkened street. "What was the hotel again? Motel Nine? Get over there. She'll have checked in today—yesterday—she's a single female, we can brute-force her room number from the camera feed at the front desk." He paused. "And while you're at it, keep your eyes open for Angela Hagen or Kurt Douglas."

"What?" Sonia was outraged. "Are you saying we've been rolled by Rita? That little chiseler—"

"I'm not saying that Rita Douglas is disloyal, but we aren't the only HUMINT organization with people who can jaunt, and the opposition know a lot about Rita and her attachments. I got word this afternoon that Kurt and Angela dropped off the map. Angela caught a flight to Frankfurt, which is abnormal behavior on her part: and Kurt hasn't been seen for forty-eight hours. It *might* be a coincidence. Kurt could be lying dead in his bedroom, and Angela might have suddenly developed an urge to play tourist. But I wouldn't bet on it. Someone just moved the pieces on the game board."

An hour later, Sonia Gomez and a young Federal police officer called Martin walked into the Motel Nine where Control had stashed Elizabeth Hanover. Sonia's escort seemed gawkily self-conscious about playing host to a visiting American agent: she hoped he wouldn't turn out to be a problem.

The bar was dark and deserted, the lobby almost empty save for a couple of night owls using the free wifi. Sonia walked up to the front desk and the receptionist on night duty greeted her politely enough: "Hello, would you like to check in?"

"Secret Police." Gomez beckoned her escort over. Martin wordlessly produced an ID card. His uniform alone should have been sufficient, but as Sonia was discovering, they tended to do things by the book in Berlin. (Except for jaywalking. *Everybody* jaywalked, especially in the eastern half of the city. It seemed to be a national sport or something.) Sonia shoved a glossy photo-print under the receptionist's nose. "We are looking for this woman. We believe she checked in this morning—"

"Excuse me." The receptionist squinted at her: "do you have ID?"

"She's with me," Martin intervened smoothly. A rapid-fire exchange ensued in German, leaving Gomez irritated at being shut out. The receptionist took the photograph and disappeared into the back office. "He is checking the records," Martin murmured. "Please be patient. He cannot let us examine them ourselves without a letter from a judge."

Gomez bit her lip and waited. Seconds ticked by. Presently the receptionist returned. "Excuse me," he said. "Do you have a name for this woman?"

"No!" Snapped Gomez. "She will be using a false name—" She stopped, frustrated.

Martin cast her a reproving glance. "My colleague is correct," he told the receptionist. Then paused. "Ms. Gomez, how would she have paid?"

Sonia thought for a moment. "She wouldn't. Someone else paid for her room. She probably doesn't have a passport or ID card, so she will have used some other form of ID. A phone, maybe?"

"Ah!" The receptionist cheered up. "Then I think I can help you. An English woman called Elizabeth Jordan checked in this morning using her phone as ID, claiming her wallet had been stolen—her room was paid for in advance by her parents."

"Can we see Ms. Jordan's room?" asked Martin.

"It's urgent," Sonia added. "She may be intending to harm herself."

"Oh dear." The receptionist looked unhappy and switched back to German. Martin produced his ID card again: it vanished into a scanner for a brief moment before the receptionist gave it back. "I'll have to come up with you," he said. "You must knock first. If there is no reply, then I am authorized to gain access."

A few minutes later they stood outside an anonymous door in a dimly lit hotel corridor. Martin knocked on the door, somewhat diffidently. "Police," he called, pitching his voice low, with an embarrassed glance at the 'do not disturb' lights glowing outside the other bedroom doors. "Police, please open your door." Another knock.

"She's not going to respond," Sonia said quietly. "She's not here."

The receptionist looked perplexed. "Then what are we—"

"Open the door," said Martin. "We can't be certain she is not here unless you open the door. Please?" A moment of indecision, then the receptionist fumbled out a keycard and laid it against the door handle. The door unlocked, motor whirring: Martin pushed inside, the lobby light switching on automatically. "Nobody here," he said. "The bed is not used."

"Wait." Sonia slipped into the room behind him, pulling on blue latex gloves. She flipped light switches, checked the bathroom, then poked around the bedroom systematically. "What's this?"

Stuffed in the trash can under the desk was a messenger bag. Gomez carefully pulled it out. "Look." She held it under the desk lap. There was a hole in one of the lower corners, a perfect circle surrounded by scorched fibers. She opened the bag and sniffed. "It still smells of powder." She stared at the local cop. "Does evidence of a firearms discharge count as probable cause in Germany? Because we've got it."

Martin nodded. "I'll have a word with the boss," he said. "This will open *lots* of doors."

NEW LONDON, MANHATTAN ISLAND,
TIME LINE THREE, AUGUST 2020

The staff car drove Miriam and Erasmus out of the barracks and onto the back streets of New London. It circled for a few minutes before parking. Guards hauled the Burgesons out and marched them into a sprawling office building. Miriam noticed sandbagged firing points manned by tense Commonwealth Guards in battle dress. A few of them glared at her as she passed, openly hostile. Arc lights flooded the killing ground in front of the offices, bleaching the broken glass and debris to the texture of a newspaper photograph.

They passed through a guard room and an office before their escort dragged them up in front of a twitchy-looking lieutenant. The officer checked them off on a list, then led their party deeper into the office complex. Miriam's apprehension began to unwind slightly. This was a police admin/payroll office, not a dungeon. You didn't give prisoners a tour of the bookkeeping department before you executed them, did you? Also, they were still on the ground floor. *They can't be that careless,* she worried, *can they?* Or maybe they could: her people hadn't exactly over-shared the details of how world-walking worked. While the ordinary police had followed DPR instructions on how to safely contain para-time intruders by keeping them underground or on a high floor, the Commonwealth Guard's SCEP didn't play nice with other agencies. *Maybe they have a bad case of not-invented-here?*

Their escorts came to a halt outside what was clearly a waiting room. It was furnished with low chairs and an incongruous side table that looked as if it should be set with tea and cookies. Then they were waved inside. "Where are we?" Erasmus asked hoarsely, his shoulders hunched. For a moment, Miriam hated her captor's marginal consideration. Erasmus obviously expected a beating, gripped by bad memories from previous decades.

The lieutenant merely blinked myopically. "The brigadier will see you shortly," he said.

"What brigadier?" Miriam asked, but he simply shook his head. The guards took up positions outside the open door, hands on their holstered pistols. She raised her still-cuffed wrists. "Is this strictly necessary?" She asked.

Their captor frowned at her, clearly uncertain. On the one hand, she was a prisoner. On the other hand, the prisoner was both a Party Commissioner and old enough to be his grandmother. He fretted for a few seconds, then reached a decision. "Your word that you will not try to escape?"

"I promise," Miriam said, very deliberately, "that if you release me, I will wait patiently to see your superior. I won't be any trouble for you." She shot a sidelong glance at Erasmus, whose expression—of surprise?— barely registered before he nodded.

"I will abide by those terms also," he said gravely. "My word, as a Commissioner of State for the Party of the Revolution."

"Well then." The young lieutenant produced a key and solemnly unlocked their handcuffs.

Miriam rubbed her stinging wrists and resolved to intercede on the lieutenant's behalf if the opportunity ever presented itself. He might be too stupid to walk and chew gum—much less stand guard over valuable prisoners—but punishing him for an act of decency would be profoundly unfair. In any case the real fault lay with his superiors. They'd tasked him with securing a world-walker but had neglected to make sure he understood how to do so.

She risked a cautious glance at Erasmus, who nodded amiably at her. He sat down. She settled on the seat beside him and folded her hands neatly in her lap. When the Commonwealth Guards had stormed the reviewing stand and dragged them away, they'd searched her for the obvious things—knives, guns, wallet, watch—but they hadn't strip-searched her, and they'd missed the locket hanging on a ribbon under the collar of her blouse. Now she assessed her chances. She could easily palm it and world-walk before the guards could stop her. *I can make it. But Erasmus . . .* her elbows hurt. Her knees hurt. Her hips were the hips of a fifty-year-old. She wasn't unfit, let alone an invalid, and given a bit of time to prepare she could carry him with her to the bug-out time line her locket's knotwork coded for. The DPR had designated the uninhabited alternate Manhattan Island next door as a panic room for their personnel. They'd built shelters and planted stockpiles of supplies there. But while the young lieutenant had foolishly unlocked her handcuffs, she doubted his guards would give her the opportunity to physically lift Erasmus. They were careless, but not *that* incompetent.

She could escape, but she'd have to leave her husband behind.

Minutes passed. Miriam casually unbuttoned the collar of her mourning gown, as if relieving some minor discomfort. She tugged the locket out, positioned it above her collar bone, but made no move to open it. Erasmus noticed and glanced sidelong at her: she shook her head minutely. *I'm not deserting you yet.* He gave her a slow, lingering look. "Don't engage in false heroics," he warned her quietly. "If you can save yourself, you must do so. I don't want to take you down with me like Annie."

Miriam stared at him. "But—" she began, then bit her lip. Nearly forty years ago, Erasmus and his first wife had been caught by the Imperial secret police, in the wake of a popular uprising. They'd both been sent to the labor camps. Erasmus survived long enough to be released: Annie had died. "I . . . yes."

She *could* escape. It was her *duty* to escape: to find Brill, find Rita, to take the scattered DPR survivors in and establish a control center, then direct the fightback against the enemy. And she could see, plain as day, what would happen if she did so. The self-righteous Commonwealth Guards would see it as clear confirmation of her guilt, evidence that she intended to subvert the revolutionary succession. And they'd have her husband as a hostage. If they threatened to execute him . . . *I mustn't put us in that situation,* she realized.

They settled back to wait. Finally, the inner door opened. "Bring them in," someone called. Miriam stood, and for a shameful moment her determination wavered: but then the ambiguous moment passed.

"Commissioner Burgeson. And the *other* Commissioner Burgeson." The office beyond the waiting room was unexpectedly cramped. An unshaven, middle-aged man in a Commonwealth Guard brigadier's tunic, unbuttoned at the collar, sat behind a desk overflowing with papers. Junior officers and specialists sat at bulky communications terminals and cipher machines on either side of the room. "I'm going to make this quick. *You—*" He pointed at Erasmus—"are not under suspicion, and will be allowed to resign your post and live in quiet retirement. We thank you for the work you have done on behalf of the Revolution—but you can best serve the cause by making one last broadcast and then stepping down. *If* you cooperate, then we may be able to show your wife some leniency, even though the evidence of her guilt is quite incontrovertible . . ."

He seemed to be ignoring Miriam, treating her as an invisible adjunct to her husband. "Really?" She raised an eyebrow at the brigadier. Erasmus shook his head frantically, but she pushed on: "What exactly am I supposed to be guilty of?"

"Treason, of course." Brigadier Richards placed his hand atop a fat sheaf of papers secured with treasury tags. He turned to Erasmus: "This isn't a coup," he said, "but a counter-coup. We're pre-empting your wife's plan to restore the monarchy—"

"What?" Miriam didn't attempt to conceal her confusion. "That's not what's—"

Richards waved a finger at her: "We know all about your scheme! Your husband's attempt to bamboozle us with some cock-and-bull story about a spaceship was too little, too late—"

"But—" Erasmus tried to interrupt, but Richards rolled over him.

"You sent Major Hulius Hjorth, part of your inner circle, to smuggle

Elizabeth Hanover out of Berlin! We know you're hiding her in your household, with yet another moonshine story about her being your long-lost daughter from another time line—"At least he didn't prefix "time line" with *so-called*; he wasn't one of the endlessly irritating para-time denialists—"Ready to take over when you arrest the Council of Guardians as they meet to select a new First Man after the funeral. We've even got the interviews with the Princess that you prepared to broadcast tomorrow—"

"Rita's tapes?" Erasmus echoed. He looked at Miriam. "Get away with you!" He said, as if it was Richard's story he was dismissing. But Miriam knew better. Her knees wobbled: her head spun at the total craziness of the brigadier's misinterpretation, at the disastrous implications of his error. He'd been ranting for less than a minute and he'd already shaken her resolve to stay. Erasmus was telling her to flee, and the worst of it was that he was right—she *had* to run, lest Richards' selective disbelief wreck everything.

"Are you sure?" She asked, clutching at her collar.

Erasmus nodded, then looked at Richards: "you're an idiot," he said succinctly. "My wife isn't a traitor. Juggernaut is real but those tapes were *faked*, we needed to convince the French that we've got the Princess—the truth is—"

Miriam tugged at the locket in her fist, snapping the fine chain it hung on, and flipped it open. She stared at it blearily. The knotwork refused to come into focus at first, and when it did her head pounded. *Shit, there's an obstacle*. She stood and staggered away from the chair. The Brigadier rose. "Where are you—"

She looked at the locket again, and this time her jaunt succeeded.

JUGGERNAUT, LOW EARTH ORBIT, TIME LINE THREE, AUGUST 2020

A couple of hours after Juggernaut over-flew the funeral in New London, Huw was just about prepared to concede that everything aboard Juggernaut was going tolerably well. The various teams were working their systems. There had been no new and notable system failures, they'd tracked down and patched or isolated the leaks and short-circuits that the violent launch had thrown at them, and the mission plan was on track. The situation on the ground was anything but under control, however.

"What the *fuck* are they playing at down there?" Demanded Sergeant MacDonald, then cast Huw an apologetic look: "sorry, sir."

Huw smiled tightly, or grimaced—at this point fatigue made it a fine distinction. "What now?" He asked, sealing the zip-loc squeeze bag of gluey oatmeal he'd been trying to eat.

"I've got a, a General Minsky on the uplink from New London? A Commonwealth Guard General, that is. He's ordering us to land immediately and hand over command to lawful authority."

"He wants us to land." Huw said flatly.

"Sir, he says if we don't land immediately we will be judged to be in mutiny and he'll have us shot down." MacDonald was clearly biting his tongue.

"Put him on to my loop," Huw said, then lost control momentarily. A hiccuping snort of laughter escaped before he could stifle it. *The general wants us to land.* "Juggernaut to ground, commanding officer Huw Hjorth calling New London. Is that General Minsky?"

A hissing of airwaves filled Huw's headset—the ground link away from Maracaibo was old-school VHF radio—then a loud throat-clearing rattled his ears. "This is General Minsky, Commonwealth Guard, speaking on behalf of the Law and Dignity Restoration Committee. Captain Hjorth, you are in breach of lawful authority if you do not land *immediately—*"

"Can't." Huw listened for a few seconds while Minsky chuntered menacingly into his microphone. "This is a Juggernaut-class vehicle. We are propelled by atomic explosions. Not only is Juggernaut not designed to land—at the end of the mission we're scheduled to abandon ship and return to Earth in re-entry capsules—but if we attempted to land, we'd kill everyone on the ground within a hundred miles. And then we'd crash. So . . . your call."

Minsky was silent for almost a minute. "You will cut short your mission and return in your re-entry capsules, then," he said tensely.

"I'm afraid I can't do that, either." Huw grinned mirthlessly. "We are due to overfly St. Petersburg in a few hours. Obviously it would be a bad idea to abandon an asset like Juggernaut where the French might steal it. Nor can we abandon it prematurely, with over a thousand nuclear charges on board. We can only maneuver if we world-walk to an uninhabited time line, otherwise we will black out radio communications around the world for several days. You don't want that, either."

"You are being deliberately obstructive," Minsky snarled.

Why, whatever makes you think that? "Tell me, by what constitutional theory does this, uh, Law and Dignity Restoration Committee, assert authority, General? The Commonwealth Guard is not in my chain of command. As Explorer-General—and this is an exploration craft, not military—I report to the DPR, which is part of MITI. That in turn reports to the Central Committee and the First Man. Was your committee established in accordance with a decree issued by the First Man, a motion passed by a quorum of the Radical Party Central Committee, or in compliance with the provisions of the Continuity of Government in Wartime Act?"

"Stop quibbling: we act by order of the Party General Secretary in defense of the revolution! The First Man's office is vacant and members of the Central Committee are accused of treasonably conspiring to reinstate the monarchy. Where do *you* stand?"

"I obey my chain of command and the rule of law, not some dubious committee convened on hearsay and rumor and acting without legal authority, sir. I don't propose to debate you further: I am tasked with displaying the Commonwealth's might in outer space, to deter our enemies from attacking while our attention is distracted by the current turmoil. This is going to occupy my next several hours. I urge you to use the time to return to your barracks and submit to the lawful authority of the Party. Again, speaking as an officer in the DPR, I deny the existence of a conspiracy to restore the monarchy. The only conspiracy I see here is yours. Juggernaut over and out."

Huw shook his head. "Fools," he grunted.

"Sir? Is there anything else?" MacDonald asked.

"Yeah, get me a line to Olga Thorold as soon as you can. In the meantime, we'll proceed as planned with the St. Petersburg overflight. Afterwards, we transfer to time line twelve for inclination adjustments. Then, we'll see. If this Law and Dignity Committee nonsense is what I think it is, well, I have a suggestion but I want to clear it with the highest legitimate authority I can reach."

Something about this coup smells familiar, Huw told himself. School of the Americas familiar, Operation Condor familiar, CIA banana republic playbook familiar. There were American emissaries in New London. State Department diplomats, not just Rita. Huw had spent years in the United States, had attended college and grad school there. Adrian Holmes was ambitious enough, and the Commonwealth Guard paranoid enough, to mount a coup. But would they have thought to do so without someone whispering in their ears? *What if Rita was a feint, a distraction to get the Burgeson's—the technocrat faction's—attention?* The United States rarely attacked its perceived enemies directly, and outright warfare was not a viable strategy to pursue against a nuclear superpower. Not when a mixture of flattery and lies, promises of cooperation and warnings against the enemy within, could induce a rival to tear its own guts out.

"If Olga agrees with me about who is behind this, I think we can get them to back off," Huw said aloud. "But I want a sanity check. I'm not going there on my own." He kept the rest of his plan to himself for the time being: *nice space station you've got; wouldn't it be a shame if someone parked a battleship on its airlock?*

NEW YORK/BALTIMORE, TIME LINE TWO, AUGUST 2020

FEDERAL EMPLOYEE 004930391 CLASSIFIED VOICE TRANSCRIPT

DR. SCRANTON: Rita reported back and it's . . . it's a mess.

IRVING: What level of mess are we talking about? I thought the plan was to *make* a mess?

DR. SCRANTON: (Shaky laugh.) *Just a little.* (Pause.) The good news is, the State Department's gambit worked and there's a coup in progress in the Commonwealth. The bad news is, the faction running it aren't realists—they're the revolutionary, uh, the Commonwealth Guards. Kind of equivalent of the Iranian Revolutionary Guards, or the Waffen SS. With nukes.

IRVING: That's understood. State's been telling them exactly what we need them to hear, anything to discredit Miriam Beck—I mean Burgeson. We're running the standard Condor playbook through them: they're moving in on behalf of the Party committee to bring stability, that's the theory. When the dust settles our man Holmes will be in charge and the world-walkers will all be rounded up—

DR. SCRANTON: But it's not going to settle! Jesus, this is a *total* fuck-up. During the military parade for the funeral—you remember all those Soviet May Day parades? When they used to reveal their latest toys?

During the funeral MITI—Miriam Burgeson's people—unveiled a nuclear-powered spaceship called Juggernaut. It made an overflight of the funeral in low-Earth orbit. It's a copy of something called Project Orion that NASA was working on in the fifties and sixties: Rita caught it on video, it's *not* a hoax. It's so freaking big it's naked-eye visible *from the ground*, the flight crew include world-walkers, and they've got enough nukes to fight World War Three all on their own!

IRVING: You're shitting me.

DR. SCRANTON: I wish I was, sir.

IRVING: Orion, wasn't that some kind of crazy Cold War project?

DR. SCRANTON: Yes. JFK cancelled it in '63, but the world-walkers figured out a way to make it work. Remember they're a true State-Level Actor? Not penny-ante rubbish like Iran or North Korea, this is more like the Soviet Union before they went into decline. They've got an immensely powerful and secretive government agency with a huge black budget for industrial espionage and tech development, like DARPA on steroids crossed with the NSA. They were in a position to build the thing in secret, without significant oversight, and they did that.

So we've got this para-time superpower in the throes of a coup, and the faction we're backing are trying to round up the world-walkers, but the world-walkers have just unveiled a *doomsday machine*, and it's already operational and under autonomous command by the faction we're actively trying to rat-fuck. Pardon my French.

IRVING: Let's hope they don't blame us, then. Things could get a mite tense.

DR. SCRANTON: Why *wouldn't* they blame us? Do you think they're stupid?

IRVING: Let me think. Hmm. Okay, for the time being I want you to put a hold on active ops in the Commonwealth: I need to go brief the President. That's a *total* pause. I'll yell at State to cool things at their end, too. Smith can continue angling for that princess and the spies in Berlin, he should totally do that, but right now you're to treat Commonwealth soil as radioactive. We play nice with whichever faction comes out on top until it's time to stick the knife in. Meanwhile, I want a full report on this space thing—Juggernaut?—so I can kick it up a notch. POTUS is going to want to set policy, and set it fast. And I need you up here tomorrow for the next NSC/DHS joint committee session.

DR. SCRANTON: What are you thinking?

IRVING: I'm thinking that now they've got a para-time second-strike capability, we've got to make them aware of our own. Meanwhile we've still got the alien crap to deal with. Maybe we can kill two birds with one stone? But only if the Commonwealth don't panic and kill us all . . .

END TRANSCRIPT

MARACAIBO COMMONWEALTH AIR BASE, TIME LINE THREE, AUGUST 2020

As the courier jet lined up on the main runaway at Maracaibo Air Station, Olga tightened her lap belt and tried to relax. From the front of the passenger compartment she had a clear view over the pilot's heads, right through the glazed nose and vacant bombardier's position. Runway lights glared in parallel lines as the turbojets spooled up to an eerie shriek and the plane began its take-off roll.

Ten years ago, the bomber variant of this jet—loosely based on the Tupolev-16 and its civilian conversion, the Tupolev-104—had been the most advanced weapons system in this time line. It was primed to deliver packaged nuclear annihilation to Paris and St. Petersburg at high subsonic speed, slashing past enemy interceptors that were still powered by piston engines. Today it was ludicrously obsolete, with only the passenger variant still flying. It had been replaced by submarine-launched ballistic missiles, and now Juggernaut: platforms that MITI-sourced breakthroughs had provided for the Commonwealth. But right now this unarmed and obsolescent ex-bomber was the most dangerous aircraft in the Americas, as far as the Junta was concerned.

Olga tiredly propped her eyes open as the lights began to sweep past to either side of the flight deck. (Like many uneasy flyers, she had an irrational feeling that if she took her eyes off the horizon the plane would crash.) The howling jets added a grumbling roar, and she reached up to adjust her ear defenders. It was a little quieter back in the main passenger compartment where the racket was muffled by additional soundproofing, but Olga disliked the tiny windows. *It'll be better when we have proper jet airliners in production*, she thought, but the 747-workalikes were a lower priority than defending the revolution against its enemies: they were still only flying as prototypes. At least the cockpit view was spectacular. The converted military aircraft hurled itself at the horizon, chasing the moon's reflection in the waters of the lake. It might be no faster than a regular airliner in time line two (and much noisier and more polluting), but it *felt* faster. *And with this view, if they try to shoot us down at least I'll see it coming.*

Not that she expected to be shot down—at least not deliberately. The Commonwealth Guard were a gendarmerie, not a navy or air force. They operated patrol boats and rotary wing craft, even some short-range anti-aircraft defenses: but they had neither cruisers nor fighter jets. They weren't set up to fight a war against external enemies. Meanwhile, the Air Defense Force with their interceptors and missile batteries seemed to be loyal. And Olga had a deadly weapon of her own, in the shape of the courier jet's radio operator and her equipment.

She must have dozed off shortly after take-off, for the next thing she knew, the flight attendant was tentatively tapping her shoulder and her neck ached: "ma'am? Ma'am?"

"Wha—what's up?" Olga blinked and tried to sit up. It was a struggle.

"Ma'am? Sparky says there are some messages waiting for you. I'd have let you sleep but a Flash priority signal just came in, and your man said you were waiting for it?" The flight attendant cast a wary eye back along the cabin towards Jack's seat.

Olga managed a nod. "Yes, he's absolutely right," she said, holding up a hand. "Help me with the tray table, please?"

The steward set up the table in front of her, then hurried forward to retrieve a fistful of print-outs. "Can I get you anything else?" He asked.

Olga frowned as she saw the origin header on the top sheet: DPR GHQ MOST URGENT and then a flag to show the transmission had been encrypted. "A coffee, please." The situation reports from the capital had finally caught up with her. First up was a standard situation status update: could be better, could be worse. The ministers (including Miriam) had been rounded up by the conspirators. Lots of low and mid-ranking personnel had made it to safety, including Brill. She'd survived more than one coup in the Gruinmarkt days, and was canny enough to have prepared contingency plans for trouble during the transition period. The junta seemed to be politically isolated and on the defensive, barely more than Adrian Holmes consolidating the Party Secretariat with the support of echelons inside the Commonwealth Guard. The regular army general staff were muttering about illegal orders and restoring lawful authority, and the Chamber of Magistrates—the publicly elected parliament—had condemned the plotters. Everyone was loudly declaring their loyalty to the revolution. So what had stirred up this mess in the first place?

Then Olga got to Brill's report about Rita, and the message she'd brought from the US National Security Advisor, and she began to swear.

"Ma'am?" It was the steward again.

"What is it?" She tried not to snap, but the tension bleeding through into her voice clearly made the man nervous.

"Sparky says she's got Juggernaut on-air? Relaying to you? Can you take a call?" He offered her a headset trailing a long, coiled cable.

"Yes." Olga fumbled with the headset, then got the microphone in place. "Hello? This is Olga Thorold speaking."

"Hi, Olga, this is Huw, aboard Juggernaut. We're good to overfly St. Petersburg in about two hours and forty-six minutes, just checking for any updated instructions? I have a modest proposal for what to do with Juggernaut after this pass—"

Huw's plans had a tendency to be ambitious and alarming, but under the circumstances, Olga was willing to listen to suggestions from the devil himself. "I'm all ears. I mean, go ahead."

"Okay, here's what I propose to do." Huw told her, and to her own great surprise, Olga couldn't pick any holes in the idea. "It serves notice on the bastards," he pointed out. "But there's nobody in a position to green-light it for me, except you. So I need a sanity check."

Olga shut her eyes briefly. "Do it," she said. "Sir Adam is still dead with no replacement in sight, Most of the Committee are in captivity, the chain of command is disrupted. I *think*—" She quickly checked off her own reporting chain—"yes, you've got command authority for Juggernaut and I'm not going to tell you not to go ahead at this point. Just try not to start a nuclear war."

She opened her eyes again and gazed out at the blue, empty unrolling beyond the nose canopy. *Still not dreaming,* she thought. "Show of force it is."

BERLIN, TIME LINE TWO, AUGUST 2020

"So," Kurt said watching Liz. A mild smile tugged at his lips. "I suppose you are wondering what happens next."

Elizabeth kept her back straight as she perched on the edge of the over-stuffed armchair. "I am sure you have a plan, otherwise Control would not have commended you to me," she said primly. "Angela has made it clear to me that you are natives of this world, seeking asylum with the Commonwealth, and *they* appear to trust you. But that will do for now, because it's late and I need to rest." She yawned. "Is there a bed?"

"Yes, I forgot." Kurt glanced at his wrist, where he wore a compact time-piece. "It's nearly three, how did it get to be . . . ? Ah, jet lag." He shook his head. "Yes, there's a bed, if you'll follow me, Miss Hanover."

Liz glanced at Angie. "He's my girlfriend's grandfather," Angie told her. "You can trust him as much as you can trust me, or anyone here."

Girlfriend's grandfather? Liz wondered as she stood up, *what an odd way of saying . . . something.* She'd been conscious, albeit footsore, while they were scampering all over the city, up escalators and down subway platforms. But now she was in the warmth of a home, her brain kept trying to switch off like a light bulb. Hearing was muffled and sharp simultaneously: sight was fuzzy, and whenever she tried to pay attention to anything, her eyelids tried to ambush her and close up shop.

She followed Kurt into the hallway. He walked with the creaky preci-sion of an old man whose joints hurt, although in St. Petersburg she'd have taken him for no more than fifty. He drew her attention to a door ("bathroom," he said), then opened another door for her. "Your room for the night." It was indeed a bedroom, although small and under-decorated. The electric light fixtures and flat television seemed odd luxuries to her, and there were curtains drawn across the windows. But the walls were painted an unadorned off-white and the carpet was of cream-colored wool with no border decoration. More evidence supporting her hypothesis that the people here were puritan nonconformists with a fetish for plain living. "Angela will be in the room opposite, I will take the living room sofa," Kurt told her. "I'll wake you in the morning."

"Thank you, I—" Liz yawned. She'd been about to ask for towels and a nightdress and hot water, but pulling her boots off seemed vastly more important in the moment. Kurt withdrew silently and closed the door. She barely had the energy to do more than take off her footwear, move her pistol under the pillow, and turn out the light. Then she collapsed on the bed and the darkness claimed her.

Liz was exhausted when she went to bed—it had been a long and troublesome day—but to her irritation she only slept for four hours, then found herself lying awake as the early morning light crept around the edges of the curtains. *What am I doing?* She asked herself. Two days ago, it had seemed perfectly clear. The Major would pick her up and smuggle her to an aerodrome in another world (one she had only the most hazy conception of), then fly her away to the Commonwealth. But now—

Everything had gone wrong. First the Major arrived to rescue her and was shot for his pains. Then she'd had to deal with this strange new Germany while being pursued by agents of a shadowy not-Commonwealth America. And now she didn't know *what* to think, not in the slightest. What little conversation she'd had with Angie was like a glimpse into a topsy-turvy world populated by the hereditary servants of a long-dead ogre-republic. They were eager to escape from their not-Commonwealth America, which sounded like a warped parody of the Commonwealth itself. (Not that she'd ever been allowed to visit: she just assumed that everything her father and her tutors told her about the Commonwealth was a pack of lies.)

Time to find out, she thought, throwing off the quilt. She hadn't undressed and felt quite remarkably frowsy. but she pulled her boots on anyway. She made use of the bathroom, then went looking for someone to talk to, if anyone else was awake yet.

Despite walking softly, Liz found Kurt was ahead of her when she reached the kitchen. There was a clock on the wall (recognizable, although it took austerity in design to a new extreme, showing her two very plain hands and a white face bare of any numbers). It was only half past six. Kurt had been bent over some sort of glass-and-plastic contraption that hissed and muttered to itself, occasionally spitting puffs of steam. Now he straightened up and looked at her. "Coffee?" He asked.

"Yes, please." Liz bobbed her head. Kurt reached into a cupboard for a couple of cups, which were incongruously recognizable, and now she realized the smell of coffee was coming from the machine on the counter.

"It will be ready in a minute," Kurt told her, then paused, as if perplexed. "Did you sleep well?"

"Well enough." Liz took a deep breath, cringing slightly as she realized she had neglected to powder her teeth. "What happens now?"

"We must stay ahead of the Americans, which means moving regularly." Kurt pulled a squat glass jug from the machine and poured coffee into the plain, cylindrical mugs. "Milk? Sugar?" She nodded to the former. "We'll be off right after coffee. A passport is being arranged for you. Once it arrives we will board a commercial flight to Venezuela, where the Commonwealth maintains a covert presence. I don't know the details of how you'll arrive in the Commonwealth, but the DPR will take you back to New York—I'm sorry, New London—to be welcomed by the Commissioners. Because you are unfamiliar with airport security, Angela will fly with you."

He passed her a mug of coffee. She sipped it cautiously. It was bitter and weak, but better than nothing. "What about you?" She asked.

Kurt shrugged. "I'm still awaiting instructions."

"What about the Major?" She persisted.

"Ah, the Major." He looked at her warily. "What does the Major mean to you?"

Liz raised her chin. "He put his life on the line for me, and took a bullet for his pains. Are they going to discard him? The Commonwealth, I mean? Because—" She took a sip of coffee to cover her turmoil—"that would be a bad sign. For me, I mean. And for you." She paused. "I think loyalty is a two-way street."

"That is a refreshingly original attitude for a politician in this time line. It's a long time since politics was dominated by personal considerations here. Not since the collapse of the imperial system, more than a century ago." Kurt smiled at her expression of mixed incredulity and discomfort. "Luckily you are dealing with Mrs. Burgeson, not the Commonwealth government. She won't leave the brother-in-law of her deputy—a close personal friend of hers—in enemy hands. Beyond that, I can't tell you anything."

"'Do you have other business?'"

"I couldn't say." Kurt watched her sip her coffee, unblinking. "You *do* look a bit like her, you know. A lot, in fact."

"Like who?"

"My granddaughter. Adoptive granddaughter, that is. Rita."

"The woman who's impersonating me in the Commonwealth?" Liz twitched at the idea of a body double. It felt horribly inappropriate, even though she understood the reasoning behind it.

"Yes. Politics *is* personal, however much democracies might like to pretend that it isn't. However much my former superiors in the Socialist

Republic might have tried to brush it under the carpet. That's what this is all about, you see. Republics governed by the rule of law—like this version of Germany, or the United States, or the Commonwealth—try to pretend that everything is determined by legality and individual merit. They like to believe it has nothing to do with heredity, or accident of birth, or who went to school with who. Everything is supposed to be orderly, like planets orbiting the sun, each in their predictable track. But the conflict between ideals and personal loyalties warps the entire structure, like an invisible sun passing through the solar system, its gravity dragging orbits out of alignment and causing havoc. A sufficiently powerful extended family—like Rita's, like the world-walkers—can bring worlds into collision and smash civilizations they can't even see, all by unwittingly exerting their hidden influence."

He ran his fingers through his thinning hair. "I dedicated the best years of my life to serving a republic that no longer exists. Now I'm old, I find that everything comes down to family and friends. You have already made a choice, a difficult one, between obedience to the dictates of family and . . . something . . . some other cause. I hope it works out for you. As for Rita?" He shrugged. "She was offered employment and trained by the US government *precisely* because her birth mother is Mrs. Burgeson, a leader of the Commonwealth, a leader of the Clan of world-walkers in exile. They tried to turn Rita into a weapon against Miriam. It was badly done because bureaucracies *really* can't handle family ties, but—" Kurt's pocket buzzed like an angry wasp—"excuse me." He pulled out a phone and glanced at it. "Aha. Your new passport is coming." He swallowed another mouthful of coffee then put his mug in the sink. "I will wake Angie and we should leave." He smiled again. "When you get to New London, you should compare notes with Rita. You may find you have more in common than you realize."

THE SOLAR SYSTEM,
TIME LINES ONE—ONE BILLION, 9000 BCE TO 2020 CE

The human Forerunners were not a single civilization, or even a single hominid subspecies. By the time they encountered the Hive they had spawned multiparous tribes and nations, fought wars, built empires, risen to glory, collapsed, and risen again—repeating the process innumerable times. On many of the Earths they colonized, they found pre-existing hominid populations, and dealt with them as colonial enterprises have always dealt with indigenous peoples. Writing, philosophy, and science were lost and rediscovered over numerous millennia and millions of versions of Earth: civilizations rose and fell. In outer space, the Forerunner clade never made it much past Mars, for why should they bother? What was the point of striving to cross the endless gulf between stars when there was an uninhabited empire of galactic proportions, ripe for occupation and colonization, right on their doorstep?

(Humans: glorious, brilliant, visionary, and enlightened; also cruel, short-sighted, barbarous, and foolish. As on one world, so on a myriad.)

Perhaps nine thousand years ago, around the time of the great inundations at the end of the last ice age on the world of Rita's birth, some offshoot of the Forerunners first encountered a version of Earth that had been colonized by the Hive. And they tried to deal with them as colonial enterprises have always dealt with indigenous peoples—which is to say very badly for the indigenes—except that the Hive were no more amenable to human colonial conquest and genocide than a super-volcano or an asteroid impactor.

It is no longer possible to know whether the ancestors of the Hive experimented with jaunting between time lines in whatever star system they started out from: their origin is long forgotten. Quite possibly they did so, in which case the Hiveish world-walkers remained isolated in their own solar system, seeing no need to cross the interstellar gulfs. But the Hive were a spacefaring eusocial superorganism, radiation-hardened and able to estivate while their seed ships drifted between stars. They were not inherently limited to one planetary system, or even to one species. But when the Hive captured and anatomized Forerunner hominids, they also acquired the machinery of para-time empire, and at some point recognized its utility. And they modified the underlying transport mechanism to suit their own ends. A single world-walking worker bot was not terribly useful, but a Hive-scale gate could allow a cluster of bot-like workers, queens, and soldiers to swarm through into another Earth. It was a far faster means of expansion than suspended animation and a slow cruise between star systems, so the Hive exploded into the affine space of the Forerunner multiverse like a plague of metal-armored ants bearing energy weapons.

In the wake of that catastrophic first contact, thousands of world-spanning civilizations died.

Seen from the perspective of the Hives, the Forerunners—and the related hominid subspecies they had somehow emerged from—were an abomination. They were tribal primate omnivores with a voracious appetite not only for biomass, but also metals and rare earth elements. Forerunners swarmed across the multiverse like a disease, breeding rapidly and expanding indiscriminately, bringing down biospheres and importing zoonotic diseases. In every time line where the dreaming apes took hold they precipitated a mass extinction event. Even the more enlightened Forerunner empires—ones that understood the environmental value of not shitting in the bed they slept in—were bad for the Hive, competing for resources and killing Hive workers when they stumbled across them.

The Hive did not rely solely on brute force to protect themselves against the Forerunner para-time empires. Biological weapons worked wonders against the hominid world-cities. Some of them were modified viral and bacterial plagues (fungi proving slightly too slow to be of use—Forerunner medical sorcery could generally find a treatment before such infestations took hold). Others were more esoteric. Plagues that attacked human food crops were generally good. So—in the view of the more patient Hive-associations—were prion diseases that mangled the self-replication facility of the artificial sub-cellular organelles required for jaunting. Hominid populations restricted to a single time line could be isolated and mopped up in detail later, after the broader para-time population was eliminated.

A war of extermination raged across an infinitesimally tiny corner of the multiverse. Mere millions to billions of time lines were affected, and only on the one blue-and-white planet: a metaphorical termite mound locked in mortal combat with a parenthetical australopithecus, insignificant and invisible and far beneath notice to the world-girding orbital megastructures of the *true* high civilizations of para-time.

On millions of Earths, humanity (and meta-humanity) died horribly. But on tens of thousands of others, undiscovered Paleolithic tribes carried on about their mundane lives, finger-painting on cave walls and carving beads and stones to adorn themselves. And in many millions more, the industrial might of planetary civilizations built doughty barriers against the invading Hive-bots. Their five dimensional fortresses housed medical thaumaturgists able to program software patches for the advanced prosthetic immune systems of their world-walking cyborg infantry. In thousands of time lines, their industrial redoubts in high orbit rained scorching nuclear fire on the Hive, followed by invasion shuttles dropping smart matter weapons and jaunt-capable drones atop the burning wreckage of the enemy beachheads. The hive were daunting but not invulnerable: nukes and malware could slaughter them wholesale, guns and lasers could kill them retail. A grand overall strategy emerged, if only by implication: the surviving Forerunner civilizations sought to sever the grid of communicating time lines, to build a four-dimensional wall that would deny the Hive access to the vulnerable heartlands of humanity. Millions of Earths could be abandoned in flames if necessary, or toppled into premature ice ages, to serve as a Maginot empire, a static bulwark against invasion. Unoccupied, uninhabited, these dead worlds would provide the enemy with no maps showing the way back to the loose federation of human time empires.

But the Hive had already injected their poisons into the human combatants. Far behind the lines, the slow, stealthy targeted prion infestations progressed, propagating silently among the Forerunners and crippling the jaunting ability of their children's children, replicating and expressing their deadly payload generations later.

And as is so often the case when an army faces inevitable defeat at the claws and mandibles of an exterminatory alien enemy, a steady trickle of deserters and refugees fled the conflict zone. Running for safety in the uncharted wilderness of time lines that had not yet been explored by the Forerunners or the Hive.

PART THREE

HANG TOGETHER

Nothing is as dangerous for the state as those who would govern kingdoms with maxims found in books.

—Cardinal Richelieu

Mistaken Identity

It was turning out to be a memorably eventful day for Rita.

Dr. Scranton handed Rita off to a pair of taciturn DHS officers, who had been briefed over a satellite phone by Colonel Smith. Then she disappeared in a whirl of rotor blades, back to her critically important White House briefing in Baltimore. Agents Fenn and Garner whisked her across town to a police station, where a team of their colleagues had relocated much of the Unit's equipment from the Philadelphia site. She had time to snatch a burrito and a quick shower, but turned down the offer of a helmet and body armor: if she had to be sneaking around New London, she'd prefer to do it wearing Commonwealth-appropriate clothing, even if it was formalwear from a state funeral. Before she knew it her escort were hurrying her along to a cordoned-off downtown site. An ambulance with open doors awaited, beside steps leading up to a hastily-erected platform on top of construction scaffolding. It was just below nose height to Rita, a meter and a half above ground level. Beside the platform, an unrolled air mattress slowly inflated on the grass—just in case she had to come back in a hurry and missed the edge of the platform.

This is dumb, she told herself, not for the first time. *Dr. Scranton is panicking.* The smart move would have been to wait until the coup blew over, then infiltrate Mrs. Burgeson's office after getting a handle on her night-time movements and arranging a distraction for the security guards. But something about the picture troubled Rita. Eileen didn't seem particularly prone to panic. Rita's previous experiences of her were that she was icily precise and frighteningly astute. You didn't get to her level without being the sharpest knife in the box, so Rita worried: *what else is going on that I haven't been told about?*

She slid across the back seat of agent Garner's car. "Are you clear on the ground plan, going in?" She asked.

"Wait one." Garner touched his earpiece. "Yes, Ms. Douglas. We locked in the coordinates. The platform should be level with the ground in time line one. From there, you can jaunt straight across to the room below the Commissioner's office. We're going to wait here for exactly one hour. If you don't come back before then—"

"I'll exfiltrate some other way because you'll be gone. Check." Rita glanced out at the gathering darkness, then unlatched the door. "Got my inertial mapper—" They'd swapped batteries while she'd been on her break—"and my camera."

"You'll need this, too, ma'am." Garner handed her a nylon holster. "Sign here."

"Wait, what—" Rita frowned. "I don't need a gun! I mean, I'm not going to shoot anyone. If there's trouble, I jaunt—"

"Orders, ma'am. You're going into hostile territory in the middle of a war. You don't go unarmed. We don't *let* you go unarmed."

"Well . . ." Rita took the tablet and thumb-printed the dialog box. "Thanks, I guess." She'd learned enough about guns on the FBI course to know that the fastest way to get yourself shot was to carry one. Going armed was guaranteed to escalate any confrontation, and unless you were an expert shooter, you'd come out of it worse. Any guards she ran into while burgling a government building in a military coup would, by definition, be trigger happy. So she bit her tongue and decided to rely on her ability to jaunt *really* fast if people shot at her. She took the pistol—a Glock with a twenty-round magazine and laser aiming device—just to convince agent Garner that she was complying with his checklist. But then she had to make sure that it was properly loaded and that the laser's battery was charged. And then she had to check that her inertial nav was loaded with her waypoints and zeroed, and that the rest of her gear was ready. And by the time she'd done all that, it was getting dark.

"Phone," said Garner, passing her a handset.

"Rita?" It was Dr. Scranton.

"I'm on-site and pretty much ready to go. Do you have any updated instructions for me?"

"Yes, that's why I'm calling." Dr. Scranton actually sounded *flustered*. Her voice was uncharacteristically scratchy. "I've been in a meeting with the National Security Advisor all afternoon, and I've got revised orders for you—I'm emailing them through to Agent Garner now, along with a new list of transfer points for you to upload to your inertial mapper. Short version: we want you to find Mrs. Burgeson's people and set up lines of communication so we can maintain contact with them. Most likely they'll have someone watching her office. And I have a message for you to pass on to them, from the President. Or, rather, the National Security Council, as chaired by the President—you know how it is with committees—but signed by her."

"A message from the President?" Rita asked, reflexively impressed despite her growing awareness that even senior politicians were just regular people, burdened with everyone else's unrealistic expectations.

"Yes, it's for Mrs. Burgeson, or Mrs. Hjorth, or whoever's running the shop over there. We expect to have Elizabeth Hanover in custody within twenty-four hours. But we're willing to negotiate for her, and to hand over other persons of interest to the DPR, in return for certain considerations. If they, for their part, are willing to negotiate in good faith."

"You've got—*wow.*" Rita shook her head. *Miriam's going to be really pissed,* she realized. "Anything else?"

"Yes. Be sure to tell them we got the Juggernaut message loud and clear."

"What message?"

"Rita!" Dr. Scranton sounded as exasperated as her fifth-grade math teacher. "Who do you think that overflight was aimed at? A couple of hundred thousand funeral attendees who could barely see a dot in the sky, or a rival superpower with a space program and the ability to send a nuclear strike through para-time? *We got the message.* I'm relying on you to tell them that we're realists, and we're willing to discuss terms for détente. Trust but verify, treaty negotiations, common ground, nuclear hotlines, that sort of thing."

"I'm—" *baffled,* Rita thought—"confused. But I can tell them that. Uh, better put it in writing?"

"The email is on its way to your tablet right now. You can even take a print-out." Eileen's tone was as dry as the interior of the Atacama desert. "Any other questions?"

"Uh, nope. Okay, upload a set of waypoints to my inertial mapper, print-out message for Miriam Burgeson, try not to get shot. I think that's it?"

"The President wants you to know that she's counting on you. Good luck and god speed." Dr. Scranton hung up.

"Well?" Garner asked as she handed his phone back. His expression was unreadable.

"All *right*," she said, suppressing the impulse to twitch uncontrollably at the expectations laid on her shoulders. "You should have some updates for me on the laptop. Let's do this thing before I chicken out?"

It took ten minutes to download her new instructions and produce a paper print-out of the message from the President. The paramedics standing by had been briefed, but the DHS officer accompanying her up the ladder kept eying her sidelong, as if he was checking her out for horns and a forked tail. As she stepped up, he asked, "so you're a world-walker?"

"I'm a *government* world-walker to you," she shot back. "And I don't exist. No selfies, no tweets or we're *both* in big trouble."

She could see him absorbing this. World-walkers weren't exactly popular: but then he nodded and gave her a thumbs-up. "Gotcha. Break a leg, or whatever it is you do."

"I may well do just that, if you move this thing before I'm back," she told him. Then Rita jaunted—

—Dropped nearly fifty centimeters, jarred her ankles, and stumbled against a tree.

She bit back a curse as she looked around. Manhattan Island in time line one at night was an overgrown jumble of vegetation, harsh-edged shadows cast by the light of the moon. She removed her unwanted pistol and carefully placed it on her arrival spot, then cast around, checked her inertial mapper, and tried to jaunt again. Harsh pain stabbed at her temples. *Of course* the ground level here was lower so her feet were intersecting with the floor. Not far away she saw a deadfall. Clambering atop it took a minute: then she keyed up the engram for the Commonwealth and jaunted again.

This time there was no headache and she didn't fall far. Her feet landed on a carpeted floor. She was inside the ministry building. It was night and the power was out. All the light there was to see by was filtered through windows. She'd jaunted inside in some sort of reception area. The moonlight revealed a scene of frozen chaos. Drawers had been pulled from desks and up-ended. A filing cabinet lay toppled on its side, heaps and drifts of paper spilling across the carpet. Chairs were overturned, the side table smashed as if there'd been a fight. This office had been vandalized rather than searched, ransacked by intruders who wanted to score a brutal point rather than achieve any lasting goal.

Her skin crawling, Rita backed towards a wall opposite a big sash window. Glass crunched beneath her booted feet. The door to the corridor was ajar, a narrow rectangle of darkness in the gloom. *Where is everybody?* she wondered. Had the ministry been evacuated? If so, why hadn't the Commonwealth Guards posted troops here? If not, where are the skeleton staff? *This stinks.* Not for the first time she rued her questionable life choices. She wondered if she'd been set up as a pawn in some kind of 'motivational' scenario aimed at sending a message to the Commonwealth— one where she was the punch line.

Nothing for it. She tip-toed towards the doorway then paused to listen. She didn't hear anything, but that didn't mean she was safe. Nor did the lack of visible CCTV mean there were no alarms. Tech in the Commonwealth was unevenly distributed, and they weren't as backwards as they seemed at first glance to a visitor from the United States. Rita knelt and carefully touched the floor beside the doorframe. A slight hump in the carpet told her all she needed to know. There was a pressure pad on the threshold, doubtless connected to an alarm system. It was a low-tech solution, but just as efficient as cameras. Knowing if it was still active, but best to assume that an out-of-hours misstep would bring guards running.

Twitching the door open, Rita carefully stepped over the patch of raised carpet and out into the corridor. She hadn't been in this part of the building, but she'd glimpsed it on her way past, days earlier. Back then it had been a well-lit hive of activity. Now it was dark and empty. Pulling out a pocket flashlight, she briefly lit up the passageway as far as the lobby. Nothing jumped out at her. There were no guards, no tripwires or sentry guns. The floor was tiled, hard beneath her heels. She made her way to the lobby and paused again to check for light beams. Memory told her the lobby was secured by an armed guard in a sentry box: it was hardly likely to have an alarm system as well. But the sentry box was overturned and the imposing front doors to the interior of the ministry were smashed in. They hung drunkenly from their hinges, held in place by a padlock and chain. There was a dark stain on the carpet at the foot of the staircase leading up to the second floor offices. *Probably just spilled coffee,* she lied to herself, then shuddered.

Rita took the stairs as fast as she could without making a noise, keeping to the carpet until just below the top. She paused for another flashlight check, which revealed the telltale raised profile of another pressure pad. Stepping over it, she kept to the edges of the corridor as she made for Miriam's office. There were additional signs of struggle on this floor. Doors hung open to left and right, revealing damaged walls and overturned furniture. The paintings on the walls hung askew or had fallen to the floor, their frames broken. At the intersection of two passageways, Rita found a forlorn barricade of overturned desks that had been shoved aside by some terrible force. There were, as far as she could see, no bullet holes—which was a small comfort.

She finally arrived at her mother's executive suite. The carpet thickened, and the paintings on the walls were larger and boasted more rococo embellishments on their frames. Some of them had been slashed, the faces of the portraits' subjects vandalized. The carpet sucked damply at her boot soles. *There's nobody here,* Rita told herself nervously. *I need to check it out before I go home and tell Dr. Scranton it's a wash.* The idea of searching the streets of New London for her mother's people in the middle of the chaos and turbulence of a coup seemed monumentally idiotic at this remove. The urge to cut and run, to leave the abandoned ministerial building with all possible haste, was suffocating. *This is stupid,* she told herself, stiffening her spine. *There's nothing here.*

She opened the door to her mother's outer office and stepped inside.

—"Hey, " A man's voice, unfamiliar, said—

Rita tried to step backward.

"Freeze!" A different voice shouted at her. The room around her lit up like the surface of the noonday sun, dazzlingly bright. Boots pounded down the corridor behind her: she looked round, to see men with guns aimed at her. "Move and we shoot! Hands up!"

Oh no, not again, Rita thought dismally, and raised her hands.

The man sitting in the chair where her mother's desk should have been—it had been dragged carelessly aside, the expensive computer monitor tumbled on the floor beneath it—rose to his feet.

"Well, well, well," he said, indecently smug: "and who do we have here?" He wore the black uniform of a Commonwealth Guard officer, the stylized silver axe-and-cane insignia glinting at his collar and chest. Rough hands grabbed her and held her still as he walked towards her. He loomed over Rita. "You've caused a lot of trouble! But we've got you now," he announced to the room. His breath smelled of fried onions and a sour reek of cheap tobacco. He took a step back and looked past her shoulder: "bring her," he told the guards, then walked along the corridor. Glancing back briefly, he couldn't resist gloating: "coming here was rather predictable, don't you think?" More guards surrounded them as he led the party towards the rear of the building. "Notify HQ channel four, I'm bringing her in," he told a messenger. (Their acknowledgement, a hasty "yes, Major," didn't do much to dispel Rita's confusion and dismay.) To the other guards, the Major added: "I'll ride with her in the car."

"Where are you taking me?" She asked as they handcuffed her wrists behind her back.

"To explain yourself to the Committee for the Defense of the Revolution," he sneered, "your *Highness.*"

CENTRAL BERLIN, TIME LINE TWO, AUGUST 2020

Gomez and Martin got back to the Colonel's temporary office space on the USAF base at Tempelhof shortly after three in the morning. They found Smith still awake and burning the midnight oil. Major Schenk of the Bundespolizei was crashed out, cat-napping in a recliner while Smith stared bleary-eyed at a secure data terminal. It was, an ancient PC with soldered-shut USB ports and a hard-wired connection to the DHS's fusion center intelligence aggregators. "Sitrep," Smith grunted without looking up, a lapse in civility that told Gomez everything she needed to know about his exhaustion.

Gomez came to attention in front of his desk. "Found probable cause, sir! Reviewed the hotel lobby video, saw our suspect leaving around ten o'clock in company with Angie Hagen." Sonia paused. "Probable cause consists of a discarded messenger bag showing signs of recent firearm discharge inside, consistent with Major Hjorth's equipment load-out."

Colonel Smith nodded, then twitched erect and looked directly at her. "Missed by two hours," he said, then yawned cavernously. "Okay, we're getting closer. Major? Major Schenk!"

Schenk sat up slowly. "You found—" he paused, then switched to German. Martin replied rapidly. Schenk nodded, then switched back to English. "Evidence of firearm discharge will make things easier," he said.

"They might be armed, so it becomes a matter of hot pursuit for firearms offenses, in the interest of public safety."

Smith stretched. "Good." He thought for a second. "Do you have gait detection yet, on the subway security cameras? Or general deep learning object recognition?"

"Gait? You mean, walking? Yes, I believe they can do that, with a warrant which we shall have by mid-morning. What objects do you want to track?"

"Sonia?" Smith looked at her. "At ease, you're not in the army now."

"Sir." Gomez relaxed her stance. "Sir, we found some discards in the messenger bag. A couple of cartridge cases, some paper wadding, crumpled receipts from a department store. Someone—presumably Elizabeth—bought a fancy hand-bag and a bunch of clothes. We've got hotel lobby video, so that fancy bag-matching algorithm might just work."

"Yes, that got us Major Hjorth in New York, didn't it? The recognizer training set is part of the DHS deep learning library, hosted in gov.cloud: if we can get access to the camera feeds and upload them to the service, we should be able to find her."

"Bag-matching—" Schenk peered at the Colonel. "You're serious?"

"It's no weirder than facial recognition or gait recognition, is it? Bags are actually much more individual and distinctive than faces, and provide a bigger target for cameras."

Schenk scowled. "As I have been telling you, we cannot run a constant dragnet, it is not constitutionally permissible. Nor is feeding camera streams to an out-of-EU service. But with probable cause, and a specific time, if you can run your recognizer as an instance on someone else's servers here in the EU . . . can you tell me what we are to look for?"

"Sure." Smith thought. "They won't have gone direct to their next safe house, they'll have tried to throw off a tail. But we know Angie didn't hire a car. I'm willing to bet they'll have caught the U-bahn or S-bahn at least once, and they'll be going to a private dwelling rather than another hotel—breaking the pattern. So how about we look for the bag as a primary match, and Angie Hagen's face as a secondary, leaving public transit station exits between eleven p.m. yesterday and three a.m. today? If we find a final exit node we can then follow them using any nearby street cameras. I'm guessing they'll have a safe house near a couple of transit stations, maybe a bus interchange, and one or more major traffic arteries. Lots of getaway routes."

Schenk was making notes. "Is that all?" He asked, dead-pan.

"That's the easy bit!" Smith yawned. "We need to hit the cellphone base stations around our runaway's hotel. Ms. Hagen will be carrying a phone, even if she made the Hanover woman ditch hers. Once we find which stations they passed through, we can look for phones connecting to local base stations around the same time. Then we triangulate on her, and that's how we'll find where they've gone to ground."

JUGGERNAUT, LOW EARTH ORBIT, TIME LINE THREE, AUGUST 2020

"All right, people, let's get started," Huw spoke over the crew voice loop.

Everyone was back in their seat, survival suit helmets sealed. The access tunnels between capsules were closed and latched, the engineering team had removed the requisite number of propulsion charges from the main magazine and armed them, and the thermal radiators and most of the radio and radar antennae had been cranked back behind their protective covers. The world-walkers were instrumented and had taken their pills: the medics were monitoring them, ready to intervene. Even Huw was doped-up, standing by as backup world-walker in case an emergency jaunt was needed while the regulars were at their safety limit. His helmet air supply was feeding him a higher partial pressure of oxygen than usual, to compensate for the depressed blood pressure that had given him a headache. "Flight stations, report—"

The voices merged into a steady stream in his headset. "Propulsion: go. Engineering: go. Surgeons: go. Jaunt: go. Nav: go. Point defense: go. Radar: go. Life support: go—"

No anomalies. Everyone sounded tense. "Juggernaut is go for jaunt," Huw confirmed. "Jaunt team, time line one, transfer on countdown."

BERLIN, TIME LINE TWO, AUGUST 2020

It was a quarter past seven in the morning in Berlin: a quarter past midnight in New York and Caracas.

Liz was sipping her coffee when a muted buzzing noise caught her attention. It was followed by a timorous knock on the front door.

"That will be your passport," said Kurt, giving her a stern look. "Stay here." He entered the front hall and a moment later she heard the door open, and a quiet discussion in German. The door closed and Kurt returned. He handed her a small, green booklet then pulled it back momentarily when she reached for it. "A-ha, just a second."

"What?" She demanded.

"This is a—" Kurt seemed almost at a loss for words as he opened the booklet and stared at the inside front cover, then flipped to the flyleaf—"it's *real?*" He said, disbelieving.

"What?" She stared at him.

"It appears to be a genuine Indonesian passport—"

"Indones—where? What is that? Is it a real country?"

"It doesn't exist in your time line? Java and New Guinea and their islands are a nation, here—they used to be part of the Dutch empire in the East Indies—"

"*The Dutch* had an empire?"

Kurt's cheek twitched as if he was suppressing a smile: "Not any more, it seems. Attend. This is an emergency passport of the Republic of Indonesia, issued from the embassy here in Berlin, in the name of Ayu Sibabat: mother, Javanese, father an English expatriate—" he squinted at her face. "It *could* work," he said doubtfully.

"What," she tapped her toe, "is the problem?"

"Nothing, maybe. We just have to hope that German passport officials are not experts on Indonesian society." A tired look settled over his features. "There is an entry visa for Venezuela here," he flipped to a page with a card clipped to it, "and I have e-tickets for our party: you, me, Angie, others. You have been studying in Venezuela but accompanied your classmate Angie and her grandfather—that is I—to Germany for a vacation. Now you are returning to university." Elizabeth's head was spinning. Women could attend university? Attend a university *on another continent*, vacationing on a third land mass, without a chaperone? She was about to ask him to pause while she assimilated everything, but Kurt's briefing continued to wash over her. "Your original passport was lost, so the embassy issued this temporary replacement, good for one trip."

She caught up. "It's a forgery?"

"No: it's real enough. But when you pass through immigration control, you will be scanned, and when the passenger manifest of the missing flight is published they will rapidly realize that someone bribed an embassy official. It must have cost a fortune, especially at such short notice."

Missing? she wondered, then got distracted: "How rapidly is rapidly?"

"The Venezuelan and German authorities will have to coordinate—it may take them a day or two. The helper in the embassy will have to run, and fast." Kurt looked slightly dazed. "In my day, we would never *dream* of burning an asset in a foreign embassy unless it was a screaming emergency! The end of the world."

Liz had a premonition of the uproar her arrival in New London would cause. "Maybe it is." Then another thought struck her. "How are we going to get there?"

Kurt shrugged. "One step at a time. The first thing you learn in the game is to trust Control. Get ready to go, I am waking Angela now."

A minute later Angie strolled into the kitchen stretching and yawning, her clothes sleep-rumpled, a pair of oddly technical low-heeled boots in one hand and a phone in the other. "What time is it?"

"Too early." Liz smirked. "Are you going barefoot?"

Angie glared at her. "Watch this." Using some kind of magic she had her boots on and laced before Liz could blink twice. "Voila! Learned that in the army."

"The—" *Army?* Liz blinked thrice—"do I want to know?"

"I enlisted so the veteran's benefits paid for my higher education." Angie glanced at the corridor: "ready to move out!" She called.

Liz grabbed her shoulder bag, gun and all. "No, leave it," Kurt told her. "Why?"

"Enough with the questions: there will be bags waiting for you at the airport. For now, take nothing."

"No." She set her jaw mulishly. The pistol was her one guarantee of independent action—

Kurt sighed. "Must you question everything?"

"If I didn't, I wouldn't be here!"

"Well, then." He shook his head. "We are entering an airport, one of the most tightly secured spaces accessible to civilians. There are dos and don'ts, and I do not have time to train you. Things in your bag might be illegal—the wrong liquids, nail clippers, a pen knife or something that might be mistaken for a weapon. Easier to leave it. Our lamplighter has bags waiting for you that contain only things an Ayu Sibabat might have on her person that will not see her arrested."

A pen knife she could almost understand, but—"*Liquids?*"

"Yes, they're afraid of liquid explosives or poisons. Airliners are fragile so they are very serious about it. So. Leave the bag."

"This is nonsense." But she put the bag down and followed Angie and Kurt into the early morning light regardless. Her head was spinning. "What now?"

"To Brandenburg Airport," Angie declared, "by taxi."

"Try not to gape," Kurt warned her: "according to your cover documents Ayu Sibabat has flown before."

"Unless you're rich, flying sucks," Angie commented. "We're not rich, so be prepared to be treated like cattle. if they search you, it's undignified but it's not personal: just try to stay calm."

"I called a taxi," Kurt added. "A contact will be waiting for us with appropriate-looking luggage when we arrive at the terminal. Before we go in, you need to understand the airport check-in process—"

One of the melted-looking cars pulled up beside them, with an illuminated sign on the roof. Angie helped Elizabeth into the back while Kurt made conversation with the driver, deliberately distracting him. The driver didn't notice Liz's white knuckled death-grip on the door handle, but Angie did. "Problem?" She asked quietly.

"I have only ridden in one of these once before, with the Major . . ." Who was bleeding out at the time. Liz forced herself to relax.

The roads became straighter, wider, and faster as they headed out of the city, finally merging into a horizon-spanning ribbon of cement surmounted by illuminated signs that flashed by faster than the view from an express train back home.

Finally they came to a vast, echoing shed of a building, somewhat like a railway station, with desks and queues of tired travelers in place of platforms and trains. The details were all different, but the organization was tantalizingly familiar. Officials in the liveries of shipping lines and gendarmes in black with complicated-looking stubby guns strapped to their chests patrolled the chaos. Baggage carts, all alike, bearing piles of oddly shaped suitcases, all different. A middle-aged woman holding up a sign: DOUGLAS PARTY. Kurt made a beeline towards her.

"Ah, there you are!" The woman smiled broadly. "These are your carry-ons," she said confidingly, and passed out shoulder bags all round, "and your checked bags."

"What are the contents?" Kurt raised an eyebrow.

"New clothing with labels cut off, toiletries included. I put the clothes through a tumble dryer to crease them. The phones and tablets in your carry-ons are pre-loaded burners." The woman looked at Elizabeth. "There is some reading matter on your tablet!" She might as well have been speaking Greek.

"Will I ever see you again?" Elizabeth asked.

"I hope not!" The woman smiled brightly: "if you do, we'll both be in prison."

"Oh. Then . . . thank you for your efforts."

To her surprise the lamplighter leaned forward and hugged her. "Good travels," she murmured. They parted, Kurt led her into the check-in queue for the Lufthansa flight to Caracas, and Elizabeth never saw her again.

JUGGERNAUT, LOW EARTH ORBIT, TIME LINE TWO, AUGUST 2020

The screen at the front of the command capsule continued to display a view of the Pacific Ocean. It provided a peaceful, turquoise backdrop, lightly brushed with clouds, unrolling hypnotically as Juggernaut hurtled south-east, departing French Imperial airspace. Huw had spoken for ten minutes, reciting his script in both English and French. It was almost exactly the same speech he'd given as Juggernaut passed over the First Man's funeral parade. It was anybody's guess how widely the broadcast had been heard, for installations around St. Petersburg had attempted to jam Juggernaut's much small emitters, but the message itself had been received loud and clear. Early warning radar and crude missile guidance systems had lit up Juggernaut's hull for the entire duration of its pass over the French capital, and when the Imperial SIGINT intelligence service compared his words with recordings from New London, they'd confirm that it wasn't just playing on a tape loop—Juggernaut was indeed crewed.

"Nav. Countdown to jaunt commencing. Sixty seconds."

"Jaunt. Wolf ready to go."

"Thirty. Twenty. Ten—"

Bill jaunted, taking Juggernaut with him. There was no discernible sensation, but outside the screen the pattern of clouds over the ocean blinked into a new configuration.

"Nav. Jaunt confirmed. On orbit in time line one."

"Flight stations, report—"

Juggernaut's orbit was now tracking north again, back towards the equator as it passed Central America, then east towards the overgrown ruins of the Gruinmarkt. Minutes passed, then, "Nav, call for maneuvering."

"Inclination burn coming up in three minutes. Propulsion—"

"Everybody stand by for jolt in twenty seconds."

"Sixteen rounds rapid, fire in the hole!"

World's scariest piñata, Huw thought dizzily as a surge of acceleration shoved him down into his seat, *and I get to be the candy. Let's hope the hull holds up.* Juggernaut's structure groaned and rattled with every surge that followed a propulsion charge detonating. The shock absorbers worked fine, and the strain gauges showed they were well within tolerance, but it was still disconcerting—if not downright alarming.

After the sixteenth detonation, Huw took a deep breath. "Nav, are we on track?"

"We should know in about ten minutes, sir. Exposing the star trackers now—looks like the inertial platform drifts excessively when subjected to repeated jolts." Outside, the screen showed the limb of the Earth gradually shrinking and curving more tightly. The series of blasts had kicked Juggernaut into an elliptical orbit, with an apogee—highest point over ground—nearly three thousand kilometers up. They'd have to perform another maneuver in a couple of hours in order to achieve the much lower, nearly circular orbit they were aiming for.

"Okay, get back to me when you have something. Alan, how's Engineering?"

"No red lights." Alan Stevens sounded tense. "Waiting to see if all the seals are holding, but nothing's failed so far . . ."

"Good: raise me immediately if there's anything to report." Another deep breath. "Jaunt, how are you doing? Bill?"

"I'm good. Got a grade three, though." A headache bad enough to report.

"Okay, you're off the roster until the surgeon clears you. Who's up next, Rufus or Jenny?"

"It's my turn," Jenny Wu said diffidently. Not because she was particularly shy and retiring, but if Huw had to guess, it would be because the next, critical jaunt would be the first time she'd carried Juggernaut with her. "I'm green, sir. Uh, I mean I'm over the nausea."

"That's good to know. Radar, do we have an updated elements list?"

Radar: "we got the list of updates from our back channel nearly forty eight hours ago. We should be safe, as long as we arrive on track with the target at inclination 51.64 degrees and altitude 250 American miles above mean sea level. They keep that orbit as sterile as possible."

Huw snorted: "Not after we visit. Everybody, take ten then we'll go round the stations again. Prepare for what's coming next."

Hours blurred passed, as Juggernaut flew onwards. Engineering worked hard, tightening loose fittings. Medical cleared Jenny for duty. Finally, it was time for another maneuver. They lit off five bombs this time, shifting their inclination from the equator and cancelling the elliptical component of Juggernaut's velocity vector. A quarter of an hour later, Nav checked back in. "We're on the nail, sir. Altitude plus or minus two thousand meters, trailing the ISS's path by about twenty kilometers."

One of the few items Miriam's organization had failed to acquire for Juggernaut was a working Kurs docking navigation system. Another was an APAS-95 docking adapter and capture ring. Such specialized aerospace hardware didn't exactly grow on trees. But without them, Juggernaut didn't have the minimum equipment to safely approach and dock with the International Space Station. It would be like trying to park a main battle tank in a multi-story car park sized for compact cars. Moreover, firing up the nuclear propulsion system in time line two would fry thousands of active satellites operated by dozens of different nations, endearing the Commonwealth to absolutely nobody.

But Juggernaut had its own approach radar and a limited ability to maneuver using old-fashioned rockets. And Juggernaut didn't need to get within even a kilometer of the ISS to make front page news around the world.

"Great." Huw fought the urge to rub his hands together. "I expect Roscosmos Control in Moscow will have some choice words for us when we show up on their doorstep." *And NASA will flip their lid.* He paused. "How recent is our launch schedule?"

"It was last updated six days ago, sir. There's an Orion loading up for return right now, but it's not due to undock until next week. And Expedition seventy-two isn't due to lift off from Baikonur until there's a free docking port—there's a traffic jam, ever since they cancelled the Node module replacement two years ago."

Huw chewed his lower lip. "They only found out we exist yesterday, much less that we're coming to visit, so they won't have had time to send up a surprise for us." *Unless our OPSEC is so piss-poor that they've known about Juggernaut all along.* Rita's lack of awareness of the Commonwealth suggested otherwise—she wouldn't have been arrested on her third visit if DHS had any situational awareness on the ground. Nevertheless, it was his job to keep track of even the low-probability options. *It's no wonder Brill is so paranoid, worrying about this kind of spy stuff all day, every day.* He dismissed the distraction and spoke. "Jaunt control: prep for a quick in and out. I'm putting Jenny on first jump, Rufus on standby for a quick retreat. Radar, immediate scan on arrival and alert Jaunt if there's anything unexpected. Rufus, until I tell you to stand down, proximity avoidance protocol is in effect: bug-out back to this time line *immediately* if anyone sees anything. Don't wait for confirmation, we'll hold a post-mortem afterwards. Everyone button up and prepare for maneuvering. Coms, get the VHF-1, VHF-2, and Soyuz-TM beacon frequencies dialed in: I want us to be squawking as we jaunt through."

He paused, scanning his checklist as he chose his next words carefully. "Fire control, hold safe, I repeat, hold safe. There will be *no* shooting under *any* circumstances, because it's an unarmed civilian station, and also because it's an *International* one. We're not here to make enemies, we're here to make a point."

Jensen, one seat over, cleared his throat: "and exactly what point are we making, sir?" He asked.

Huw grinned broadly at him. "Isn't it obvious?"

Nav broke into the chat: "We're coming up on twenty minutes out from our transfer window, sir."

"All right. Let's show them what we've got . . ."

MANHATTAN ISLAND,
TIME LINES THREE AND FIVE, AUGUST 2020

Jaunting hurt.

Miriam jaunted very seldom these days—the risk of a fatal ischemic attack or stroke increased with age—and she was unprepared and unmedicated.

She doubled over, stumbling on the uneven ground. An ice pick stabbed at her right eye, and migraine-bright flashes of light swirled at the edges of her vision, leaving her gasping at the pain.

The bright and silvery agony subsided in waves that echoed her heartbeat, and after a minute she was able to straighten up and take stock. There were trees everywhere in the uninhabited time line, blocking her line of sight in all directions. But the older ones were all charred on the same side—the bomb line had ended at the northern tip of Manhattan Island, when the B-52s jaunted back to the United States with empty weapon bays. Judging by the degree of damage, she was maybe half to two-thirds of the way down the eastern side, just outside the walled cantonment of New London in time line three, somewhere around Fifth Avenue and Broadway in time line two. Which meant—

Miriam turned due east, and started walking (or rather, stumbling tiredly) through the undergrowth towards the banks of the Hudson.

It was a humid, hot day, and the biting insects were out in force. She was nearly fifty years old and regrettably unfit (a party commissioner's working life did not allow much time for exercise, and the Commonwealth hadn't yet discovered the benefits of gym sessions for office workers). She was underfed, borderline-dehydrated, and dizzy, so it took her most of two hours to make her way downslope towards the river. But as she walked she remembered to periodically check the charred tree trunks about a meter above head level: and eventually she spotted what she was looking for.

The discreet metal hook and wire trailing into the grass led her on a brief hunt through the undergrowth, but eventually she followed it to an olive-green metal box half-buried under a pile of twigs. She opened the lid, picked up the handset inside, and spun the hand-cranked generator. "Hello, is anyone listening?" she asked.

The field telephone crackled distantly, then emitted an electronic beep. "Password," someone said, their voice disguised by a frequency shifter.

Miriam snapped: "I don't know the fucking password, this is an emergency and I need pickup *now*." She glanced inside the lid of the box. "I'm at Terminal 0221," she added. "Miriam Burgeson, Commissioner of State."

"Holy—" The voice cut off abruptly. A few seconds later another voice came on the line. "Boss?"

"Colonel." Her shoulders relaxed as an invisible and hitherto unnoticed weight slid from her back. Colonel Haig was one of Brill's people, former

Commonwealth military permanently seconded to the DPR. "I got away, but they're holding Erasmus and about half the Commission. A Brigadier Richards was threatening me with a show trial. Can you organize a pickup?"

"Absolutely! I'll have Captain Roberts send a team to retrieve you immediately. They should reach you within half an hour. Mrs. Hjorth is in the secure location and he'll take you to her. I'll send a courier to warn her you're incoming."

"Okay, I'm hanging up. Call me if you need me." Miriam put the handset down.

Field telephones were a century-old technology, and if properly laid they were nearly undetectable when not in use. Even so, here in the backwoods of time line one, the world-walkers exercised extreme caution: the US knew this to be the former home of the Clan, and although it had been nuked until it was no more habitable than the exclusion zone around Chernobyl, they kept up regular surveillance overflights.

Miriam found a tree to lean against and rested her aching legs. Then she waited.

A civilian with no particular background in woodcraft, Miriam knew better than to expect to spot a team of special forces soldiers sneaking up on her. Nevertheless she tried, and was predictably surprised when Captain Roberts cleared his throat behind her left shoulder. At least she managed not to startle, which was good for her dignity, if not much else.

"Commissioner Burgeson," he murmured. "Are you able to walk?"

"Yes." Miriam forced herself upright. "I may be a little slow."

"If you jaunted in the last hour, I have spare Prep-A pills," he told her.

"That would be good." He passed her a small pill case and offered his canteen to wash the meds down. "We don't have far to go," he added, then raised his voice: "Arnesen, take point: Berry, Rosen, rear." They moved off slowly, working their way down-slope towards the river.

The advance team who'd surveyed the island and installed the field telephones had cleared a site alongside the Hudson. A small military landing craft—a side-wall hovercraft—was parked on a mud bank, its front ramp extended. "Please take a seat, ma'am." The soldiers boarded: a diesel engine clattered into life and the landing craft lifted off the water and turned down-river.

"Where are we—" Miriam tried to ask, but then the woman seated at the first officer's station opened a book of eye-warping knotwork designs and she had to close her eyes. She swallowed as her eardrums popped and the hovercraft dropped, bouncing hard off the water in whatever time line it had just transitioned to—"Going?"

"Not far now!" Roberts shouted in her ear—the hovercraft was loud. They accelerated again and she opened her eyes in time to see the shore of an uninhabited version of Queens rushing past, and then a wall, watchtowers, and a broad ramp at the water's edge. The landing craft howled as it left the river and climbed the apron, slowing as it came ashore. Finally the front ramp came down and the engine cut off, leaving her ears ringing.

Ten minutes later Roberts led her through a door in a rusty chain-link fence surrounding a cement building, windowless at ground level and with narrow firing slits above. It was a pocket fortress stranded in a clearing in an uninhabited forest, and it didn't look new. Roberts brought her to an office door and discreetly waited outside as she went in. "When did we set this up?" She asked Brilliana: "I don't remember authorizing this."

"Fifteen years ago." Brill greeted her from a desk where she'd set up the basics: secure data terminal, laptop, radio telephone. "Remember the early days? Olga signed off and we kept it strictly need-to-know." By implication, it had been part of the Clan survivor's bug-out plan, a last-ditch retreat in case the Commonwealth turned on them. "It was moribund until six months ago, but then we recommissioned it as a ground station for the Juggernaut program—we wanted one geographically close to New London but two jaunts away. It's a lost line item in your budget reports, but a really useful one right now." She looked to have aged a decade in the past six hours. "What news from the capital? Is Nel safe? Is 'Ras . . ."

Miriam flinched. "Nel was with Rita and they haven't got Rita so I assume she's safe for the time being. My husband was still alive less than two hours ago."

"Oh God, Miriam, I'm so sorry . . ."

"Don't be." Her tone was clipped, voice over-controlled. "He told me to get out. He knows the score. I'm not abandoning him." To her own ears, she sounded slightly wild. "I've got to go back, or they'll conclude their worst fears are true. It's a clusterfuck, Brill, the Commies only moved because they think we're trying to reinstall the monarchy. They're still not sure Juggernaut is real and they think Rita is Princess Elizabeth—they found the tapes and believed them—"

"—Oh *shit*—"

"—So now we've got to produce the princess—and Rita. It's the only way to prove to them that they're different people. And I've got to turn myself in or they'll conclude I'm guilty and operate on that assumption, which will make putting Rita or the Princess in front of them that much harder, if not impossible."

"Shit. Shit." Brill did not swear habitually: it was a sign of stress. "Okay . . . so, about Ms. Hanover, I have an update? It's stale news—nearly two hours old—but she's with Kurt and his team and they're on the move, so I authorized Extraction Plan C."

"What?" There was a visitor's seat: Miriam sat down heavily. Plan A was the aborted scheme with Yul in the pilot's seat. Plan B involved overland travel to Monaco then a private jet—not possible with the DHS already hot on Elizabeth's trail. Plan C . . ."Isn't that the *really risky* one?"

"Yes, a blind in-flight jaunt with an unbriefed and untrained pilot. We'll be tearing up and burning a lot of assets if we do this—we won't be able to run agents into Germany or Indonesia for a long time to come. Thing is, Homeland Security have got Yul and Paulie. At this point we have to assume they've rolled up our entire stateside east coast network, and they're probably hours away from doing the same in Germany. We've only got one remaining world-walker there, so I'm pulling them out and using them for Plan C. Unless—" She bit her lip—"you think we'd do better to surrender the Princess to the United States?"

Miriam thought for a few seconds. Concentration came hard, requiring her to swim against the turbulent currents of her anxiety. If the Colonel got his hands on Elizabeth Hanover, the temptation to flourish her in the Commonwealth government's face would be nearly irresistible—and right now, that meant the Guard junta. Smith didn't seem to be overly conscious of the internal flash-points and conflicts within the Commonwealth. But he wouldn't hand her over immediately, or even soon, and might even send her back to her father's court—*what's the worst that can happen?* Miriam asked herself. If Plan C failed, if the plane crashed, the Princess would die alongside Kurt and Angie (*don't think about her as Rita's partner,* Miriam cautioned herself: *don't get emotionally involved*), but they'd be no worse off in real terms than they already were. And if it worked—

"Plan C it is, as long as it seems viable. You have contact with Continental Air Defense Command? Are they still loyal?"

Brill nodded grimly. "Yes, and their loyalty is a critical element of Plan C—I'll notify them. We can do this. Just as long as the pilots don't fuck it up." She checked her laptop. "They can be airborne inside four hours, and on final into Maracaibo in another eleven hours. If there's a courier jet waiting, that's another five hours to New London—but we may be able to do better if there's enough lead time to set up an air bridge and in-flight refueling, maybe put her in the back seat of a fighter jet—"

Miriam shook her head: "do whatever it takes to get her here as fast as possible. On my orders, by any means necessary. You're in charge here: I'm going back to New London to end this, or die trying."

"Miriam! You *can't*—"

"I can and I must. I cut and ran: it looked incriminating as hell. Also, there's a morale aspect to consider. Producing the Princess alongside Rita will exert far more pressure on the junta if they've been told repeatedly that it's what we're going to do—right now they think we're lying, proving we're not will blow the wind out of their sails. Listen, right now I am starving and I need a nap. But I have to go back and face the music if we're going to have any hope of de-escalating this crisis without a civil war. Oh, don't look at me like that: I'm not going to jump in front of a bullet. But I've got to lead this thing from the front, and if anything happens to me, here's what I expect you and Olga to do . . ."

BERLIN, TIME LINE TWO, AUGUST 2020

Once Major Schenk kicked it up a level and someone got a judge out of bed to sign a warrant, the search gathered pace rapidly. There was now a central control room for monitoring the platform CCTV cameras on both of Berlin's two disjoint subway networks (a legacy of the Cold War and the city's partition into East and West sectors). They could upload their feed to a special anti-terrorism fusion center in Cologne. Even better, the ATFC could download the neural networks DHS had developed to recognize designer handbags and their miscreant owners. Finally, the Five Eyes center in Cheltenham, England, was already up to speed on cellphone location mapping. Within an hour Cologne Center had multiple hits on Liz's bag in proximity to a close facial match for Angela Hagen, emerging from three different transit stations within a couple of hours. A half hour of expensive number crunching (an operation that occupied two-thirds of a million processor cores in the GCHQ internal cluster) identified two cellphone IMEIs that had pinged the network in the vicinity of each other along the correct time line for the facial match. Finally, the search ramped down, and by 7:15 in the morning, the search had narrowed to a single block in Charlottenburg.

That was close enough for the Major. He and Colonel Smith headed out to join the GSG 9 unit that was already en route to the target.

GSG 9 was the elite tactical unit of the German federal police. They trained with the Israeli Sayeret Matkal and the British SAS, they tackled terrorist threats and hostage situations, and they were armed to the teeth. But they were quaintly obsolescent (and downright gentlemanly) to Colonel Smith's eye. Lacking Homeland Security's access to the NSA's unblinking oversight—the eye of Sauron, DHS's critics called it—they couldn't turn all the neighbors' wifi hotspots into wall-piercing radar. Regular cops had to manually direct traffic away from the quiet residential street, for there was no blanket authority to override vehicle automation here. Nor could they remotely lock or unlock all the doors in the neighborhood. It was, in fact, a dismayingly old-fashioned raid: muscular men and a few women in body armor hanging around the entrances to an apartment building, ready to go in on foot, without a single killer robot or wall-piercing pain ray in sight.

They'd tracked the target to the fourth floor. But it wasn't clear which of the three apartments the owner of the phone (and the handbag) occupied. "That's okay," Major Schenk assured Colonel Smith. "We're getting the tenant list through shortly and that should clarify things."

"Can't you just send in the drones?" Gomez complained: "She's got a gun!" *Tase first, ask questions later* was Sonia's catch-phrase. They'd been up all night, and before leaving the office she'd sunk three double espressos. Now she was vibrating noticeably.

"Let's let the locals handle this one," Smith told her. "When in Rome, etcetera. Major?"

"Of course." Major Schenk nodded, but kept a wary eye on Gomez.

"Ah, Heidi—" He switched to German for a hurried conversation with a middle-eastern looking woman in hijab and body armor, toting a laptop in a tactical sling. "Yah, yah, this is all good." The Major gestured at the computer screen. "Apartment eleven is occupied by Herr Klein and Herr Altman, a pair of programmers. Apartment twelve is occupied by Frau Lemke, a pensioner. Apartment thirteen is occupied by Fraulein Henke, a secretary. Hmm." The corners of Schenk's mouth turned down.

"Is that all you've got?" Gomez demanded.

"That is how the police register lists the occupations of the tenants. Registration is mandatory, you understand, but we are forbidden to collect general data about the public."

Smith snapped his fingers. "Rentals dot com?" He asked.

"Yes, most probably someone is subletting their apartment, it is legal for up to fourteen days. Or they are renting out a single room while staying in residence. It is frowned upon, but—" the Major shrugged—"what can you do?"

Gomez muttered something about helicopter gunships and Flying Ginzu missiles. Smith massaged his temples. It didn't seem to have occurred to his over-eager subordinate that one of the people they were after was the daughter of a foreign head of state—a man the US government might have to negotiate with at some future point. "Major? What guaranteed *non*-lethal options are open to us?"

Schenk shrugged then turned to his laptop-toting assistant. She closed the lid on her machine, nodded briskly, and hurried off.

"What?" Asked Smith.

"I told her to go and knock on the door." Schenk looked smug. "Apologizing for the surprise fire inspection, and requesting to count the heads."

"What?" Gomez glared at the Major in disbelief. "But they're armed! They could be hiding! There might be bombs!"

"We are armed also," Schenk said firmly, "so it is *very important* that there is no shooting, isn't it. Follow me."

The Major plodded stolidly into the lobby of the apartment block then tackled the staircase with the determination of an endurance hiker. By the seventh flight of stairs, Smith was flagging, his sixty years telling. Finally Schenk paused just below the landing giving access to the fourth floor apartments and held up a hand. Ahead of him, two regular officers in state police uniforms were waiting. "*Du kannst jetzt anfangen,*" said Schenk: one of the cops nodded, then moved to press the buzzer beside the door to apartment eleven.

The occupants took their own sweet time answering. After a minute, the cop buzzed again. After a minute or so and a second lean on the buzzer the sound of someone stumbling about answered them: then the door opened, to reveal an extremely sleepy bear wearing a stained tee shirt with a sarcastic gamer slogan and nothing else. He yawned, tugged his shirt down to conceal his beer belly, exchanged some words with the cop, then closed the door and went back to bed.

"Not number eleven," Schenk muttered. He glanced at Gomez: "He and his partner work from home. Programmers, they only just went to bed, he says. So, to the next . . ."

Apartment twelve's occupant answered much faster. Frau Lemke was a desiccated but bright-eyed and energetic pensioner, the kind who appeared to be made entirely of spring steel and bungee cords. She was eager to chat, mostly about the comings and going at apartment thirteen, which were numerous and confusing and not what one might expect of an office worker. It became apparent that a succession of strangers with backpacks and wheelie bags turned up at odd hours, crashed around the kitchen, and departed on the morrow. Frau Lemke was astonishingly helpful and rather difficult to get rid of. It took three rounds of reassurances that there was nothing to worry about, even about the foreign tourists who turned up at three o'clock in the morning, before the door-knocker finally managed to get her to go back inside.

"Well," said Schenk. "And now, we extract the mussel from the shell."

"How?" Sonia demanded. "She's armed, remember?"

Schenk shrugged, then turned to one of the uniforms. "*Marcus, bitte schalten sie den strom und das wasser. Und die telefone.*"

"What?"

"Patience, please." Schenk beckoned them down the stairs to the next landing. "Their cellphones are intercepted with a, what you say, a Stingray." He held up a finger. "I instructed Marcus to cut off the electricity—" another finger went up—"and water—" a third finger—"and finally the land-lines. For the internet, you see. Now we go downstairs and wait for everybody to come out."

"But that could take hours!" Gomez exploded.

"How many hours is a life worth?" Schenk glared at her: "last year, German police officers fired *only eleven bullets* in anger. All police officers *combined*. In the same year your police shot and killed more than three thousand civilians, half of them innocent bystanders. No innocents will be shot in *my* city because of *your* impatience." He glared at her until she finally looked away, then snorted. "Come sit in the car, there is coffee— decaf for you—and when we have drunk it, the Colonel—" he nodded at Smith—"will phone our flighty little songbirds and coax them down from the trees."

Breakout

"Please tell me this is just a bad Hollywood special effect. Someone's pranking us."

The President looked slightly queasy as she leaned over the shoulder of the Air Force liaison to peer at the screen in the situation room.

"Uh, I'm sorry, ma'am." The liaison—a captain—looked just as unhappy as everyone else. "This is coming from the camera on the Canadarm Two attached to the main station truss frame. Mission Control at Baikonur in Russia is relaying it to us. So unless someone's hacked the downlink from Space Station Freedom, this is really happening."

"Baikonur." The President looked pained. "This isn't a hoax."

John Irving cleared his throat. "Absolutely not, ma'am."

"How much warning did we have of this?" Her tone was clipped and chilly, very far from the warmth and sincerity she exuded in public. When she was under pressure, she reverted to habits ingrained during her time in the Air Force.

"We got a heads-up in this evening's transfer packet from BLACK RAIN: intel on this thing only developed in the past few hours." Irving sounded abashed. "Dr. Scranton's been very clear that BLACK RAIN was dangerously far ahead of State's baseline tech estimates, that their industrial espionage program isn't their sole source of innovation. It looks like she was right." He caught Eileen's eye and shook his head very slightly: *keep your head down.*

"But what *is* it?" demanded the President. "And what's it doing here?"

The White House situation room (or rather, the situation room in Baltimore while the real White House was under reconstruction) was crowded this morning. POTUS was an early riser, usually up before five to start her work-out while listening to briefings recorded by her staff. When the duty officer had called the emergency session she was rested and ready, unlike Dr. Scranton and the members of the NSC subcommittee, who had been up all night analyzing the incursion in time line four.

In the days since the ERGO-1 incursion, the politics around the alien invasion in time line four had festered and turned toxic. State was being briefed. The Joint Chiefs were not only being briefed, they were having turf wars. Air Force overflights had been pushed further and further back from the incursion, forced to rely on long-range optics and sensors from higher and higher altitudes. They weren't happy about it. The Senate had gotten involved by way of various committees, and were using it as an excuse to get stabby over the President's perceived weakness on foreign affairs again. It was an election year, and the President had other fires to fight. It was eating Eileen Scranton's time, dragging her away from her other responsibilities—including the crisis in the Commonwealth.

Meanwhile the coup in the Commonwealth progressed in a haze of accusations, confusion, anger, and menace. Normally an engineered coup in a rival power was a well-understood tool of foreign affairs. But the now-destabilized Commonwealth posed unique risks, not least an armada of nuclear-armed strategic bombers with world-walking bombardiers. They were sitting on runways in a dispersal time line unknown to anybody here, quite conceivably waiting for a signal to go Full Doctor Strangelove, and *nobody* wanted to open that particular can of worms. But State had dived into the Commonwealth paddling pool without asking DHS for a sanity check. Indeed, State seemed to think the Commonwealth were some kind of yokels, like one of the central Asian 'stans, and had been gaslighting the Commonwealth Guard rather than taking Dr. Scranton's more cautious approach of trying to induce the DPR to discredit themselves. The memories of the long face-off with the Soviet Union had faded from institutional memory over the last quarter of a century, leaving the State Department suffering from delusions of imperial omnipotence It was bound to get them bitten on the ass hard, sooner or later. And now the worst had happened.

"Greetings from the people of the New American Commonwealth," the audio loop repeated: "this is Commonwealth deep space vehicle Juggernaut. We come in peace—" And come it did, slowly creeping up on the ISS in orbit, at a steady two meters per second. It was barely faster than walking pace, but that was no consolation to Mission Control, who had a collective nervous breakdown when the gigantic intruder appeared.

Especially as it was almost all the way inside the two-hundred-kilometer sterile zone around the station when it flickered into existence. And gigantic was no understatement—this thing was *huge*.

The silence had drawn out for too long. "Our source described it as a nuclear impulse-powered space battleship," Eileen admitted. (Irving's sharp glance said, *it's your head*.) "Apparently the Department of Energy, and then NASA, looked into a similar technology in the 1960s. They shelved it because it would have violated the atmospheric test ban treaty, and also because EMP from the propulsion system would have fried every satellite already in orbit."

"Right, right." The President frowned at her. "But that's only the first question. How is it *here*? I thought they relied on human world-walkers just as couriers?"

"I can't speak to how they got it here, but we *do* know it was developed by MITI, their industrial espionage and para-time exploration ministry, and we've had some recent indications that they can carry larger structures when they jaunt—we captured a world-walker with a pilot's license and a light plane—"

"Jesus," one of the generals interjected softly. His gaze was fixed at his tablet.

The President turned her gaze on him. "What?"

"It's, uh, it's a version of Project Orion, ma'am. I was just catching up on what that means. Turns out it's nuclear armed, *by definition*. It works by detonating nuclear devices behind a recoil plate. It's probably carrying more firepower in its magazines than our entire strategic deterrent."

"So we're receiving an ostensibly friendly visit from a nuclear-armed space battleship, launched by a superpower who *just happen* to be in the throes of a military coup we helped engineer?" The President's voice was dangerously even. "Just when I thought it couldn't get any worse. What are our options? Space Command, you first—"

"Sorry, ma'am." The general from USSC shook his head vehemently. "Navy could probably touch it with a Standard-four, but it's right on the ISS's doorstep: even if we managed a direct impact, the debris plume would take out the space station. And that's assuming they've got no situational awareness. There's no such thing as a stealthy missile launch, and they'd have a couple of minutes to decide whether to jaunt out of the way of the warheads or return fire." *With nukes* went without saying.

"What about infowar?"

The officer from Cyber Command was already noping out, her posture totally negative. "This isn't like that movie *Independence Day*: we know *nothing* about their systems architecture. All we can tell is that it's hardened against proximity to nukes. It's probably not computerized in any way we can make use of. They're showing us they've got compatible radiofrequency comms, but they've been spying on us for decades and they want us to hear them. Given weeks to months, we might be able to come up with something . . . but we don't have that time."

"Navy? Air Force?" The President went around the room, confirming—on the record—that the military options ranged from risky to nonexistent. By the time she got to the Coast Guard, she simply shook her head, then announced: "let the record show that we have no reliable military options at this time." An assessing glance at the Defense Secretary followed. "I want proposed solutions on my desk no later than five p.m., with preliminary costings and time lines from everyone with skin in the game, for how to deal with *future* visits from ships like this. *If* we're still alive next week, I'll take the most promising proposals to the House. Cost is no object: Manhattan Project rules apply, nuclear options will be considered because the other side already went there and *fuck* this shit." She slumped momentarily and took a deep breath, then looked around the room. "Pardon my French. We're still alive, so the situation might be retrievable by diplomatic means. But someone's going to swing for this."

Sitting near the back of the room, Dr. Scranton suppressed a shudder.

"Meanwhile. Our second strike force is already at Defcon Two and on alert at their dispersal sites in our other time lines, yes?" Air Force nodded. "Good. Keep it that way. I want our ASAT capability up and ready to make life hot for our visitor. Even if we can't hit them, we can make them dance. Notify the ISS crew to prep for evacuation, but sit tight for the time being."

"Ma'am, it takes hours to ready a Soyuz capsule for return, and if the astronauts undock—"

"Understood." She made a cutting gesture. "Our visitors may interpret any departure as a sign that we're getting ready to shoot at them, so they're *not* going to undock. They're just going to get ready. In their space suits, in the capsules, whatever. If I have to choose between losing a space station with six astronauts, or losing the eastern seaboard, I'll sacrifice the station in an eye-blink. But I leave it to you people to coordinate with NA-SA—or whoever is running mission control—to give us the best possible shot at keeping them alive, if things break bad.

"Meanwhile, we are not, repeat *not*, starting a fight with the Commonwealth. The risk of escalation is sky-high and there's nothing to be gained by it. Furthermore, unlike the last lot of murderous bastards from the Gruinmarkt, this bunch seem to understand deterrence, and they say they want to talk. I can work with that.

"Which brings me to the other elephant in the room—the alien thing. Overnight status report? Defense?"

"Yes, ma'am. Admiral Reeve, if you please?" The Defense Secretary cued one of his aides.

The Admiral took over. "Planning for Operation Holysmoke is more or less complete, and the USS *Maine* has eight UGM-133 missiles with the ARMBAND-enabled warheads ready to launch once she reaches her patrol sector. She's already underway as of this morning—"

"Question." The President interrupted: "how long is that going to take? How soon can they be ready to launch?"

Eileen sat up, suddenly feeling a hot prickle of fear-sweat in the small of her back. UGM-133 were Trident missiles—strategic nukes—and ARM-BAND meant they were para-time capable. Fitting ARMBAND world-walking boxes to bombers or transport aircraft was well-established, and ERGO-1 was a modified ICBM payload, but to have it weaponized and fitted to ballistic missiles *already* meant somebody had been thinking ahead.

"Er, a while, ma'am. Trident missiles have a minimum range of roughly two thousand nautical miles—they're solid fuel rockets, once you light them you can't switch them off—and our boats normally creep around at three to five knots to minimize the risk of detection by hostile submarines. It'd normally take a couple of weeks for the *Maine* to start her patrol, but if she makes a speed run with cover from surface assets—we've got a carrier group in the area—she can be on station in a little under eighty hours."

The President's voice flattened. "Do it. I'll talk to the Speaker of the House about an emergency enabling act and fast track it through an emergency sitting of Congress if necessary." She caught herself. "In case you were wondering, the target is *not* the Commonwealth," she added, looking round the table as if challenging everyone present to argue with her. "I will *not* authorize a nuclear first strike on a civilized human time line under *any* currently foreseeable circumstances. We made that mistake once and we're still living with the consequences. An alien invasion by beings who refuse to communicate is another matter. They initiated hostilities and we need to prevent them from using whatever they find in Camp Singularity to backtrack to us. It also demonstrates resolve to the Commonwealth leadership—they showed us their big stick, we'll show them ours.

"Now I want to talk to State and Homeland Security: the rest of you, you're all dismissed."

Taken by surprise by the President's abrupt termination of the meeting, the NSC delegates scrambled to leave. The President disappeared through a side door with a couple of Secret Service bodyguards, probably to use the bathroom during the break in proceedings.

Eileen sat tight through the stampede towards the door. "Well, that went better than I expected," Irving observed quietly from the seat next to her.

"Sir? I don't see how it could have gone any worse."

"Oh, but it could." The Homeland Security Secretary gave her a lizard-eyed stare. "You'll notice that nobody advised her to start a shooting war with the Commonwealth. We should be grateful. The Joint Chiefs are just young enough to *personally* remember what happened last time around. And the President's canny enough to spot an Abilene paradox developing and shut it down hard." The Abilene paradox was a syndrome common to committees, where everyone went along with a consensus nobody actually supported because they were afraid of rocking the boat. Abilene paradoxes almost always broke bad: the Cuban Missile Crisis, the Watergate scandal, the decision to nuke the Gruinmarkt. "I'd rather not have to explain to my grandkids how we panicked again and lost several major cities this time around, instead of just the White House and the Capitol."

Eileen nodded, just a jerk of the chin, acknowledging his point. "We're not playing against a little league team this time."

"Exactly. So let's get ready to offer her a new Plan B," Irving said, waving her towards the front of the room.

By the time the generals, admirals, and assorted Defense Department suits had left, the room held only a dozen players. These included Irving and his Homeland Security people, and Secretary of State Marcia Wallis and her team. Finally the last attendees filtered back in: the President

286 ■ CHARLES STROSS

herself, her chief-of-staff, the White House chief counsel, and a couple of staffers. (Behind the President trailed the usual extras: secret service agents, a White House IT support worker, and two Air Force officers with the nuclear 'football.') It was about as close to a fireside cabinet meeting as the twenty-first century presidency got, and Eileen, who wasn't in the habit of attending briefings at this level, felt distinctly exposed.

The President turned her pale, blue gaze on Irving. "John. What have you got for me?"

Eileen's boss cleared his throat and began to describe the situation in Time Line Three to the President. The President had been an Air Force pilot during the first Gulf War. She was the first woman to make it into the Oval Office, and also the first Democrat since 2000. Despite being midway through campaigning for re-election and dealing with two simultaneous para-time emergencies, she was maintaining an even keel. She was famous for quoting Ginger Rogers when asked what it was like, being the first female president: "You've got to be able to do anything the men can do, only twice as well, backwards, in heels." *It could have been so much worse*, Eileen realized. *We could have ended up with another cookie-cutter war hawk, or an elderly billionaire with no grasp of the big picture.*

". . . Which is where Dr. Scranton comes in, with an update on our interactions with the Commonwealth. Eileen?" Eileen suppressed a startle reflex.

"Dr. Scranton." The President smiled briefly. "Infodump me."

"Uh, yes, ma'am." Eileen swallowed. "My unit is the main DHS contact group for time line three and a fusion center stakeholder for activities directed against the Commonwealth's Department of Para-historical Research. Also known as the DPR, which is their para-time industrial espionage agency. Right now we've been concentrating on developing political leverage against DPR and their ministerial sponsors, MITI, who are also the state level actor behind Juggernaut. This . . . visit . . . appears to be them signaling an escalation—as a prelude to negotiating for the return of a very high value asset we're in the process of acquiring." *At least I hope Colonel Smith's acquired her, or we're in a world of hurt.* "Unfortunately this stuff is all pre-planned, and our advance planning and the State Department's advance planning have clashed at cross-purposes."

"What *exactly* were you trying to achieve?" Asked the President.

"The, uh, the classic CIA playbook? Straight out of Operation Ajax, the 1953 Iranian coup, with a side-order of the post-Warsaw Pact Color Revolutions? It's a standard protocol. First, we unearth or fabricate an internal threat to the target government, by whichever faction we want to take down. Homeland Security is focused on the individuals running MITI and the DPR right now: State have gone stirring up trouble elsewhere. Then we leak it to their internal rivals—typically the army, but in this case State went for a different organization, called the Commonwealth Guard— and make it look like an existential threat. In this case, DPR gave us an opening by encouraging a defection that could plausibly be painted as a precursor to the restoration of the previous government. Anyway, by the playbook, after we identify a likely fuel we fan the flames of paranoia."

"This previous regime . . . which one are you talking about?"

"The crown-in-exile of the New British Empire, ma'am. The DPR arranged for the Princess to defect. She was supposed to show up during the First Man's funeral and swear allegiance to the Commonwealth. We put a stop to that, but we lost track of her in Berlin—we're trying to retrieve her right now. The current objective is to return her to the French Empire and her father, the claimant to the throne. Our plan was to position it as a huge failure by MITI, discrediting the former Clan world-walkers in the Commonwealth, weakening the Commonwealth para-time capability, and buying us a shot at turning their main local rivals into allies. But while we were setting this up, State began feeding the Commonwealth Guard disinformation to make it look like the Clan remnants were actually planning to use the Princess to front a royalist coup. They're former nobility from a feudal kingdom, after all."

"Right." The President looked thoughtful.

"Ma'am?" Irving prompted after a few seconds.

"Did it *not once* occur to you that there might be unpredictable blow-back from interfering in Commonwealth internal politics?" The President was quietly furious. "Did it not occur to you that you are not omniscient? Our intelligence sources in the Commonwealth are so poor that they were able to hang that *thing* above our heads—" her finger, pointed skyward, indicated she was referring to the visiting Juggernaut—"without warning. Did it not occur to you that neither you nor the State Department get to make foreign policy on the fly? That there's a difference between pursuing a bunch of narco-terrorists, or even hunting spies, and actively destabilizing the government of a nuclear-armed para-time superpower?"

"Yes ma'am." Irving fell mute. "But they're—"

"They're above your pay grade," she snapped. "This administration does *not* endorse destabilization operations conducted without proper oversight. It *especially* does not countenance such operations if they target a power that out-guns us! Once the Navy carries out Holysmoke—drops a bunch of nuclear missiles on the alien incursion—we can plausibly claim we've got a working para-time second strike deterrent. A deterrent that can match the one *they've* got, currently parked next to the ISS. That means we can stabilize the situation through diplomacy, *if* there's a stable regime to nego-tiate with. Dig out the files on SALT and START and read up on how we and the Soviets climbed down from the precipice. But cowboy games like this crap about a runaway princess *isn't helping.* And neither is gaslighting the people we need to sign treaties with." She paused again, then looked at Irving: "I expect to have your resignation letter, signed but undated, on my desk within the hour. I'll decide whether to act on it once the current crisis is resolved, or as soon as I think it will make a positive contribution to improving relations with my counterpart." She looked at Dr. Scranton: "yours too, and whoever is running this idiotic destabilization scheme—"

"—Colonel Smith—" Irving chipped in, to Eileen's disgust.

"—*Whoever.* If hanging you out to dry will save us from a nuclear war with the Commonwealth, I will not hesitate to do so. On the other hand, if you can figure out a way to defuse this mess safely, then you can retire with dignity and this will never be mentioned in public. Either way, you'll never work in government in any capacity ever again. Or in the private sector, as a contractor. My successors will be dealing with the Common-wealth for a very long time to come, and I don't doubt that they bear grudges just like the rest of us.

"Go write those letters. Then draft me a memo on what steps we can take *immediately* to take the Commonwealth off the boil."

BERLIN, TIME LINE TWO, AUGUST 2020

Eric Smith was getting edgy. "It's been half an hour," he complained. "That's enough time, surely?"

They were down by the Police control van, waiting outside the darkened apartment block. "I agree," Major Schenk conceded. "One would hope they are awake by now."

"They haven't come out," Smith said. "What are you going to do about it?"

"Ring the doorbell—as usual. If there's no movement, we will gain entry. Wait here."

Schenk collected a pair of cops and left the Colonel cooling his heels in the early morning light. "Dammit," Smith muttered. He stared at his phone for a few seconds, then dialed a contact. "Smith here. What's the latest on our guests?"

He listened for a while, then hung up.

"Sir?" Gomez asked, just as Schenk came barreling out of the apartment entrance, looking distinctly peeved. "Hey, what's wrong?"

Schenk ignored her, addressing Colonel Smith instead. "The apartment is empty. There are signs of a hasty departure. They took nothing! My men found a gun."

"I see." Smith looked at him. "How long ago?"

"There are cups of coffee in the kitchen, still warm. We *barely* missed them."

"And there was a gun." Smith nodded to himself. "It just keeps getting better, doesn't it? What are you doing now?"

"It goes back to the control center." Schenk sounded frustrated: he was finally losing his calm. Perhaps it was the fact that the people he had been unwillingly co-opted into tracking had been armed. Or perhaps it was the way they were always one jump ahead. "A scene of crime team is on its way, but they could be a while."

"You're on the run, you know you're being followed, where would you go?" Smith gave Gomez a significant look. "The airport."

"But . . . I don't understand." Gomez looked startled. "She's been abducted by world-walkers and spies, dragged off to a strange world, so what the hell does she think she's doing? Where is she going?"

"She's going *home*." The Colonel waved his phone for emphasis. "It's not a kidnapping and it's not blackmail: Major Hjorth called it an *extraction*, she's a willing defector. She wants to go to the Commonwealth. So they must have sent Kurt Douglas to run the emergency retrieval operation. Mrs Burgeson must have roped him and the girlfriend in. Ex-Stasi, he's got the tradecraft background . . . *fuck*."

"Stasi?" Schenk looked astonished. "Is this some kind of joke?"

"I *said* we shouldn't trust her, sir." Gomez couldn't resist getting the last word in.

Smith screwed his eyes shut. *She's giving me a headache,* he thought. He opened his eyes again: "let me remind you that we needed Rita, Sonia. And we still do. She's got connections in the Commonwealth. Plus, we had Kurt and Angie under our thumb until . . . when?" He jabbed a finger at her: "I want you to find out when they went active, and whether they have any other *special friends* who came crawling out of the woodwork at the same time." He went on to add, thinking of the last update Eileen had given him, "we may be running out of time. We blocked their first exit route when we scooped up Hjorth, but they must have a fallback."

He started dialing again. "Hello Central, Smith here. I'm tracking a party of three fugitives, Kurt Douglas, Angela Hagen, and a Jane Doe, previous alias Elizabeth Jordan—she's in the system—they're probably heading for a nearby airport, flying long-haul to somewhere in the Americas. Not CONUS. Uh, a previous contact arrived from Caracas, so check outbound flights—"

Smith caught Sonia's attention. "We're going back to Tempelhof," he told her. "Get the jet in the air ASAP, back to Baltimore. Sort out custody of Milan and Hjorth, they're coming with us. Hostages, now."

"Crap." Sonia took a deep breath. "Look, is this a potential hijacking situation? I did the course at Quantico—"

Smith held up a hand. "Sonia. Really, just use your brain for a moment? Where are they trying to go?"

"The Commonwealth—"

"*Precisely.* Specifically, the Commonwealth capital, which is in the same place as our New York. All we need to do is figure out their route—where they've got a world-walker waiting to meet them—and get there first. And a Gulfstream is faster than a regular airliner." He took a deep breath. "Once we know which flight they're on, we can get ahead of them. It'll be close, but not impossible. There will be no airborne interceptions, no passenger airliners being shot down, no drama. We'll pick them up when they arrive in North America. Just tell the base to prep our prisoners for transport and ready our plane for immediate departure."

"Yessir."

He could tell from her expression that Sonia was pissed. But she got on the phone as instructed, and after a moment Smith climbed down from the parked police mobile headquarters van. "Major Schenk, I need to ask a little favor of you . . ."

BRANDENBURG AIRPORT, BERLIN, TIME LINE TWO, AUGUST 2020

While Colonel Smith and his team were cooling their heels in an East Berlin stairwell, their quarry was desperately trying not to attract the wrong kind of attention as her companions led her through the airport check-in process.

Elizabeth Hanover was accustomed to traveling by train, airship, and carriage. She had attended floating parties aboard the Royal Yacht as it shuttled between Monaco and Sevastopol, flown aboard the royal flying boat on grand tours of outlying provinces of the empire. But prior to this mirror-world Berlin, she'd always travelled as a princess. Her unnoticed entourage had rolled a red carpet ahead of her dainty slippers and ensured that all inconveniences were held at bay.

Traversing the Berlin subway was scant preparation for the organized chaos of a major international hub. Brandenburg Airport had opened on schedule in 2012, expanding the existing Schönefeld terminal until it rivaled Heathrow and Charles de Gaulle for the title of busiest airport in Europe. Nothing in Liz's home world came close: travel was costly, and air travel in particular was still the exclusive preserve of the rich.

Half an hour of shuffling brought Liz to the front of a queue. The row of counters to either side seemed endless. Uniformed functionaries checked papers while travelers loaded their bags onto endless belts. The process made little sense to her, but she smiled obligingly when Kurt asked for her passport then handed it to the man behind the desk. Suitcases were loaded, leaving her with just a small tote to carry. "Security next," Angie murmured in her ear.

"Security?"

Security was another rude shock to Liz's sensibilities. There was more queueing, then orders to remove her boots and put everything except the clothes she wore in a tray and to walk through a strange contraption. *When in Rome*, she reasoned, and copied the people in front of her, many of whom seemed equally bemused by the experience. Finally she was

allowed to put on her shoes and jacket again. She followed her companions into yet another vast hall, this one lined with shops like the ones at the
railway station. To either side, numbered bays filled up with passengers
and emptied rhythmically, like the pulsing of a vast, multi-chambered
heart. "We're flying out of Gate D25," Angie told her, not glancing up from
her phone. "This way."

The hall was so vast that it had moving walkways, flattened versions of
the escalators in the railway station. As they travelled, Liz caught glimpses
of enormous airplanes lined up beyond the floor-to-ceiling windows.
They were sleek and swept-winged, like the most modern Imperial warplanes, but even the smallest of them dwarfed anything she'd ever seen
in the Empire. "They must each hold *hundreds* of passengers," she mused
quietly.

Angie overheard her. "Ours will be one of the larger ones."

"But *why?*" Elizabeth asked, still struggling to understand: "where is
everybody going? The can't *all* be emigrating!"

Angie blinked. "They're not, but we are." She paused for a moment.
"People don't vacation on other continents where you come from, I guess?"

"But it must cost—how do they all afford—" Elizabeth gave up.

They came to an open area full of uncomfortable seats and waited some
more. Another queue formed before a desk where uniformed airline staff
checked passports and the printed scraps of paper that were tickets here.
(Some people presented their phones, instead.) Joining the queue, they
shuffled down a sloping corridor and through a doorway into one of the
gargantuan aircraft. Kurt and Angie showed her where to put her bag and
sit, and how to strap herself in. A television in the back of the seat in front
of her played a short movie about safety, then showed her a display of controls not unlike the Major's phone. As the Airbus began to taxi, she found
there was even a view from a television camera atop the ship's tail. She
watched the airport roll past to either side and realized to her astonishment that their gargantuan vehicle was part of a queue.

"Says here—" Angie tapped a page of text on her own screen—"this airport handles thirty million passengers a year."

"But that must mean—" Liz blinked. *Everyone flies. It's no more remarkable here than catching the train.* The perspective shift was painful. *The
Commonwealth is far ahead of the Empire, and yet these people are as far
ahead* again. *If they* ever *discover us—*

The rumbling engines burst into a full-throated bellow and she was pushed back into her seat, as the huge aircraft accelerated faster than a racing car. A minute later its nose rose alarmingly. Liz clenched her fingers on her armrests, afraid something had gone wrong: but nobody else took fright at the way the giant liner leapt into the sky like a fighter.

"In about an hour they'll serve us a terrible meal. Afterwards they'll dim the lights so everybody gets sleepy," Angie warned her. "If you want, you can watch TV or listen to music on headphones."

"What if I need the—"

"There are toilets behind us, but you're supposed to stay in your seat most of the time." Angie paused. "And keep your seatbelt fastened. There's a surprise coming up before we arrive. Might be some *turbulence*." Her tone was foreboding, as if the prospect was something rather worse than bad weather.

"What do you mean?" Liz asked.

"Don't worry. Everything is taken care of," Kurt said sleepily from her other side. "The DPR know what they're doing."

NEW LONDON, MANHATTAN ISLAND, TIME LINE THREE, AUGUST 2020

Erasmus Burgeson prepared to argue for his life.

From the moment he'd been dragged up in front of Brigadier Richards, he'd felt the noose closing around his neck. Richards was a classic authoritarian follower, a rigidly hidebound rules-follower who craved stability and order above all. He'd made up his mind before he set eyes on Erasmus and Miriam: he was absolutely sure that he'd uncovered a monarchist restoration plot, and nothing was going to argue him out of it.

Miriam had flipped her locket open and vanished with a quiet pop of displaced air. Sensible woman. There was nothing to be gained by staying to face a show trial. But that left Erasmus facing the furious general on his own, empty-handed and speechless. Richards ranted for a bit while the guards physically held Erasmus. Then the brigadier turned to questions that Erasmus couldn't answer. Repeatedly screaming *"where is she?"* while pointing a pistol at his head was not a question he ever wanted to hear again, but he was certain that if he lived much longer he'd hear it frequently in his dreams.

"She's a world-walker," the lieutenant eventually summoned up the nerve to volunteer. "She went to fairyland or wherever they're from, didn't she?"

This earned the lieutenant a severe tongue-lashing, but the revolver was returned to its holster. Richards might be fanatical and rigid, but he wasn't totally detached from reality. In the meantime the telephones in the outer office kept ringing and message slips kept piling up on the desk, and the shadows cast by the sunlight filtering in through the window grew steadily longer.

Eventually Richards had enough. "Take him down to holding," he snarled at the guards. Fixing Erasmus with a hanging judge's baleful eye he added, "I'll deal with you tomorrow. Once we've caught the Princess. Complicity in your wife's treason. Good-day, *sir.*" To the lieutenant: "dismissed."

There was, it turned out, a basement full of holding cells underneath the Commonwealth Guards' headquarters. Cells with thick-poured concrete walls and blank steel doors, no windows but a permanently burning light, furnishings a thin mattress and a bucket. They took Erasmus' shoes and stripped him to his underwear before they shoved him inside and slammed the bolts shut. It was very quiet in the cell, for which he was grateful—in the emperor's prisons there had never been anywhere to hide from the screams and pleas of those who were being tortured that day— and Erasmus was under no illusions about what came next. His fate was in other hands, but his wife was safe, which was good, and would be working to secure an end to the coup, which was better.

All he had to do was wait, and survive whatever tomorrow brought. Eventually Erasmus slept.

The guards came shortly after dawn. They returned his clothes, then handcuffed him and took him away in the back of a van with blacked-out windows. Their mood was tense, and they were clearly under orders not to speak. But they treated him with an unsettling, simultaneously cringing but aggressive deference, as if they were unsure whether they might be ordered to obey him or execute him.

He closed his eyes as the van made its tentative way through checkpoints in the administrative zone of the capital city, trying to compose himself. *I'm not afraid of death,* he tried to tell himself, but it didn't help. He'd witnessed executions in the camps, had himself lived as a fugitive under sentence of death for years before the revolution—he was inured to the shadow of the noose. He'd been terrified of losing Miriam, although that seemed unlikely now. However, he was tormented by quiet anxiety for friends and family members, and increasingly worried by the specter of what could happen in the wake of a coup. He'd read accounts from time line two: of sports stadia turned into execution grounds, of industrial death factories that dwarfed anything the Crown had built in the Canadian hinterlands. And he knew the men he faced too well to harbor any illusions about their self-restraint. Brigadier Richards was their attack dog, typical of the breed. The Commonwealth Guard were the Praetorians of the revolution. They promoted from within their ranks, self-selecting for their devotion to principle over personality. They had a tendency towards asceticism that veered alarmingly towards that of an archaic religious order of chivalry, or the warrior monasteries of old Nippon. They were not noted for their tolerance of deviationism from the cause of Democracy and Equality. Merely having been the First Man's secretary during the revolution was no guarantee of safety.

The van stopped. Doors opened: the guards lifted him out and marched him along a corridor, past checkpoints, then through halls he recognized. The People's Palace, home of the Magistrate's Assembly. *Just the right venue for an auto da fe.* His heart sank. But rather than taking him to the chamber, the guards turned aside and led him into the warren of legislators' offices behind the assembly. They came to another checkpoint, where there was much saluting and signing of forms as they handed him over to a much smarter detachment of Guards. "Where are we going?" He asked his new custodians.

"The Junta want to see you, *sir.*" The sergeant put a subtle emphasis on the honorific, somehow inverting it. "This way." They brought him to a small, airless room with dirty windows that had been painted over on the outside. A boardroom table had somehow been shoehorned into this space. Three seats lined one side: a somewhat less comfortable seat stood before them. "Sit," they told him, then unlocked his handcuffs and took up positions inside the door.

A few minutes later the door opened again. Three men in the uniforms of very senior officers in the Commonwealth Guard entered. One of them was Brigadier Richards, predictably choleric and unfriendly. The other two—"Citizen Commissioner," said Richards, "these are the chairman of the Protectorate Committee, General Anton Minsky. And the secretary of the Committee, General Carlos Ecker." He took the third seat along, clearly positioning himself as the junior member of the triumvirate, and waited until Minsky and Ecker sat, before taking his own position.

Erasmus closed his eyes briefly, and nodded. The sense of déjà vu was suffocating, taking him back twenty years and more. It had been a long time since he'd faced a police interrogation, and never one with so much at stake before, but the experience never left you. "Gentlemen. I gather you wanted to see me?"

"Commissioner." Minsky smiled affably and laced his fingers together. "We appear to have a problem."

Erasmus nodded again, keeping his face still.

"We are here because of information received to the effect that your ministry and the Ministry of Intertemporal Technological Intelligence have colluded in treason—specifically, to arrange the restoration of imperial rule by inviting the heir to the monarchy to return here." Minsky's affable smile remained. "Would you care to explain yourself?"

Ah. That.

Erasmus thought for a few seconds. "You know you're wrong, don't you? It's always a hazard, confusing agents-provocateur with informants . . ."

The temperature in the room seemed to drop several degrees.

"Be that as it may." Minsky's expression hardened: "We would have been guilty of gross negligence if we hadn't moved. And now—" He shrugged. "We are *not* wrong. There really *is* a plot to return Elizabeth Hanover to Commonwealth territory. Your ministry was engaged in creating documentary footage of her, for broadcast. This would tend to confirm the existence of a plot. Something went wrong, didn't it?"

"Where is she?" Erasmus leaned forward, fascinated.

Richards cut in: "Our people are questioning her now."

It was such an obvious bluff that Erasmus didn't bother to rise to it. *If you don't know where she is, which means you can't simply shoot her . . .* he shook himself. "It was going to be the propaganda coup of the century, to have Miss Hanover herself appear at Sir Adam's funeral. She was to pay her respects and swear allegiance to the Commonwealth, accept citizenship, and renounce the throne in return for an amnesty. It might even have started a trend, you know. Better a citizen in heaven than a prince in hell and all that: and what is a pretender in exile, without an heir and a court?"

"Well, that's a bit of a problem, isn't it?" The speaker was the other general, Ecker. Bald, monocled, he bore an un-military air of abstraction. A *detective*, Erasmus pegged him. *Or secret police.* "And you can see our dilemma, I hope. A willing defection leading to Miss Hanover swearing her undying support for the Commonwealth would be indistinguishable, right up until the final stage, from a restoration plot, would you agree?"

Erasmus was about to reply—a reply appeared to be expected at this point—but Brigadier Richards interrupted again. "Facts, citizen comrades, we must deal *in facts.*" He sat up and puffed his chest out. "We know that Princess Elizabeth of the House of Hanover was declared missing in Berlin three days ago—the French and their allies are on fire. Around that time, a woman bearing an uncanny likeness to Miss Hanover appears in New London, staying in the home of a director in the DPR. She is introduced as your wife's daughter by an earlier undocumented marriage that your wife had not previously seen fit to mention, and makes public appearances on this basis, but also records television broadcasts declaring herself to be Elizabeth Hanover. Let me put it to you, Commissioner Burgeson, that if the DPR was party to a conspiracy to restore the crown, such a story would be the perfect cover once they brought the heir to Commonwealth soil. Miss Hanover herself is young, pretty, and entirely lacking in the dubious baggage attaching to her father. The outraged squawking from St. Petersburg is just a pre-arranged smokescreen."

Erasmus gaped as Richards crossed his arms and glared at him, smugly triumphant. "You're jo—no, you really *believe* that?"

Minsky peered at Erasmus. "Leaving aside the question of whether your wife's mysterious 'daughter' is actually the thin end of a royalist wedge—we have also been made aware that your wife was *running a covert space program.* These facts were drawn to our attention nearly simultaneously, in the immediate aftermath of the First Man's death. We were on the alert for restorationist plots, of course, and attempts to rig the succession. But a space program with corpuscular weapons coming out of its ears, under the control of a former member of the aristocracy of the world from which her world-walkers came? They *were* aristocrats, Mr. Burgeson. Some would say it would only be natural for them to bend the knee before a crowned head in expectation of their privilege and power being restored. The refusal of Explorer-General Hjorth to obey our lawful orders to land his vehicle and surrender to Commonwealth authority can be viewed as mutiny in the face of the enemy. He claims this Juggernaut machine is impossible to land, and if abandoned could conceivably fall to French possession—but there is no evidence to support this."

Ecker sighed and looked mournfully sympathetic. "Everywhere we looked, we found you and your wife in the middle! What are we to *think*, Mr. Burgeson? What are we *to do*?"

"Well, for starters, we were loyal servants of the revolution *before it happened*, and perhaps you should consider the possibility that we have not suddenly decided to sabotage the Commonwealth and undo the work we've dedicated the past two decades to?" Erasmus tried to sit up, but his back was sore. "I agree that you have to go by capabilities, not inferred intentions, but I think it should be possible to prove that Miriam's daughter, Rita, is *not* Princess Elizabeth—unless you think the royals are world-walkers?"

"Balderdash," began Richards, but Minsky held up a hand.

"Continue, please."

Erasmus took a deep breath. "Juggernaut is a MITI program. I've been aware of it for some years now. This stuff isn't totally secret: the Chamber of Magistrates were briefed months ago. It was due to fly *next* year, not this, but in view of the risk of foreign aggression during the succession period, the oversight committee agreed to push ahead with an early launch as a show of strength. I can't answer your assertions about the reliability of former aristocrats—*non-British* ones—in command positions, but they've selflessly served the Commonwealth for many years. Again, why would they change now? Especially as the Hanoverian crown is not *their* monarchy. The technical issue of whether Juggernaut can be landed ought to be cut and dried, yes? I'm sure your questions can be answered by the DPR and Air Defense Force staff involved, at the Maracaibo air station and other para-time installations it provides access to.

"Juggernaut was due to overfly St. Petersburg next: I think you are in a better position to know the outcome than I am, but as we don't appear to be radioactive dust blowing on the wind, I assume it was a success."

"A giant dagger hanging over our head," said Richards.

"A giant dagger hanging over *the United States'* head," Erasmus retorted. "Who do you think it's really aimed at, our own people? Don't be silly. The French? Elizabeth's defection was supposed to shut them up. The real threat is from the *other* revolutionary republic with para-time capabilities and empire-building aspirations—"

"Who your wife *claims* her daughter is a spy for," Ecker said, with gruesome geniality. "I find your attempts to find an explanation for everything consistently make it look worse, Mr. Burgeson. Either she's an enemy of the state or she's a spy for an enemy state, which is it to be? Either Juggernaut is a secret weapon aimed at one enemy or it's a secret weapon aimed at another, but either way it's *highly* fortuitous that it came to light now, is it not?" He added, after a momentary pause, "come now: if you were in our shoes, what would we do with your faction?"

("Troublemakers," grumped Richards.)

"What are—" Erasmus mastered his tongue and shut his mouth abruptly, considering. "Well, you could shoot us." He shrugged, self-deprecatingly. "But that wouldn't help."

"Why wouldn't it help?" Minsky smiled again, like a shark: "We shot Leon Sánchez. We're going to shoot Adrian Holmes, after we try him."

"But he—oh. I thought he was your leader?"

Richards cleared his throat. "Yes: so did he. That's why he's under arrest until we can put him on trial and shoot him. Can't be doing with conniving schemers."

"Well." Erasmus began to rock, unaware of his appearance he was so deep in thought. "Well. Let me see." He was thinking for his very life. "It always helps to define our common goals, don't you find? And I think right now we can agree on these objectives: to cement the lawful transition of powers in the Commonwealth, to defend the revolution, and to ensure the legitimacy of the government."

He stopped. Minsky nodded. "Do go on," said the general, as polite as any prosecutor deposing the accused in a capital trial. ("I believe we're making progress," Ecker noted.)

"Well." Erasmus licked his lips. "I do not believe you gentlemen would have taken steps to seize power if you didn't have an exit strategy. Something like, oh, purge the traitors. Then prompt the rump Commission to appoint a new First Man. Then announce an amnesty while you return to barracks? That's one option." He glanced at the men across the table and swiftly moved on. He felt like a mouse in the dock beneath the unblinking gaze of a court of owls: "or you might conclude that the entire current Commission is too corrupt or compromised to reinstate. And that it would be best to dismiss the government and Magistrates, and operate as a junta in the long term. I would, in all honesty, counsel against that course of action for various reasons—" *not least among them because this interview could end with me in front of a firing squad wall*—"most notably, a junta wouldn't have the legitimacy of the Constitution behind it. That would ultimately create a power vacuum. And the logical person to fill it, if and when you falter, is John Frederick." He smiled, a trifle embarrassedly. "Back to square one, which I stress *none* of us want to see. So I think your best option is to finish your purge as fast and bloodlessly as possible, then step aside."

Dead silence met this delivery. It dragged on for endless seconds. Then, finally, Minsky spoke, his tone neutral, even light-hearted: "Jolly good, Commissioner! That is actually what we are minded to do, as it happens, and it is to your credit that you reached the same conclusion about the undesirability of operating as a junta. But I have just one more question for you before we leave to consider our next plan of action:

"Can you think of any good reasons why we shouldn't just shoot you alongside Mr. Holmes?"

GREEK PALESTINE/THE GRUINMARKT, TIME LINE ONE/NEW ENGLAND, TIME LINES TWO AND THREE, 200 BCE/1630–1830 CE

The multiverse is prolific: the multiverse eats its young.

Every quantum event that produces divergent outcomes that a human-scale observer perceives forces a split between time lines. But most such divergences are insignificant: and they ultimately re-merge. It doesn't matter how a butterfly flaps its wings if nobody sees it, and eventually the bug collector goes home and memories fade and only the significant paths remain detectable.

Layered atop this sea of diverging and reconverging possibilities is another observer effect: the jaunt mechanism developed by the Forerunners has a certain minimum resolution. You can't jaunt on top of yourself, and you already exist in a superposition of quantum states. In a move to tame the untamable, the Forerunners restricted their para-time mechanisms to work in fixed increments across a higher-level graph of possible states which could be reliably selected by a secondary mechanism embedded in the visual recognition circuitry of world-walker brains. Topological deformations—knots—were a convenient way of encoding a move through the manifold of parallel versions of reality in a way that one or more Forerunners could share.

When a brain hosting the jaunt mechanism recognized a knot—or trigger engram, as the DHS researchers named them—the exotic matter circuitry hidden inside their neurons flipped into an excited state and triggered a cascade throughout every cell in their bodies, shifting them into sync with the target continuum. The mechanism itself shielded them from one implication of jaunting—that by doing so, they inadvertently created a macroscopically different time line. Or at any rate it did so when the machinery was working as designed.

The war between the Hives and the Forerunner empires was already ancient when a series of setbacks—of battles lost and worlds destroyed in the firebreak of depopulated universes between the factions—rippled through the manifold. In its wake it scattered refugees and fugitives like the seeds of a myriad new universes.

One of these setbacks was a major loss. A once populous high-tech civilization was besieged and then reduced by a sizable and unusually energetic Swarm. The Swarms, in the large, evolved to confront new threats by adopting subtly different strategies: this particular encroachment specialized in high energy physics, injecting microscopic artificial singularities into fortified enemy Earths to collapse them into peanut-sized black holes. These served as a source of energy for the Swarm, which used them to power numerous invasion gates, through which they attacked the neighboring wall of para-time fortresses.

The Dome in time line four was an annex of one of these fortresses. The Hive had made several attempts to breach the fortress, but the repeated attacks on time line four were successfully repelled by its defenders. They built a dome atop the invasion gate to monitor and seal it. But despite their local successes, the Hive ultimately prevailed when they changed tactics. They flared the black hole by dropping vast amounts of mass into its accretion disk, then channeled directed bursts of hard radiation through all the gates they'd established. Having killed the defenders and slighted their fortresses, they paused only long enough to ensure that these time lines were unoccupied by hominids—a fimbulwinter caused by dropping a handful of medium-sized meteorites on the planet sufficed—then moved on, leaving behind a minimal watch on the hole that had powered the successful attack on the fastnesses of time.

It was a messy fight, and the Hive warriors were less than 100% successful in their clean-up operation.

When the fortress fell, a number of Forerunner defenders were caught
outside it. For reasons now unknown, at least one of them—possibly an
entire team—were thousands of kilometers away, on the other side of the
Atlantic Ocean. Perhaps they were experimenting by putting a geospatial
gap between themselves and the point of contact with the Swarm. Or
perhaps they were looking for a route through to a different time line . . .
possibly one that had no prior contact with the war.

What can be known at this time is that they didn't die in the aftermath
of the Swarm's victory over their fortress: they were sufficiently far away
to survive the incineration of half a continent, the fallout plumes and the
choking haze of upper atmosphere dust that dropped the time line into
an ice age. But there was little to sustain them. So one or more of the survivors made their way to an adjacent uncontacted time line, where they
found iron-age civilizations bickering and squabbling around the eastern
coastline of the Mediterranean Sea.

A butterfly's wing flapped: and a new time line was born—in which for
reasons now unclear, history burst its banks and meandered into a different course in the territory that would later be known as Roman Palestine.

We do not know the fate of the first world-walker to open up the time
line that gave rise to the Gruinmarkt. They didn't leave an obvious im-
print at the time, no world-walking family, no invisible sun warping the
orbit of civilizations around it. But in the wake of the Macedonian invasion of those territories, things went differently, and eventually the Seleu-
cid empire suppressed certain troublesome tribal peoples who insisted on
worshipping a single deity rather than the approved Hellenistic pantheon.

Judaism was stillborn in that time line: nor did Christianity (or anything
recognizable as Islam) make an appearance. The worship of Mithras and
of Ahura-Mazda spread in the east, but failed to make in-roads in the west,
where a Norse-derived faith took hold. When the longships reached the
Americas with their freight of smallpox and plague and Viking settlers, it
was the worship of Lightning Child and the One-Eyed Father and the Eagle Mother that they brought to the lands named Nordmarkt, and Sudt-
markt, and Gruinmarkt.

Parallel Earths exist in multitudes. Under normal circumstances, the
probability of any one time line not already home to Forerunners receiving

a visit by a second refugee—or deserter—would be as close to zero as to bear no scrutiny. But this was not a normal age. A shield wall of civilizations was steadily crumbling, eroded from the inside by a stealthily seeded prion plague.

The jaunt mechanism inside the self-replicating organelles the Forerunners had seeded themselves with relied on intricate artificial enzymes to copy the quantum dots—artificial exotic matter—that it worked through. The eruption of prion disease—malformed proteins that caused their own peculiar structural deficiency to be adopted by their intracellular neighbors—was the outcome of a carefully concealed genetic time-bomb created by a particularly brilliant Hive's bioengineers. The Swarm weapon had lain dormant for dozens of generations before it activated across millions of worlds in parallel. The symptoms were destructive: the jaunt organelles of the afflicted still worked, but jaunting would trigger sudden hypertensive crises, stressing the victims' cerebrovascular circulation until they hemorrhaged and died.

The faster and more often they jaunted, the faster they died: and when and where enough of them died, the Hive arrived to finish the job.

The bioweapon outbreak and subsequent Hive invasions of the sixteenth and seventeenth centuries, as the Europeans of time line two counted dates, did not exterminate the Forerunners. It's very hard to destroy a galactic empire, or a human diaspora on a similar scale scattered across hundreds of millions of parallel time lines rather than star systems. It was, at worst, equivalent to the extermination of a civilization spanning the planets of a globular star cluster: death and destruction on an incomprehensibly vast scale, but ultimately signifying nothing. The contemporary Forerunner civilizations—no longer the ones that had first encountered the Hive: the Hive evolved—lost perhaps a fractional-percent of their population. And another fractional percent who survived the first attack ran and hid, brain-struck soldiers deserting their posts, civilians grabbing whatever they could carry on their person and taking to the time roads.

A man who called himself Henryk Lofstrom ran and hid in a small kingdom on the north American coastline.

History does not record his world of origin, or his original language, or much of anything about him. History starts with his great-grandson, Angmar Lofstrom. Angmar is known to us: he was a world-walker, and despite the hypertensive headaches he suffered whenever he jaunted, he was functional. He was probably—the genetic evidence supports this—the child of a marriage of cousins, because he could jaunt, and none in his parents' generation could do so.

Behind the cipher of his dead great-grandfather lies a gulf of lost knowledge. It is unclear precisely how Henryk came into possession of the trigger engram for transit between the Gruinmarkt and the New England colony of Massachusetts. Presumably it happened some time in the early eighteenth century, early enough for the butterfly to flap its wings again: evidently the wind of its passage gave rise to a hurricane in Scotland and split the time line yet again. In one alternate, the Stuart crown held Scotland in 1745. The English crown—held by descendants of the Elector of Hanover—entered exile in the colonies in 1758, when England lost a war on two fronts against the Auld Alliance. Others of Henryk's descendants settled in the New British Empire, while those of Angmar's line survived by dodging the bandits of the Gruinmarkt and the press-gangs of New England.

Angmar's children prospered, and after skipping a generation the family trade re-emerged: the Hive bioweapon had damaged the jaunt trait badly enough to render it recessive and lethal if over-used, but not to destroy it. For a while, the loose tribe of his descendants and their relatives by marriage were only modestly prosperous. But then came the railroads and the telegraph and the repeating revolver and the United States. And soon enough they became wealthy beyond the wildest dreams of their neighbors at home in the Gruinmarkt.

So: three time lines, loosely sharing a common thread of visitation by damaged Forerunner refugees. Then explorers from the Gruinmarkt discovered a fourth adjacent time line, sterilized and abandoned by the Hive, home to a dormant gate into Hive-occupied para-time. Not long afterwards, the United States government rediscovered and began to excavate the Dome.

And then . . .

The Center Cannot Hold

As the hours passed and the Airbus drilled on through the stratosphere, Elizabeth fell into an uneasy sleep. The airliner tracked south west over the Iberian Peninsula and North Africa, before turning west to cross the open waters of the North Atlantic. The food service was not so much disgusting as bewildering: *people* eat *this*? was her first reaction, followed by *why is my knife bendy*, and shortly thereafter, *where do I put everything*? But it was all she was getting, that much was clear, so she swallowed it down with grim determination. Afterwards she figured out the headphones by copying other passengers, then hunkered down to watch TV. A strange knotty design greeted her when her screen came on, so that at first she thought it was broken, but after almost a minute it displayed one of the increasingly familiar menus, and she ended up watching some sort of theatrical fairy tale romance. (It turned out people in this time line had *really weird* ideas about royalty: *weird* and *wrong*. She resolved to write the Disney Corporation a stern letter.)

They had seats in the economy section two thirds of the way back, side by side between the cabin wall and the left passenger aisle of the widebody. Kurt had the aisle seat—his old man's bladder evidently troubled him—and Angela had chosen the window. Sandwiched between them, Elizabeth eventually dozed off into an uneasy slumber. So she didn't have an opportunity to spot the DPR agents seated elsewhere on the plane: the middle-aged woman in a smart suit in business class, the thirtyish man traveling alone in premium economy. She had no idea that the man in row twenty was a lamplighter, a covert world-walker whose job had been to travel in advance and arrange accommodation and equipment drops for the Major. She didn't notice the woman in row eleven, although if they'd spoken, she might have recognized her as the voice of Control. Nor did she notice the world-walkers carefully close their eyes or glance aside when their seatback screens displayed the knotwork logo—a dated and ineffectual attempt to kill world-walkers taking commercial flight. (Had it ever worked, the consequences would have been both different and vastly more damaging from those the TSA security planners had imagined.)

Elizabeth, Kurt, and Angela were not traveling alone: an entire DPR support team was evacuating on this flight. Under normal circumstances it would have been a horrendous OPSEC violation, inviting their arrest on arrival. But the circumstances were anything but normal.

And the flight would never arrive.

Advance Passenger Information was a mandatory requirement for all intercontinental flights. It detailed the passengers identity documents, origin, and destination, and had to be filed in advance. Thanks to a well-paid member of embassy staff in Berlin and an even more highly paid airline security officer in Caracas, the team's records had been filed late but approved for entry. The security officer had confirmed that, this being a Lufthansa flight, there were no sky marshals aboard. (US-bound flights flew with armed agents in the cabin but the EU had no requirement for this, and neither did Venezuela.)

Exactly seven hours into the flight, about a thousand miles out from Caracas, the woman in row eleven tapped her tablet screen, connected to the airliner's satellite internet feed, and logged in to a commercial business messaging server.

A minute later, the man in row twenty twitched as his phone vibrated in his pocket. He woke suddenly, tapped the screen: then, like the businesswoman, he connected to the internet and logged onto the same server.

He thumb-typed: GO/NO GO?

Control was busy checking a chatroom for updates: a packet of files was waiting for her to download. It contained up-to-the-minute weather reports and a digital flight bag application with runway maps, radio frequencies, and other highly technical information that she was utterly unqualified to understand.

WAIT, she replied. DOWNLOADING OUR WELCOME KIT. In another window she typed: LH0057 OUTBOUND ON SCHEDULE, CONTROL READY. She hit the link to download the digital flight bag in the background.

On the ground in Caracas, in a Commonwealth safe house, DPR oversight would be tracking her flight's progress via the internet.

A minute later she got a reply: GO GO GO.

The flight bag download was mostly complete: it paused, 48/62Mb complete, and she forced herself not to hiss impatiently. Finally it resumed, the counter blurring until the update was finished. She briefly logged into the flight bag app to make sure the new weather and navigation information was installed: then she switched back to chat.

PORTAGE IS GO, she typed.

Received, the app confirmed. Then the internet went down, and with a shudder and a shimmy the Airbus hit severe turbulence and dropped like a stone.

There were screams of dismay, the crash and rattle of a trolley falling over in the nearest galley. In row twenty, the young man winced in pain and hunched over his phone, the screen of which displayed an eyeball-sucking knotwork.

LH0057 was a long flight. The captain had taken the controls during departure and initial stages of flight. Now he was sleeping in the crew rest area behind the flight deck. Up front, the second officer was designated pilot flying, while the first officer monitored the controls. They weren't totally relaxed, for the flight was passing through the intertropical convergence zone, a belt of turbulent weather that frequently spawned storms and squalls around the equator. The jaunt brought a sudden onset of turbulence because the air pressure and wind direction were different in the new time line. A downdraft dumped them a hundred meters in a couple of seconds. The autopilot disengaged, the master caution warning sounded, and the overspeed warning lit up: but the pilots reacted appropriately, kept the plane under control, and resumed level flight. As the captain scrambled through the cockpit door, the master caution warning ceased and everything settled down. But now there was a new problem.

"I've lost GPS," said the first officer. "Also satcom and VHF—everything." He poked at the radio controls.

"Huh." The captain turned round and quickly scanned the circuit breaker panel while the FO checked the flight data computer warnings. "Nothing here. Messages?"

"Nothing, Everything went down simultaneously with that jolt."

They got busy working the checklists.

There was controlled chaos in the cabin as the flight attendants rushed about, checking passengers for injuries, securing overhead bins that had burst open, and clearing up spills of food and drink. Most of the passengers had been strapped down, the seatbelt sign illuminated while the Airbus flew through the belt of storms: a few had nonetheless been thrown out of their seats. Control watched and waited patiently. *Fifteen minutes,* they'd told her. *Give the crew fifteen minutes first.* Fifteen minutes to stabilize the flight, pick up the pieces, deal with minor injuries, and realize they weren't in Kansas anymore.

She checked her watch, checked the charge on her tablet (eighty-two percent, dropping slowly, wifi was connected to the plane's in-flight service, but there was no connectivity via satellite internet). She sipped her bottled water. Finally, the fifteen minutes were up. She reached up and pushed the icon to page the cabin crew.

Five minutes. Nobody came. Obviously they were still busy.

Frowning, Control unfastened her lap belt and stood up. *That* got a reaction, and not a particularly friendly one.

"Please return to your seat at once, mein frau, we are experiencing—"

"World-walkers." She sat down before the other woman could freak out. "I have been told to inform you that this plane has been abducted by a world-walker—not me. The pilots have lost contact with the ground. We will be intercepted by fighters in another half hour and guided to a military airfield. When the pilots request it, I have a digital flight bag for them."

Now she had the cabin crew's undivided—and unfriendly—attention. Nobody likes a hijacker.

Control complied with their demands obediently, allowing them to zip-tie her to the seat. Once they secured her, the panicky tension subsided somewhat. "When we land, you will be handed over to the Venezuelan national security police," the purser advised her: "you shouldn't joke about hijacking—"

"I'm not joking." She smiled, to take the sting out of her rebuke. "There is a world-walker among the other passengers, I'm just the messenger." *Half-true.* "Check with the flight deck, ask if they can talk to anyone, anyone at all. We are flying in another time line. You'll see: the radios are down because the Commonwealth doesn't use the same frequencies."

Minutes passed. A couple of cabin crew hovered, clearly worried by her. She tried to relax. Finally a woman in a pilot's uniform made her way down the aisle. "Who are you and what is happening?" She demanded.

"A world-walking agent of the New American Commonwealth has transferred this aircraft to another time line—you felt the turbulence, yes? Air pressure and temperature differences. You've also lost all navigation and communications contact with the outside world." The pilot's face was stony. "We are about two hours away from the South American coast and have fuel for perhaps another hour beyond that while you try to work out what to do. *Or*—" She pointed her chin at the storage bin in front of her— "there is a tablet with an electronic flight bag in there. It's loaded with radio frequencies, METARs updated an hour ago, runway and taxiway maps, and all the necessary information for you to land at the Commonwealth Air Defense Arm's Maracaibo Air Station."

The pilot scowled at her. "And if we don't want to go there?"

"Good luck landing at Caracas International—Caracas doesn't exist in this time line." Control shrugged. "Also, the Commonwealth are expecting us. Fighters should already be airborne to accompany us in." The second officer reached into the storage rack and retrieved her tablet. "Password is four zeroes," she added helpfully.

The pilot turned the tablet on and squinted at it, then opened an app and began to page through the options. "This all seems to be . . ." she stared at Control: "*why?* Why are you doing this, this hijacking?"

Control raised her eyebrows. "That's above my pay grade," she said, slightly ruefully. "I just do what my government tells me to." *Government.* She could see the word sinking its barbs in, the implications flowering in the pilot's imagination. "There is a diplomatic situation. Once it is resolved we will return you, your passengers, and your aircraft to your original destination, with apologies. You are not hostages and we will provide compensation for delays and damage in accord with the terms of the Montreal Convention."

Control saw the pilot's expression flicker into momentary disbelief as the cabin intercom announced: "second officer Heyne, return to the flight deck."

Heyne straightened up: "Later," she said, then strode rapidly towards the front of the plane.

Control closed her eyes and tried to relax. So far, everything was going exactly according to plan.

NEW LONDON, MANHATTAN ISLAND, TIME LINE THREE, AUGUST 2020

The Commonwealth Guards hauled Rita into the back of an armored car and drove through the back streets of the capital for a while. It was night, and the car lacked windows, and every time Rita tried to ask a question or say something, her guards pointedly ignored her. Their treatment bespoke contempt rather than mere indifference, as if they had some reason to actually *hate* her, but had been told she was not to be harmed. The atmosphere in the vehicle was venomous, and after a while she cowered silently in her bucket seat.

They brought her to an imposing building, then immediately led her down a couple of flights of stairs into a corridor lined with blank-faced metal doors—a prison, she realized, but not like the cell the transport police held her in when she first arrived. She was searched. They took the tablet and inertial navigator, muttering darkly about spies and evidence of her treachery, then removed her shoes and finally her handcuffs. Then they slammed the door on her.

"Fuck," Rita mumbled, rubbing her abraded wrists. *What a mess!* There was a thin mattress on the ground, but instead of sitting she gave the corners of the ceiling a close inspection for cameras. There was nothing that she could see, apart from a mirror-glass insert in the door. So she stood with her back to it (*watch* this) and activated the e-ink display on her wrist, cued up the knotwork for time line one, tried to jaunt, and winced. *Blocked.* Quite possibly her cell was underground, at least at this point—the only place she could try to jaunt without being in view of her jailers.

Now she began to worry.

There was no way of knowing how long they held her, but after a while she slept, and she awakened only when the door banged open and the guards came for her. She was sleepy and disoriented, so didn't try to resist as they hustled her into an interrogation room—she was getting tiresomely used to them—and made her stand in front of a desk. They kept their hands on her, as if worried she might try to strangle herself if given half a chance. Finally a middle-aged man with too much gold and silver braid on his uniform strode in and sat on the other side of the table.

"Good morning, *your Royal Highness*," he began: "I am Brigadier Richards, and you had best tell me *everything* about your conspiracy." A nod at the guards and heavy hands shoved her down on a chair that hadn't been there moments before. "It will go easier for you if you do," he added ominously.

Rita blinked. "You really think I'm Elizabeth Hanover? You're making a mistake."

"I don't think so: I know it for a fact." Richards fixed her with a glare. "We captured the tapes for your treasonous broadcasts, you know. There's no point denying it."

"Well, you're wrong. I'm a federal officer in the Department of Homeland Security of the United States of America, as you'd know if you examined the mission-specific equipment your people stole when your goons arrested me." Best not to mention the verbal message Dr. Scranton had given her for her birth mother's ears. She tried to keep a slight tremor out of her voice. "Those broadcasts were faked. I'm a trained actor, I was asked to record them because—"

"—Because you're assisting a coup against the Commonwealth that will put you on the throne," Richards cut her off. "You can stop this nonsense. We investigated: Mrs. Burgeson never had a child in the United States with her first husband, Mr. Beckstein. You're out of your depth and over your head. The conspirators have all been arrested. Royal grace and favor won't save you now!"

"Are you even *listening*?" Rita demanded, her voice rising: "I'm not a goddamned princess! I'm a citizen of a foreign power, acting as a diplomatic go-between! My mother's people were brokering a defection by this princess you're after when she went missing, so they asked me to act as her for the TV cameras until they can find her—"

A gun appeared in the brigadier's hand. "Very well, have it your way. If you are not the Princess, but an agent of another time line, you will prove it now or I will shoot you."

"I, uh—" her mouth was dry, her heart hammering. "I need to stand." She pushed up against the hands holding her down, and after a moment the guards stepped back—out of the line of fire, she barely registered.

"Let me." She prepared to key the jaunt sequence again.

"If you really are Mrs. Burgeson's daughter and you fail to return immediately, I will shoot a member of your family in your place," Richards added, with the detachment of a clerk telling her there was a fee to pay.

"This may not—" she focused: her vision blurred and there was a stabbing between her eyes—"Oww, can't jaunt here, are we underground? I need to be—" Richards' gun jabbed at her face like the gaping mouth of a striking snake as she stepped sideways (guards shifting closer to the door)—"here"—

Focus. And *jaunt.* Fail, and headache.

"I've seen enough," said Richards. "Take her back to the cells. No, stick her with the other Specials. Can't shoot her yet, there needs to be a trial first." Meaty hands grabbed her arms and locked them behind her back. The brigadier smiled triumphantly. "It'll be your next television appearance, Your Highness."

MID-ATLANTIC AIRSPACE,
TIME LINE THREE, AUGUST 2020

"LH57, this is Commonwealth Center, do you read—"

Heyne paused her fingers over the VHF radio controls. "That's it," she said. She'd been searching the indicated non-standard frequencies for a signal for a couple of minutes, and she'd finally found it.

"*Scheiss.*" Captain Kraftman was old school enough that he *never* lost it: swearing in the cockpit was a sign of extreme displeasure. "Put me on air."

"Okay, we're ready to transmit." She unmuted the two-way connection. "LH57, Commonwealth Center, we read."

"Standby." A different voice came on: "LH57, this is General Anders. I expect you have questions."

Kraftman glanced away from the instruments, out the side window at the silver delta shape keeping pace the starboard wing. He swallowed. Weird turbulence and a passenger with a frightening story were bad enough, but a warplane of a type he didn't recognize spoke for itself. At least now he had an outlet for his fears, an external voice on this neighborhood's air traffic control channel. "This is Captain Kraftman, Lufthansa World Airways. I want to register a protest in the strongest possible terms. We have two hundred and ninety-two souls on board and you are jeopardizing their safety. If that fighter fires upon us it, it will—"

"The fighter escort is there for your protection."

Kraftman was speechless for a moment. "Explain, please."

"I'll explain in person when you are on the ground. In the meantime, it is essential that you land as soon as possible. Do you have the digital flight bag we supplied?"

Kraftman glanced sideways. Heyne was bent over the tablet, copying radio frequencies and waypoints for navigation beacons into the flight computers.

"Yes."

"You will want to fly the approach on manual, this being an unfamiliar air station to you. To set your mind at ease, all other traffic is presently subject to a full ground stop—the only craft in the air within a thousand miles are you and your escort. I will hand you over to military approach control shortly. Once you are on the ground, you will hold at the end of the runway and prepare to be boarded. We will offload certain passengers—they will make themselves known to you, this is not an arrest situation—and then you will be towed to the terminal buildings. We will provide accommodation and hospitality for passengers and crew while making arrangements for your continued journey. Is that satisfactory?"

General Anders wasn't offering any alternatives. "It'll do," Kraftman acknowledged grumpily. *For now.* Another sidelong glance out the window. The delta-winged warplane was clearly not built for stealth, but was area-ruled and had big air intake ramps, suggesting supersonic performance. It was like something out of the 1970s. *I thought they were supposed to be backward?* He pondered the question for a moment, before dismissing it to focus on more immediate concerns. He made eye contact with his first officer: "I need to talk to the passengers. Johan, you have control . . ."

NORTH ATLANTIC AIRSPACE,
TIME LINE TWO, AUGUST 2020

The C-37A—a Gulfstream 500 in US Air Force drag—was already airborne, crossing Scottish airspace en route to the North Atlantic, when Colonel Smith's satellite phone rang.

He stared at the caller ID as if he could change it by force of will alone. "Smith here. Sitrep."

"Colonel? Fusion center, I have an update on your persons of interest, and, uh, it's not good—"

Smith jotted a note on his tablet then hung up. "Damn," he mumbled: then "damn," again. He went online via the satellite data link and began looking up radar tracking reports.

He caught Sonia Gomez staring at him. "Yes?"

He side-eyed the passengers in the back. Two rows behind them, Ms. Milan sat beside the Major, who was stretched out on a recliner with a drip plugged into his arm—well enough to travel with medical support, not a flight risk without someone to push his wheelchair. Sonia slid into the seat opposite him. "Is something wrong?" She asked.

"You *could* say that." Eric ran clawed fingers through his thinning hair. "We're screwed." He took a deep breath. "Center got confirmation that Kurt Douglas and Angela Hagen, in company with a woman who's a positive gait match for Elizabeth Hanover—alias Ayu Sibabat, Indonesian citizen traveling on a confirmed-genuine passport—boarded a Lufthansa flight to Caracas five hours ago. They got the drop on us. LH57 is currently over the Atlantic, about four hours out. *Fucking* Venezuela, that was Major Hjorth's infiltration point, *fuck*."

"Can we stop—" Sonia stopped.

"Not short of shooting down a German airliner with nearly three hundred people on board, no," Smith said acidly. "And the Germans would figure out we were responsible within hours when they cross-checked the passenger list and spoke to the federal police. But even if we were willing to go there, we don't have any assets within range that can be scrambled fast enough to generate an intercept." Venezuela was not only ill-disposed towards the current US administration, it was out of range of fighter aircraft flying from the United States without tanker support. Tanker support took hours or days to set up, and the Navy didn't have enough carrier battle groups to keep one stationed in the middle of the Atlantic.

He shrugged, then picked up his phone again. "Ops, this is Smith, I need to talk to Dr. Scranton. Is she—the White House, yes. Got it. Holding." He made eye contact with Gomez. "It's gone diplomatic," he told her.

Gomez visibly wilted. An instinctive hard-liner, she held low expectations of the Democrat President. Smith, in contrast, had differently low expectations. He'd seen a lot of politicians in his time, and the current POTUS was both brilliant and smart—which in his opinion was a bad combination, as it made her hard to second-guess and prone to seeing three sides to every black-or-white issue. "What happens now?"

"We wait—Eileen? Hello, yes, thank you. We're inbound over the Atlantic, six-plus hours out. What's the latest?"

MARACAIBO AIR STATION, TIME LINE THREE, AUGUST 2020

"—Your captain speaking. Due to a security alert, we are unable to proceed to Caracas International Airport as scheduled. Instead, we are being diverted to a nearby air force base, where we will be landing in approximately eighty-five minutes time. We are no danger and the aircraft you may be able to see off our left wing is there to escort us. I apologize on behalf of Lufthansa World Airlines for the delay to your journey, and once we land, ground staff will arrange onward travel to your final destination."

Kurt blinked tiredly. "That must be the politest way anybody's ever been told they've been hijacked," he muttered, keeping his voice low.

"High—jacked?" Elizabeth was puzzled.

"Kidnapping, air piracy." Kurt's mustache twitched. "Whatever they call it where you come from."

"The turbulence must mean we world-walked." Angie was blocking the view, so Elizabeth nudged her. "Can I see out?"

Angie gave way reluctantly: "I had to do a bunch of aircraft recognition modules when I was in the army, and it's definitely not anything I recognize."

"Look at the tail markings," said Liz. "That's a Commonwealth jack." A slash of red with a superimposed golden starburst split the silvery slab of the interceptor's tail fin, visible in the glow shed by the airliner's passenger windows. The Commonwealth warplane was a silver arrowhead almost half the size of the Airbus, with ominous arrow-like missiles slung under its broad delta wings.

Cabin crew began to move down the aisles. "Please lower your window blinds," a worried-looking attendant told them. "We'll be serving breakfast in just a few minutes—"

The crew came up with distractions to keep the passengers in their seats and occupied. Trays loaded with small appetizers were handed out, coffee poured, landing cards distributed with stern, but friendly instructions to fill them in (even though the plane was no longer even in the same universe as the Venezuelan Republic that had issued the paperwork). There was, oddly, no sign of panic, no shouting, no attempts to rush the cockpit. Clearly everybody had already come to the conclusion that there was no point protesting. They were being diverted, they were going to land, ignore the ominous war machine on the other side of the shuttered window, leave it to the professionals.

Liz noted that neither Kurt nor Angie seemed in the slightest bit surprised. Indeed, neither—once she stopped to think about it—was she. The Major had planned to fly her out in a light plane, after all. This was just a messier, ad-hoc version of the same plan.

Descent and landing came quickly. The weather was good and the runway seemed endless: they slowed gradually, and finally drifted to a stop in the middle of a wilderness of concrete. "Please keep the window blinds lowered," instructed the purser. "Air stairs are being brought out to the runway. We will debark shortly and be bussed to the terminal." A pause. "Will Kurt Douglas make himself known to the cabin crew, Kurt Douglas to cabin crew—"

Elizabeth found herself escorted firmly but politely to the big doors in front of the wing root, along with Kurt and Angie and two or three other passengers she didn't recognize. (Stretching her stiffening arms and legs as she waited, she enviously eyed the leg room and pillows in business class.) The crew didn't seem to know whether to treat them as guests or prisoners. Eventually there was a muffled thump from outside the door. A couple of crew members swung it out of the way to reveal a mobile staircase. As Liz stepped onto the platform, the heat struck her in the face like an open oven door. The concrete was baking hot even at night. Soldiers in Commonwealth uniforms—regular army, she thought—moved around the foot of the stairs as a staff car drew up. She spotted other vehicles: fire tenders, ambulances, tracked infantry vehicles. One of the soldiers, an officer, ascended the stairs. "Elizabeth Hanover?" He asked, politely enough. From his epaulettes, she pegged him as an Air Defense Forces Colonel in his early thirties. A high flyer, then.

It was now or never. "That is I," said Liz. "Does this territory belong to the New American Commonwealth?" It was a formality, but she wanted a positive acknowledgement.

The officer nodded. "I am Colonel Grayson, chief of staff to General

Anders, commanding Maracaibo Air Station. The General sends his re-
grets, but he is currently occupied elsewhere. I need to be clear—are you
here of your own free will? Do you understand that by entering the Commonwealth, you are in violation of the General Exclusion Order of the
thirteenth of November, 2003?"

For a dizzying moment Liz wondered if she was doing the right thing.
"Yes! That is, yes I am here because I would like to claim asylum in the
Commonwealth, at the invitation of the Ministry of Intertemporal Tech-
nology and Innovation."

Colonel Grayson looked as if he was unable to make his mind up
whether she was a Faberge egg or a live hand grenade. Then he blinked,
and his slightly perplexed expression came back into focus. "Welcome
to the Commonwealth, in that case. I have orders to send you to the
capital directly—I'm sorry we can't give you time to recover from your
flight, but they want you in New London *yesterday*. Please follow me?"
His gaze tracked past her. "And the rest of your party, Mr. Douglas, Miss
Hagen . . ."

It seemed like an immense amount of fuss to make over one young
woman striking out on her own, but Liz wasn't naive enough to imagine
it was all about her. It was actually about her father, or rather the penum-
bra of her father's station, the stifling mantle of responsibility that had settled on her shoulders as it became clear that she was the only heir he was
going to get. She'd have been lying to herself if she didn't secretly enjoy
the attention—at least at first, and some of the time. (It had only become
onerous, and then frightening, when the implications sank in as she came
of age.) She strolled down the staircase behind the Colonel, Kurt, and Angie and the other anonymous passengers trailing her, and every eye was
upon her as the Colonel escorted her to the command car.

She leaned back as it whisked them across the air station. It wasn't as
smoothly silent as the automobiles of the otherworld's Germany, but the
ride and speed were superior to anything the French Empire could offer.
Their driver sped past a row of parked jet interceptors in their dispersal
bays, then in through the open front doors of a gigantic hangar to park
beside another set of steps, leading up to a very different aircraft. A technician held the car door open. Liz was immediately half-deafened by the
roar of ground starter trucks waiting to blast air into the engine nozzles of
the courier jet.

"Best I could do, I'm afraid," The Colonel shouted in her ear: "you should be there in six hours, just after dawn!"

"What *is* that?" Angie looked appalled as she took in the glassed-in nose and outrigger undercarriage.

"Diplomatic courier, converted intercontinental bomber," The Colonel shouted. "On board now, smartly does it!" Evidently he felt less need to be polite to Liz's hangers' on.

Liz climbed the shorter air stairs then ducked through the hatch into the cramped interior. At the front of the cabin, the pilots, flight engineer, and navigator were already running through their checklists. A uniformed attendant—military, not civilian—showed them to their seats and handed them ear defenders. A minute later, the hatch sealed shut, and the courier jet lit up its jets with a thunderous howl. There was, Liz thought, *no* chance of anyone sleeping on this flight. But as the plane began to taxi her eyelids slid shut and she proved herself wrong.

MANHATTAN ISLAND,
TIME LINES THREE AND FIVE, AUGUST 2020

The Marine Corps V-22 Osprey materialized out of thin air over an uninhabited alternate Manhattan Island with a minimum of fuss. It was high enough up that the passengers' stomachs merely lurched briefly before the pilots caught it. Bright morning sunlight streamed in through the windows, forcing Eileen Scranton to squint in order to see her escort. She was traveling with an army captain called Briggs (who'd been read into the DRAGON'S TEETH program), a sergeant Jackson (ditto), and four *very* young-looking infantry privates (actual DRAGON'S TEETH troops, first intake). There were also a couple of Marine Corps loadmasters who seemed oddly unhappy about being treated as a glorified taxi by DHS and the army.

Eileen was the only civilian in the group, and the only one in civilian clothing.

"How does this work again, ma'am?" asked Jackson.

"It works like this, I hope." Eileen smiled toothily as she pulled out a ruggedized phone with a stubby aerial extender and turned it on. Jackson side-eyed his captain, who nodded minutely. "If you're worried about them shooting us down, don't be," Eileen added. "This area is uninhabited in this time line—the Gruinmarkt started about a hundred miles north—and they had nothing that could touch us. As for the Commonwealth, if they wanted to touch us we'd already be dead: they've got MANPADs."

(One of the kids swallowed, visibly: another of them asked a question over their group channel—probably *what's a MANPAD?*)

Eileen hefted the brick of a phone, watching the screen as it searched for a base station in a theoretically-uninhabited, theoretically-primitive time line. *Nothing . . . nothing . . .* and *signal.*

It made sense to plan for contingencies. If the Commonwealth weren't keeping an eye on this territory, they were criminally negligent, and a couple of solar powered GSM base stations up trees that could be turned on or off when they were expecting visitors was a very economical way of putting out a doormat.

A couple of seconds later, a text message popped up on the phone: IDENTIFY YOURSELF.

"And we have *contact*," she murmured, before carefully standing and making her way towards the cockpit.

An hour later, Dr. Scranton found herself sitting in a control room in a well-camouflaged building in an unidentified time line, opposite a woman who had been on the FBI's MOST WANTED list for almost eighteen years. Mrs. Hjorth turned out to be a middle-aged, greying blonde in a long black dress with a mud-stained hem. There were dark shadows under her eyes. Evidently she'd come here straight from the funeral parade, on foot. To look at her you wouldn't imagine her to be a foreign spymaster—Eileen's opposite number, as near as made no difference. "Creamer, no sugar, thanks."

Brilliana Hjorth poured, slid a metal travel mug across the table, then raised her own mug in a tentative toast. They were alone in the room, their respective entourages waiting outside. "So. What brings you here, Dr. Scranton?"

Eileen froze for a moment before it registered: of course, Rita would have said who she worked for. "I'm following up on our last message."

"Your last message."

"Yes—I assume you heard from Rita?"

A flicker of consternation crossed Mrs. Hjorth's face. "Not since yesterday—before the shooting. I gather she took my daughter to a place of safety, then went to report to you?"

Oh. Crap. "Yes, she did." Eileen considered her next words. "We sent her back with a message last night, after dark. For you, or Mrs. Burgeson, whoever's highest in your reporting chain." She paused. Mrs. Hjorth waited. Eventually, she broke: "Did you hear from her?"

"No." Brilliana picked up a phone handset. "Central, Hjorth here. Rita Douglas was supposed to report in last night. Can you put out a call? All points, notify me immediately if anything comes in." She hung up. "That *might* shake something loose." She gave Eileen a look. "I assume your message was important, if you're following it up in person."

Double crap. So Rita had gone missing, message undelivered. "No biggie, just a heads-up from the President." She moistened her lips. "We have a problem," she said, trying to regain her grip. "We're not playing games any more. Deadly serious, now."

"A problem." Brilliana's voice was dry as moon dust. "Another one?"

"Humanity." Eileen frowned. "*Humanity* has a problem."

"I think you'd better explain."

"Gladly." Eileen reached into her briefcase and withdrew a document wallet of glossy photographs. "You told us about Juggernaut. Turnabout is fair play: we have a . . . an equivalent project. *Had* a project. Past tense."

She slid the first photograph onto the table. A mountain valley, slopes shrouded in conifers: in the bottom of the valley a dirty white dome, with a jagged crack running down one side. "Most time lines are uninhabited, but some time ago we discovered this ruined—"

Brill tapped the picture. "Yes, the Dome. We visited, let me think, eighteen years ago? It's close to DC, right?"

Eileen was taken aback. "You recognize it? The Clan found it?"

"Yes. It was during our initial exploration phase—before the, um, unpleasantness. We took a quick look, but it was an adjacent to time line two and before we had time to go back—we were only there for a day or so— the shit hit the fan. After which all two-jump adjacents except this one were off-limits, for obvious reasons. What did *you* find?"

"Pandora's box." It was a long story. To her credit, Mrs. Hjorth refrained from interrupting, but made quick shorthand notes on a spiral-bound pad. When she finished, Eileen found her mouth was dry. "So. Any questions?"

"Yes. While I appreciate that this is a steaming pile of ordure on your doorstep, with all due respect, I fail to see how this is *our*—the Commonwealth's—problem." Brilliana glared at Eileen across the table.

"Meanwhile we are in the middle of a crisis, which your organization's meddling has made considerably worse. While I do not set policy and can't speak for my government, I think I can safely say that thanks to your interference we don't have the resources to help you even if you weren't trying to undermine—"

"—We have the Princess."

"What?" Brilliana recoiled.

"It's true." Eileen mentally crossed her fingers. "Smith is in Berlin, where he's picked up your cousin, the Major. He's also in custody of a spy, Paulette Milan. And it's only a matter of time—a couple of hours—until he has Elizabeth Hanover too. I'm here to say that we're prepared to do a trade. We'll give you Milan, Major Hulius, *and* the Princess, as a down-payment. This—" she tapped the stack of glossies—"is a clear existential threat to us all."

"Huh." Brilliana looked thoughtful. "What do you want?"

"A lot of fiddly details. Arms verification and limitation treaties, mutual inspection, trust but verify—stuff we worked out with the Soviets in the eighties. But the centerpiece will be a mutual defense treaty aimed at non-human incursions from para-time."

"Juggernaut. You want Juggernaut."

"A joint strike."

"To cauterize the Dome, right?"

Dr. Scranton nodded.

Brilliana was silent for a dozen seconds. Then she began to shake. Alarmed, Eileen thought for a moment she was ill: but then she realized Brill was *amused*. "You crack me up," she told Eileen. "For a moment I thought you were serious." She picked up the phone again. "Central, Hjorth. What is the current location of Elizabeth Hanover, latest update?" She listened for a few seconds. "Thank you."

"What?" Eileen looked at her.

Brilliana Hjorth smirked. "It seems some things are universal: death, taxes, and minions who make excessively optimistic claims. Elizabeth Hanover is aboard one of our aircraft, and due to land at Long Island Air Defense Station in less than two hours. You might want to question the veracity of your Colonel Smith's reports on other matters, too."

Eileen gave her a tense smile. Inwardly, she was fuming. "I can assure you, we *do* have Paulette Milan and Major Hulius Hjorth. The—Princess—I admit was perhaps forward." *You idiot, Eric!* "But I'm serious about us changing our tune. The President was very clear on the subject. We can't—" *mustn't*—"fight a war on two fronts, and the fact is, you—the Commonwealth—our relations are a mess of our own making. Right now, here and now, you and I are talking. We *can't* talk to, to *that*." She jabbed at the uppermost picture of the Dome. "You know what imperial bureaucracies are like, how you get power struggles between institutions? Like the one in the Commonwealth right now—there's one in Baltimore, too. And I have to tell you, we—DHS, my people—are coming up a day late and a dollar short. My boss, the Secretary of Homeland Security, would prefer to deal with Mrs. Burgeson, who is at least a known quantity who operates within established parameters, than to have to take a back seat while the State Department dickers with the Revolutionary Guard or Commonwealth Guard or whatever your enemies are called, who are largely unknown to us and presumed hostile as well." The words stuck in her throat, but they were true, or at least true enough for diplomatic purposes. "Tell us what you want from us in return for de-escalating and making sure we never get into a mess like this again."

Brilliana seemed to be on the brink of replying when one of her phones rang. She picked it up. "Hjorth here . . . yes? A sitrep?" She frowned, then looked at Eileen. "Where *precisely* was Rita supposed to come through?"

"We, uh, we sent her through into your ministry building? We thought you'd have Mrs. Burgeson's office locked down."

"Oh *scheisse*. Uh, Control, Rita was supposed to go to Mrs. Burgeson's office. Did you—really? Really? All right, let me know if you hear anything else." She hung up then stared at the phone for a moment.

"What happened?"

Brilliana's face sagged as if she'd aged a decade in the past minute. "We did *not*, as it happens, hold the MITI headquarters building. But we had it under observation. Looks like you handed Rita over to the Commonwealth Guards on a plate. What a clusterfuck."

"Well then—" Dr. Scranton paused. "Does Mrs. Burgeson know?"

"Not yet." Mrs. Hjorth wasn't telling her something important, but Eileen couldn't work out what, unless it was more bad news about the Burgesons. "But I need to report this to her as soon as possible. She needs to know they've got another hostage against her." She stood up. "Are you ready to meet her?"

"I—yes." Dr. Scranton froze. "But why now?"

"If you're *serious* about wanting our help for that infestation, you need to pitch in and help sort this mess out. And the first step is to help us convince the Commies to go back to their barracks. Which, as it happens, I think you *can* contribute to." Brill stood up. "How many world-walkers with capabilities like Rita have you got trained? And are you willing to assign them to a, a joint peace-keeping operation? Think carefully before you answer, because what we do about *that*—" the Dome, again— "depends on the outcome."

LONG ISLAND AIR STATION,
TIME LINE THREE, AUGUST 2020

Miriam waited at the end of the runway with her ministerial entourage and a judge from the supreme bench, anxiety clenching her stomach into a tight knot. They were escorted by a detachment of regular army troops: the army was loyal, so far, to Party and parliament. *So far.* Erasmus was still a hostage, Rita was missing, her people on the run or arrested and held in horrible conditions. It was almost unbearable to be forced to wait like courtiers on the whim of a spoiled princess, but that was what she was here for. *Swallow it*, she told herself. She'd done far worse over the years, to get where she was today. The most she could hope was that Elizabeth Hanover was, if not biddable, then at least not a complete brat who'd risk other people's lives on a whim.

The big courier jet kicked up a shrieking storm as it turned towards the waiting hangar, then came to a full stop. The engine noise spooled down, and a belly hatch opened near the back of what had once been a bomb bay. Stairs dropped down, rails unfolded, and then a couple of uniformed attendants descended to help the passengers out.

"Please stand back, ma'am," one of the guards told Miriam, as they formed a protective line in front of her.

"Not necessary," she said tensely. The stooped, slightly gaunt figure of Kurt Douglas she knew. The next—a blue-haired woman—*Rita's friend?* And then—"okay, we're good here," she told her guard: "we need to do this. Showtime, folks." With that, she stepped out from behind their shelter to approach the returning Princess, at the head of a TV camera crew and outside broadcast team. Then did a double-take.

Miriam had seen plenty of newsreel footage of the Pretender's daughter over the years: a brown-skinned girl surprisingly similar to her Rita, but still-faced and serious, preposterously gowned and coiffed, escorted everywhere by ladies-in-waiting and courtiers. Court fashions had only become more baroque and ostentatious during the years of John Frederick's exile, so that the Princess would have looked barely out of place as a visitor at the court of the Sun King.

"Rita—" Miriam began, then stopped dead as the woman on the air stairs met her gaze. *Holy shit*, she thought, stunned by her appearance: *she went native in a day?* "Sorry." She took a deep breath. "Elizabeth Hanover, I presume? I'm Mrs. Burgeson from the Ministry of Intertemporal Technological Intelligence. I'd *like* to welcome you to the Commonwealth, but—" she gestured at the soldiers—"we're having some issues right now. If you'd like to come this way?"

"Issues?" The Hanover girl—*no, woman*, Miriam corrected herself— stepped down from the ladder, ignoring the TV crew who had just captured the first footstep by a member of the royal family on North American ground since 2003. "What kind of issues?" She demanded, assessing Miriam as Miriam assessed her right back.

Miriam had been expecting a princess, not a punk. Elizabeth—in black biker-styled jacket and mirrorshades, with her hair in a scrunchie and chrome-studded black boots—looked like she'd be more at home at a metal fest than a royal court. *Someone* badly *wants to cut loose*, Miriam realized. *Well.* She'd been expecting a spoiled princess, but Kurt had, it seemed, delivered a real rebel, maybe even a future feminist icon. She felt a flush of gratitude and a sense of warmth that took her quite by surprise: Elizabeth put her in mind of her own younger self much more closely than tight-lipped, circumspect Rita. "There seems to have been a misunderstanding by some elements of the Commonwealth Guard, who interpreted your arrival as a conspiracy to restore the crown," Miriam said drily. Behind her the camera crew maneuvered for a better angle.

"Gad, no!" Elizabeth's deer-in-the-headlights expression spoke volumes more than any oath of allegiance. "Listen, if the Commonwealth can no longer give me asylum, can you at least send me somewhere other than St. Petersburg?" The microphone boom swung perilously close to her face. "I didn't run away to avoid having to marry a pox-ridden lecher, or because my father wouldn't buy me a palace for my birthday, or some kind of stupid trivial nonsense like that. I ran because I also realized he's—my father—is on the wrong side of history, and I'm sorry, daddy, but I think that's the wrong place to stand." Elizabeth turned her face slightly askew from Miriam, so that she spoke directly to the camera. Her oratorial delivery *had* to be planned, and for a moment Miriam teetered on the edge of panic as she realized Elizabeth was out of control. But then the Princess continued: "I believe in the Commonwealth. I believe in the rule of the people, by the people, and the peaceful transfer of power, and the ability of men and women of good will to work together for a better future. I believe we are living in the early days of a better nation, and I want to be part of that nation, to help build something new, not remain stuck in the past like a fly embedded in amber, struggling as it suffocates."

What. The. Fuck. Miriam blinked, close to tearing up with relief. Elizabeth's speech was pitch-perfect, almost as if Erasmus had scripted it for her. Her delivery was a credit to a royal who'd been rubbing shoulders with diplomats and politicians since she learned to walk, but the *content*—and her exotically alien outfit—were mold-breaking. *Holy crap, this is really happening! We're going to be all right.*

"I'm ready to swear the oath of renunciation now, if you'll have me," Elizabeth added, meeting Miriam's gaze directly.

Miriam glanced round, forcing herself to get a grip on her emotions. She was on camera and history was in the making: this wasn't the time to lose her shit. "Judge Gordon, please?" She called Mr. Justice Gordon forward. He wore his gown over a bulletproof vest, tugging it close with as much gravitas as could be mustered in the face of the wind blowing over the runway—its hem flapped as if he were about to take flight. She took up a position to Elizabeth's left as the judge gravely produced a bound copy of the Basic Law, and invited Elizabeth to place her hand on it as she affirmed her intent to renounce her birthright in return for Commonwealth citizenship.

Miriam kept her face fixed in a politely attentive smile, aimed at Gordon. Behind him, she registered the cameras moving in for a close-up shot: behind the crew, she saw their director flash her an exultant thumbs-up and mouth, *it's a wrap.*

The short ceremony concluded and the lights on the cameras went out. "Okay, let's get out of here," Miriam announced shakily. "Jack—" to the director from MiniProp—"was it good?"

"I think so. We'll find out for sure in the next hour or two, won't we?"

He looked smugly appreciative. "It's a pleasure to work with you, your—ah, Miss," he told Elizabeth.

"It *was* live?" Miriam checked anxiously.

"Yes, it went out on all channels simultaneously, and it's going to loop four times an hour for the next six hours. Nothing short of a total power grid black-out is going to stop the message."

Elizabeth wore the slightly glassy-eyed expression of an adrenaline crash. "Is that it?" She asked. "What happens now?"

A pair of armored cars were approaching at a crawl, doors open. "We get you to a place of safety where the Commies can't get their hands on you, while the army brass try to talk the Guards down from the cliff-edge they're dancing on. That was a really good speech, by the way, it should take the wind out of their sails very nicely." She took Elizabeth's hand. "Come with me. I think everything's going to be all right now." She couldn't quite keep the wobble out of her voice. Elizabeth responded by squeezing her hand.

From her other side, the green-haired woman, Rita's Angie, closed in. "Where's Rita?" She demanded. "I thought you said she'd be safe here!"

Miriam winced. "Believe me, *I* thought so too, and making sure of it is my next priority." *That, and helping the Commonwealth Guard leadership down off the parapet they must be nerving themselves to jump off.* "You should come along—you too, Kurt. We've got a busy day ahead of us."

INTERNMENT CAMP, UPPER MANHATTAN ISLAND,
TIME LINE THREE, AUGUST 2020

A coup d'état might be messy, but the chaos left behind as one collapsed was hardly an improvement. As one more tiny piece of the debris of empire, Erasmus Burgeson was most certainly in a good position to appreciate this—but not to enjoy it. When General Minsky had asked *"Why shouldn't we shoot you?"* he'd stammered for a few seconds, then froze, his tongue tied.

"Well?" Asked the general.

Think. Erasmus racked his brain for something to say in his defense. *Why shouldn't we shoot you?* It came to him that perhaps Minsky expected him to grovel, to provide yet more proof that the civilian administration was a hot-bed of scheming politicians. But then—

"I refuse to argue for my own neck at the expense of the revolution," he said slowly, straightening his back, remembering the long-ago searing pain of the birch whips the old regime's camp guards wielded. "This is larger than any of us. This is the Commonwealth's first transfer of power. Its first opportunity for a *peaceful* transition. You may dislike me—I have no control over that—but if you take this as an opportunity to settle personal scores, then you will set a precedent. By doing that, you risk proving that Commonwealth politics *is* personal, just as much a matter of wealth and position as the politics of the nobility it replaced. If you shoot me out of hand, then you grant your successors a license to settle politics by the privilege of the gun. Which makes you an enemy of the revolution—*my* revolution, the one I'd be happy to die for. If you want to shoot me, lay charges in front of a judge and hold a trial first. Otherwise you're a fucking traitor."

Erasmus met Minsky's unblinking gaze, and his heart hammered and his palms were moist. *I'm never going to see Miriam again*, he realized, a wave of nausea gripping him. *I just told him I can't be bought. I just handed him a loaded gun.*

But then the General did something unexpected. He inclined his head fractionally, as if acknowledging a worthy opponent. Then he looked past Erasmus' shoulder, at the guards behind him. "Take him away: we'll decide what to do with him later."

They didn't shoot Erasmus, but he was under no illusions that they loved him. After listening to him for a few minutes of heart-stopping bullshit—*please don't shoot me, think of the optics*—General Minsky casually told him to shut up, then ordered the guards to take him back to the cells. Quite possibly it had been staged purely to set him off-balance: there had been no intention to have him shot. But equally possibly, maybe his arguments *had* carried some weight, at least sufficient to fend off a bullet the very next day. And then again, perhaps the triumvirate were just keeping him around until they felt secure enough to hold a show trial and formal execution.

The trouble with revolutions, in Erasmus' experience, was that they seemed to induce a horrible kind of competition between opposing teams of zealots. It was time-consuming and hard work to prove your merit through good governance, but easy to demonstrate your loyalty by shooting those who compromised their ideological purity in order to keep the public fed. The Party had managed to beat back the rise of the thuggish Freedom Riders and the Security Commission during the dark days after the revolution, but the Commonwealth Guard were subject to the same totalizing incentives as any other armed formation outside of government control. They *might* return to barracks without any further bloodshed, but Erasmus wasn't optimistic. The best he could hope for was that Miriam and her daughter had got away and that enough of the Commissioners had escaped to deny the Guard the legitimization of a clean sweep.

They didn't take Erasmus back to the cell he'd spent the night in. Instead, they weighed him down with fetters, loaded him into the back of a truck, and drove him around for a bit before unloading him inside a forbiddingly fenced-off compound—clearly a real jail that had been seized and repurposed by the Guard. "Inmate for P-Block," his escort told the turnkeys. "This is Commissioner Burgeson. He's one of the specials."

"Heh. Sign here." Clipboards were exchanged, keychains rattled, cage doors slammed. Erasmus tuned it out. The petty degradation of jail was nothing new to him. He'd spent more than a third of his adult life in and out of imperial prison camps and prisons before the revolution. They marched him down a succession of fenced-in alleyways, then through another razor-wire-topped fence and into a low building with glass windows and no bars, curiously un-prison-like. There was something half-familiar about the layout. He took a good look at it: this would probably be his home for some time. Possibly his last home and final resting place if they opted for indoor executions.

His guards brought him to an unfurnished room, bounded by a pair of doors. They removed his manacles, then shut the outer door on him. He looked around. One of the doors led to a basic bathroom with shower, sink, and toilet. In the other direction there was a cramped living room with a pair of battered armchairs and a table to eat at, were there any food to be had. Beyond it, a bedroom with two narrow beds and a chest of drawers which proved to be empty. The windows all looked out over the yard and the front door was locked, but it was surprisingly spacious, ridiculous luxury for a prison cell. This . . . Erasmus recognized the layout. *It's the old world-walker internment camp!* He almost chuckled at the irony of being locked up here. These were the Clan's refugees' original quarters when they came to the Commonwealth. Not a prison, but an internment camp for suspicious alien refugees.

After the revolution, Miriam had brokered a deal between the survivors of the world-walker Clan and the Emergency Government. The Clan sought—and got—asylum from their enemies. They got better living conditions than many of the aristos and troublemakers who'd been rounded up: proper rations, heat in the depths of a bitter winter. But they'd still been housed behind high fences, with relatives held hostage in basement rooms while the world-walkers ran errands. Trust, citizenship, and free movement came later: political power, *much* later.

Erasmus parked himself in an armchair by the window, and settled down to wait.

The day wore on tiresomely. Erasmus had never been great at dealing with enforced inactivity, but had enough experience not to be too discomfited. What was going to happen to him next was fairly clear: he was more worried about everyone else. The gates to the camp were invisible from this inward-looking window, but he could see movement in the windows across the yard. A lot of prisoners seemed to be arriving today, and at one point he recognized the distinctive silhouette of Commissioner Irving, who he knew for a fact had been captured on the reviewing stand and held in the barracks with the Burgesons. "The specials" the screws had referred to were obviously special political prisoners. Hostages, in fact if not in name.

If only there was some way of getting a message to Miriam, or to her world-walkers! The Commonwealth Guard would get a very unpleasant surprise when all their precious P-block inmates went missing. The joke was on them: the camp had been totally porous to the world-walkers. Back when they built it the revolutionaries had been unaware of how to secure world-walkers—in a cell either below ground level or high enough up to risk broken bones if they tried to escape. Miriam had told him other stories, about doppelgänger locations—traps situated in the same location in another time line, so that unwary world-walkers would find themselves in an oubliette full of razor wire or poison gas. But you needed world-walkers to create such traps, and the Commonwealth had been beyond clueless in the early days. The Clan refugees had stayed where they were put during the early days because their home time line was lethally radioactive and in time line two they were wanted as terrorists: they had nowhere else to go. It seemed like the Commonwealth Guard junta were just as ignorant as the Provisional Government had been back in the day.

It was early afternoon and Erasmus was growing stiff and increasingly hungry when there was a rattle from the front door. He pushed out of the armchair, wincing slightly—his knees and back tended to seize if he sat in one position for too long—and was on his way into the vestibule when the door opened. A prison officer stepped inside and scowled at him: then two more guards, holding a swaying figure upright between them.

"Rita." He blanched. "Is she—"

They shoved Rita towards him. "'Ere, she's yours," said the officer. She was handcuffed and looked drunk or intoxicated. Rita moaned quietly, and Erasmus stepped forward to take her weight while the guards unlocked her. The screw gave Erasmus an indecipherable look: "we've got eyes to see the televisor with, you be sure an' remember when this's all over." To Rita: "there you are, *Miss Burgeson*, you'll be right as rain soon enough." Then they retreated and locked the door again.

Rita groaned again. Her eyes were screwed shut against the light. "What's wrong?" He helped her towards the living room.

"Got a migraine." She shuffled as if she was Erasmus' age.

"How did they—" He paused. "Let me get you some water." The kitchen had few utensils and no food—someone had made a half-assed attempt at weapon-proofing what had been built as family accommodation in a gated community—but he filled a cardboard cup from the sink and carried it to Rita, who had taken the armchair and was sitting hunched, clutching her forehead. "Here."

"Thanks. Don't suppose you have any Motrin?"

"I'm sorry, I've no idea what that is."

She chuckled then winced. "This is a *really odd* prison."

"Your mother lived here for the first couple of years." It just sort of slipped out.

"What? And why are *you* here?"

"They're using it as an internment camp again. For hostages—members of the government awaiting trial." And because she looked bewildered he explained.

"Fuck." She winced again, this time at his expression. "Sorry. Look, you mean to say Miriam got away, so, what, they're holding you hostage against her?"

"Exactly that." He forced a smile. "Which means she's still at large, which is good news. But what about you? Did they abuse you?"

"Not—" she rubbed her eyes—"not unless you call forcing me to try and world-walk while underground because they're too ignorant to realize—" her eyes tracked towards the window, widened. "Tell me that's not what I think it is?"

Erasmus smiled tightly. *Now* Rita's headache made sense. He'd seen Miriam after a failed jaunt. It wasn't pretty. "Tell me what else happened. How did they catch you?"

When Rita described Scranton's idiotic orders for her to find Miriam by walking into the most obvious trap in the history of obvious traps, Erasmus resisted the urge to swear. But when she went on to recount Brigadier Richards' belief that she was, in fact, Elizabeth Hanover, he gave in to the urge to vent. He stopped when she got to Richards' threat of a show trial. But then he shook his head. "Something's not right."

"I'll say." Rita seemed to be recovering from her headache. "We're stuck in a prison camp waiting for a show trial, but they housed us together—"

"Hedging their bets against—" he made a cutting gesture—"no, that's not right. What the screw said, something about the televisor. He called you *Miss Burgeson*. And they housed us *together*."

She met his gaze with a puzzled expression. "Yes, so? Oh—wait. *Richards* is convinced I'm her, but the guards . . ."

"The guards disagree. Because of something they saw on the television." Erasmus nodded to himself. "I think you'd better world-walk. When you get to time line one—you're right, this location is utterly insecure for world-walkers—find Brill or Miriam, I'm guessing they'll be watching this site. Time is of the essence, they need to jailbreak all the prisoners *immediately*." A gathering sense of urgency took hold: "I'm not a betting man, but if I was, I'd say your mother got the real Princess Elizabeth up in front of a TV camera and blew the restoration plot narrative the junta is running on, right out of the water. Which in turn discredits them. Minsky is probably sanc enough to stand down, but I'm not sure about Ecker. Richards is a zealot, he'll shoot everyone before he can bring himself to admit he was wrong. Listen, can you tell Miriam—"

Rita pushed herself to her feet. "No, *you* can tell her." She rolled up her left sleeve, then stood in front of him. "Climb on, we're leaving."

Crisis on Infinite Earths

A day late and a dollar short:

The junta was meeting en banc in the office of the speaker of the Magistracy. Outside, all was superficially calm. There were no demonstrations or protests in the capital—not with two divisions of ferocious Commonwealth Guards patrolling the boulevards and avenues of New London, backed up by a motorized shock brigade and their tracked armored vehicles. But the pictures from elsewhere on the continent on the bank of television screens at the side of the junta's meeting room were anything but peaceful.

In Fort Petrograd, the Guards were mewed up in their barracks. while the city's mayor declared a Radical Party Emergency Committee. He denounced the junta before a crowd of thirty thousand citizens, who were camped out on the broad city plaza before San Francisco Bay. In Dunedin, the sprawling transport hub on the shore of Lake Michigan, more thousands marched. They were chanting demands for democracy and liberty, outside a city hall where the local guards commander held the councilors and their families hostage, the situation entirely beyond his ken. In São Paulo, the same, with the added twist that the State Governate had come out in support of the Party Commission. They denounced the Commonwealth Guards as traitors and ideological deviationists—an accusation both hurtful and incomprehensible to the increasingly volatile Brigadier Richards.

"We *are* the loyalists!" He shouted at the screen. "Why are you *lying* about us?"

General Minsky took a more cynical view. "History is written by the victors," he pointed out. "But it can also work the other way round: those who write the news win the war of public opinion."

"You sound like that lying shitweasel Burgeson!"

Minsky fixed the brigadier with a reptilian stare. "Really? Yes, I suppose I do. He's a good model, don't you think? You should practice sounding like him, too. It'll work a lot better than swearing at the—what did he call it—peace and reconciliation commission, won't it?"

"You're going to do it." Richards took deep breaths, snorting bullishly. "You're going to take his rope and tie it round your neck!"

"I know when to *back off*," Minsky said acerbically. "If I let you shoot him . . ."

"If we did, it'd stiffen our spines, what?" This was, from Colonel-General Gomez, who until this point had remained silent. It was an unwelcome interruption to Minsky's line of thought.

"Wait, what's this—"

Something new was coming up on one of the television screens: a color view of a swirling blue and white mass—the world's surface, as seen from a platform outlandishly high up. In fact, two million feet up, and rising at a speed of seventeen thousand miles per hour. "—New broadcast, relayed worldwide by powerful transmitters aboard the Ministry of Intertemporal Technological Intelligence's communication satellite—"

Richards made an inarticulate sound somewhere between a snarl and a groan. But he fell silent as the assembled officers turned to watch the televised display, slack-jawed at this intrusion from another century. But there was worse to come—

—A brown-skinned young woman centered in the screen, addressing a judge and the other Commissioner Burgeson—the one who escaped. The shape of her nose and cheekbones were instantly recognizable from a hundred earlier newsreels, despite her current outlandish attire. She stood on a concrete expanse of runway before a Commonwealth jet aircraft, one hand raised, the other positioned on a book.

A babble of undisciplined interruptions: "What channel is this?" "Get this off-air immediately!"

"Gentlemen!" Minsky barely raised his voice, but the babble subsided.

In the background, the woman in the black leather jacket and oddly mirrored spectacles was speaking: "I believe in the Commonwealth. I believe in the rule of the people, by the people, and the peaceful transfer of power, and the ability of men and women of good will to work together for a better future. I believe we are living in the early days of a better nation, and I want to be part of that nation—"

"—That's torn it—"

"—How did *that* get here?"

"Fucking world-walking nonsense—"

"Game over," Minsky said flatly. "I submit that our opponents hold the high ground, both moral and astronautical. Those earlier show-reels—"

"She's an imposter!" Richards snapped.

"No, she *isn't*." Minsky stood up. He looked around the room, then stared directly at Richards. "Remember Cromwell's injunction, Brigadier? They wouldn't *dare* broadcast that, that . . . *declaration* if they couldn't produce her in public. The woman in the show-reels at the Propaganda Ministry—the one awaiting trial—*she* is the imposter. She *told* you she was an imposter! If *this* one is an imposter, then why the bizarre stage-dressing and costume? We knew they were smuggling her out of Berlin using world-walkers: the story hangs together. But all that is behind us now. If they can prove her identity, we will have to concede the truth of Mrs. Burgesons' outlandish claims. That they've finally pulled the fangs of the Pretender's scheme, to obtain French support for a Restoration. What's more, they've made a technological breakthrough so vast that it beggars the imagination. The terms they are offering are surprisingly lenient: a Special Commission to investigate what went wrong with the succession. We will come out of it badly—but do you really want to ignite a civil war, just to avoid having to admit that we were mistaken?"

MANHATTAN ISLAND, TIME LINES THREE AND FIVE, AUGUST 2020

It had been a very long time since Erasmus had last ridden on anyone's back, much less a world-walker's. Miriam's people were too precious, too limited, and Erasmus too senior, to indulge in impromptu jaunts. For the past decade they'd had better means of carrying large payloads—freight hovercraft, zeppelins, airliners. Also, the floor of their room wasn't at the same level as the ground outside. "We're probably going to drop some distance when you jaunt," he warned Rita. "If I'm on your back you'll twist an ankle for sure."

"Twist an ankle or wait for a firing squad? Mm, *hard* choice." She stepped in close and wrapped her arms around his chest. "I've got you. Hang on, knees up."

"What—" Erasmus tensed and his ears popped and he slipped, ankles jarring painfully as his feet landed. "Where?" He blinked and looked around. "Oh." They'd landed in woodland, low shrubbery and fallen vegetation all around.

"Welcome to the Gruinmarkt, or what's left of it," Rita said. She sounded relieved. "Now we've just got to find someone. I could take you to New York—my New York—but I don't think that would be wise, do you?"

"I don't suppose so," he said thoughtfully. Rita looked surprisingly chipper for a world-walker who'd just jaunted. "How are you feeling?"

"Up for a walk." She shrugged. "How are you?"

"If you know where we're going, lead on."

"This is just a guess—" Rita inspected the trees—"but that direction's north, so if we're still on Manhattan Island we should head *that* way." East. "Look for signs of, well, anything. The worst case is, we can get back to New London. Just not inside a concentration camp." She muttered something under her breath that sounded suspiciously unladylike (*fuck my life*, perhaps), then started to pick her way between the trees.

Erasmus followed her gingerly. A twisted knee or sprained ankle here would be very bad. He was awed by the ease of their escape but driven by a sense of urgency on behalf of the other specials. In his experience the moment of greatest risk for any hostages during a coup was when the wheels fell off. He and Rita were free, but if they didn't find Miriam's people in time to stage a rescue—

They'd been on the move for what felt like half an hour when Rita stopped suddenly. Erasmus had been following her beaten path and nearly walked into her. "Halt! Identify yourselves," someone called.

"Rita Douglas." A pause. "And Erasmus Burgeson." She reached for his arm as he stood beside her.

Erasmus' heart seemed to stutter: for a breathless moment he wondered if he was about to die. Then the invisible speaker's tone changed. "Mr. Burgeson, please step forward and be recognized? Oh. Oh! We've been looking for you, sir. Your w—the other Commissioner Burgeson—is going to be very relieved." A camouflage-clad figure stepped out from behind a tree trunk. "One moment." A burst of static as the soldier spoke rapidly into a blocky hand-held walkie-talkie. "One-two alpha, pickup requested for the other Commissioner Burgeson. Uninjured, one other—what was the name again?—Rita Douglas, both walking." To Erasmus: "where were they holding you?"

"The old internment camp outside the cantonment. Who exactly am I talking to?"

"Thought so. Lieutenant MacDonald, sir, DPR security regiment. Mrs. Hjorth will be eager to debrief you as soon as we can portage you to HQ."

They didn't have long to wait. They were already close to the river: a littoral hovercraft and a team of heavily armed soldiers whisked them away, and half an hour later Erasmus found himself leading Rita into a busy control center in yet another time line.

"Ras!" Brill rose and embraced him, but Rita froze in the doorway, eyes wide.

"Angie?" She said it on a rising note, almost a question, as the other woman shot up out of her seat and opened her arms.

"Oh god *Rita*," Angie grabbed her and held her close. "You're okay? Really?" Angie stared at her anxiously.

"Hey, I'm not the one who's been LARPing spy games in Berlin—!"

"—No, you're the one who's been locked up in New London! Come here, you." Angie hugged her again, then kissed her hard. "I was so worried—"

The two young women were lost in the moment. Brilliana shrugged apologetically at Erasmus, as if to say, *what can you do?* Their reunion sucked all the air out of the room, so much so that it took a few seconds before Erasmus noticed the woman in American costume who remained seated at the table, watching expressionlessly.

"Who's this?" He asked.

"Oh, right. Erasmus Burgeson, this is Dr. Eileen Scranton. Head of Rita's chain of command in US Homeland Security." Brilliana gestured at the stranger, who finally stood and extended a hand for Erasmus to shake.

"Mr. Burgeson." Scranton smiled thinly. "I've heard quite a bit about you."

"Likewise." He nodded.

Rita looked as if she wished the dirt floor would open up and swallow her. "Oh crap—"

"—Is this—" Angie began.

"—Yes, yes she is." With a silent subtext of *I am in* so *much trouble*. She drooped visibly, letting go of Angie's shoulder, but they continued to hold hands.

"Dr. Scranton is here to discuss co-operation on matters of mutual benefit," Brill said elliptically.

"That's about it," said Dr. Scranton. She seemed drily amused by Rita's embarrassment. Less so by Angie, who she quite pointedly avoided making eye contact with.

"I—" Erasmus paused—"see." He met Brill's gaze, baffled. *This woman has been single-mindedly trying to kill your people and destabilize the Commonwealth for years!* He wanted to shout: *what the* hell *are you playing at?*

"Were you released or did you escape?" Brill asked bluntly.

He shrugged "Rita—" Rita looked slightly less embarrassed as he explained. "The junta is holding the captured Commissioners hostage in the old internment camp," he continued. "We're not certain how many, or in what condition, but the guards referred to special prisoners. Also, they were aware that Rita is not Elizabeth Hanover—"

"—The junta thought *you* were—" Angie interrupted. She sounded astonished.

"That was the plan! And it worked for a while."

"With unpredictable side-effects," Erasmus added. "If the camp guards know, then we don't have much time. The junta's claim to legitimacy is based on a conspiracy theory that we can disprove."

"*Have* disproven," Brilliana pointed out. "It's going out on every TV channel in the Commonwealth. The Guards haven't figured out how distributed networks operate. Let me show you." She moved the large tablet on her desk so that Erasmus could see it, then showed him a full-screen video.

"Wow. I can see why everyone thinks I look like—" Rita trailed off. "Was she *supposed* to say that?"

"It wasn't expected, no." Brill looked indecently smug. "But I'd say it's an all-time win. Oh, and Juggernaut worked, too."

"But it puts us on notice," Erasmus said with deep foreboding. "It's possible that the junta will fold, but it's *also* possible that—"

"Hostages, yes." Dr. Scranton wore a very peculiar expression. "We might be able to do something constructive about that. Let's talk terms . . ."

NEW LONDON, MANHATTAN ISLAND, TIME LINE THREE, AUGUST 2020

"I'm just stepping out for a minute," Richards rose from his seat at the committee table. "Call of nature."

Ecker nodded absently: he was busy scribbling on a message flimsy as an adjutant waited anxiously. General Minsky was focused on the bank of televisions, which were now re-running footage of a preposterously long-drawn-out series of corpuscular detonations—subatomic petards swamping the camera every second or two as something vast ascended from a burning wasteland atop a monstrous chain of fireballs. Everyone else in the room was either too busy or too junior to matter, or already committed.

Richards marched to the exit, nodded at the guards who saluted him on the way out, then entered the washroom and waited patiently at the far end.

Colonel-General Gomez joined him a minute later. "It seems the girl was telling the truth," he muttered as he stood in front of the urinal next to the brigadier.

"Evidently." Richards forced his jaw to relax. "Which makes it *worse*. She's a spy for the Americans." *With all that implies*, he left unsaid.

"It seems we have a choice of evils. Yes?" Gomez side-eyed him nervously.

"The French we know how to deal with," Richards said dismissively. "Rope, lamp-posts, you know the drill. But another empire from another universe, with super-science and allies among the Peoples' Commissioners?"

"Minsky is just about ready to throw in the towel," Gomez muttered. "We'll have to move fast." He paused to button his fly.

"Don't worry, general, this is not unforeseen. Can I count on your discretion?"

"Absolutely."

"I need you to take a motorized infantry formation to the former VIP internment camp on the North East Side and secure the prisoners. *In particular*, I need you to secure the Burgesons good and proper, both father and adoptive daughter. He's a traitor and she's a spy, but we might be able to use her briefly when it's time to stage an accident for the Princess. What we *can't* afford is for anyone to escape."

"Understood. What about the waverers?"

"Leave them to me."

Gomez and Richards left in opposite directions, Gomez heading for the motor pool and Richards to the guards' ready room.

Richards was fuming by the time he found his adjutant, Colonel Jefferson. Jefferson had holed up in a meeting room with his own assistant and a squad of troops, all armed. "Sir?"

"It's time," Richards grunted. "Give me that." Jefferson's squad sergeant leaned across an unlocked gun rack and handed the Brigadier a submachine gun. Richards checked it out then loaded it as he looked around. "We have a problem," he announced. "Certain members of the leadership cadre are wavering in the face of the counter-revolutionary faction who are attempting to seize power. You might have heard wild rumors circulating about the Pretender's daughter swearing an oath of allegiance to the Commonwealth. This is a baseless lie: we have her body double under lock and key, and videotapes to prove the so-called oath was a fabrication." He raised his voice: "I intend to take direct control of the junta and ensure adherence to revolutionary principles. Are you with me?"

"Sir! Yes sir!" snapped Jefferson: his men followed suit.

"Our first task is to arrest the waverers. If they resist, you must shoot. Once they're in custody we will transport them to the North East Side internment camp to await trial. We will also ensure the security of the prisoners there, who include traitors and spies. Colonel Jefferson! Requisition motor transport and get it ready to move out. Bring as many bodies as you can. Lieutenant, sergeant, the rest of you—with me, we have waverers to arrest."

Circumstances called for decisive action and the time for subtlety was past. Richards marched back to the control center at the head of his troops, shoved the door open, and aimed his gun at the conference table. "Gentlemen. You've been sitting here for too long: you are dismissed."

General Minsky half-rose, then froze in position. He seemed curiously unsurprised. "So this is the way it's going to be?" He asked.

"Yes, yes it is," Richards announced to the room. "Lieutenant, arrest these men." Behind him the shock troops spread out, guns leveled. The communications clerks and junior officers in the room were clearly not prepared to die for their principles—more evidence, if evidence were needed, of the lack of moral fiber among the junta's followers. "Disarm them."

General Minsky seemed resigned, but Ecker had other ideas, and the sneaky devil unholstered his pistol under the table and snapped off a shot without any warning. The first bullet missed, but Richards' men were on-edge and several of them lit up immediately, spraying the room with automatic fire. The cacophony only lasted a couple of seconds, but by the end of it everyone on the other side of the table was dead or dying. The air was acrid with the stink of powder and bloodstains were splashed halfway up the walls, as Richards leaned over Ecker's prone figure and looked down on General Minsky. Minsky looked as unsurprised in death as he had moments before. "Fools," Richards grumbled. His ears were numb and ringing with tinnitus. "Everybody reload!" He shouted, turning to face his men. "To the transport pool, at the double!"

What a mess, he thought. Minsky could have been an asset, with some attitude adjustment. If only Ecker hadn't lost his shit. There was no avoiding it, now: he had to go for broke, or the putsch was dead in the water. *We'll have to kill all the hostages to prove we mean business.* Then deal with the French. The revolution *would* be saved, one way or another.

INTERNMENT CAMP, UPPER MANHATTAN ISLAND, TIME LINES THREE AND FIVE, AUGUST 2020

"You want us to what, *exactly*, ma'am?" Captain Briggs asked.

Dr. Scranton looked behind her, making eye contact with a South-Asian woman in mall ninja drag—black fatigues and non-regulation boots. The younger woman nodded and Scranton cleared her throat. "Your trainees. I understand they can't hit a barn door at twenty paces, but can they carry a passenger and jaunt? Because if so, they've got a new mission." She either didn't notice, or deliberately ignored, Briggs' glance at Sergeant Jackson. "This is Rita Douglas. She's the pilot program for DRAGON'S TEETH—intel community, not army."

The young woman cleared her throat. "There's an internment camp up near East Harlem in the Commonwealth version of New York where the coup plotters are holding a bunch of senior politicians who they kidnapped. I escaped from it earlier today, with one other inmate who knows the layout. It's guarded, but the guards don't have a clue about worldwalkers and it's laid out more like a gated community with barbed wire and checkpoints than an actual jail." She looked at Dr. Scranton for direction. "I think the guards are wavering. There's no telling which way they'll jump."

Dr. Scranton took over. "The coup in the Commonwealth is rapidly falling apart. The inmates are hostages—members of the government who were captured by the plotters. It has been determined that it is *currently* in the best interests of the United States government to render military assistance to the civil authorities in time line three." She side-eyed the intenselooking middle-aged woman conferring with an entourage of staff at the other side of the compound. "Here's how we're going to do it . . ."

Half an hour later, as they watched a bunch of Commonwealth soldiers boarding a functional-looking hovercraft, Jackson caught a moment with his captain. "Sir, what the *hell*? Are we helping the enemy now?"

Briggs looked weary. "They're not the enemy—at least according to whoever's in charge of this clown car."

"So suddenly we're an aid mission?"

"Would you rather go back to hunting aliens with a bunch of high-school drop-outs?" Briggs gave him a hard stare. "Get your people ready."

"Yes, sir." Briggs was walking towards Douglas.

Jackson shook his head and went to gather up his flock. They were down to just four Dragon's Teeth enlistees: Bernstein, Zuck, Mills, and Jensen. *If I'd known there'd be no shooting, I could have brought Flynn as well,* he thought, but it was too late for that. Add the Douglas woman—she was older than the kids and Scranton seemed to rate her, which was a positive—and that gave him five world-walkers. *Why can't they do the job themselves?* he wondered.

"Listen up, children, we have a job to do," he announced. Bernstein instantly went alert: the others took a couple of seconds to snap to it. "It's an easy one—for you. No alien murderbots, just good honest heavy lifting." The Douglas woman was heading their way. "This is Ms. Douglas from Homeland Security and she's going to brief you now."

INTERNMENT CAMP, UPPER MANHATTAN ISLAND,
TIME LINES THREE AND FIVE, AUGUST 2020

"Mapper?"

"Zeroed." Rita checked the display on the replacement inertial mapper Captain Briggs had made her sign for. ("It's an army asset, ma'am: they'll have my ass if I don't get it back," he told her apologetically.)

"Helmet camera?"

Rita flipped the tiny head-up display down in front of her right eye. "Camera running."

"Ready?" Briggs sounded calm. Behind him, Angie looked as if she was ready to chew on barbed wire and spit out razor blades. (She wasn't coming along on this mission, and she'd told Brill exactly what she thought of this decision. "Sorry, but you can't jaunt," Brill had replied, shutting her down hard. So she was sitting it out in the bleachers, fuming quietly.)

"Yeah, ready to go. And . . . I'm out of here." Rita jaunted.

It was mid-afternoon and the sky was a dull overcast, with a tension in the air from a thunderstorm that was currently rolling in from the Atlantic. She stood in the middle of a dusty street, nobody about, a high brick and cement wall surrounding the block on the other side. She glanced up and saw fence wire. *Check.* This was it: she'd come within about ten meters of the internment camp itself. In the distance, a shout. Rita wasted no time. She swept left then right with her helmet, then jaunted again, straight back to the staging area they'd prepared.

"We're right on their doorstep," she reported. Checking her mapper, she turned and aimed. "The perimeter wall is about eight to ten meters in that direction, running at right-angles."

"Excellent." Brilliana snapped instructions and two of her staff sprayed markings on the ground, then began to pace off the edges of a rough rectangle where she indicated. "That should be inside the wall, but we need to look around before we send the transport over. Are you game?"

"I can do it." Her mouth was dry. *I've done this before*, she reminded herself: she'd jaunted into a patrolled security cordon to gather intelligence. *Let's hope the guards aren't trigger-happy.* Her pulse was still pounding.

Brill noticed something and relented slightly. "You can take five," she told her. "I don't want to break you. I know how hard it can be."

Rita was about to snap back at her—*no you don't*—but then she remembered that *yes*, Brilliana probably *did* know. She hadn't always been a middle-aged administrative functionary. "I'll be okay," she said tensely. "Let's get this done."

"Not just yet." Brill looked her in the eye. "I want you to know that what you're doing is really important. Not just to me—no, this is important to *everyone*. If it works, it's going to defuse the coup before it turns nasty, nastier. I know it's a lot to put on you, but it's also going to go a long way towards convincing the new First Man that the United States isn't an automatic threat, that coexistence is possible. It's not every day that an individual gets to bend the orbit of worlds towards peace, but you're doing it." She glanced aside. "Miriam checked in, she told me to tell you she's proud of you."

"Yeah." Rita swallowed. "Thank her for me. I should get going now."

The second jaunt brought Rita out a couple of meters inside the perimeter wall, facing a high chain-link fence topped with more razor wire, beyond which lay the outer wall of a two-story building with bricked-up ground floor windows. Brill had told her about it. Rita ran sideways to the corner of the fence, then jaunted back again. Mark, jaunt, and repeat. After ten minutes she'd circumnavigated half the perimeter wall, stopping when she came in sight of the front gates and the guard checkpoint. The guards, if present, were watching the entrance, not the dead ground between fence and curtain wall. Back again, she waved to the surveyors who were trailing her with powder spray paint cans and a theodolite, marking the perimeter of the irregular polygon on the ground. "Corner!"

Half an hour later Rita was crouched in the front of a DPR assault hovercraft, on a bench seat between Sergeant Briggs and a pudgy kid in glasses and a US army uniform he wore like a costume party outfit. The hovercraft was one of three open-topped eight-seaters the size of a minibus. Half a dozen DPR troops climbed in behind her, armed with carbines, bolt-cutters, and first aid kits. "Are you ready?" Briggs asked her.

"Not my first rodeo." She side-eyed the drill sergeant. "If there's shooting when we arrive I am *totally* out of here—mission's a bust. That's per Mrs. Hjorth: if you want to argue, take it up with her."

Briggs nodded. "No argument here." He glanced at the pudgy kid. "How about you, Zuck? Ready to jaunt?"

Zuck swallowed and bobbed his head. "Yessir."

The hovercraft's engine roared into life and its skirts inflated: the kid looked as if he was ready to wet himself. Rita laid a hand on his bared forearm, where the e-ink tattoo was visible. "You should try to relax! If we need to make a quick getaway it's easier to focus if you're calm!" She shouted over the engine noise.

The kid nodded, wide-eyed. Rita glanced at her wrist, where her own display was showing a countdown timer. "Okay, jaunting in ten seconds. Five. Three, two, one—"

Rita jaunted, and the world outside the hovercraft changed. "Go! Go! Go!" Yelled the DPR team leader. The driver lowered the front ramp and he and his men jumped out. A moment later another hovercraft flashed into existence beside them with a thundering roar, to be joined seconds later by the third. Her driver raised the ramp and gave Rita the signal: she jaunted again. This time there were eight soldiers waiting for a ride. They shuttled back and forth until they'd moved the best part of a platoon of DPR troops into the courtyard. Other supporting workers followed: medics, a camera crew, and extra people Dr. Scranton had brought in from the United States. Finally, the driver cut the hovercraft's engine and the vehicle settled to the ground. "Now we wait," said a familiar voice behind her, and Rita nearly jumped out of her skin.

"Alice?" She demanded.

"Mrs. Hjorth sent me." Inspector Morgan had changed into army fatigues and was toting a submachine gun, but otherwise looked much the same for having weathered a coup. "I *am* your bodyguard."

"Welcome—" Something caught Rita's attention and she focused on the next hovercraft over. "Okay, here comes step-dad." Erasmus Burgeson was climbing down from the machine, assisted by a pair of soldiers. He caught her eye and beckoned.

"I imagine he's here to convince the prisoners that this is a rescue attempt," the Inspector commented. Her gaze searched the buildings overlooking the yard. "Can't say I like this location. It's all right as long as the guards don't start shooting."

"So let's get inside." Rita stood up and walked down the ramp to meet up with Erasmus. "Showtime!"

INTERNMENT CAMP, UPPER MANHATTAN ISLAND,
TIME LINE THREE, AUGUST 2020

Brigadier Richards glared at the locked gates of the compound as if he could open them by force of will alone. "Get us inside," he demanded.

His adjutant nodded. "Yes sir. Sergeant, get those gates open." Behind them the rear door of the APC clanged open and boots hit the ground, barely audible over the grumble of the motor. Richards stared up at the internment camp walls some more, looking for sharpshooters, then clambered into the commander's cupola of the vehicle for a better view.

Richards' men had grabbed what they could from the motor pool at HQ: a handful of armored personnel carriers, a couple of infantry fighting vehicles (APCs with turret-mounted auto-cannon for fire support), and half a dozen trucks. But there were no tanks, just a garbled message from an agitated NCO who said they were all committed to covering the bridges from Long Island and the mainland. Apparently the regular army had moved a brigade's worth of heavy armor into position overnight. They were demanding the Commonwealth Guards' unconditional surrender on behalf of the government, or some such nonsense. Richards was having none of it, but when life handed you lemons you'd damn well better make lemonade. So he got his troops on wheels or tracks and drove north, to get to the captured counter-revolutionary criminals before their cronies could try and free them.

Nobody moved in the streets as they passed through the gates around the imperial cantonment. Civilians generally had more sense than to scuttle around under the guns of a Guards armored column, and for the most part they were observing the curfew.

As they had approached the former internment camp, Richards grew tense. It was clear enough that the mutinous back-sliders General Minsky had brought into the grand project of renewal were falling apart. *As much spine as a jellyfish between the lot of them,* Richards told himself, although he kept the sentiment to himself. Party Secretary Holmes had been the first to express misgivings, so soon after the move on the reviewing stand during the parade that even the limp-wristed Ecker had agreed he needed to be locked away for the duration. But then the Army and Air Defense forces had refused point blank to have anything to do with the revolution. The Navy top brass were absent without leave: their ships were all at sea, waiting it out under communications lock-down. The two Admirals who'd responded to the junta's urgent communiques had declared their loyalty to the Commonwealth and their intention to defend it at sea against "foreign opportunists"—a barely disguised brush-off.

Now that Minsky and his crew were dead, and the junta's operations in the capital devolved entirely onto Richards' shoulders, he felt angry and resentful. MiniProp and MITI had colluded to deceive the Commonwealth Guard about their intentions, as if the Guard were disloyal to the First Man's principles! And half the Peoples' Commissioners had been in on the conspiracy. There was no question that heads must roll before order could be re-established.

"Sir! Guard house secured." A squad of soldiers had cracked the chain-link gates and swarmed inside the checkpoint. Now Richards' carrier rumbled forward and waited while his men opened the inner gate. The driver pulled into the courtyard beyond and parked. "Area secured."

Richards climbed down into the courtyard and walked towards the administrative block. This side of the complex wasn't accessible to inmates and appeared to be undefended. Guards swarmed around him, securing the offices and ready rooms. "Nobody in here, sir," his captain reported. "We've swept both floors. No sign of booby traps."

"Hmm." Outwardly calm, Richards was confronted by another frightening possibility: that the guards had abandoned their posts—or even thrown in with the traitors. "Proceed and search the prisoner blocks. If there's any armed resistance, shoot to kill. Otherwise, call me when you find where the rats are hiding."

Richards hung back prudently, waiting with his close protection detail while the troops searched the complex. It wasn't so much a gated community as a small town—at its peak it had housed over a thousand families, not to mention their guards. But most of the barracks had been emptied years ago, one wing briefly repurposed as a lunatic asylum before it closed for good as the new neuroleptic medication became available. Now only one quadrant was in use as a detention center.

He didn't have long to wait before his adjutant's walkie-talkie crackled into life. "We've found someone in the yard behind Detention Wing B, sir. Unarmed, says he wants to talk to whoever's in charge."

"Identify him," Richards snapped. His bodyguard hovered closer as he marched briskly towards the covered walkway leading to the Detention

Wings. It was surprisingly quiet in the open air, the sound of the breeze stirring distant branches vying with the distant grumble of APC engines and an odd warbling whine, like a telephone call-discontinued tone.

"Sir, he claims to be a People's Commissioner, Commissioner Burgma—no, Burgeson?"

Richards snorted. "I'll deal with him. Don't let him leave."

To get to the yard where his men had found the Commissioner—sitting on a wooden chair, as carefree as a lark—Richards had to go through another abandoned checkpoint and then the prisoner accommodation. Which showed signs of hasty evacuation not very long ago at all. Doors hung open, tables with meals abandoned half-eaten, mugs of coffee still cooling. The prison warders had pulled out, along with the prisoners they were supposed to guarding. *Contemptible*, Richards thought furiously. If Burgeson thought he'd be open to negotiation he was going to get a short, sharp shock.

"Sir, area is secured. The prisoner says he wants to parlay. Do you want us to bring him inside?"

"No." It wasn't far. And while Burgeson seemed to be alone, Richards was willing to bet his left nut that he was being watched. For what he had in mind, a public demonstration would work best. "Take me to him."

The Minister of Propaganda sat alone on an armless wooden chair in the middle of the exercise yard. He seemed perfectly composed despite the dozen heavily-armed soldiers surrounding him. (All but two kept their weapons pointed outward, too sensible to form a circular firing squad.) They squinted up at the walls of the housing block, as if expecting a surprise attack. As Richards approached, Burgeson raised his head and smiled amiably. "Brigadier."

"Where are they?" Demanded Richards. "What have you done with the prisoners?"

"Me?" Burgeson cocked his head to one side. "I've done nothing. There's been too much *doing* lately, and not enough talking. Wouldn't you agree?"

Richards twitched his submachine gun towards Burgeson's face before he got a grip on his bubbling anger. The warbling whining sound echoed in his ears. "I've got your number! This is a set-up. You organized the restoration conspiracy to give yourself an excuse to seize power! I don't know where you've hidden the traitors but—"

The whining sound rose to a crescendo, echoing from the walls around the yard. Richards swore loudly and looked round. His guards scrambled for cover as strange flying machines hurtled across the roofline, closing from all directions. He turned back to the Minister of Propaganda in time to see him on his feet, leaning on a short, wide-hipped figure in an unfamiliar uniform. He squeezed the trigger a fraction of a second too late, sending a hammering stream of bullets to splinter an empty chair: he never even saw the high frequency beam-shaping wireless hotspots the American engineers had installed behind the upper floor walls, flooding the exercise yard with terahertz radar signals and wifi guidance beams.

Then the borrowed DHS drones locked onto their targets and unloaded their payload of fragmentation grenades.

LONG ISLAND AIR DEFENSE STATION, LONG ISLAND, TIME LINE THREE, AUGUST 2020

By the time the C-37A landed after its third flight sector, Eric Smith was groggy with exhaustion. He'd been up since the early hours in Berlin and ended the day in Baltimore, six time zones later, only to learn that his princess was in another time line. They'd touched base long enough to find a replacement flight crew and for Smith to report in person to a very irritated John Irving. Eileen was still down the rabbit hole on the other side of the looking glass or wherever, and POTUS wanted an in-person update, *stat*. So Smith had climbed back aboard the government Gulfstream, in the company of a uniform carrying a black box which, he was assured, was a working ARMBAND unit—primed and able to jaunt the plane straight into Commonwealth airspace once it was airborne. (And *fuck secrecy*. Not that the Commonwealth could possibly be unaware the ARMBAND technology existed: but the violation of security principles still made Smith's skin crawl.)

He caught thirty winks while Gomez stood watch over their equally frazzled prisoners and the flight crew and supercargo did something that made the bizjet bounce around the sky like a frog in a liquidizer. He was still asleep when unfamiliar fighter aircraft took up position off either wing and escorted them in to a sprawling military airfield that had replaced the Hamptons in this time line. The squeal and bump of wheels on concrete woke him up as they touched down. And then they were following a guide car to a parking area at the other side of the airfield from a row of parked interceptor aircraft, and a surprisingly familiar air stairs and a reception party as the crew opened the Gulfstream's door—

"Colonel Smith? I'm Captain Jacobs, and I'd like to welcome you to the Commonwealth on behalf of the Department of Para-historical Research. My colleague would like to see your passports, now."

He couldn't put his finger on exactly why for a few seconds, but something about the reception party gave him a drenching shock of déjà vu. Brutalist concrete architecture, unfamiliar retro-looking supersonic jet fighters waiting to scramble from their dispersal bays, soldiers in emphatically non-NATO uniforms . . . and a southern accent? It was like something out of an old cold war movie: the United States in the wake of a Soviet invasion, minus the fake Russian accents. "I . . . yes." Smith stifled a yawn.

"Long flight?" Jacobs' sympathy was unaccountably irritating.

"From Germany." Colonel Smith handed over his passport and Jacobs handed it to a woman in another strange uniform—tailcoat, bicorn hat, and a leather case with a fold-down flap that held official rubber stamps and ink pad. She scrutinized his passport as if she'd never seen one before (*of course: she hasn't*, Eric realized blearily), then flattened it under a glass plate and photographed it, before stamping it and handing it back.

"And your companions, please."

Smith frowned. "Two of them are undocumented detainees—I don't have passports for them, but one of them is believed to be a citizen of yours."

"I've been briefed. Can I come aboard to verify their identity?"

"Better not, we'll bring them out. Ah, your citizen is in a wheelchair. He was shot in the chest a couple of days ago. He's stable but requires medical attention."

"Right." Jacobs turned to one of his troops: "Morecomb? Call Medical and tell them to get a hospitaler out here." Back to Smith: "I still need to check your people's papers. Precedent is important."

Fifteen minutes later, Major Hjorth was on his way to the base medical facility in an ambulance with unfamiliar markings—they were called hospitalers here, apparently—and Smith, Gomez, Captain Jacobs, and Paulette Milan were on their way to a different kind of facility in the back of a black staff car with a pronounced Soviet vibe.

Smith leaned back against the leather bench seat and tried to stay awake by focusing on his companions. Across Gomez' tense lap, he could see

Milan staring out at the air base in apparent wonderment. The traitorous bitch probably couldn't believe her good luck, he decided. Before the abrupt about-face from the White House she'd been looking at thirty to life in a Federal supermax cell, if not the death penalty. But here she was, jet-lagged and gift-wrapped as a token of amity. *We're just giving her back to them,* Smith pondered. *Not even a gesture at a trade-off.* He blinked. *Unless State got something out of it without telling us?*

The car drove for several kilometers around the airfield perimeter road, passing missile emplacements and the domes of air defense radar installations—their apparent modernity confirming Smith's fears about the Commonwealth's defenses (although the signal processing computers beneath them were certainly behind the American state of the art)—and then through a clump of residential facilities. Finally they arrived at a squat office block. "Please follow me," said Jacobs, as guards stepped forward to hold the car doors for them. A sign over the entrance told Smith exactly where he was: about to enter the headquarters of the DPR. It felt profoundly weird and not a little bit frightening to be here, like walking into the KGB headquarters building on Dzerzhinsky Square in Moscow.

The strangeness of the Commonwealth gave way to an incongruous sense of dissonance inside the building. The familiar—reception desks, flags—were undermined by strange localisms. Weary-looking professionals in comic-opera uniforms, insignia with no equivalent in time line two. Jacobs led them past a security checkpoint then into an elevator, down and along a corridor, and finally into a windowless meeting room. It might have been a Federal building in Baltimore, except for the alien flags and the old-fashioned filament light bulbs. Jacobs knocked. A moment later the door opened: "Enter."

"Eric, Sonia." Dr. Scranton rose from a seat beside the woman at the head of the dark oak conference table. "And you must be Colonel Milan." Paulette Milan—so recently a prisoner—looked glassy-eyed, but managed to nod.

The women beside Dr. Scranton stood. "Hey, Paulie!" She smiled. "Long time no see!" To Smith she added, "I'm Brilliana Hjorth." Her smile disappeared. "I don't see my brother-in-law. Where is he?"

"Base infirmary, ma'am." Jacobs looked apologetic. "He's poorly but stable."

Paulette butted in. "He was shot by a French soldier while he was assisting the, uh, Princess in her defection. His vest took most of the impact but it collapsed a lung."

Mrs. Hjorth unwound slightly. She nodded and dropped back into her seat. Her eyelids were pouched and saggy, her hair just a little too fly-away. It seemed the head of the formidable enemy intelligence service had been getting by on as little sleep as everyone else, and Smith took a malicious comfort from the knowledge. "Please, grab a seat," she told everyone. To Paulette: "over here, please." She gestured at the vacant chair on her left.

"I . . . uh, wow." Paulette walked around the table and took her seat, then looked at Mrs. Hjorth. "Where's Miriam? What's going on? I mean, I've not been getting much news lately." She sent Smith a sidelong glance that spoke volumes, none of them friendly.

"The Burgesons are currently *somewhat* busy," Brill said gnomically. "Including Rita. Olga will be along shortly, but has limited stamina. Needs must, which is why Miriam delegated short-term negotiations to me—that is, DPR/DHS liaison. An end to backstabbing, mutual repatriation of nationals—"

"I'd hardly call a Lufthansa Airbus full of assorted German tourists and Venezuelan nationals any of *our* business—" Eileen sniped.

"—It'll make you look good to the EU, what more do you want?"

"You're holding some of our citizens!"

Brill smirked. "You mean Kurt Douglas and his team?"

"They're Americans, you can't just kidnap them. We want them back, to answer for—"

"It's not kidnapping: they asked us for political asylum, and we're granting it." Brill's smirk broadened. "They're not doing so as American citizens, but as citizens of the German Democratic Republic. If you don't like it, you can take it up with Erich Honneker's ghost."

Eric couldn't hold it any more: "this is bullshit! The GDR doesn't exist!"

Sonia Gomez' reaction was less temperate: she swore viciously. "I told you they were spies and fucking traitors. We should have shot them!"

Her outburst brought Smith a couple of seconds to regain self-control. "I see where this is going." He stared at Dr. Scranton. His boss stared back at him gnomically. "It's gone political, hasn't it."

"It went political *ages* ago, Eric, that's why we're here."

"Then if it's political, why am *I* here?"

Eileen kept her poker face on: "you were requested as an official observer, Colonel."

"By me." Brill waved her hand. "It's a kind of 'keep your friends close and your enemies closer' sort of thing. We needed an observer who is consistently untrustworthy but principled enough to do the right thing."

Eileen nodded slowly. "The President and the NSC took a high-level decision to hit the reset button on relations with the Commonwealth while you were in flight, Eric. We need them, they need us, nobody needs a nuclear war."

"So . . . ?"

"So Kurt Douglas' geriatric spy ring—a bunch of toothless pensioners on walkers—can fuck off to a Commonwealth nursing home, along with those of their families who want to follow them. We're better off without them. Same goes for you," she added in Paulette's direction. "No offense. We cancel any and all ongoing ops in the Commonwealth, and the DPR stops sending spies into the United States." (As *if any espionage agency in the history of ever would honor such an agreement*, Smith silently thought to himself: *pigs* will *fly first*.) "We're to give the DPR limited access to DRAGON'S TEETH resources for joint missions—" before Eric could explode she held up a hand—"that's already happened, or should be happening round about now."

Eric stared at his boss as if she'd taken leave of her senses.

"What's in it for us?" He demanded.

Dr. Scranton looked at Brill, who shrugged. Then she looked at Eric: "the DRAGON'S TEETH thing sets a precedent for cooperation. In return, we've asked the Commonwealth—or rather, we've asked Mrs. Burgeson—for access to one of their assets."

"What asset?"

Mrs. Hjorth raised a bony index finger and pointed it at the ceiling. "The one my husband is aboard right now, in orbit about three hundred kilometers above us."

Eileen nodded. "They've agreed to assign Juggernaut to a joint operation. You're here to observe the post-coup cleanup and report to me, while I report to the NSC and we get a proper liaison structure in place. And then things are going to get *interesting* . . ."

The Guns of August

"So, they're buying the proposal?" Irving leaned forward across the conference table.

"I . . ." Dr. Scranton winced. "Yes, inasmuch as *we'd* buy anything *they* tried to sell *us*, if you follow my drift." She forced herself not to rub her eyes, which were dry and sore from days with insufficient time for sleep and self-care. "Giving them the goodie bag—" the captured DPR agents— "didn't hurt. Blowing cover on DRAGON'S TEETH and helping with their coup problem helped. But I think coming clean about the incursion worked best: they get 'we can hang together, or hang separately'."

"Good." The President didn't sound terribly relieved, though. She cleared her throat. "So. State will take point on establishing diplomatic relations." The tension Eileen had noticed in the President's face when she first arrived at the meeting was creeping back. "I'm going to proceed on the basis that it's a done deal. However, despite this week's TV coverage of their space dreadnought, we're going to catch heat from idiots who still think we're dealing with a bunch of narco-terrorists. We've got the paratime equivalent of flat-earthers and anti-vaxxers out there, and they're baying for blood."

CNN and Fox both had news anchors melting down in front of the cameras. First there had been the view from the ISS, video of a huge, incongruously futuristic space dreadnought closing in on the space station—an odd kind of retro-futurism, a futurism that bespoke roads not taken by any space program NASA had budgeted for. It had triggered a Sputnik moment, an acute and sudden awareness that someone had stolen the ball and gotten halfway to the horizon while the home team slept. Then, while Eileen had been hammering out a working arrangement with Mrs. Hjorth, the President and the White House press secretary had orchestrated a planned disclosure. The hopper incursion at Camp Singularity actually drove Juggernaut off the top of the news for twelve hours. It lasted right up until *someone*—Eileen strongly suspected Mr. Burgeson's hand was at work: he was a master of psychological warfare—leaked footage of tanks rolling in a foreign capital, stentorian instructions to keep calm and carry on in the name of some sort of authoritarian coup. (Thank you, Erasmus, for framing the Peoples' Commissioners as pro-democracy good guys beating back a coup: a cliché that would play well in Peoria.) At which point the penny dropped and the press corps finally worked out that the giant space dreadnought and the alien invasion were somehow connected to the military coup in another time line, and the whole thing turned into the biggest hairball of incoherent media screaming since 7/16.

"We're running a trade surplus of helpful idiots right now," the President continued. "NASA say they can easily build something like Juggernaut in twenty years, tops, for less than half a trillion dollars. The Navy say they can do it in ten, but they want to go cost-plus with the usual contractors. The DoE say the propulsion system relies on nuclear bombs that nobody knows how to build, and we can't test them without violating the Comprehensive Test Ban Treaty. Meanwhile North Korea is threatening to build their own and colonize Mars. Oh, and Elon Musk says he can do it with rockets if NASA just gives him that ISS re-supply contract he's been lobbying for. The worrying part is they're all serious, and it's an election year. This is a *madhouse*."

The President sighed. She looked remarkably laid back for someone whose fingers were making chicken-strangling motions below the level of the tabletop. "God give me patience. Dr. Scranton, is Mrs. Burgeson playing us? Or do we have a workable arrangement?"

"Sir?" Eileen glanced at John Irving: but her boss shrugged, subtly passing the ball back to her. "Uh." Eileen steeled herself. "I . . . *on the balance of probabilities*, yes. We're not dealing with medievals here. The Commonwealth is a post-Enlightenment project with a written constitution and rule of law, at least when they're not recovering from a failed coup. Prior to the coup, I'd have said they would go for it. Now—it's a mess. The political maneuvering, the Kremlinology, it's all opaque. We screwed up earlier, but we walked it back and they seem to be listening. We'll know more after the swearing-in, when the new First Man picks his cabinet. All I can say for now is that Brilliana Hjorth promised to kick it up a level."

Her brow furrowed. "It depends if Mrs. Beckstein—I mean, Burgeson—if she's confirmed in place in the new cabinet. If not, we could be in trouble. But right now I expect them to go along with our proposal."

"Did you ask about getting one of our astronauts on board?" Asked Irving.

Eileen nodded. "They say their docking adapter is incompatible. They also said, if *we* had Juggernaut, would we want to invite a Commonwealth officer to hitch a ride?" She paused for a second. "Then they said yes, but only to a civilian observer. And there are strings attached."

"Whatever they are, we'll pay." A brief pause. "Dammit."

"If it gets them to sign the treaty and agree to the joint operation, it's well worth it," Irving commented philosophically. "We're asking them to put skin in the game. Otherwise, our only option is a solo nuclear strike on an Advanced Persistent Threat that's at least a century ahead of us. We need the Commies on board—"

"—Commies." The President frowned. "For God's sake don't call them that in front of any cameras, John! The last thing we need is Fox News framing this as Cold War 2.0."

"I don't know." Irving crossed his arms: "Without the Cold War, could Nixon have gone to China? It's a handy metaphor, and metaphors are easy to spoon-feed to idiots. And it has the advantage that the Cold War ended peacefully."

"Huh." The President nodded to herself, half-closing her eyes in thought. "Yes. I could work that message. Détente, the lowering of tensions. We should definitely frame it that way for domestic consumption. Yes." She nodded once more. "Let's play that old tape again and see how it sounds in a new century . . ."

NEW LONDON, MANHATTAN ISLAND,
TIME LINE THREE, SEPTEMBER 2020

Almost a week had passed since the Commonwealth Guard coup collapsed in a bloody rain of fratricidal in-fighting. When the regular army drove back into New London, the remaining Guards surrendered peacefully. The majority of the arrested politicians and officials were shaken but uninjured: the junta had intended to use them in a series of show trials to justify the coup, and had consequently kept them alive. The mission brokered by

Brilliana and Dr. Scranton that Rita had been involved in was one of a half-dozen scattered rescue operations around the capital. There had been relatively few deaths, and the damage to offices and buildings was mostly cosmetic.

It was a good month to be a glazier or cleaner, though.

The coup might have been suppressed, but that meant more work for the Burgesons, and for Brilliana Hjorth. Olga Thorold arrived back in the capital just in time for the mop-up, before over-working and putting herself back in a sick bed. Angie, Kurt, and Kurt's irregulars from the Wolf Orchestra were shuffled off to the visiting officers' accommodation at the Long Island air station, under the supervision of Inspector Morgan, whose remit within the Transport Police now appeared to include monitoring refugees from parallel Earths.

For her part, Rita moved in with Angie, after an extremely awkward debriefing interview with Colonel Smith. ("Am I fired?" She'd asked him point-blank: his refusal to confirm or deny—while Sonia Gomez stared daggers at her over his shoulder—was singularly unreassuring.) He'd left her with the distinct impression that if she returned to the United States without a diplomatic visa she might well be arrested. It wasn't an understanding she was keen to test. Go hang with the former East German spy ring, or return to the chilly bosom of the Department of Homeland Security: hard choice. When she'd raised her family ties (Franz, Emily, River) with Inspector Morgan, she'd been told their names were "on the list," whatever that meant. It was frustratingly, infuriatingly, inconclusive—which apparently was normal for refugees during times of political change.

But she wasn't left to her own devices for long. Or at all: Inspector Morgan kept introducing her to researchers from the DPR who wanted to know all sorts of things about everyday life in the United States. (And it was *really hard* to refuse to describe the Girl Scouts Camp she'd attended when she was fourteen on grounds of national security.) It also turned out that she had fans in the Propaganda Ministry: if nothing else she could get work as an actor. Finally, she received the occasional note from her birth mother, who was as busy as only a senior government official during a succession crisis could be, culminating in yesterday's summons.

And so, eight days after they were reunited, she and Angie sat among the audience in a stuffy ceremonial hall in New London, waiting for the new First Man to be formally announced.

"I'm nervous," Rita admitted.

"Thanks." Angie clasped her hands together to keep from fidgeting. "You're the one with the acting experience! How do you think *I* feel?"

"If you feel anything like I do, you probably itch." Rita ran a finger around the collar of her blouse. "I feel like I'm playing dress-up, even when I'm not wearing an outfit supplied by the Ministry of Propaganda wardrobe department—"

"It's a theatrical costume." Angie was philosophical. "Makes you look like you belong here. How do you think *I* feel?" She looked as out of place as a Star Trek extra in a Battlestar Galactica re-run. Rita reached over and tugged a ringlet, adjusting Angie's wig. Close-cropped blue hair was sufficiently outlandish that their MiniProp handler had insisted on a hairpiece for their joint photo op. Erasmus's people had kitted them out in what passed for suitable attire for properly turned-out Commonwealth society ladies. Ironically, Angie was less irritated by it than Rita.

Rita was still trying to get a handle on how Commonwealth attitudes to sex and gender differed from those of the United States. The revolution just two decades past had junked a huge volume of traditional law and custom, but public attitudes were still playing catch-up. Erasmus had delicately hinted that having a high-profile interracial lesbian couple in the spotlight would be *socially and politically useful,* but Rita stubbornly resisted being pushed towards a career as an opinion shaper and influencer. She'd had enough of *that* for one lifetime, even though she could see why Miriam and Erasmus might want them to play the part of a respectable politician's daughter and her friend. But in any case, being a public role model was a valuable public service at this event and at the many similar ones she had a dismal feeling she was going to be required to attend in the future.

"Suits you." Rita flashed her a grin: for a moment Angie mimed punching her, but then leaned in close enough for Rita to feel her hot breath on her cheek. Rita's heart stuttered for a moment. "Remember we're in public."

"Later, then." Angie folded her hands again, and turned to face the front of the chamber attentively. "Look, it's Liz." She pointed. Rita followed her gaze. The former princess was sitting in the next row, smartly but almost aggressively plain in her suit, head tilted towards—*is that Kurt?* Rita blinked, feeling inexplicably betrayed. But of course Ms. Hanover would be making connections here. Or perhaps Miriam had maneuvered Kurt into making himself *useful* by taking Elizabeth in hand, just as she was trying to orchestrate Rita's life. It seemed to be what Mrs. Burgeson did to people: put them together to make useful connections. Angie nudged her. "We should go and say hello after the announcement, she's as much a stranger here as we are—"

A ripple went through the viewing gallery as the door at the back of the chamber opened. The Commissioners who still held membership in the Council of Guardians—the surviving ones—entered. Everyone stood. Rita leaned against Angie, taking comfort from her stolidity. Erasmus and Miriam stood close to the middle of the group. Probably their position meant something, but Rita hadn't seen enough of Commonwealth politics to have a clear handle on it. She'd seen barely anything of her birth mother since the coup. Her requested presence here felt like a flimsy pretense at familiarity, almost offensively impersonal. "Look. The camera lights are on."

This was really just a staged photo op. Nevertheless it was the kind of photo op that had people in the know queuing around the block, and bribing the doormen to be allowed to stand in the background. The Ministry of Propaganda had organized it in just the past day. The audience was packed with dignitaries. Colonel Smith was here, a couple of rows back from Elizabeth Hanover. (When Angie had first introduced her they'd done an awkward social tap-dance. "Maybe *I* could impersonate *you*, over in your United States," the former princess had joked. "You're welcome to try, if you want to be arrested for spying," Rita had replied.)

One of the colorless Commissioners in the front row walked to the podium and began to speechify. Rita tensed. It was Adrian Holmes: the very man she'd been unpardonably rude to at the funeral viewing, and who she'd been led to understand had conspired with the Commonwealth Guards. *Oh, this isn't going to go well,* she thought. Then he began to recite, with the oddly rolled vowels of a priest reading a liturgy: "Hear ye, hear ye. By the authority of the Central Commission of the Founding Party of the Commonwealth . . . I, Adrian Holmes, General Secretary of the Party Commission, call this session of the Council of Guardians to order. All stand, for the declaration of democracy—"

Rita found the procedures here simultaneously alien and familiar. The history and politics of this time line had diverged from her own almost three centuries ago: some of the forms and language of the Commission *sounded* like congressional procedure, but other things kept her on edge. The Commonwealth had purged their legal code of Latin jargon while the United States still clung to it. And the Declaration of Democracy that everybody recited was straightforward, couched in modern language. "We create this nation anew on the basis of equality and fraternity, to collectively exercise our liberty as fellow citizens of a republic—"

The session settled into a half an hour of routine boredom until Holmes got to the matter of the succession. "We are gathered here today to vote on two matters. First, on the authority of the Council of Guardians, to approve the Party's proposed candidate for the office of the First Man."

Angie leaned close to Rita. "The First Man, is that, like, the President?"

"Nearly," Rita muttered. *More like a secular Grand Ayatollah.* "Wait."

Holmes read from a script. "The Council of Guardians has met in closed session to consider candidates from among their number, and all but one have been eliminated in the first round. I call now for the Council to swear in as First Man—"

"—*What?*" Angie whispered in Rita's ear, scandalized at the lack of public participation.

"—It's like the Vatican—" Rita replied.

"—a man who served Adam Burroughs, the founder of our better nation, as his personal secretary. During the days of the eighty-six—" the previous, abortive revolution against the Crown—" He was imprisoned by the Imperial regime, escaped and worked selflessly as a Party cadre during the repression that followed. After the revolution he served the Commonwealth most ably as Commissioner for the Ministry of Propaganda—"

Rita blanked. "Wait. What." Fireflies were twinkling in the press gallery on the other side of the auditorium. "Wait, that can't be right—"

"—Burgeson, we call upon you to—"

Angie was gripping her arm with fingers like steel cables. "Is that what I think it—"

Rita squinted past the strobing glare of cameras to look down on the floor of the chamber as Erasmus rose and, back stooped, walked slowly towards the podium.

"—Love, your step-father is *the new president?*"

"Grand Ayatollah," she corrected absent-mindedly. She felt numb. *Surely they'd have told me?* But no: and now Miriam's remoteness, and then the insistence on Rita and Angie being turned out like Commonwealth-style preppie heiresses made more sense.

There was cheering. Angie was pounding her on her back; everyone was on their feet. But Rita sat alone, paralyzed by a sudden realization. She'd chosen to make a new life for herself here—sliding into it as the path of least resistance, borne along in the wake of Angie's asylum claim and Kurt and her family's exile. She'd somehow imagined that she could still be herself, Rita Douglas, aspiring actor and accidental spy. But Erasmus was to be the new First Man, and her other mother was the First Lady of the Commonwealth.

"Holy shit." Rita stared at the stage in horrified realization. Despite impersonating a princess for a week, she had zero clues how to be the First Lady's daughter.

"'C'mon," Angie whispered in her ear, pulling her to her feet: "They're going to want you to join them up there in a minute."

"But I can't—"

Angie kissed her cheek: "you *can*. I'll be right beside you. Think how much good we can do together? I've got your back."

Rita could see the uniformed ushers closing in on them and tensed.

Angie held her hand. "It's going to be all right," she reassured her.

"Okay." Rita took a deep breath and straightened her spine, then smiled professionally. *"Showtime—"*

Then she took her first step forward, towards the role of a lifetime.

JUGGERNAUT, LOW EARTH ORBIT, TIME LINE TWO, AUGUST 2020

Two days after the inauguration a different formal exchange was in progress, high above the clouds over Argentina.

"Juggernaut, Control, airlock fully depressurized, external hatch four is open. Stevens and Cortez standing by."

Huw hovered over the comms panel, listening in as Sergeant MacDonald juggled channels adroitly.

"Expedition 70 Control to Juggernaut, confirmed. Soyuz is undocked and preparing for ferry sequence. Denisovitch and Kurta in DM, pressurized: Jensen suited in Orlan-MKS for EVA transfer from OM, OM unpressurized. Jensen reports PLSS says four hours eighteen minutes to bingo air, temperature nominal. Over."

Stevens came over the Juggernaut communications loop: "should be plenty." He sounded slightly tense, for he, too, was waiting, suited up, inside a depressurized airlock.

Huw took a quick poll of the ship's stations. Then he reached past MacDonald: "Juggernaut, Control, Soyuz is cleared to approach. Over."

Bringing Juggernaut any closer than two kilometers from the International Space Station would be the height of recklessness. But the diplomats were making kissy-face and so a compromise was reached. Colonel Alice Jensen, a former USAF pilot turned NASA astronaut, would come aboard Juggernaut. She'd use a Russian space suit similar to the ones the Commonwealth had cloned, using a Soyuz capsule as a ferry. It'd require the Soyuz to fly perilously close to Juggernaut under manual control, without docking radar. Jensen would try to space-walk across the gap between the depressurized Orbital Module and Juggernaut's airlock. Normally ISS spacewalks were planned a couple of years in advance and choreographed painstakingly, but this time they'd cannibalized bits of a pre-rehearsed checklist. The ISS would be down one crew member for a couple of months, until the next Soyuz arrived. But in return the US government would get a witness on Juggernaut during its expedition to time line four.

Stevens and Cortez were waiting in the larger vehicle's airlock to help. "I see it," Stevens reported. "Soyuz range check?"

"Juggernaut reads one nine three zero meters, closing at two meters per second." Slow enough to track easily, but still fast enough to damage both spacecraft if they collided.

"Brown pants time," MacDonald remarked, muting his microphone.

"Don't jinx it." Huw scanned the boards again. "Juggernaut, Control, is Alice in the loop?"

"Jensen here, Juggernaut." A slightly breathy voice, the whir of suit helmet fans audible in the background. "Standing by."

"Juggernaut, airlock crew, sitrep."

"Cortez here, I'm on the ball. Over."

Cortez would be waiting in his suit, just inside the airlock, clutching their improvised docking aid: a foam ball trapped in a net at the end of a carefully coiled length of nylon rope.

"Range check."

"Four hundred and twenty meters . . ."

"Fifty meters."

"Soyuz thrusters Z-axis minus two hundred, go."

"I'm opening the OM hatch now . . ."

The Soyuz had closed to just twice its own length away from Juggernaut's open airlock. Cortez—fastened to a hull anchor point—pushed the ball towards the open hatch. The rope unreeled behind, but his first three attempts at playing zero gee basketball missed. "This—" Cortez huffed quietly—"is harder than it looks, people."

The open Soyuz hatch was only eighty centimeters in diameter, and the rope tugged the ball unpredictably off course. But on the fourth attempt Cortez made the throw: "I've got it!" Jensen announced. "I've got the ball!"

It took another twenty minutes for her to safely fasten the rope to her suit and exit the Soyuz hatch, then for Stevens and Cortez to reel her into Juggernaut's own airlock. Finally, Stevens spoke up: "external hatch closed and latched. Are we green inside?"

"Cross-check—confirm hatch closed." Verity, waiting inside, could see the screw jacks that held the ship's air in. "Integrity check. Standby to re-pressurize."

"You have control," Huw told Jenny Wu, who was standing by in the co-pilot's seat. "I'm going to welcome our visitor aboard." He pulled his feet up and rolled towards the main access tunnel. "You can take prep for jaunt and powered flight."

"Aye aye, sir." Jenny glanced sidelong at him, then cracked a broad grin. "Do you ever get the feeling you're living in that American TV show—Star Trek, isn't it?"

Huw rolled his eyes. As a civilian world-walker, Jenny took—and got away with—more liberties than the ex-military crew members. "Frequently, but don't tell anyone I said that. Otherwise they'll expect me to pay for a ho-lodeck upgrade."

"My lips are sealed." And then Huw was through the hatch, heading to the main docking node, ready to start the final countdown.

UNDISCLOSED PATROL AREA, NORTH PACIFIC, TIME LINE TWO, SEPTEMBER 2020

The *USS Maine* had been on extended patrol in its assigned area of ocean for nearly three weeks when the firing orders arrived.

Like any other ballistic missile submarine, the *Maine* spent most of its time impersonating a hole in the ocean—impellers slowed, reactor and turbines at idle, dawdling along at walking pace beneath two hundred meters of water. It followed a seemingly random track across an area of the ocean about the size of western Europe. Its planned path was shared with a *Virginia*-class attack submarine shadowing her at a distance, ready to attack any foreign warship or submarine that approached the Trident boat. Every three hours or so the *Maine* would ascend to what passed for periscope depth these days—actually fifty meters below the surface, but close enough that a sensor buoy trailing behind the submarine could rise to the surface and expose its sensors to the sky for a few seconds.

Three hours was approximately the time it took a satellite in low Earth orbit to complete two orbits—a satellite such as TRIPWIRE, the positive command channel for the Trident force. Most of the time TRIPWIRE lurked in orbit in an undisclosed time line, safe from anti-satellite weapons, but each listening period coincided with a scheduled window when TRIPWIRE might jaunt into time line two and broadcast an encrypted data burst as it passed over the submarine's patrol area. It did this at least once a day, just to confirm the system was working. But today, the encrypted message wasn't a test signal.

The normal state of affairs aboard a Trident submarine is that the crews drill incessantly, but very rarely fire any missiles—when they do, they are loaded with dummy warheads and aimed at a target range. (Test firings are rare because a UGM-133A missile cost nearly as much as a fighter jet.) The order to rise to firing depth and launch its eight specially modified missiles was therefore unprecedented in the experience of the *Maine's* captain. No ballistic missile submarine had ever launched a salvo of live nuclear-armed missiles. (Indeed, no ballistic missile submarine had launched even a single live nuclear warhead since the early 1960s, before the Atmospheric Test Ban Treaty put an end to such events.) However, the order wasn't unanticipated—he and the other officers on both watch crews had been briefed before they left port. The missile crew on duty set to work punctiliously, running through their checklists and uploading the final parameters to the flight guidance computers aboard each rocket stage.

History does not record precisely what transpired aboard the USS *Maine* that day. The actions of a navy crew deploying strategic weapons in combat are tightly classified. We know from anecdotal reports that Captain Henry took the unusual step of addressing the crew during the heightened readiness state prior to the launch. We know that he explained that this was a planned strike at another time line, that the North American Commonwealth was *not* the target, indeed that the NAC were partners in a joint operation—we don't know whether everyone believed him. As the clock counted down towards zero hour, the *Maine* ascended until she was just twenty meters below the surface, under way at roughly two knots.

At zero time minus five minutes, the *Maine* opened eight of the missile hatches along her upper hull, exposing the pressurized canisters containing her missiles to the sea. Of similar proportions of a tube of lipstick, each missile weighed over sixty tons at launch. Igniting such large rockets inside a submarine would be suicidal: instead, at the bottom of each tube, a flash boiler would generate a piston of live steam that forced the missile out of its tube. Each rocket breached the surface and ignited its first stage in turn, launching at thirty second intervals.

A Trident D5 missile is a three stage, solid fueled rocket. Each of the stages ignites in sequence, and once burning they can't be switched off. In consequence, Trident has a minimum range, as well as a maximum. To strike targets close to the launch site (close is relative—the minimum range is well over two thousand nautical miles), the missile ascends steeply before following a plunging trajectory. For more distant targets, the missile follows a flatter, longer curve. As it flies, it adjusts its course using a star tracker and an inertial platform. Two minutes after launch, as the third stage ignites, the missile is already traveling at over 20,000 kilometers per hour: it's a brutal ride. Finally, once the third stage burns out the MIRV 'bus' takes over—a maneuvering section that adjusts its trajectory minutely to aim and release each warhead on an unpowered trajectory towards a separate target.

Each of the eight warheads on each of the *Maine's* eight modified missiles was equipped with an ARMBAND unit. Five minutes after separation from the missile bus, they jaunted, vanishing from X-band radar as they coasted across the Pacific north-west coast.

An observer keeping careful watch, from a position in orbit around the Earth of time line four, might conceivably spot the incoming train of Mk-5 reentry vehicles—but it was unlikely. The RVs were cold, coasting without rocket propulsion. Each warhead was a black cone approximately two meters tall, small enough to fit in the bed of a pick-up truck. Nor did they emit any significant amount of radiation. Every day, thousands of meteorites of similar size re-entered Earth's atmosphere and burned up long before they reached the surface. The individual Trident boosters had ascended on trajectories pre-planned for MRSI—multiple rounds, simultaneous impact—but the warheads were staggered by fractional seconds to prevent fratricide (in case the neutron pulse emitted by one warhead prematurely activated a neighboring warhead, causing it to mis-detonate).

The Hive incursion in time line four had placed artifacts in orbit around that version of Earth. However, the Hive was focused on ground-level search operations, spreading out in concentric rings across the North American continent in an attempt to locate and destroy the Forerunner intruders who had awakened them from their thousands of years of hibernation. What sensors they had in orbit were pointed downwards: for the hive knew that if the Forerunners had a strategic weakness, it was that they seldom bothered to venture far above the atmosphere. Para-time was their preferred battle space. For the hive to encounter hominids in space was not completely unprecedented, but a very low probability event.

Less than twenty minutes after the countdown aboard the *Maine* reached zero—over a period of less than ten seconds—sixty-four W88 thermonuclear warheads rated at a little less than half a megaton each plunged back into the atmosphere. They converged on the Hive incursion around the gateway in time line four, where once the Dome had quietly rotted. Each of the W88s arrived within a hundred meters of their aim points, falling in two waves. The first tight group of four H-bombs were set to detonate at ground level on the valley floor around the Dome, and they were followed by a second wave of sixty warheads, fuzed to detonate between one and five kilometers up. The first wave vaporized what was left of the Dome and Camp Singularity: the second wave brought hell on Earth to a circular area the size of New York, where molten steel ran like water and trees ignited like Fourth of July sparklers.

The destructive effect of a simultaneous time-on-target attack using W88's was comparable to that of a two hundred megaton super-bomb. It set the sky on fire from horizon to horizon, shortened the mountain peaks on either side of the valley at ground zero, lit forest fires fifty kilometers outside the kill zone, and achieved one other thing—

—It drew the Hive's complete and undivided attention.

JUGGERNAUT, LOW EARTH ORBIT, TIME LINE FOUR, AUGUST 2020

Zero hour minus eighty minutes, and in the sunset skies above the Juggernaut launch pad in time line twelve, a spectacular light show rose in the west.

The night sky in time line twelve had been illuminated by spectacular aurorae as far south as the Tropic of Cancer since Juggernaut's ascent into orbit. The Earth's magnetic field had trapped a radiation belt of charged particles emitted by the nuclear explosions, and they took days to weeks to decay. Now Juggernaut was back in orbit, using time line twelve as a dumping ground for more fallout as it maneuvered under power, cranking its orbital inclination so that at zero hour it would overfly the wilderness where Maryland existed in the inhabited time lines.

"Bumpy ride, eh, Colonel?" Huw glanced sideways at the NASA astronaut in the observer's seat.

Alice Jensen rolled her eyes at him. "This is *insane*," she replied, grabbing her seat restraints. *Thump*. A giant boot kicked them in the backside, followed by a chorus of squealing and rattling metal—internal fixtures within the command module, rather than the hull structure itself, Huw fervently hoped. "You don't even keep a—" *Thump*—"sterile cockpit?"

"Only if you're part of the flight ops team: I'm more of an—" *Thump*— "onboard mission director. Not a lot to do right—" *Thump*—"now." They were chatting with open helmet faceplates, throat mikes muted while the actual flight crew and the nuke crew handled the planned maneuver. Huw kept one eye on his status board, but Davis and Jensen were running the flight deck while Saunders was in charge of feeding atomic propulsion charges to the mortar that kicked them behind the pusher plate. Until it was time to world-walk—or engage in other non-routine activities—Huw's team didn't have much to do. *Thump*.

"How many more—" *Thump*—"to go?"

"Uh, thirty-six—" *Thump*—"nope, thirty-*five* now." *Thump*. "Then we take ten minutes for damage control reports—" *Thump*—"and if we're good to go, that's—" *Thump*—"when things get—" *Thump*—"exciting."

And what could be more exciting than sitting in a tin can with nuclear explosions going off under your ass at one second intervals?

Juggernaut, rising in the west atop a trail of brilliant violet flashes, trailed a ghostly aurora as it reached its zenith over the wild shores of an uninhabited Cuba then hurtled east across the Atlantic.

Ten minutes later, Huw called for a go/no-go report from each of Juggernaut's stations. Everything was running to plan, and the strain and damage from the propulsion charges was within tolerance. But what came next had the potential for disaster. "All right, everybody, team leads? I want you to distribute the checklists for BLUE FRIDAY. That's, BLUE FRIDAY, people." He caught Colonel Jensen watching him. "Morten, you are now Target Acquisition. Cortez, you are now Battery Commander." Morten was normally in charge of proximity radar, Cortez ran backup for the nuke team. Their new titles reflected new roles—roles they'd trained for but hoped never to need to execute.

"Battery, you have unrestricted release control on my word." Huw reached for his control panel and inserted a key in an unobtrusive slot, then turned it: "mark."

"Battery, guns are hot."

"Target Acquisition, ready on your word."

Huw flipped down his copy of the checklist. "Target Acquisition, maintain EMCON on insertion but power up threat receivers A and B, internal power only. At Tango time minus thirty seconds, we are going to go dark and stay that way until Tango time plus thirty seconds, at which time Target Acquisition will go live. It's going to be a messy radiation environment, people.

"Battery, set up fire plan Alpha, time on target, six rounds rapid. Queue up fire plan Beta, time on target, six rounds rapid. Then alternate until you run dry."

Jensen's eyes were wide, but she bravely resisted the urge to ask, so Huw took a couple of seconds to explain: "we brought a couple of six-guns. *Big* six guns." Thirty centimeter naval guns with six-round autoloaders, designed to fling their payloads well clear of Juggernaut before their highly specialized nuclear warheads detonated. "Fifty kiloton nuke-pumped X-ray lasers, with dirtied-up eighty kiloton EMP mines as a whisky chaser."

"I, uh—" Jensen was aghast.

"Juggernaut was no more designed for a first strike than those fancy Tridents your people are bringing to the party," Huw added. "So it's a good thing we're on the same side, isn't it?" He turned back to his checklist without acknowledging Jensen's jerky nod.

An hour seemed like an age: an hour passed like no time at all, grains of sand trickling through an hourglass with frantic speed. Finally the countdown hit the point of no return. "Jaunt crew, go."

Bill Wolf was on jaunt, with Jenny Wu on standby to abort back to their safety time line. Jenny narrated: "Bill's ready in three, two, one . . . clear." Outside Juggernaut's TV cameras, the cloud patterns flickered and rearranged themselves. "Established on time line four. Retreat jaunt on hold at T minus ten seconds."

Tension seemed to squeeze the breath out of the command module crew. They were now two hundred kilometers above an alien-occupied time line, hurtling across hostile territory at eight kilometers per second. Somewhere high above them a swarm of deadly black cones were plunging down at just under orbital velocity, slamming towards a forested valley floor two thousand kilometers ahead of Juggernaut's ground track. If everything ran to plan, *if* the Americans were dealing in good faith, the volley of W88s would detonate just sixty seconds before Juggernaut flew over the Dome.

"Target Acquisition, picking up unrecognized signals, seems to be a mix of X-band and W-band frequencies, very low entropy, multiple sources at high inclination. TR-A doesn't have a match for any known codecs."

"Can you get a count on them? And orbital elements? How many are we talking about?"

"I got, uh, nine over the horizon now, one going dark in thirty seconds. They're all above us, that's all I know for now, inclinations range between forty-two and sixty-nine degrees. Update: lost signal from bogie one, two new sources—bogies ten and eleven—coming up. Also, there's a ground signal source dead ahead, right on top of our target zone. Sitting fat and happy, chattering away."

Huw chewed his lower lip. "Battery, call the release checklist for SLEDGEHAMMER."

"SLEDGEHAMMER confirmed." Cortez sounded unnaturally calm. "I need your lock code, skipper."

"Lock code—" Huw read eight numbers from his checklist. "Confirmed lock code."

"Lock code confirmed. SLEDGEHAMMER is armed."

"Nav, Battery, update trajectory elements for SLEDGEHAMMER."

He caught Jensen's eye, muted his mike again. "It's a *really big* bomb in a stealthed re-entry capsule. Two hundred megatons with a Cobalt-60 chaser. We'll release it once we confirm the situation on the ground, before we maneuver: it should impact one orbit later."

Jensen shook her head. "Your boss is *clearly* a fan of *Doctor Strangelove*."

The live countdown on Huw's board dropped into double digits, then towards single digits. Finally, the duty pilot made the call: "button up now, all cover. Light show in ten seconds." Protective shutters slid across most of Juggernaut's cameras and instruments, the same ones that had protected the ship during its first flight. Circuit breakers tripped, isolating all the external antennae. For the next minute, Juggernaut would drift, almost blind, above a nuclear hellscape. But not *entirely* blind: Huw's command module had a couple of sacrificial TV cameras with heavy filters. And so the command crew got to watch.

Skimming over the cloud tops above time line four's equivalent of the southern states—covered in sub-arctic forests, the gleaming white flare of the ice cap just visible on the limb of the Earth's face, far to the north— everything looked peaceful to Huw's eye. Over the past days he'd become accustomed to the ever-changing cloudscapes of all the Earth's he'd visited, although the shifting beauty of the view never failed to take his breath away. He felt his pulse race as he held his breath, waiting for—

—There.

He saw a flicker on the horizon ahead, like four bolts of lightning plunging from the top of the atmosphere to the ground, if lightning ran laser-sharp and struck from the edge of space. Then the view blanked for a few seconds. Then the screen refreshed, pixelated for the first moments: then it cleared to reveal a portal into hell. *Four* portals, incandescent bubbles of unholy fire that merged and overlapped in the middle, coiling and tumbling dead center in the screen.

"Target Acquisition, confirm multiple EMPs, detonation nominal—"

More flickers of lightning plunged from the zenith, like robot angels falling towards their individually targeted hells. Each flicker grounded in a flare of whiteness that froze the screen in a mess of pixels before cooling and expanding. As the deadly rain continued, the earlier fireballs tumbled and ascended, sucking up debris plumes to form the characteristic stems of mushroom clouds.

"Holy crap," somebody said aloud over the common audio loop.

"Keep it sterile, folks," Huw heard himself say. The mushroom patch was expanding ahead and below as Juggernaut's orbital trajectory took it closer.

"Twenty seconds to unbutton," called the duty pilot.

Huw cleared his throat. "Battery, SLEDGEHAMMER release on your count."

"Confirmed: starting timer on SLEDGEHAMMER. Guns waiting on Target Acquisition, fire plans alpha and beta ready."

"Unbutton in ten . . . eight . . . six . . ."

Juggernaut's sensors came back online as the shutters withdrew. Below and gradually receding to stern, the field of deadly fireballs rose, cooling and expanding as they reached the stratosphere. Then the first alerts came in.

"Target acquisition, I have fifteen repeat fifteen X-band sources on passive. Starting up search radar."

"Battery, SLEDGEHAMMER separation is commencing. Maneuver inhibition is in effect." Juggernaut's main drive and maneuvering jets had to stay offline while the eighty-ton warhead eased away from its berth on the outside of Juggernaut's mainframe. A collision with the huge bomb wouldn't detonate it—probably—but it might damage both the weapon and the mothership.

"A turret, gun reports ready—B turret, gun reports ready."

"Target acquisition, confirm seventeen contacts on primary search radar. Ground signal discontinued—wait, bogey four is maneuvering!"

Huw's stomach lurched. "Uplink to Battery as you get a fix," he said. "Plenty of time." *No, there really isn't,* his inner voice was screaming. Colonel Jensen was clutching at her armrests in the seat beside him. "Drive, stand by for Battery's all-clear on SLEDGEHAMMER sep."

"Target acquisition, bogey seven is accelerating—bogey ten and bogey six also. Uh, they're making about six gees. Infrared plumes, looks like they're using rockets."

Oh thank fuck. Huw suppressed a shudder. Dr. Scranton's uploaded briefing about the events on the other side of the Gate had been nightmarish.

The bogeys they'd seen maneuvering around the black hole hadn't been rockets—they had some kind of magic space drive. But if it was powered by the hole, and the hole was on the other side of a gate being buffeted by several megatons of nuclear hell right now, there was a chance—

"Battery, SLEDGEHAMMER is one hundred meters clear and dropping ahead." Near a planet, orbital velocity got faster the closer you were to the surface. By shoving SLEDGEHAMMER away and down, the weapons crew ensured that Juggernaut could light up its main drive without cooking the bomb in a stream of fast neutrons. "Commencing fire plan beta, six rounds rapid."

Thud. The jolt from the modified naval gun was nothing like the punch of the drive charges, but it still rattled Huw's teeth in his head. *Thud. Thud. Thud*—Each conventional powder charge flung a nuclear weapon away from Juggernaut at over three hundred meters per second. They were on a timer, counting down one minute from the last round, and when they went off simultaneously they'd create a storm of microwave interference that ought to screw up radio and radar for a while.

"Propulsion, ready for powered maneuver during EMP. Countdown started, fifty seconds—"

"—Target acquisition, I have five candidates for fire plan alpha. Uploading now."

"—Battery, targets dialed in, commencing fire plan alpha—"

"Propulsion, powering up in three . . . two . . . one . . ."

Thump. Thud. Thump. Thud. Thud. Thump. The stream of jolts—both from the main drive and the gun launchers as they ejected their directed nuclear weapons—merged into a hellish cacophony, then settled down into a continuous pummeling of propulsion charges as Juggernaut accelerated and rose towards a higher—and therefore slower—orbit. Below and ahead of them, the dark cylinder of SLEDGEHAMMER fell slowly towards its re-entry window. Above them, the star-bright pinpoints of the Hive satellites flared and twinkled, maneuvering to converge with Juggernaut's projected orbit. Around them, there was a sudden purple flash of light as half a dozen nuclear EMP mines detonated. Then six more flares as the X-ray lasers spat out bursts of energy targeting the nearest bogies.

"Target acquisition, bogie four is tumbling."

"Battery, fire plan alpha, bogie seven—"

"Target acquisition, bogies six and twelve have stopped accelerating."

What? Huw perked up. "Have you got a read on their delta-vee?" He asked.

"Yes, looks to be approximately seven hundred meters per second, sir. Either they're fuel-constrained or they're really good at faking it."

"They're not that subtle." As Juggernaut accelerated, the bogies had continuously modified their own trajectories to keep lock—behaving like particularly dumb guided missiles. Huw made a decision: "Nav, set up a series of reboosts totaling not less than seven hundred meters per second and take us clear of all the bogies Target are tracking. Battery, halt fire plan alpha. We're going to try and run their fuel tanks dry."

Until they can bring something more through the Gate. But the Gate was still obscured by mushroom clouds, and it'd take the enemy entities orbiting the hole some time to scramble more assets.

Huw checked the timer on SLEDGEHAMMER. "All we have to do is keep them focused on us for another seventy-three minutes." Until the hammer dropped, digging a five-kilometer deep crater and dumping a mountain of intensely radioactive debris on top of whatever mechanism anchored the Gate.

The hour passed in a curious mixture of dread and boredom. It seemed to Huw that space warfare was very odd: a mixture of long periods of free-fall drifting, minutes of pounding acceleration—like sticking your head inside a church tower while the bells were ringing—and moments of gut-freezing terror when Target Acquisition picked up another bogie, or when Damage Control reported that a strain gauge on one of the main structural trusses had exceeded its design margin. (The strain gauges were doubly-redundant: its twin instrument said everything was fine. Huw went with the second opinion, and prayed.)

Nearly an hour and a half had passed since the initial Trident missile strike. There was no visible sign of the Hive intrusion, although Target Acquisition was still tracking twelve drifting satellites. Seven of them had ceased maneuvering while on trajectories bound to re-enter within minutes, suckered in by Juggernaut's navigators: two of them were streaking through the upper reaches of the atmosphere over the South Pacific, shedding debris. Five had disintegrated or disappeared from radar after receiving a blast from one of Juggernaut's directed energy weapons. Another four targets were on orbits that would take them halfway to the Moon before they looped back down, by which time Juggernaut would be long gone. That left three to worry about, although they'd ceased maneuvering and were well clear of Juggernaut's flight path for the time being.

They were down to the last five minutes. Juggernaut coasted high above the Earth, nearly a thousand kilometers up and fifteen degrees closer to polar orbit. The clouds ahead were a soot-streaked red-glowing mess, lit from beneath by the wildfires ignited by the second wave of warheads. They'd used nearly two hundred propulsion charges and seventy-two weapons charges. The magazines still held enough bang-cans to get them home, but the ship was creaking and groaning after every shot like an automobile with a damaged suspension. Everyone had suited up for the duration with helmets closed, and after three hours of being shaken around, Huw felt grimy and sweaty. His suit smelled of stale farts and fear. He badly wanted a chance to run a thorough damage control check with space walks and multiple repair teams, then rest up for a day. It felt like they were living on borrowed time, every scheduled maneuver a round of Russian Roulette. But—

"Battery, bridge? SLEDGEHAMMER is on final approach. Re-entry commencing in eighty seconds." A pause. "Sixty seconds. SLEDGEHAM-MER on internal guidance."

"Jaunt—" Huw cleared his throat—"prep for bugout on my call, hold at ten seconds."

"Jaunt ready." It was Bill, the duty world-walker this time.

"Target Acquisition—" Morten's voice was shaky with stress—"bogey sixteen is emitting in V-band again, high power. Bogey—no, bogeys five, six, nine, ten, and eleven are all emitting! Bogey sixteen delta vee changing, they're under way again. Uh, the primary target is—"

Directly ahead of the falling SLEDGEHAMMER, the clouds lit up with an eerie blue glow, like the Cherenkov radiation surrounding the fuel rods at the bottom of a reactor cooling pond. "Oh fuck my life—" someone said aloud, and the sentiment was so apt that Huw couldn't bring himself to reprimand them. The glow brightened steadily.

"Is that something coming through?" Jensen asked.

"Unclear." Huw paused. They'd made a single complete cloud-skimming orbit since the initial attack. Time for the enemy presence beyond the Gate to prepare a response? They might not be able to use their tame black hole for maneuvering on this side, but what if—

"Battery, I want you to throw out everything you've got on fire plan beta *right now,* jam those satellite signals! Just mess it the hell up!"

"Battery, fire plan beta in effect. SLEDGEHAMMER is in re-entry plasma blackout. Firing—" *Thud. Thud. Thud.*

"How long—" *Thud*—"does SLEDGEHAMMER take to descend to—" *Thud*—"detonation altitude?" Asked Jensen, sounding far calmer than Huw felt.

"About a minute. Should be any time—" *Thud*—"now—"

The sky above the Hive incursion, already a luminous mystery, suddenly flashed white from horizon to horizon. Part of Huw's status board flared red, and the master caution alarm kicked off, buzzing urgently.

"Battery, mines about to cut loose in fifteen seconds from my mark."

Huw shook his head. The gunlaunchers fell silent and a different alarm began shrilling, DEPRESSURIZATION SECTOR FOUR. "Jaunt, execute bugout immediate!" The cloudscape was dimming towards a hideous yellow, as if the surface of the sun had fallen to Earth. In the middle of it a fireball bloated outward, slowing and reddening as it climbed. It was so large that its lower margin touched the ground even as its upper edge rose above the atmosphere and expanded outwards.

"Jaunt in five . . . four . . . three . . ."

Was it his imagination, or did something carve an impossible knife-edge straight line through the fireball, rising from the surface and blazing a trail into space for a couple of seconds? Perhaps a microscopic black hole, injected into the suddenly-hostile time line to put an end to the human infection? Or perhaps it was nothing at all. Huw blinked, unsure whether eye fatigue or damage to the TV sensors was deceiving him.

"One, and jaunt—"

And they were once more flying over friendly skies.

NORTH AMERICA, TIME LINES TWO AND THREE, 2020 CE

Humanity survived—for now.

Of the three time lines settled by refugees or deserters from the Forerunner alliance that is the subject of this tale, two survived first contact. (The third—ironically the first to initiate contact with another time line, and the least technologically developed—fell victim to the hubris and un-sophistication of its leadership and the paranoia of their contactees.)

Both surviving time lines hosted civilizations that had already advanced beyond the constraints enforced by reliance for energy on wind, water, and muscle power. The stress of discovering that they were not alone spurred a dangerous rivalry. Ironically, because their ability to jaunt had been blighted by the Hive's bioweapons, they were unable to freely expand and explore and, as hominids were wont to do, unwarily enter the Hive's time lines. Instead, they exhibited a propensity to explore the dimensions less often travelled: both civilizations ventured into Earth orbit and beyond at an unusually early stage.

Eventually these civilizations stumbled across the wreckage of a Hive beachhead in the wreckage of a shattered Forerunner fortress. Then one of them breached the chrysalis containing the hibernating remnants of the Swarm that had attacked it, dreaming away the centuries in tight or-bit around the black hole on the other side of its Invasion Gate. A small Swarm had been left to stand a lonely watch for any possible Forerunner counter-attack through the Gate. It might have slept for many more cen-turies, had not the military of time line two sought to exploit the potential of the hole as a first-strike weapon against time line three.

The Hive were mainly a space-bound clade. Attempts by hominids to tackle them on the high ground usually failed, for primates tended to adapt poorly if at all to radiation and microgravity. Nor had they mastered the techniques of using black holes as a power source for their vehicles. So the Hive's response to a tentative visit from a hominid probe was well-practiced and swift: smash the enemy vehicle, send a new attack swarm through the Gate, expand, seek evidence of the enemy's home time line, convert the planet into raw materials to support a new Hive and the black hole to power it, then iterate until the home world of the infection was destroyed.

What the Hive in time line four were *not* prepared for was a rapid, ag-gressive response from the orbital high ground. The hominids of time line two had spent most of a century refining their orbital bombardment systems, and those of time line three had spent decades desperately play-ing a game of catch-up. The planners behind the DRAGON'S TEETH mission had done their job properly, and successfully prevented the Hive from gaining access to the engram coding for time line two. The Trident strike obliterated both the Dome and the surrounding crude structures, denying the Hive any insights into the intrusion. Then a giant ridiculous vehicle abruptly appeared in orbit and opened fire on their positioning and communications vehicles. Restricted to primitive rocket motors in the absence of a hole to power their quantum-entanglement momentum transfer mechanisms, the satellites were unusually vulnerable. Just as the mother-Hive on the far side of the Gate flung them a lifeline in the shape of a newly-generated power hole, the hominids detonated an unusually energetic device right on top of the Invasion Gate's buried anchor point, cutting that time line off completely from the Swarm time lines.

After inadvertently covering their tracks, the spacefaring humans aboard their leaky, creaky, preposterous battleship fled back to their benighted backwater, ready to declare victory.

And having set a precedent for refraining from mutually assured destruction between time lines, the diplomats of the United States and the Commonwealth settled down to the serious business of promising not to murder one another. Which was a victory, of sorts.

NORTH AMERICA, TIME LINE FOUR, 2020 CE

As for the Hive, the Hive survived—for now.

The game wasn't over, of course. Time line four still hosted a small number of Hive elements, including Queens and Memories. (Whenever the Hive opened up a new time line, survival dictated speedy dispersal of the perquisites of expansion and replication.) The newly formed hole would orbit this Earth inside its lithosphere for centuries, gathering mass and energy and providing a potent source of power for the expanding local Hive. The hominids would inevitably be back, be it months or decades in the future—curiosity was their greatest weakness—meanwhile the isolated Hive waited and, waiting, laid its plans.

There would be a reckoning.

AFTERWORD AND APOLOGIA

Thank you for reading *Invisible Sun*, the last book in the *Empire Games* trilogy, which concludes the *Merchant Princes* series. I began writing what was to become the first book in the series, at the time titled *The Family Trade* (finally published in reassembled form as *The Bloodline Feud*), in mid-2002; I'm finishing the copy-edits to *Invisible Sun* in early 2021.

It's been a long slog, and this book is unconscionably late. I'd like to apologize and explain why, before I thank everyone who's been involved along the way.

Short version:

Invisible Sun seems to have been written under a curse.

Longer version:

The original trilogy—published as six slim books with high fantasy covers—came out between 2003 and 2009. When they were later picked up by Tor UK (a separate company within the same multinational publishing group), I convinced my UK editor, Bella Pagan, to let me reassemble them into the original intended form, as three much fatter techno-thrillers. These books—*The Bloodline Feud, The Traders' War,* and *The Revolution Trade*—are my preferred edit: I learned a lot about writing in the ten years between starting the first book and editing the revised edition.

I'd burned out around the time I finished them in 2009: at 640,000 words, the series was already longer than *War and Peace*, never mind a slim volume like *The Lord of the Rings*. By 2011 I'd just about caught my breath again, and my editor at Tor in New York, the late David Hartwell, charmingly and mercilessly badgered me into agreeing to write a second trilogy in this same universe. I got started at the beginning of 2013 and had a first draft by mid-2014: the goal was to publish in 2015 or 2016, so I wrote them as a single near-future story set in an alternate 2020 that had evolved from the setting established by the first books (which told a story that ran, in book-time, from 2001 to 2003).

Incidentally, some of the eccentricities of this book are due to it being a fossilized relic of a science fictional future I invented in 2013—a parallel universe to be sure, but still a predictive examination of a seven years hence 2020. It has fatphones, not iPhones or Androids, although that's down to divergent time lines (time line two in the Merchant Princes multiverse clearly diverged from our own long before 2003, and modern smartphones postdate that year). There are hopelessly utopian-seeming aspects to this future, from the perspective of our own, fully experienced 2020. Time line two features a United States led by a competent female president (who is not Hilary Rodham Clinton). There's no COVID-19, no QAnon, no Brexit. But on the other hand, our actually-existing time line doesn't feature a radioactive hole in the middle of Washington, D.C., a cold war in para-time, or an alien invasion. I guess we got the better deal . . . maybe?

Anyway, edits happened and delays followed, and eventually *Empire Games* and *Dark State* surfaced a year or so later than planned. And then I was working on *Invisible Sun* (the circa-2014 first draft was weak: it needed a rewrite) when David Hartwell died—suddenly, unexpectedly, and horribly.

Leaving aside the human dimension (David was a friend of mine: I'd known him for over fifteen years at the time), losing an editor is one of the worst things that can happen to a book. Luckily there was a contingency plan in place. As he was close to retirement, David had already established a succession plan for his authors. Bella was to take over as editor for *Invisible Sun*, while the US side of my publication track at Tor would go elsewhere. So I eventually got back to work on it, started another rewrite—and my father died.

Losing a parent is sad, unpleasant, and depressing, but in my father's case it wasn't entirely unexpected: he turned 93 in 2017, a couple of weeks before the end. He had a long and fulfilling life. However, it took the wind out of my sails. I had to shelve a different book I'd been working on for twelve months: I'd lost my appetite for *Invisible Sun*, but nevertheless managed to get back to work—then a close friend of mine died suddenly. And my mother had a series of debilitating strokes, ended up in nursing care, and died almost exactly two years after my father. (She was 90.)

Can you guess what's coming next?

Working through one death is manageable, working through two courts burn-out, but working through three or more . . . it wasn't fun. The fourth rewrite of *Invisible Sun*, in the wake of my father's death, sucked mightily. But on the other hand, I had no more parents to lose (and my surviving editors were both relatively young and healthy): what else could possibly go wrong? Coming out from beneath a cloud of terminal illnesses, I set to work and finally finished a solid draft in early 2020—one where all the pieces came together to provide a satisfying conclusion for the series—just as I began hearing disturbing news reports about a new respiratory virus spreading in Wuhan.

(Reality was clearly taking the piss.)

Invisible Sun was originally intended to be published in 2015–2017. Each real-world death took a twelve month toll on my productivity. Then COVID-19 added an additional six to nine months on top, by hampering my publishers' ability to produce books. But if you have read this far, it's a safe bet that my epic run of terrible, bad, no-good, horrible luck has ended! No dinosaur-killing asteroid has landed: no invasion of extradimensional hive robots has occurred. *Humanity has survived the publication of this book.* (At times, this did not seem terribly likely.)

Is this the end of the *Merchant Princes/Empire Games* series?

In a word: maybe. And then again, maybe not.

This is certainly the end of the series for the time being. There will be no more books about Miriam and her family, or about Rita and her contemporaries. When I originally wrote a pitch for a four-book series back in 2002, planning four doorstep-sized novels, I had something very different in mind. *Empire Games* replaces the originally-planned third book in that series, and the big-picture inserts towards the end cover background that was going to be revealed in the fourth book: that fourth book won't (can't) be written now.

I might set other stories in the multiverse of the Clan at some future date, but if I do so, it will be in the shape of a stand-alone novel or novels that don't connect up to the *Merchant Princes* series. At just under a million words in print and ebook, and just over eighteen years in the writing, the series is over.

This book, and the entire series, would not have existed without two people: David Hartwell, my editor at Tor from 2002 until his untimely death in 2016, and Caitlin Blasdell, my literary agent. Caitlin laid the seeds for it by challenging me to come up with an alternate history/parallel universe story: David then tended the field until the seeds sprouted, reaped the harvest, and came back for more. But editors don't work in isolation. At Tor UK, Bella Pagan (who had previously been my editor at Orbit UK for my SF and Laundry Files books) encouraged me to re-cut the first books for UK publication, then took up the challenge of editing *Invisible Sun* after David's death. At Tor USA in New York, Patrick Nielsen Hayden took over as my editor after David, and is somehow keeping all my balls in the air during this time of crisis. Finally, as my agent, Caitlin is also my editor of last resort, and has lent her polish to the final drafts of this book.

Over a twenty-year period, I have benefited from the comments and feedback of innumerable test readers and friends, many of whom I am embarrassed to say I have forgotten. However, I'd like to specifically single out for thanks Rebecca Judd (who did a huge amount of work turning the first series into a coherent cross-referenced Scrivener project I could work on), and her partner and my close friend Hugh Hancock. Hugh died tragically and suddenly in 2018: he was in his early 40s.

GLOSSARY OF TERMS

Accretion disk
A "whirlpool-like" disk of extremely hot gas that gathers around a black hole. As matter is sucked into a black hole, it heats up until the radiation pressure from the inside of the accretion disk balances out the attractive force of the hole. It thus limits the rate at which a black hole can absorb matter. As most black holes rotate, the accretion disk is dragged round at very high speed: temperatures range from several millions of degrees up.

ARMBAND
Device used by US military and DHS to transport aircraft between parallel universes. The mechanism is secret; believed to include neural tissue harvested from world-walker "donors."

BLACK RAIN
Code name assigned to time line three (home of the New American Commonwealth) by the US government.

Bogie
The chassis or framework carrying wheels, upon which a railway carriage rests. *Also* an unidentified, mostly probably hostile, aircraft (military usage).

Clan
An umbrella organization consisting of five (previously six) families of world-walkers, formerly residing in the Gruinmarkt in time line one. Coordinated the world-walkers' inter-temporal trade and smuggling activities, provided security, and a framework for the arranged marriages required to keep the world-walking bloodlines alive. The Clan was effectively

disbanded in 2003, and the survivors sought asylum in time line three (with the New American Commonwealth).

Corvée for the Clan Postal Service
An obligation of world-walkers from time line one (who were members of the Clan). They had to make themselves available to transport goods between time lines a certain number of times every month. The organization is now defunct.

CVS
A big, well-known American pharmacy chain

DHS
US Department of Homeland Security: in time line two, the agency responsible for transportation security, counter-terrorism, and para-time security (interception of world-walkers). Also responsible for organizing security of government and corporate sites in other time lines, and countering threats from all other time lines.

DPR
Department of Para-historical Research: a para-time industrial espionage agency established within MITI in the New American Commonwealth.

ELINT
Electronic Intelligence; covert intelligence gathering by electronic means (as opposed to HUMINT).

Engram
Among world-walkers, a knotwork design that can trigger the world-walking ability to transport them to another parallel universe.

Family Trade Organization
Precursor to the Office of Special Projects. It was a cross-agency organization established within the US government in 2002 in response to the discovery of world-walkers and the Clan.

FISA Court

United States Foreign Intelligence Surveillance Court: a US Federal court established to oversee requests for surveillance warrants and other espionage-related secret legislation.

Gruinmarkt

A small kingdom on the eastern seaboard of North America in time line one, founded by Viking colonists between the twelfth and fourteenth centuries. Home of the Clan. It had reached a late, mediaeval-level of political and economic development before it was destroyed in a nuclear holocaust instigated by the United States.

Hochsprache

A Germanic family language spoken in the Gruinmarkt; now effectively extinct, remembered only by former members of the Clan.

HUMINT

Human Intelligence: intelligence gathered by means of human agents and informers (see also SIGINT, ELINT)

ICBM

Inter-Continental Ballistic Missile.

MITI

Ministry of Intertemporal Technological Intelligence: a government agency within the New American Commonwealth. This body is tasked with accelerating technological development by disseminating new developments discovered in other time lines.

New American Commonwealth

Successor nation to the New British Empire, which ruled North and South America and Australasia in time line three from 1761 to 2003. The New American Commonwealth is a revolutionary republic created by the former Radical Party to pursue the goal of spreading democracy throughout time line three.

Niejwein
Capital of the Gruinmarkt. Destroyed in 2003.

NRO
National Reconnaissance Office: US government secret agency in time line two responsible for launching spy satellites and developing photographic/radar intelligence from satellites.

NSA
National Security Agency: the US government agency in Time Line Two tasked with SIGINT and ELINT, the interception and decryption of enemy communications. Noted for monitoring all phone, internet, and data communications worldwide.

Outer family
Among the Clan world-walkers, the world-walking trait is recessive: only the children of two active world-walkers inherit the ability. However, the children of a world-walker and a non-world-walker may be carriers. The offspring of two such carriers may have the world-walking ability. Such carriers were monitored by the Clan and known as "outer family" members (the Clan had a strong interest in maximizing the pool of possible world-walkers available to them).

Para-time
Umbrella term for parallel universes diverging from a point in time. The cause of divergence may be some quantum event which may have multiple outcomes with macroscopic (observable) effects.

POTUS
President of The United States

RFID
Radio Frequency ID: "smart" inventory control tags found on many items of packaging or clothing. RFID tags can be interrogated remotely and used to identify the item they are attached to, unlike bar codes (which need to be scanned at close range). Same underlying technology as contactless payment cards.

SCEP

Special Counter-Espionage Police: a government agency within the New American Commonwealth of time line three. The organization is tasked with tracking down subversives, spies, and agents of both the British Crown in Exile and the French Empire. An agency of the Commonwealth Guard.

SIGINT

Signals intelligence: intelligence obtained by analyzing metadata derived from enemy radio, telegraph, internet, and other signals.

TL;DR

"Too Long; Didn't Read" (sarcastic dismissal of a long explanation or glossary, like this one)

USAF

United States Air Force

World-walker

A person equipped with the ability to controllably teleport between parallel universes. It's an inherited ability, the hereditable mechanism presumed to have been invented by a high technology civilization elsewhere in paratime.